The Pride of the King

Thanks for being there for me all these years!

Amanda Hughes

Copyright © 2011 Amanda Hughes

All rights reserved.

ISBN:10 1463589123
ISBN-13:978-1463589127

DEDICATION

This book is dedicated to my children who never lost their faith in me.

ACKNOWLEDGMENTS

Special thanks to Ronnell Porter for cover art and design.

New Orleans 1748

Chapter 1

Lauren De Beauville needed a hurricane. She was never satisfied with gentle rainfall or a passing shower. To feel alive, Lauren always needed a tempest, and that is what she received on her wedding day.

A flash of lightning flooded her room as the nuns glided in to prepare Lauren physically and spiritually for the sacrament. They arranged her hair and placed an exquisite white veil on her head. Tiny lace roses bordered the wispy garment and intricate beadwork cascaded down the back, but Lauren did not notice the beautiful veil. Her heart was pounding with terror because she was about to marry a man old enough to be her grandfather.

After morning prayers, the nuns lead her to the convent sanctuary which smelled thick from incense and candle wax. Father Toussard, The Abbess, and several novices were waiting for her with folded hands. Lauren was baptized in this sanctuary, she wore the veil of a young communicant at this alter and today, at fifteen, she stands here as a bride.

A loud click echoed through the church as Monsieur Heathstone, the groom, snapped his pocket watch closed. The elderly man stepped out from the shadows, pursed his lips and whispered something to the priest.

Father Toussard straightened up, clearing his throat. Joining the couple's hands he opened his book and began to perform the marriage ceremony in English. Everything is for the benefit of this monster, thought Lauren. *Her wishes did not exist. She was not even worthy of being married in her own language.*

She wondered what her sister Simone was doing, if she was watching the whole charade from some dark corner of the chapel. *Would she ever see her again? Would she ever see the convent again; the only home she had ever known?*

She looked around the chapel for the last time. There were candles everywhere, most of them tallow but a few, those around the altar, were made of exquisite beeswax. There was no stained glass in the sanctuary. The fledgling colony of New Orleans could not afford such frivolities.

Lauren loved the little church. The Ursulines praised the great cathedrals of Europe, but those grand monuments to God meant nothing to her. This is what she loved. Her eyes rested on a small statue of the Virgin Mary. Many times in the past, she had turned to Our Lady of Prompt Succor, but today it seemed that the Virgin was mute and disinterested. *Why has Mother Mary allowed this to happen?*

"Mademoiselle De Beauville, Mademoiselle, if you please--" encouraged Father Toussard. Lauren jumped, realizing that the time had come to take her vows. Calling on every bit of strength she could muster, Lauren straightened her back, took a deep breath and repeated the words of the priest.

Lauren De Beauville would never forget September 4, 1748. It was a day that would begin with dread and trepidation and end in terror and panic. She would witness two disasters that day, marriage to a man she detested, and the destruction of the only home she had ever known.

* * *

A crack of thunder greeted Lauren as she emerged from the chapel door. She was now a married woman. Before she could pull up her hood, Monsieur Heathstone hustled her out into the horizontal rain. It was practically impossible for her to keep her eyes open as the drops pelted her in the face. Her garments were a poor match for the downpour, and she was soaked within minutes, her skirt hanging heavy with mud.

Street vendors were frantically packing up their wares, seeking shelter from the intensifying storm. Even the colorful peppers and apples looked drab and dreary today. Only the catfish and oysters seemed to enjoy the deluge.

Heathstone rounded a corner, pulling Lauren along behind him and entered L'hotel de la Marine. Lauren had seen it once when Sister Giselle had taken her to the docks to pick up a shipment of silk worms. It was large and well kept. The logs stood vertically; the posts set directly onto the earth. It was two stories in the back with a small dining room addition in the front.

Although the dining room was empty when Lauren entered, it was not cold. Monsieur Berne, the proprietor, had taken great pains to make the inn cozy. There was a fire crackling and several tables were set with candles and high-back chairs awaited customers. The interior walls were plastered and whitewashed, and a massive cherry cupboard stood in the corner. Pewter plates and tankards filled the shelves, and the drawers in the bottom held Madame Berne's fine table linen.

Monsieur Berne was bending over these drawers as Heathstone and Lauren burst in, the wind banging the door. He was a stout, jovial fellow and greeted them heartily. Heathstone had chosen this inn because the proprietor spoke English, a rarity in the province of Louisiana.

"Come in! Come in!" he roared in English. His large stomach preceded him as he advanced, arms outstretched. "You have returned with the lovely bride! The weather--is it not severe?"

In spite of the owner's jovial demeanor, Monsieur Heathstone did not smile. He sat down in front of the fire indicating the same to Lauren. The smile dropped from the innkeeper's face. The French did not like the English in New Orleans and Heathstone's attitude did not help relations.

Monsieur Berne continued, "If it's food you want, I have only three eggs and a half a loaf of bread. No one is getting through in this storm, so I have nothing to cook." He wiped his brow and looked out the window. The wind was now blowing branches off the trees and unsecured items tumbled wildly down the street. "May the Virgin Mary protect us all!" prayed the innkeeper as he turned toward the kitchen.

Heathstone grumbled something, sinking down into his chair. Lauren arranged her soaked skirts and looked across the table at him. His appearance and surly attitude disgusted her, and she was grateful he had shown little interest in her so far. Nevertheless, the thought of bedding him tonight terrified her.

The nuns had shared nothing with the girls regarding procreation. Her twin sister, Simone had made it her business to learn about the facts of life early and passed what she learned on to Lauren.

She watched Heathstone pull a hankie out of his waistcoat and blow his nose. Her heart began to pound furiously. *Where will he take me? What will he do to me?*

Suddenly, there was a loud crash outside and water started streaming down the plaster behind the massive cupboard. "Oh Mon Dieu!" cried Monsieur Berne rushing into the room. A tree had fallen on the dining room addition. Too unsympathetic to help the worried innkeeper, Heathstone shrugged and turned back to the fire.

Lauren watched the innkeeper push a ladder in front of the cupboard, climbing up to inspect the damage. "It is *not* good," he moaned in French. "I don't know how--"

Suddenly, he screamed, and the cupboard toppled over upon him. A torrent of water came smashing through the walls of the inn turning Lauren and Heathstone over in their chairs. It slammed Lauren against the opposite wall, pinning her against the plaster. She choked and sputtered, her lungs filling with water. The pain was excruciating as the furnishings trapped her against the wall, her ribs snapping. Heathstone was swept away under the water. The innkeeper was caught behind the huge cherry cupboard, screaming in pain as the floodwaters rushed into the room.

Suddenly, the logs of the inn began to crack like toothpicks as water filled the room pushing the cupboard and the innkeeper through the timber frame of the house. Monsieur Berne was killed instantly. His body resembled a rag doll, bumping and banging into debris as it washed away.

Lauren spilled out of the hole too, into the street, the current carrying her away in the storm. Struggling desperately in the black water she gasped for air, the wind raging all around her as debris flew past her head. Her heavy woolen skirt began to tangle around her legs. Suddenly, a maelstrom sucked her under and the roar of the water filled her ears. Her lungs felt as if they would burst. A branch caught her skirt, trapping her underwater. She struggled frantically, pulling and tugging on the material trying to free herself and surface for air, when someone grabbed her hair and dragged her up. It was Heathstone.

"Grab my hand!" he shouted, reaching for Lauren. He was clinging to a floating log. She caught his hand, but it was slippery and her heavy skirts dragged her out of his grasp and under again. As the waters pulled her down a second time she thought, "If I swim away, I will be free. If I take his hand--"

She made her decision. It was worth the risk. Lauren stayed under as long as her lungs would allow, riding the ravaging current. When she finally burst to the surface, he was gone. She grabbed a log that sailed past, pulling herself on top of it. Suddenly, she realized that this was no log at all, but a decomposing corpse. Lauren stared at the shriveled face in horror, then hurtled it away. Dead bodies were everywhere; surfacing from the St. Peter cemetery, worm-eaten children, decrepit adults, skeletons and coffins rushing by on the torrent.

Swiftly, she grabbed a casket and tipped the box, looking inside. It held a corpse about her size, and without hesitation she dumped the body into the water. It was painful and grotesque pulling herself into a coffin, but she knew that now she would survive. Bruised and battered, she put her head down on the soaked wood of the coffin and fell into a swoon.

Lauren fell in and out of consciousness, confusing dreams with reality. The storm swept the casket down the torrent slamming it against uprooted trees and debris, tipping and bumping it madly. In a fog of delirium, Lauren tried to recall where she was and why she felt pain. *Just yesterday, she had fallen from the giant oak tree by the convent wall. Maybe she had been injured.* Try as she might, she could not remember the events of the day and she fell back into a swoon

Chapter 2

Everything had changed for Lauren De Beauville in one day. It was only a day ago; Lauren was sitting in a large oak tree in the convent courtyard watching the people on Le Rue Conde. Sister Gertrude called her name and she jumped, slipped and began to tumble. Frantically, she grabbed for branches falling down through the tree, slamming onto the earth below with a thud. The air expelled so abruptly from her lungs that she could not breathe until the nun pulled her upright.

"My dear, my little one, are you hurt?"

Coughing and sputtering, Lauren pushed tangled volumes of hair from her face. "I think I'm alright, Sister," she said breathlessly. She rose to her feet, and brushed off her apron. "Oh please, don't tell anyone, Sister Gertrude. I promise I won't climb--" Lauren caught herself. She was about to lie to a nun and that would mean damage to her immortal soul. She did not intend to stop climbing trees and to say otherwise was a falsehood.

Sister Gertrude smiled. At the same age, she would have been in that tree. She liked the tall willowy girl with copper-colored tresses.

Lauren returned her smile.

She has a reckless smile, thought Sister Gertrude. *It is the smile of a pirate.*

"Mother Marie Margarite would like to see you in an hour," she said.

Lauren's tawny eyes grew wide. Everyone knew the Abbess only talked with the girls when it was a very important matter. Maybe this was it, Lauren thought, maybe they had found a placement for her. She was old enough to leave these walls, to find her true home and make her way into the world as a lady of distinction and education.

"Don't be late!" said the Sister cheerfully and she turned, leaving Lauren alone in the garden.

She sat down on a stone bench as if reeling from a blow. She had been waiting so long for this day and news about her future. Over the past weeks, she had felt it coming. She had grown restless and irritable, snapping without reason at her sister, and it had been harder than usual to attend to her studies.

Lauren had always been a restless, impulsive girl. She approached everything at breakneck speed, embracing new experiences with enthusiasm and delight until the inevitable boredom struck, and she yearned for new adventures again.

Lauren and her twin sister Simone had called the Ursaline Academy for Girls, home for ten years. They had only dim memories of the rice plantation and their French-born parents lost to them long ago. The gentle Ursulines raised the orphaned twins tutoring them in religion, academics and social graces. Lauren would miss her home at the convent, but she and Simone had to go. The time for seclusion and sanctuary was over.

Waking from her thoughts, she jumped from the bench and raced into the dormitory, slowing her pace when Sister Bona came around the corner. Lauren threw the door open of her room and found Simone with her head on her arms, looking out the window. Her brown eyes were bloodshot and her blonde hair was falling out of the knot at the back of her neck.

"What's wrong?" Lauren asked.

Her sister shrugged.

Lauren rolled her eyes. "Oh, I see we are taken with melancholia again."

"I don't want to fight with you today, Lauren," Simone said, without looking up.

"I don't either," said Lauren. "I bring good news. Mother Marie Margarite wants to see me today. I'm sure it's about a placement. I wonder where it will be. Of course, she will place us together. What do you think, Simone?"

Simone turned away. She was in no mood to talk. Lauren suspected she was having trouble with her young man, Joffrey. Twice a week, boys came to the school to do repairs at the convent and immediately Joffrey noticed Simone. Young men frequently noticed Simone. Her face resembled the angels painted on the wall of the sanctuary, sweet and ethereal, but her full curved body was unmistakably of this world.

Although twins, it was hard to tell that Simone and Lauren were sisters. They bore little physical resemblance to one another and their personalities differed as well. Simone was pensive and sultry given to frequent brooding and melancholy, whereas Lauren was carefree and impulsive. Simone agonized over beaus; Lauren had no time for boys. In spite of all their differences, the girls were best friends.

"Did you hear me? What do you think Simone? Will they keep us together?"

Simone did not answer. She looked up at the sky, "The clouds have an odd turn to them today. I wonder if there will be a storm."

"Oh, don't be foolish. The sky is blue," barked Lauren as she marched to the window and thrust her head out. The clouds did look strange, Lauren had to admit, but it was nothing more than a curiosity. *Leave it to Simone to overreact.*

There was a sharp rap at the door and the girls knew that their rest period was over, and it was time to help with the evening meal. "I'll meet you right after I talk to Mother Marie Margarite," said Lauren. She bit her lip, hesitating a moment before going on, "I'm sorry if you are having trouble with Joffrey. I'm not very good at listening."

Simone looked surprised, "What are talking about? Joffrey? He's a thing of the past," she said, dismissing the subject. She turned and walked out of the room.

Lauren reported to the convent kitchen to dice potatoes. The room was bustling with activity, but she was in a world of her own full of anticipation and excitement about her new life. She stared out the window dreaming of her future. *Of course, they would send her to France. The nuns always sent young ladies of breeding to France. They never stayed in New Orleans. It was too backward.* At the very worst, Lauren thought, she would go to a plantation to serve as a governess, but even this held appeal. She would be free of the convent walls.

Suddenly, someone barked, "Lauren, the potatoes!" It was Sister Therese.

Lauren mumbled her apologies and went back to work. The nuns expected every girl, regardless of her background, to work at the Academy. There were twenty girls in residence at the convent; fifteen French girls, three Negroes, and two Natchez Indians. Each had a job to do and they bustled around the kitchen clattering pots and pans, rolling out dough and chopping vegetables. The nuns made certain that the students were proficient in everything, practical as well as scholarly. The Ursulines were the first religious order in the history of the Catholic Church to educate girls. Society had always viewed the female mind as inferior, but the Order took exception and began opening academies in spite of the criticism.

The Ursaline Order arrived in the Colony of New Orleans in 1727 and in a short time built a convent, hospital and an academy for girls. Now, two decades later, the good nuns educated not only French girls of wealth and privilege but slave girls and local Indians. They believed that all young women were entitled to an academic and spiritual education, not just the wealthy.

Most of the girls would marry shortly after leaving the Academy but some would need to provide for themselves, so the Ursuline's instructed them in the care and breeding of the profitable silk worm. Many went on to lead independent, productive lives working on silkworm plantations.

The large stone building with shuttered windows was home to nuns and students in residence. The convent housed not only the Academy but an orphanage as well. Lauren and Simone fell into this category. Born to wealthy French immigrants who came to New Orleans during the formation of the Mississippi Company, the twin girls never knew their mother. She died giving birth to them leaving a shattered and depressed Monsieur De Beauville to raise two youngsters alone. He descended into drink and debauchery, dying penniless and riddled with disease. The good sisters took in the girls shortly thereafter.

The hour had finally come. Lauren asked to be excused from her work in the kitchen. Her palms were perspiring as she knocked on the door of the Mother Marie Margarite's office.

"Come in," said a gentle voice.

It was stuffy inside the small office of Mother Marie Margarite. Because of the wind, the Abbess had closed the window, and the smell of candle wax and lavender hung heavily on the air. The old woman sat behind a gargantuan oak desk. She folded her hands and smiled at Lauren. Although Mother Marie Margarite was a tiny woman, there was nothing small about her supervision of the convent and the academy. Her wizened face had endured years of hardship in the Old World and the New World, and because of these tribulations; she had become a strong and capable servant of the academy and of the Lord.

Mother Marie Margarite could see from her flushed cheeks that Lauren was excited. She felt more assured than ever that this placement was suitable. As Lauren entered the room, an older man stood up to greet her, holding out his hand.

"Lauren De Beauville, may I introduce Monsieur Adair Heathstone," said the Abbess. "He has traveled a long way to meet you, my dear, and we are very grateful to him for coming."

The gentleman stepped forward kissed Lauren's hand and stepped back casting his eyes down respectfully. The girl's heart bumped in her chest. *Here at last was her employer ready to apprentice her to her new engagement.* Her mind raced with possibilities about the future and the new experiences she would embrace. *It was all very thrilling.* Swallowing back her excitement, Lauren managed to calm her nerves long enough to examine the man more closely. He was of later years, clean-shaven and neat. His clothing appeared well cut but austere. Except for a few gray hairs combed over his head and a small pigtail at his neck, he was completely bald. She noted that he was very thin, almost gaunt as he murmured something in another language.

"Monsieur Heathstone does not speak French," explained Mother Marie Margarite. "He is from the English Colonies."

"I see," said Lauren. Another world, she thought. *I shall be seeing new lands, meeting new people,. Protestants even. What a delightful adventure*!

"As you know Lauren, we here at the Academy want only the best for all of our girls. We have been searching long and hard for a placement for you. Because of your somewhat depleted financial condition, your prospects have been few. But our prayers were answered with Monsieur Adair Heathstone."

Mother Marie Margarite reached out to Lauren and took her hand. The Abbess said joyfully, "Monsieur Heathstone is here to marry you."

Chapter 3

Lauren could not breathe. She pulled the office door shut behind her and struggled for air. The shocking news, the closeness of the room and the sight of that hideous man choked her to death. She could think of nothing but getting outside, outside to the garden where she could clear her mind and cleanse herself of this blasphemy. *Could the sisters not see what a mockery they made of the sacrament of marriage? The false vows she had to take? The whole thing was unthinkable!*

She staggered down the dark hall, unaware of the thunder rumbling outside. Her pace quickened as her stomach churned, breaking into a full run. By the time she threw the door open to the courtyard, she was retching violently. Rain poured over her, soaking her hair and gown as she stumbled toward the oak tree, slipping on the mud. At its base, she sank onto the muddy ground sobbing hysterically.

Someone called, "Lauren!" Lauren! Are you out here?" As dark as it was, Simone found her sister and pulled her into her arms. "Come in now!" she shouted over the thunder, "You will die of consumption out here. Come now!"

The oak tree flailed overhead as Simone pulled frantically at her sister. A gust of wind peppered rain into their faces, "I can't breathe in there. They have betrayed me!" Lauren screamed

"You must come in! The storm is worsening. I know all about it. We'll talk inside."

Reluctantly, Lauren stood up. Her hair was wet and tangled, and her gown was covered with mud. "I can't marry him, Simone, I just can't!"

Simone pulled Lauren inside and pushed the door open of the first room she could find. She pulled her sister inside a dark classroom and left briefly, returning with a basin of water, towels and a dry gown. She lit a taper and set it on a desk. The candle flickered, illuminating desks and bookcases. She soaked a towel in water and began to wash Lauren's face and arms scolding, "Vespers is in ten minutes. They can't see you like this."

"What am I going to do? I have to marry him in the morning," Lauren mumbled, standing like a compliant child under Simone's direction.

"You are going to do what you do best," her sister said. "Be strong!"

"Did you see him?" Lauren asked. "He is an old man. An old man! I am only fifteen years old."

Lauren put her face in her hands, then looked up and said suddenly, "How did you hear about this?"

"I heard some of the girls talking."

A bolt of thunder cracked, and they jumped. The tears started to stream down Lauren's face again. Simone wiped them from her cheeks and pulled a clean gown over her sister's head.

"What about you, Simone?" said Lauren, wiping her nose on her sleeve, "You're next."

Simone did not answer. Silently she combed her siblings tangled hair.

Lauren could feel heaviness upon her chest. *There it is again, that feeling of being unable to breathe. It is unbearable.* Abruptly she cried, "We must run away Simone! We must go tonight! We have no choice."

Simone blinked and opened her mouth to say something, but the words would not come.

"There is no time. We must gather our things now! Let's see," said Lauren making a mental checklist. "We must travel light. We will only need one change of clothes. I have saved a little money. We can go down to the wharf. Yes, that's it. Surely there will be someone we know--" Lauren noticed the reluctance on her sister's face and asked, "What is it? What's wrong?"

Simone murmured, "Nothing."

"What!"

Simone sighed and closed her eyes. "I don't know how to tell you this."

"Tell me what?" Lauren asked.

"Tell you, Lauren that I can't leave."

"Of course you can! Don't be foolish! We're old enough. It will be difficult at first but we'll survive. We have always done everything together. You are my sister."

"I won't leave, Lauren," Simone said firmly.

"Why not? What about seeing the world together? Everything we dreamed about since we were children." Lauren could see the troubled look on her sister's face and the anger rose within her. "Have you turned coward on me?"

Simone turned away. Lightning flashed through the shuttered window, illuminating her briefly. "Yes, I am a coward. A coward because I could never admit to you or to myself that," and she swallowed hard before continuing, "I want to be an Ursuline."

Lauren's jaw dropped, and she blinked in disbelief. "Surely you jest! What a grand joke! This must be a result of some new beau jilting you. A nun!" and she laughed. "Really, Simone, you scared me. You will be interested in another boy next week, and all this will be over."

Simone shook her head and stepped forward. The candle flickered on her face, and in spite of the determined look, Lauren continued hastily, "Stop all of this nonsense and get your things. We must leave tonight. We haven't a second to waste."

Lauren turned to head for the dormitory, and Simone caught her arm. "Why do you think I was crying earlier today?" she said. "This was not an easy decision, but I had to face the truth. I cannot run away from my destiny and neither will you. Mother Marie Margarite is right. You must marry this man. It is the will of God."

Lauren was flabbergasted. *This could not be true. Did Simone just say she should marry this monster?* There was a long silence as Lauren searched her eyes. Simone was indeed not joking. Lauren looked at Simone as if seeing her for the first time. A self-assured, committed postulant had replaced the sultry, brooding teenager. Not only was her demeanor different but her words as well.

"I cannot run away from my destiny," Simone continued, "Everything has been arranged and Mother Marie Margarite has accepted me. It is the will of God." She stepped over taking Lauren's arm.

"Don't touch me!" Lauren screeched, jerking her arm away. "Don't ever touch me again!"

At that moment, the church bell rang for Vespers. Lauren turned on her heel and left the room. Simone called to her, but she was swallowed up in the shadows.

*   *   *

After evening prayers, the nuns took Lauren to bathe her for the wedding in the morning. She followed their instructions mechanically, but it was not until she was in bed that night that she realized what was going to happen. Back and forth she tossed in bed, wrestling with her feelings. Lauren felt completely betrayed by Simone. They had planned to stay together forever, and now her sister took a path Lauren could not follow. *How could she choose such a life? How could these cold, stone walls be enough?* Maybe she never had known Simone, or maybe Simone had lived a lie.

Although she was loved and cared for, Lauren had never felt comfortable at the convent. She had always felt like a guest of the benevolent nuns and that some day she and her sister would have to move on. Always, she had envisioned a life which included Simone, but now she must search for a home alone.

Rolling over in bed, she bit her lip, fighting back tears of loneliness. Everything was changing so fast. The only thing certain was that she was alone and terrified. Her plans to run away had crumbled the instant Simone refused to leave, and now she could do nothing but wait to marry this monster, wait for others to dictate her destiny.

Chapter 4

Lauren opened her eyes and struggled to focus. She remembered everything now, Simone staying at the convent, the wedding and the hurricane. She felt the coffin bump into something, and she pulled herself up onto her elbows. The rain and winds had ceased, and the sky had cleared. Lauren at looked at the casket. The very container, which held death for so long, had saved her life. It bumped again, and she looked over the side. It was bumping a small structure, like a shed. The storm surge had washed her beyond the ruined palisades of the city into the rural backcountry.

She strained to see any sign of town, but there was only cypress and mangrove trees sheltering her like umbrellas. Lauren was afraid to get out and wade to dry land. She did not know what was swimming in these backwaters. Mustering up her courage, she threw one leg over the side of the casket. The pain in her ribs was excruciating, and she slumped back down, panting.

After several moments, she decided to try it again. Biting her lip, she threw both legs over this time, and when the casket tipped, she quickly slid into the murky green water. Fighting the urge to faint, she took a few breaths to steady herself. Algae swirled around her as she waded through the bog, pushing aside fallen branches and weeds. Her skirt pluming out around her waist, Lauren dragged herself through the muck, turning this way and that, searching for some sign of habitation. She realized the swamp was completely silent. There were no birds singing, no squirrels jumping, not even a croaking toad. It was ominously quiet as if the swamp was holding its breath.

Shaking off the feeling of doom, Lauren climbed over the tangled roots of two large mangroves and stepped out of the water onto a grassy rise. She looked up and saw a house, a large dilapidated plantation surrounded by cypress and Spanish moss, abandoned and overgrown. It appeared to have been a fine home in its day but now wore a look of melancholy and despair.

She picked up her soggy skirts and waded through the grass and weeds to get a better look. She walked up the hill and saw the river. This home, like any of the great plantations of the day, was on the Mississippi. It was a two-storied manor with whitewashed clapboard siding and faded green shutters. The roof, worn thin from years of wind and rain, had several holes in it and the porch, which spanned the front of the house, was sagging badly. Although the decay was pathetic, what contributed most to the wretched appearance of the house was the overgrown landscape. Vines covered the walls and large trees shrouded the structure, dripping with Spanish moss and ivy.

As if hypnotized, Lauren stared at the home. Goosebumps rose on her arms. She had an eerie feeling as she approached the house, hugging herself. Suddenly, she gasped. Lauren could not believe her eyes. This was her childhood home! Memories flooded her like ghosts from the past. There on the front steps of the house was a little girl with a doll. Lauren recognized Simone, not the pious and melancholy teen at the convent, but the Simone of childhood, a carefree girl of the De Beauville plantation. Her memories were dim, but she remembered this place. All her life she had dreamed about returning here and the pastoral days on the river. More than once, she fought the impulse to jump over the walls of the convent and dash back here, but it had changed.

Lauren walked around the house. Everything looked so small. She remembered the house being enormous. The grounds were not imposing now and the trees, which at one time seemed enormous, were now mediocre in height. It was no longer the pristine plantation of yesterday. Lauren's childhood home had deteriorated into a pathetic relic of the past. She squeezed her eyes shut. She did not want to be reminded that her father had gambled away their home and died of that unspeakable disease. *Why did she have to revisit this place?*

Lauren turned and staggered toward the river trying to remember something other than pain and loneliness. The rushing current of the Mississippi seemed to wash the bad memories away, and she recalled a scene, a small glimpse of her past. It was a warm Sunday morning, and she was standing by the river with her father, listening to church bells. Her hand felt so small in his hand. She remembered the sound of house slaves preparing breakfast as river traffic drifted by lazily. She could smell the sweet potatoes and fresh bread. The sun felt warm on her skin, and Lauren remembered feeling safe and protected. Knitting her brows, she struggled to remember her father. There had been no relatives to keep memories alive, so all Lauren could recall was his shadow.

The wind began to move the trees again. Lauren pushed the wet, tangled locks from her face and looked up at the sky. Odd-looking clouds streaked across the sky once more. She knew that she must find shelter again quickly. Reluctantly, she looked at the house. It was her only refuge.

Lauren climbed the crumbling stairs to the front door. Pain stabbed her in the chest when she tried to take a deep breath. Hanging onto the walls and doorframes, she passed from the faded foyer directly into the sitting room. A squirrel ran up the smoke-stained chimney scolding and chattering. The house had been abandoned for years. The oak floors were stained from a leaking roof, and the rare glass windows were broken. Pieces of furniture littered every room. It appeared as if transients had smashed chairs for kindling and the drapes had been used for bedding.

Lauren pulled herself over to a large oak table and leaned heavily onto its dusty surface. She remembered playing under this table with Simone. A heavy damask cloth had covered the piece long ago. It was long gone. It had been their fort, and they spent hours there in make-believe adventures. Lauren longed for Simone by her side. She said a prayer for her safety and reassured herself that the stone convent was practically indestructible during a storm.

Suddenly, a memory surfaced. Lauren was five years old and hiding under that heavy oak table. The De Beauville plantation house was crowded with people, and she remembered being relieved to be under the table and out of their reach. She had endured hours of endless hugs and wet, teary kisses. She remembered watching the black skirts of the ladies sweep elegantly past the table, and the men shuffled by in highly polished boots. Her stomach churned at the memory of the heavy perfume of the flowers and the sweet smell of the cakes coated in marzipan.

She hid a long time under the table until the last voice died away that day. The room was quiet and Lauren knew that she was alone in the room with her father's corpse. Her solemn father, stretched out soberly in a box, his white hands folded over his chest like a wax mannequin melting in the candlelight. Suddenly, someone reached under the table and grasped little Lauren by the arm. She screamed in terror.

"Be still!" scolded the nun, wrapping her arms around Lauren. "Everything will be alright. I am taking you and your sister to live with us at the convent."

The nun wiped her tears and smoothed her hair. Lauren looked at the corpse of her father. He was ready for his journey, and she was ready for hers.

Swallowing hard, Lauren came back to the present. She looked around the deteriorated sitting room. She took a step, and suddenly the chamber started to whirl. It seemed as if the floor came up and hit her in the face. Lauren crumbled down onto the moldy planking, completely helpless with her head spinning and her stomach churning. She was too weak to pull herself up, so she remained on the soggy wood floor staring under the oak table.

Chapter 5

The storm returned to the Louisiana country, equal if not stronger in magnitude. The trees over the De Beauville plantation crouched in self-defense, trying to maintain their grip on the earth while the wind pulled savagely at their roots. Heavily taxed waterways spilled down new avenues bursting wildly over the embankments, hastily seeking new ground. The plantation strained under the stress of the tempest. Water streamed through the holes in the roof and the wind ripped shutters from their window casements. Debris tumbled madly across the grounds of the estate, smashing everything in its path.

Lauren did not see the destruction; she remained on the floor of the sitting room, sliding in and out of consciousness. Her injuries had sapped her strength, and a small puddle of blood had pooled on the floor by her mouth. All sense of reality left her. One moment it seemed like she had been on the floor for weeks, the next a heartbeat. The storm sounded distant and remote. She felt no fear, only groggy delirium.

A low groaning sound came from under the floor, and some wood cracked. Lauren did not realize that the wind was lifting the plantation house from its very foundation. She fancied she could hear the slaves rattling pots and pans, speaking in hushed tones as they bustled about the plantation getting ready for dinner. She slipped back into a swoon.

Waking again she heard a man bark, "Carefully now! Put her down gently!"

Lauren felt a blanket drop over her body and someone brush the hair off her face whispering, "I must leave you now but I'll be back." She opened her eyes but saw no one. She fancied she had just been tucked her into her bed upstairs for the night.

When Lauren awoke hours later, the storm had ceased. She was in the sitting room, but instead of resting on the hard cold floor, she was lying on a fur blanket in front of a fire. She saw a young man leaning over the hearth, stirring something in a large cast iron pot. He stepped from the fireside to the window, unlatching a shutter. The storm had weakened the hinges, and the entire piece dropped from the house onto the ground below with a crash. Chuckling, the young man peeked at the smashed shutter below, then sat down on the sill swinging one leg up to balance his lean body.

The wind blew a lock of brown hair onto his forehead, and Lauren watched him stretch in the sunshine. The boy appeared to be around seventeen years of age, and she wondered if he had been the one to move her onto the hide.

He dozed for a while in the sunlight then noticed her watching him and jumped down from the sill. "Well you *are* awake! We survived quite a storm, but it is over now." He gestured toward the window, "Look, the sun has returned."

The young man slid across the floor and ended up sitting cross-legged in front of Lauren. He was dressed in buckskin and wore his hair tied back with a leather thong, a broad smile stretching across his face. "My name is Rene' Lupone, son of Gabriel Lupone. What's yours?"

With great effort, Lauren whispered her name, but he could not understand her. He simply nodded, knowing that it was far too early to converse with his new friend.

It was painful even to breathe, and Lauren felt sick to her stomach. She heard a door slam and a man entered the room standing over her.

"She is awake, Papa, but I am afraid she cannot talk," said Rene.'

The handsome but weathered face of Gabriel Lupone looked down at Lauren. "Where is your family, girl? We must know where to take you." He hesitated a moment and continued, "I see you wear a wedding ring. Where is your husband?"

Remembering yesterday, Lauren's eyes filled with tears, and she turned her head.

Monsieur Lupone whispered to his son, "Perhaps her husband was killed in the storm. Let her rest now, Rene'." Putting a hand on his son's shoulder, he continued, "We will return in an hour to question her further. There is no time to waste. By journey's end there could be snow."

Rene' and his father left to repair the damage done to their bateaux during the storm. The party who had found Lauren consisted of twenty-two men who had been trading flour, corn and pelts in New Orleans for the precious commodities of silk, sugar and gunpowder imported from Paris and the Indies. They made this arduous journey once a year from the village of Kaskaskia in the Illinois country to obtain supplies for their isolated colony to the north. Originally, the group had been over ninety souls strong, but the hurricane had left the convoy fragmented and disorganized, and several crewmembers had died.

For the rest of the morning the group worked at a feverish pace, mending sails and repairing holes in their flat-bottomed barge-like vessels called bateaux. The men were tired but anxious to start for home. Although it took only three weeks to paddle down the Mississippi, the return upstream took a painstaking three months. They missed their families and wanted to put the exhausting journey behind them.

Monsieur Lupone stood up, wiped his hands on his trousers and ordered, "Finish tarring that last canoe and we'll be off. There's one thing left I must attend to before we embark."

The storm had left the group with no skipper, and the men turned to Gabriel Lupone for leadership. His patient but firm disposition won their respect as well as his keen sense of justice.

He started up the hill toward the house with Rene' behind him. He turned to his son and barked, "What are you so interested in? Don't start any silly, schoolboy ideas. We know nothing about this girl, and I *cannot* be saddled with an injured female. Now go back to the crew and put the last of the pewter into those crates."

Grumbling, Rene' returned to the bateau and pitched pewter plates into a wooden box, watching the plantation house. His father was right. He was interested in this girl. She would be an inviting diversion on the way home, and he secretly hoped that they would be unable to locate her family.

Gabriel entered the sitting room and looked at Lauren apprehensively. He watched the girl sleep while he considered his options. He concluded that there was only one solution, to find her family immediately. "How are you feeling?" Gabriel asked as he squatted down in front of the girl.

Lauren opened her eyes and swallowed hard, trying unsuccessfully to clear her throat. Monsieur Lupone dipped a drinking gourd into a bucket of water and placed it to her lips.

"Where is your family, your husband? I must know so we can find you shelter."

Lauren only stared at him.

"Have you no family, child?"

Lauren shook her head slowly.

"Where is your husband? You must find the strength to tell me. Our party must return to Kaskaskia immediately. I am sorry, Madame--is your husband dead?"

Lauren licked her lips and whispered, "Dead."

"I am sorry," he said, sympathetically. "Do you live here?"

Lauren considered the question a moment then said, "No, the English Colonies."

Lupone blinked in disbelief, slapped his thighs and bellowed, "Well I can't take you there! Damn it to hell!"

He stood up and paced the room, shaking his head. He turned to the window and looked down at the group of men, loading the last of the supplies onto the bateaux. He knew they must start for home. "What the hell am I supposed to do?" he mumbled to himself.

He turned away and paced again. Suddenly, he stopped and looked down at Lauren. "It is the only way. You must come with us."

*   *   *

"Mama, come quickly! They're home!" cried the child dashing from the cabin, leaving the door open.

Madame Lupone wiped her hands on her apron and took a shawl from the peg. "Come, little one," she said softly as she picked up the baby. Glancing into the cracked mirror on the bureau, the woman smoothed her hair into place.

The years had been kind to Anne Lupone. After seven children, two miscarriages and a lifetime in the Illinois country, her pale skin was smooth and free of wrinkles. In her middle years, Anne's hair was still the color of corn silk and her figure firm. She attributed it to her happy marriage to Gabriel.

"Mama, you are so slow. You must come now!" little Justina cried. The child ran back and took her mother's hand pulling her in the direction of the docks on the Kaskaskia River. The entire village was in a flurry. The convoy had returned from New Orleans that morning and brought needed supplies as well as letters from relatives and friends in France.

"Be careful with that, Cassill, that barrel holds Madame Peron's fine china!" barked Gabriel at a pock-faced young man as he hoisted a box roughly upon his shoulder.

Gabriel looked drawn and tired. The expedition had been a success, but the trip had taken it's toll on him.

The entire convoy of eighty eight arrived safely in Kaskaskia. The storm had separated them for three months, but in the end there had been only two deaths, an extraordinarily low number for such a perilous journey.

The villagers rushed down to greet their loved ones, and when Gabriel looked up he saw Anne with the baby and Justine running toward him. The little girl threw herself into her father's arms, and Gabriel sandwiched the children against his chest as he hugged his wife. "My God, woman, I've missed you," he said, kissing her.

"Where are the other children?" he asked, anxiously.

"They are here and there," she replied. With tears in her eyes she asked, "Where is Rene'?"

"I don't know right now," he said stretching to see over the barrels and crates, looking for his eldest son. "But he is well."

Anne studied her husband. She could see the lines grow deeper in his face after each expedition, but this time when he returned the furrows were even more pronounced. "What went wrong? You seem weary."

"Oh, I'm alright. There were one or two problems to deal with," he said, with a sigh. He turned to pick up a barrel and continued, "First there was the storm, and then there was this girl--"

Suddenly, without warning, Lauren burst around the corner and slammed into Gabriel. The force of the impact knocked him back several steps.

"Oh, Monsieur, I'm so sorry!" she gasped, staggering back with her hand over her mouth. "I didn't see you. Rene' was chasing me--"

Next, Rene' came around the corner and crashed into Gabriel too. The boy apologized sincerely, but his chest was heaving with laughter.

"You see, my dear wife," Gabriel said, exasperated, "Here are the two problems that have made me so very weary this journey."

Chapter 6

Being young and resilient, Lauren made a full recovery from her injuries, but the battle was hard-fought. It was not the broken ribs or punctured lung which plagued her throughout the journey but a fever which threatened her life.

For days she lay in a tent on the bateau, tossing and turning, sliding in and out of consciousness. She was alone most of the time. The men of the convoy had little time to nurse her. They themselves battled exhaustion, illness and inclement weather as they paddled against the current of the Mississippi. Rene' had not forgotten his new friend though, and he tended to her as much as possible, inevitably having to return to the paddles. The convoy needed every strong back for rowing.

After weeks of fighting for her life, Lauren's fever broke, and she awoke to pain and weakness. There were endless days of flies biting her limbs and eternal nights of mosquitoes pursuing her flesh. In the evening, she took shelter under her blankets preferring the stale air under the covers to the feeding frenzy of the bugs. In spite of these hardships, the girl grew stronger. It was several months before she could do any kind of work on the journey, but even then as she assisted in food preparation, she was pale and weak.

Her presence put a strain on the men as well. They were not used to the company of a female, and many resented having to cover their backs in the hot sun. From sunup to sundown they pulled at the oars, their muscles aching and their legs cramping. Occasionally the men sang the song of the voyageur, but most times, they were silent, rowing back and forth, lost in the rhythm of their labor. Rowing upriver, fighting the powerful current of the Mississippi was a grueling task. Several of the group succumbed to fatigue, and one slave lost his life, dying with paddles in hand, when his heart gave out. The monotony was nearly intolerable and morale was low.

Every night the group broke camp somewhere along the river's edge. The Chickasaw Indians, enemies of the French, were native to this area, so the men of the convoy carefully scouted each campsite before lighting a fire and rolling out bedrolls. There had been dangerous encounters with these tribes in the past, and every man knew well the age-old grudge these Indians held against the French.

Dinner each night consisted of corn and bacon or dried venison. Each man consumed as much food as possible, replenishing energy expended throughout the day. There was little time for gaming or conversation after the evening meal, and the paddlers would drop heavily onto their bearskin bedrolls exhausted from the day's work. Unfortunately, a good night's rest would not follow. Bugs would plague the men, robbing them of precious hours of sleep and causing them to toss and turn. They would awaken weary and bad-tempered, condemned to the same drudgery the next day.

When Lauren finally became aware of her surroundings, she realized that the country in which she traveled had changed considerably. Gone were the cypress trees and Spanish moss as well as the sultry closeness of the Louisiana air. The temperature here was cool. The trees looked different reflecting brilliant colors in the crisp sunshine, and there was freshness in the air which filled her lungs like never before. So this strange land is the Illinois Country, she thought. The nuns had spoken of it occasionally. She had no idea this wide river traveled so far to the north, and she wondered why these people would want to live so far into the wilderness.

It was also strange for Lauren to be in the company of so many men. Her life had been exclusively with women, and it was disconcerting to be in the presence of twenty-two males. The men avoided Lauren, but she was keenly aware of their eyes on her when she turned her back. Gabriel did not like having such an attractive young female on the voyage, and he felt responsible for her safety. These men had not been with women for a long time, and her vulnerability robbed his peace of mind.

As her strength returned, so did her enthusiasm, and she found the journey to the north to be a grand adventure. The prospect of a new home filled with fresh new faces excited her, and it quelled, for a time, the restlessness that plagued her. By the time they reached the Illinois Country, Lauren was in full health and ready to approach this new life with bold resolve.

The convoy left the Mississippi River and was heading up one of its tributaries when someone shouted, "Home!"

Standing on the tips of her toes, Lauren shaded her eyes. Kaskaskia was still upriver, but she could see smoke circling from chimneys and a cluster of buildings. Standing watch on a bluff across the river was a timber fort with four bastions. Dogs were barking in the distance, and there was an air of excitement as the convoy approached the village.

"There will be time for greeting your families later," shouted Monsieur Lupone firmly. "We must unload our cargo, and then you may return to your homes."

Lauren's heart was pounding in her chest. Her eyes were riveted to the people standing on shore. *They did not look so very different from the city dwellers of New Orleans.* The women wore colorful bodices over muslin waists and ankle length skirts made of calico or wool. The men wore vests over cotton shirts and knee britches with long woolen stockings. Some were clothed entirely in buckskin, but everyone, man and woman alike wore moccasins.

The French were not the only inhabitants of Kaskaskia. Negro and Indian slaves stood on the riverbank waiting for the bateaux. Once they were at the landing, Monsieur Lupone barked orders, directing his crew and the slaves to unload.

Lauren drank in every nuance of Kaskaskia. For the first time in her life she was a participant, not a bystander watching from an oak tree behind convent walls. The village was in an absolute uproar. There were oxen pulling carts from the river, fathers carrying children on their shoulders, and women rushing to and from market gathering food for the homecoming celebration. Every resident looked relieved. Loved ones had returned home at last, and supplies had arrived before the winter winds.

Unlike the streets of New Orleans, Lauren saw little poverty here. The villagers seemed prosperous and well fed. It was obvious this backcountry was fruitful.

Similar to Southern Louisiana, the homes were constructed of a series of posts set directly onto the ground joined with *bousillage*, clay mixed with straw aggregate. Most had wood shingle or thatched roofs, a porch on two sides, and always a picket fence enclosing the yard. The smoke from the fireplaces smelled heavenly to Lauren in this crisp air, and she gathered her jacket more closely around herself.

Anne Lupone looked at Lauren, "I see you wear Rene's capot. Have you no warm clothing?"

"I have nothing beyond the clothes on my back."

Anne stopped walking and looked at Lauren, "How is this?"

"Monsieur Lupone was good enough to take me in after my husband was killed in the hurricane."

"You had no one in New Orleans to take you?"

"No--Not really," said Lauren.

"You dear little thing, you have been very brave. It must be very difficult losing one's husband."

Lauren did not want to lie to this good woman. "To be honest, Madame I hardly knew him. You see, it was an arranged marriage, and the storm hit on our wedding day. Please feel no pity for me. I cannot grieve for someone I did not know."

Anne squeezed her hand and smiled, "That makes me feel better. Now let's go home."

The Lupone farmstead sat on the edge of the common fields which stretched out in long strips toward the bluffs. A small fence surrounded the house and garden, and a large barn in back housed cattle and pigs. Several geese rushed up to Lauren, hissing and pecking at her as she stepped in the yard. She jumped aside laughing.

"It's unusual to have the house empty. The children are all down at the docks taking part in the celebration. We have been blessed with six children, and when they are all here it seems like twenty!"

Lauren looked around the cabin. Everything was immaculate. As if Anne was reading her mind she said, "Our home is very clean and organized thanks to Monsieur Lupone. As long as I have known the man, everything must be in its place." Still holding the baby, Anne walked over to a ladder and pointed up, "The little ones sleep here in the loft and you may too. Rene' sleeps down here by the fire."

"Madame, you are most gracious, but how am I to repay you?"

"We shall not discuss that today. Tonight you are our guest."

She put the baby down in a cradle by the fire and said, "Now we must worry about supper. Tonight is merely gumbo. We shall have our special meal tomorrow when the sugar arrives from the docks. We will slaughter a goose and make several sweets. Tomorrow will be our celebration."

The women set to work at the kitchen table preparing the evening meal. Anne was pleased to have another female by her side. After chopping some onions and dumping them into the gumbo, Lauren looked around. It felt good here. It felt like home. The walls were in bad need of a white wash, but the floors were immaculate and the furniture was in good repair. A walnut cupboard with double doors stood against one wall as well as a sideboard and several chairs. The sturdy kitchen table sat in the center of the room with a smooth pine top and legs made of cherry wood. Lauren noticed several pieces pewter resting on the mantle and a flintlock musket on the wall above it. The bedroom held a fine bedstead, which Anne said she brought into the marriage as a dowry. It had rich rose-colored bed curtains and a matching spread.

Suddenly the door burst open and a swarm of children rushed in followed by Rene'. The little ones surrounded Lauren, pulling at her skirt, climbing up her legs, vying for attention as Rene pushed the door shut against the cold wind. He shouted over the roar, "I can't believe that you are here! It's no surprise you fit so well!"

"Come here Rene. Let me look at you," ordered his mother. "My how you've grown!" and she patted his face. There was no doubt in the woman's mind that he had changed. Rene's figure had hardened and his face looked more mature. The dimples were still in his cheeks and the lock of hair still fell carelessly onto his forehead, but clearly, he was older. Her son had left Kaskaskia a boy and returned a man.

"Where is your father?" she asked suddenly.

"He will be late tonight. He said that I must eat and return to the docks immediately."

"Very well," she replied and started to dish up gumbo.

Rene' sat down at the table and watched with an air of amusement as his sisters and brothers swarmed Lauren. The girls fussed with her hair, and the boys were wrestling and tumbling at her feet.

"Rene,' there will be hot baths waiting for you and your father tonight when you return," said Mrs. Lupone. Turning to Lauren, she said, "I will find some clothes for you after you bathe. You cannot wear that torn gown and Rene's weathered capot."

Anne sliced a loaf of black bread, placed a bowl of butter on the table and sat down. "Come now everyone and sit down. We will say, Grace."

Lauren smiled. She liked it here. At least for now, she had found her home.

Chapter 7

December brought not only the season of Advent, but also another birthday for Lauren. With all of the changes in her surroundings, she barely noticed that she was growing into a woman. At sixteen, most of the girls in Kaskaskia were married and taking on the responsibilities of motherhood, but to Lauren, marriage meant being buried alive. She was giddy with her newfound freedom, and she awoke each day ready to embrace her life with open arms.

Throughout the month of December, she stayed with the Lupones and worked with them. Gabriel and Anne had little time to discuss a situation for Lauren, so they made no decisions. In fact, they were relieved to have the girl help them with household duties and childcare. The chores of the farm were left mainly to Anne and Rene' because Gabriel and his slave were moving supplies from the bateaux to the storehouse at the fort.

Lauren was in charge of household duties with Didier, their Negro house slave. Anne was pleased to see how quickly the girl picked up the routines of the home, and the children were overjoyed with their new nanny. Rene' enjoyed this new arrangement as well, and made frequent visits to the house telling his mother that he had better check on things.

Included in all of these new experiences for Lauren, was snow. One afternoon, shortly after she arrived, Rene' burst into the kitchen exclaiming, "Come to the window, Lauren, and look! It's snowing!"

Never in all her life had she seen anything like it. Of course, there had been the occasional flake that fell on New Orleans in January but nothing like this. The sky was positively alive with motion. Big, wet flakes drifted to the ground and instead of melting instantly, they blanketed everything, the grass, the house, the fence, the entire town.

"You must come out now!" demanded Rene,' grabbing her arms. She followed him outside, stopping on the front step to catch the cool gems. It was like nothing she had ever experienced, and suddenly a feeling of loneliness washed over her. Simone should be here. Simone should be by her side catching snowflakes with her, not strangers.

"What's wrong? You don't like it? You look sad."

Blinking back tears, Lauren smiled and said, "You imagine things. I love it!" and she stepped down the stairs.

Swept up in the excitement, the children ran past her into the yard and gathered the snow into clumps for a snowball fight. Several of them tried to stuff snow down Rene's shirt, and he hurtled them down into the snow where they landed, screaming and giggling.

Lauren could not help but be cheered by this merriment and began to laugh. She pushed snow down his shirt too, but when he attempted to do the same she screamed, "Improper! Very improper!" and ran to the back of the house. Rene' ran in the opposite direction, catching her in his arms as she came around the corner.

Suddenly in an embrace, their laughter stopped, and the smiles dropped from their faces. Rene' placed his hand at the back of Lauren's neck and pulled her into a kiss.

"I've been meaning to do that for a long time," he murmured.

Lauren blinked, and then ran up the steps to the porch.

"Lauren, wait!"

Bounding up the stairs, Rene grabbed her shoulders and said, "I'm sorry. I didn't mean to offend you. I thought--" he stammered, "I thought you might like it."

Lauren knitted her brows and said, "I do like it. You may do it as often as you please," and went into the house.

*   *   *

The anticipation for Christmas was building, and every resident of Kaskaskia made preparations. This meant days of cooking, baking and cleaning. They had to butcher chickens, turkeys and geese, make stews and doughnuts, which were, sugared and hung in pillowcases. They froze these special pastries until Christmas Eve when they were thawed and consumed at the *Reveillion*, a holiday feast after Midnight Mass.

Most of the work this time of year fell to the women of the house, Mrs. Lupone, Lauren and Didier. They worked together from sunup until sundown rolling out piecrusts, cleaning poultry, and scrubbing copper pots until they glistened. Anne and Lauren became increasingly close. Lauren had never known her mother, and in Anne she found a tender nurturing parent with a sympathetic ear. Anne listened for hours as the girl shared her hopes and dreams. Never once did the woman criticize or belittle her. Never did she attempt to give her advice or lecture. She simply allowed Lauren to experience, for the first time in her life, the unconditional love of a parent.

For Anne, the experience was similar. Agnes, her first-born girl, would have been Lauren's age had she lived, but a fever had taken her life ten years earlier. The company of Lauren filled a void in Madame Lupone that had been nagging her for many years. Gabriel observed their deepening affection for one another and grew fond of Lauren himself. He so loved Anne that if someone made her happy, then he was happy too.

"What do you find to talk about all day?" he would ask his wife.

The reply would always be, "Nothing you would be interested in."

Christmas came at last, and everyone in Kaskaskia prepared themselves for Midnight Mass at The Church of the Immaculate Conception. It was a cold night, and the townspeople trudged silently through the snow carrying lanterns and torches, speaking in hushed tones out of respect for the birth of the Savior

Rene' slid his arm through Lauren's as they walked through the dark, snowy streets. "It is very pretty here with just the lanterns and the candles in the windows, isn't it?"

"This place is like nothing I've ever dreamed of," said Lauren. "Your lives are so different here yet I feel--" and she hesitated, "I feel at home."

All through Mass, the two young people sat side by side, their arms touching. The town busy bodies craned their necks looking at Lauren, narrowing their eyes disapprovingly at the masses of curly, auburn hair that she tied up into a knot. They gossiped about *that* widow from New Orleans, speculating about her relationship with Rene' Lupone. Lauren observed their intrusive eyes and smiled to herself; she was used to the nuns. These old ladies did not scare her.

After Mass, everyone returned home for the *Reveillion*. Everything culminated in this one night, and when Gabriel threw the Yule Log onto the fire, the family cheered, knowing that this gesture signaled the beginning of the celebration. Didier set the table and put the finishing touches on the meal during Mass. Moments after they arrived home, they were feasting on meat pies, turkey, oyster soup and maple syrup tarts.

"Father, when are you going to fiddle?" asked little Pierre, the seven year old.

"When I am as full and fat as an old bear," Gabriel said, taking another piece of tourtiere. After chewing a while, he said with a twinkle in his eye, "I will play, but there will be absolutely no dancing!"

"Oh!" was the disappointed reply, but when he began to laugh, all the children raced over and jumped into his lap, pretending to hit him.

"Now Anne, my fiddle!" he commanded swatting her backside as she left the table.

In the bedroom, Anne knelt down and opened an old cherry hope chest. She folded back several blankets and there on top of her wedding dress lay Gabriel's fiddle. Carefully she lifted it out and closed the lid. Sitting back on her heels, she reminisced for a moment. *How handsome Gabriel had been the first night she had seen him.* He was playing his fiddle at a sugaring off party in Cahokia, and she knew from the moment she set eyes on him that he was the man for her. His hair was wavy and dark, his eyes a bright blue and his dress meticulous. In spite of the mistakes he made playing fiddle, there was an air of confidence and good humor about him. Gabriel had changed little over the years. There were streaks of gray in his hair and fine lines in his face, but he was still a handsome man, and she knew the women in town envied her. In spite of all the hard times Anne still loved Gabriel dearly, and not a day went by that she did not thank God for him.

"Anne! What are you doing! These children are pawing me to death!"

Anne stood up and went back to the kitchen, handing Gabriel the instrument.

"Father, let me play first," pleaded Rene,' as he reached for the fiddle, "We want to see you and Mother dance."

"Oh no," said Anne giggling. She tucked some hair back into her cap self-consciously.

"Why not?" teased Gabriel, "Are you afraid that I may dance better than you?"

"What!" she cried and held out her hands. "We'll see who the better dancer is!"

With that Rene' put the fiddle to his chin and began to play. Lauren put the baby on her lap, and the children clapped as the two whirled round and round the room.

Lauren marveled at how young the couple looked tonight. For the first time since she had arrived, she could see the beauty in Anne's face, and the handsome figure Gabriel cut. They were the first married couple she had ever known, and she realized that some weddings were indeed about love. The dining and dancing went on until dawn, and everyone dropped into bed at dawn, exhausted but satisfied from a night of merriment.

The New Year brought more celebration, but this time the residents of Kaskaskia opened their doors to their friends, relatives, and neighbors. After the New Year Mass, the Lupones stopped at the home of Gabriel's brother, Francois and his wife Justine, who was an Illinois Indian. After some refreshments, they moved on to the next house where Anne's cousin lived, and then they visited Gabriel's uncle. The family returned home welcoming several more family members and friends in the afternoon.

"Tonight is the best part of all," Rene' said, "It is the New Year gala at Monsieur Bernard's home. He is very rich and has a large home with plenty of room to dance."

Lauren sighed and sat back into her chair. Her first dance and she had nothing but old clothes to wear. As if reading her mind, Anne stepped over to her and murmured, "Don't worry. We will find something nice for you to wear."

Late in the afternoon as the sun began to drop in the sky, Anne called Lauren into the bedroom. She held up a blue taffeta gown with a cream-colored stomacher. "I was thinking this would be lovely on you. The color will go so well with your hair. Don't you agree?"

Lauren gasped, "It's beautiful! I have never worn any garment that elegant. The nuns only let us wear 'sensible' clothes."

Anne smiled, "Well you are ready for this now. After a few alterations, I'm sure it will suit you just fine."

"But is it your dress? I can't allow you to alter—"

"Nonsense, now come here," she said threading a needle.

With skilled hands, Anne quickly made the dress suitable for Lauren's figure and helped her tie a cream-colored ribbon in her hair.

"Come here to the mirror," Anne said smiling.

The mirror was not large enough for Lauren to view the entire ensemble, but there was enough visible in the cracked reflection for her to smile with delight. "Oh! I am so excited! Is it time to go yet?"

"As soon as I am ready. Now out!" Anne demanded, pushing Lauren out the door.

"Well! Well! Look at you," said Gabriel standing up as Lauren entered the room, "You are certainly more attractive than the first day I saw you, all bruised and battered at the plantation house."

He sat down by the fire to smoke his pipe, and after taking a puff he barked at Rene', "Close your mouth, boy, and find the lady a chair!"

Rene' jumped up, pulled a chair from the corner and placed it by the fire, blushing.

It took a long time to get the family of six ready, but Anne and Lauren managed to wash and dress every child and put refreshments in a basket for the celebration. Then as a group, they walked to the outskirts of town to the Bernard home.

The New Year celebration was well underway by the time the Lupones arrived. Fiddlers were playing a merry tune while couples whirled about the dance floor. Several women set up long tables against the walls filled with round cheeses, *tourtieres*, cakes, and hard cider. There was an air of excitement here, and Lauren was eager to join in. She assumed that Rene' would take her immediately to the dance floor, but when she turned around, he was gone. She searched the crowd for his face but did not see him. Everyone was chattering and laughing and before she knew it, the rest of the Lupones had vanished into the crowd leaving her alone by the huge fireplace to watch the festivities. Young and old attended the dance and Lauren noticed that several of the men had Indian wives or sweethearts. There were few French girls her age, and most of them were standing by the food tables holding babies and small children.

The fiddlers struck up a particularly lively tune and Lauren started to tap her foot. It did not concern her that she had never danced with a boy before. Simone had taught her several steps and this gave her all the confidence she needed.

Suddenly, a young man dressed in a somewhat worn linen shirt and knee britches approached her. He seemed nervous and stammered something about wanting to dance. She took his hand and followed him onto the dance floor. As she passed through the crowd, she noticed people looking at her and the men, in particular, watched her with a look of admiration in their eyes. For the first time in her life, Lauren was aware of her appeal. She tossed her head and turned to face her partner. He took a breath and swallowed hard before taking her hands. Off they sailed into the dance and Lauren felt as light as air. She glossed over her mistakes with a smile and before the dance was over, the young man was convinced Lauren was the most beautiful girl he had ever seen.

She did not reserve all her dances for this boy though, there were others who came in succession one after another. After seven dances, Lauren was finally exhausted and stumbled over to the long oak table that held the food and drink. Leaning against the table, she longed to loosen her stays.

Suddenly, there were screams of surprise and laughter as masqueraders wearing animal skins burst into the room. They were dressed up as monkeys, buffalo, and huge bears roaring and growling loudly, holding out sacks, which the master of the house filled with food. She overheard someone say these masqueraders were a Kaskaskian tradition. They begged from door to door every New Year's Day collecting food in this reveler's fashion for the upcoming Twelfth Night Ball. She heard a growl and two black paws grabbed her waist. She jumped, trying to release herself from the iron grasp of the masquerader. He pulled her out the nearest door and into a courtyard.

"What are you doing? Let go of me!" she screamed. Reaching up, she pulled off the mask and found Rene' doubled over with laughter.

"You were terrified!" he guffawed, "You didn't know it was me!"

"I did too know it was you!" she cried, trying to cover her embarrassment, "What do you think you're doing dragging me away from the party like a sack of potatoes!"

"I brought you out here because I wanted to be alone with you, that's all."

"Well I don't want to be alone with you! I'm going back to dance."

Rene' caught her hand and pulled her into an embrace. "You told me once that I may kiss you whenever I want. Is that still true?"

"No," Lauren snapped, "Not anymore!"

Suddenly, she started to giggle, pushing him away. "Stop it. It's cold out here. I want to go in."

"I'll keep you warm," Rene' said as he wrapped her in warm fur and began to kiss her.

Suddenly, Lauren lost her inhibitions. The heat of the young man's kisses intensified, and she invited them freely. He ran his hands over her body, and she was helpless to stop him.

The next moment, Rene was torn from her embrace, and an angry voice roared, "That will be enough!"

Lauren stood petrified as Gabriel dragged Rene' out of the courtyard and into the street. He looked back and demanded at the top of his lungs, "You, my girl, are coming too, now!"

Terrified, Lauren followed. When they returned home, Gabriel sent her up to the loft to bed while he chastised Rene downstairs in the kitchen. She tossed and turned all night, thoroughly ashamed of herself.

When she finally climbed down the ladder in the morning, she found a very serious Gabriel sitting at the kitchen table, and Anne standing by the hearth with a tear-streaked face. Rene' was nowhere to be found.

"Good morning, Lauren. Now please sit down," said Gabriel, gesturing to a chair at the table.

Without a word, Lauren slid into the chair, looking down at her lap. Gabriel stood up with his hands behind his back and began to pace. "My girl, you have gathered the affection of everyone in this family, and for this I am truly grateful. However, my son has taken it beyond friendship which is a very dangerous avenue for you both. Being your guardian, I must consider your reputation and your prospects for marriage, so it is with great difficulty that I say," Anne turned away and faced the fireplace, "You must go and live elsewhere."

Lauren blinked and her jaw dropped.

Gabriel continued, "The owner of the Kaskaskia lead mine, a gentlemen by the name of, Jean-Baptist Aberjon is in need of a companion for his wife. She is an invalid and in need of constant care. I have arranged for you to be employed by him. You will reside at his home. You must leave this afternoon."

Chapter 8

The snow crunched under Lauren's feet as she walked to the Aberjon residence, a bundle of clothes under her arm. She walked alone along the streets of Kaskaskia, keeping her eyes down. Anne had offered to accompany her, but Lauren insisted that she remain at home.

No one seemed to notice Lauren as she trudged down the street through the snow. It was only last night she had been the bell of the ball, but this afternoon she was nothing more than another face in a scarf. Lauren stopped in the middle of the road fighting the impulse to run but thought better of it. She made her choices, and they had led her here to the Illinois backcountry. She must carry on knowing she had nowhere else to go.

It was easy to identify the Aberjon residence. Anne told her it was by far the grandest home in all of Kaskaskia and Lauren saw it standing proudly on a hill near a frozen stream, surrounded by trees. Every home in Kaskaskia had a fence around it, but this one had a grand, ornate enclosure made of iron. The house was the only structure in the village erected of stone, and it sported three stories and two *galeries* or porches, one on the main level wrapping around the house and the other attached to the second story.

She made her way up the walkway to the front steps. She noticed the knocker on the door. The object seemed large and imposing in the cold afternoon sun. Reluctantly, she reached up and let it drop. Footsteps echoed from inside and an Indian girl answered the door. Without saying a word, she gestured for Lauren to step in and disappeared down the hall.

Pulling her gloves off, Lauren looked around the foyer. Across from the front door a set of stairs covered with patterned carpet led up to the second story and the bedrooms. She looked around to see if anyone was coming and stepped down the hall to peek. The main level had a library, sitting room, office and a large drawing room. Lauren thought the drawing room was the largest room she had ever seen. Long drapes hung in folds onto the floor, a cherry card table and chairs sat in front of the fireplace with wine glasses and two silver candlesticks. There were various armchairs around the room, and in one corner stood a harpsichord and bench. A rug was on the hardwood floor, the color burgundy and cream. It was indeed a sumptuous room, thought Lauren.

"You're Madame Heathstone?" she heard someone say.

Lauren whirled around and faced Monsieur Aberjon, a man of middle years only slightly taller than herself. The Indian girl was behind him.

"Yes, Monsieur, I have been sent by the Lupones."

"We've been expecting you."

Turning to the girl he said, "Eugenie, take her things upstairs immediately."

Lauren scrutinized her new employer as he walked over to a cabinet, took out a crystal decanter and filled a glass with amber colored liquid. His clothing was of a fine cut, and the lace he wore at his neck was of a splendid quality. His boots were polished to a high shine and his nails were impeccably clean. Yet despite this finery, Monsieur Aberjon had a coarse demeanor. It was apparent to Lauren that this man was not born to his present station in life and that he was not suited to this fancy dress. His skin was dark and leathery and his shoulders were rounded. He did not wear a wig and his bristly hair stood out straight in a pigtail at the back of his neck. His right eyelid drooped, and when he looked at Lauren, she felt a chill.

"My wife is quite weak and for the most part bed ridden," he said turning around to face her. "You will find her unpredictable and subject to--shall we say--occasional outbursts. She has little interest in anything beyond her dogs and an occasional game of draughts." Monsieur Aberjon tossed his head back emptying the contents of the glass in one swallow, "Your duties will include round the clock care and companionship to Madame, some minor household duties and of course walking the dogs. In return you will receive your room and board." He walked to the doorway and before leaving stated, "I spend much of my time at the lead mine, so I am home seldom. We have two house slaves. Talk to Eugenie or Marianne if you need anything. You will find them most helpful. Now go and meet my wife, Josephine. Her room is up the stairs and on the left."

Monsieur Aberjon left Lauren alone in the drawing room. Everyone had been cordial, the surroundings were luxurious and the arrangement agreeable, but a tiny voice whispered caution to her. Shaking off the anxiety, she looked around the room once more. She remembered Rene' telling her that the Aberjon's owned the lead mine and she deduced that excavation must be very profitable.

Never good at controlling her impulses, Lauren found herself walking toward the elegant harpsichord marveling at its workmanship. She had never seen a musical instrument of such beauty and she longed to hear just one note from the dainty keyboard.

Just as she reached out to touch a key, she heard someone say, "Madame's room is this way." Lauren jumped and saw that it was the young Indian girl again. The servant's manner continued to be quiet and reserved as she turned and walked out into the hall. After showing her to Madame's room, the girl left as silently as she came.

A clock ticked heavily as Lauren approached the bedroom door and knocked. Someone told her to come in, and when she stepped over the threshold into the boudoir, bright color blinded her for a moment. Not a variety of colors and hues but one tone repeated in every furnishing, pillow, drape and coverlet; it was the color pink. The upholstery on the armchair was pink, the wallpaper was pink, the duvet and every pillow on the bed was pink and lying on the bed in a pink wrap was an overweight, middle aged woman with long red hair hanging in tangles about her porcine face. Sitting next to her were two jovial-looking Great Dane dogs, which Lauren noted were the *only* articles in the room not pink.

"Please come in dear," Madame Aberjon said and then with a sweep of her arm asked, "Isn't the room lovely? I designed it myself. I'm thinking next year maybe red. Or do you think pink is more flattering to my complexion?"

Lauren's mouth hung open in amazement. The lady of the house was pleasant but apparently eccentric. Lauren replied, "Oh, Madame. I much prefer pink to the red."

"Smart girl, smart girl, I knew I could count on Jean-Baptiste to find a good companion. Now come over here and sit by me." She reached out a chubby hand and patted the duvet. "Now tell me all about yourself, dear. I want to know everything, simply everything."

Sliding onto the edge of the bed, Lauren began to tell the woman about her life at the Academy when suddenly Madame Aberjon shrieked, "Baroness! Get down!"

One of the dogs was eating cake off a plate on the nightstand. The distressed woman took a lace hankie out of her sleeve and swished at the animal several times before collapsing back onto the bed gasping. Frantically Lauren searched for something to cool the lady down as the dog lapped at the dainty on the nightstand completely unconcerned. She found a pink, oriental fan resting under a book and opened it hastily.

"I am reduced to helplessness," Madame Aberjon whined, shaking her head, "absolute, utter dependency."

Lauren's stomach churned as the woman's heavy perfume wafted up to her nostrils. Her long, red hair streaked with gray lay in a tangled mess all over the pillows and her wrinkled white breasts heaved up and down as she gasped for air. The bed lurched to one side as Baroness rejoined Duchess on the duvet. Lauren watched the dog lick the crumbs from its lips in a satisfied fashion. When Madame closed her eyes, Lauren made a face at the animal. The atmosphere is certainly unusual here, she thought.

"My husband just doesn't understand me," the woman whined. "He thinks that I am merely weak and languid, when in reality I am plagued by all manner of disease and suffering." Without notice, she bolted upright in bed grabbing Lauren by the arms. "Do you suppose he has gone to her today? Where did he say he was going?" she demanded, shaking Lauren.

Shocked and speechless Lauren could do nothing but stammer.

"Where did he go? Tell me!" the woman continued.

"I know not, Madame," she said breathlessly, breaking the woman's grasp and standing up. Feeling confused and frightened, Lauren took several steps backward staring at her employer.

"I've never been a good wife to him," she cried dropping back on the bed. "I'm such a disappointment, Oh Jean-Baptiste, how could you leave me for another?"

Lauren's heart was pounding. Madame Aberjon continued to cry into her pillow as Lauren backed slowly out of the room. Closing the door quietly, she looked frantically up and down the hall. *Where had that Indian girl gone?* She wanted to go to her room. She needed to collect herself. She needed to think. Lauren looked hastily in several bedchambers and at last, she found her clothing in a room at the end of the hall. Quickly shutting the door behind her, she dropped down onto the bed to catch her breath. Her instincts had been correct. There was something wrong at this house and she should run away. Madame Aberjon was a lunatic, and Lauren was now the resident caretaker of a madwoman.

Chapter 9

In spite of the hardships, days passed quickly for Lauren in her new position of companion. Madame was an extremely demanding charge, and she awakened Lauren most nights. Her days were spent feeding, washing and entertaining the invalid while her nights were spent soothing and calming the woman's anxieties. Madame Aberjon had a fear of the darkness, and every evening at twilight she would fall into a panic, clutching at Lauren's clothing pleading with her to stay by her side. The woman's personality was extremely labile and Lauren never knew what to expect, one moment she was kind and solicitous, the next hysterical and violent. On most occasions, Lauren was able to restrain the woman, but occasionally Madame Aberjon would bruise or hit her.

During this time, Lauren lost her spontaneity and carefree attitude. Her responsibilities were numerous and she found herself neglecting her own needs. Over the weeks, she lost touch with the Lupones. Rene and Anne came calling several times, but she always refused to see them. She wanted no painful reminders of her days that were gone forever. Loneliness and isolation plagued her, and she threw herself into her work, taking exceptional care of Madame.

Although Monsieur Aberjon was not home often, he did notice Lauren's efforts and thanked her with an increase in her allowance. He did not go to Josephine's room often but when he did visit her, it ended in an incident. Madame would plead with him to stay or accuse him of infidelity, and he would leave hastily asking Lauren to return in his place.

Days turned to months, and spring eventually arrived. The snow melted and birds returned. Although the roads were nothing more than greasy mud, everyone was out enjoying the longer warmer days.

"We must open your windows, Madame. The sun is out, and the birds are singing," suggested Lauren as she drew back the drapes and unlatched the window.

"Oh, do you think it is wise, dear? There could be a draft," replied the woman sliding down under the covers.

"It will be good for you. Look everyone is out--" Just as she opened the window, she saw Rene walking up to the house.

"Bon jour! It's a beautiful, spring day." he called. "You must come out with me. I must talk to you."

Lauren said nothing, only swallowed hard.

"Who was that dear? That voice sounds familiar," asked Madame.

"Rene' Lupone," said Lauren, abruptly closing the window.

"Gabriel's son has come to see me? Oh the darling! Send him in," she demanded sitting up.

"But Madame," Lauren pleaded, "surely your hair, the condition of the room. I don't think now is the time."

"Nonsense, send him up," she said, straightening her gown.

Reluctantly, Lauren leaned out the window and shouted, "Madame will see you now."

With a confused look Rene' hesitated then approached the front door. Holding his hat in his hand, he waited for Lauren to come downstairs. Taking a deep breath, Lauren pulled the heavy door open and stood face to face with Rene'. Unable to contain himself, the young man scooped Lauren into his arms and swung her around, "What has been wrong with you? We were such friends and now you will not even talk to me. I've missed you so!"

"Put me down," ordered Lauren coldly.

"I don't understand," he said releasing her. "You left our home, not our hearts. Why don't you come and see us Lauren? We miss you terribly. Even Father wishes you would visit."

"I am very busy now. There is no time for entertainment. You and your family saw to that," she said turning and walking up the stairs.

Rene' hesitated in the foyer, trying to make sense of her words.

"Well? Are you coming? Madame is expecting you," Lauren said from the top of the stairs.

He climbed the stairs apprehensively and followed her to Madame's room stopping at the threshold. The breeze from the open window carried the scent of heavy perfume and unwashed dogs to his nostrils, and he suppressed a gag. Swallowing hard he entered the boudoir and there like a sultana on her pillows lay Madame Aberjon with Lauren standing next to the bed. The dogs jumped up and inspected Rene' as Madame sat up.

"My darling boy, how delightful to see you," cooed the queen. "Look how you've grown! Your mother must be so proud."

Rene' looked around the room, unable to reply.

"Lauren. Please have Marianne prepare us some chocolate."

"Yes Madame," replied Lauren as she swept past Rene'.

Catching her by the wrist, he said under his breath, "You're not leaving me alone. Are you?"

"Why not," she said, "Your father seems to think I can endure being alone with her permanently. Why can't you for five minutes?"

Downstairs Lauren found Eugenie, the Indian slave in the kitchen kneading some bread. "Where is Marianne?"

"At market," was the girl's reply as she continued kneading.

"Madame would like some chocolate please. We have a guest."

Eugenie nodded and turned to the cupboard for Madame's dainty yellow teacups. Silently, she prepared the chocolate as Lauren watched. For the first time since she arrived, Lauren scrutinized Eugenie, although the same age the girl had experienced most of her life as a slave. She was petite and tidy, her dark hair knotted at the back of her head. She suspected that the Eugenie had little to say because of her malformed upper lip. It formed a large crease under her nose and prevented her from properly forming her words. Everything she said had a nasal quality and a lisp was prominent.

"How long have you been with the Aberjons, Eugenie?"

"Over ten years, Madame."

"What? You must be no more than fifteen years of age. That is your entire life."

"Yes, Madame."

"What tribe were you born to?"

"Chickasaw. I was captured when the Illinois raided my village."

"What of your family?"

"Dead or enslaved," the girl replied flatly. Turning to Lauren with the tray of chocolate she asked, "Is there anything else or may I take this up now."

"I'm sorry I didn't mean to pry, Eugenie."

Looking down at the floor, the girl waited to be dismissed.

"We shall go up now," said Lauren.

She was reluctant to return to the Madame's room. She knew that once the visit was over Rene' would try to talk to her. Eugenie gave a little knock on the door and entered the boudoir with the tray. Rene was sitting stiffly in one of the pink armchairs next to Madame's bed, and the dogs were at his feet.

"Where is Marianne?" demanded Madame Aberjon.

"She has gone to market for tonight's supper," replied Eugenie quietly as she approached the bed with the tray hot chocolate.

"Let me see that," the woman said pulling herself up. She inspected the tray with a scowl and said, "You have never made chocolate before have you, girl?"

Lauren sensed trouble and stepped forward on high alert. Rene' read Lauren's face and shifted in his seat. His eyes were darting from Madame Aberjon to Lauren. Even the dogs sensed trouble and left the room.

"This will not do!" shrieked Madame and in a flash sent the tray flying and its hot contents all over Eugenie. The girl screamed as the liquid hit her skin and Madame lunged across the bed tearing at her. "You little whore! You are the one he goes to at night! I'm not stupid!" she screamed as Lauren pinned the matron to the bed. "I've known for years! How dare you come in here!"

Struggling to free herself, Madame tried to push Lauren off as Rene' whisked Eugenie out of the room and down the hall to attend to her burns and scratches.

"You stay away from him! Do you hear me! You whore!" she continued to scream, "Oh my God, Oh My God! Let me go!" Madame Aberjon fell back and began to sob as Lauren loosened her grip. She knew from experience the time of danger had passed, and the outburst was over. Panting, Lauren straightened her own clothing and left the room.

She found Rene' in one of the guest rooms nursing Eugenie's burns. The girl was lying on the bed with her knees drawn up in pain. She said not a word but rolled from side to side moaning. Rene' dabbed cool water on her face and chest but nothing seemed to help her distress.

"I will care for her now. Thank you. You better go," ordered Lauren.

Rene's face was white and he asked, "Has she calmed down?"

"Yes."

"Lauren, I had no idea what she was like," he apologized, his eyes like saucers. "My family had no idea. All of these years Monsieur Aberjon has referred to his wife as an invalid, we thought she was merely frail and sickly. We did not know that she was a madwoman!"

Lauren bit her lip and shook her head, "I understand. Nevertheless, you must go."

Chapter 10

By the grace of God, there were no permanent scars to Eugenie's face and neck. With Lauren's care and Marianne's knowledge of medicine, the girl healed completely. Marianne, a Negro slave, gained her knowledge from her mother's stillroom when she was a child in New Orleans. The old woman mixed various plasters and packs to apply to the skin and slowly the blisters and scratches healed and disappeared. Marianne was a kind and generous woman who treated the girls like granddaughters.

Eugenie was able to help around the house on a limited basis, but Lauren had to watch her. The burns could turn dangerous if left unclean, so she inspected and changed Eugenie's dressings on a regular basis.

At first, the girls talked little, but as time went by, they opened up to one another and began to share their thoughts and feelings. They were a world apart in backgrounds, but they found common ground because of their age and their loneliness.

It was heaven for Lauren to giggle and exchange secrets with another girl. There had been no one since Simone, and once more she felt whole. For Eugenie the experience was different. It took her days before she could relax and contribute anything at all, but slowly she let her guard down. Ridicule about her deformity and years of slavery had taken its toll on her trust, but gradually the barriers eroded, and the girl opened up. The two would stand by the fire and chop vegetables or knead bread, talking and giggling, until Madame's bell would ring and Lauren would have to leave.

Lauren continued to care for Eugenie's burns and one evening when she peeked under the bandage she said, "We will see what Marianne has to say, but I think that you are almost healed."

She ladled some water into a basin and gathered Marianne's medicines together so she could dress the wound one last time. Eugenie's dark eyes followed Lauren as she moved around the kitchen talking and laughing. The girl marveled at the energy of her new French friend. It was not Eugenie's nature to be impulsive like Lauren yet she gave as much of herself as she could.

"You would have loved the New Year dance at the Bernard home," said Lauren throwing a soiled bandage into the fire, "Oh, I wish I could go back to that night." Lauren began to reel around the kitchen holding an imaginary partner. "It was the first time I ever danced, Eugenie. It was wonderful! Rene took me out under the stars and--"

"*And* you were caught by Monsieur Lupone," scolded Eugenie.

"You certainly know how to ruin a good story," said Lauren scowling. She dabbed a cloth in the basin of water and began to clean the girl's wounds.

"Rene' was here to see you again this morning," said Eugenie.

"I suppose I was upstairs with Madame *as usual*," said Lauren.

"Yes, I think you were dressing her at that time."

"Oh," Lauren sighed dabbing a poultice on the blisters, "I wish I could get away from here, even if it was only for an hour. I feel too young to be buried here."

The reflection from the fire danced over the girls as they sat deep in thought.

"I've been thinking, Lauren. Why can't Marianne and I take care of Madame while you go out some afternoon with Rene?"

"Oh, yes," said Lauren sarcastically. "You have nothing better to do than to take on my work."

"We could do it," Eugenie protested.

"I won't let you and Marianne do my work for me," she said indignantly.

"Then do our work sometime, so we can get away too."

Lauren straightened up and smiled, "Do you suppose we could do such a thing?"

"I don't see why not," returned the girl.

"Oh!" cried Lauren, grabbing Eugenie's hands. "You're brilliant! But what if Monsieur comes home?"

"Well-" Eugenie said, biting her lip, "Let's see. Of course! Take the dogs with you! We shall say you are walking the dogs and when it's our turn you can say we are at market."

"Oh Eugenie, you are wonderful!" cried Lauren, hugging her friend.

The following day Lauren finished her work as quickly as possible and settled Madame down for the afternoon. She removed her apron, put on a straw hat and tied green ribbons under her chin into a smart bow.

Marianne was in the kitchen when Lauren burst in. The old woman stopped turning the spit and marveled at the girl. Lauren had chosen a flowered waist with a green skirt Anne had made for her. She wore a pale yellow linen neckerchief tucked smartly into the matching green bodice. She had tied her auburn hair into a loose knot at the back of her head and her cheeks wore a blush of excitement.

"Slow down, slow down girl! Don't you be getting into trouble now," warned Marianne. She could still remember how springtime filled a young girl with fancy.

"I won't," promised Lauren as she raced around the kitchen preparing an apple butter sandwich and pouring a mug of milk. She stuffed the bread into her mouth and guzzled down the milk as she ran out the door.

"Don't forget the dogs!" reminded Marianne.

"Oh! I was so excited I almost forgot," she said with her mouth full.

Baroness and Duchess were delighted to go for a walk in the warm afternoon sun. The Great Danes danced and tugged at the leash. With several sharp commands, the dogs settled right down. In spite of Madame's spoiling, Lauren had taught the dogs to respect her, and they knew that she would not tolerate insubordination. She opened the gate and turned to look back. There in Madame's window was Marianne waving to her. Eugenie was in the kitchen preparing afternoon chocolate, and Monsieur was at the lead mine. All was going as planned.

Summer had come at last to Kaskaskia, and it seemed like the whole village was alive. It was a grand day and Lauren marveled at how fresh the air smelled. This time of year in New Orleans the atmosphere grew sultry and the fevers began, but here in Kaskaskia there was new life. There were gardens to tend, crops to plant and new babies being born.

Lauren took the dogs down through town directly to the Lupone home. Anne was on her knees weeding the garden when she came through the gate. She stood up and wiped her hands on her apron smiling broadly. "Well, well I didn't think I was ever going to see you again," she said hugging the girl, "We've all missed you terribly Lauren, but it is Rene who has been lost without you."

Lauren looked down. She had been cold to Rene' lately, and she hoped that Rene's feelings had not changed for her. Her heart raced at the thought of seeing him again.

Little Celeste' Lupone was sitting at Anne's feet smiling as she smeared handfuls of mud all over her face and gown. "Look at Celeste`!" Lauren laughed and she bent down to pinch the fat cheeks of the toddler.

"Oh, Child!" scolded Anne scooping her up. "Come and sit with me on the porch, and we'll have some cider," the woman said taking Lauren's hand. "The children are scattered everywhere today, so maybe you and I can talk."

It was as if they had never parted, and they chattered about every little bit of news or gossip that came to mind. Suddenly Anne took Lauren's hand, "My dear, can you ever forgive us? We had no idea what the Aberjon household was like. We never would have sent you had we known."

Lauren shook her head. "I have grown to love Madame Aberjon, and it has all been for the best."

Anne did not look convinced, but she allowed Lauren to take the conversation elsewhere. It was good to have the young girl back again, and she realized how much she loved Lauren. Lauren had missed Anne terribly too but never allowed herself to admit it until now. It was as if she had never left.

The dogs panted in the shade of the porch for an hour until at last Lauren stood up to say goodbye. "You must say 'Hello' to

Gabriel and Rene' before you go," urged Anne, "They are out in the commons."

"I had planned on it," returned Lauren closing the garden gate. She was anxious to see Rene`. She waved farewell and headed to the fields holding up her pretty skirts as she walked down the dusty road to the fields.

Gabriel was the first to see Lauren. He smiled and waved. He liked the girl in spite of her careless impulsive ways. She was young and headstrong yet he pitied her lack of peace. He could see that she was restless and unsettled in her heart.

Rene rushed up and took her hands. "It's so good to see you again! You look wonderful! How did you ever get away?"

"I worked something out," she said with a shrug. "Now there will be more time for walks."

Gabriel raised an eyebrow and looked from Lauren to Rene'. He knew what walks meant, and he groaned, "Now Rene'--"

"Please Father?"

"Well--" he said wagging his finger. "You know the rules. Her cheeks are far too rosy today," and he smiled.

Calling to the Great Danes, they waved goodbye and went down to the river. They sat on the shore talking while eagles circled in the spring sky. There were canoes and pirogues gliding downstream, and an occasional fish would jump snapping at a bug, but they noticed only each other.

Rene' looked wonderful to Lauren. His hair had grown lighter in the summer sun, and his body had grown taut and muscular from tending the crops. She wondered how she could have ever been cold to him with those dimples and that lock of hair falling onto his forehead. It felt heavenly to be young and desirable again, and when Rene' kissed her she felt alive once more.

"How often can I see you?" he asked running his hands over her hair and cheeks.

"I can meet you here every other day, at this time," she said.

Rene' reached up and pulled the ribbon at her chin. He slid her hat off and began kissing her again, but this time Lauren pushed him away. "It's late. I must go," and she stood up, brushing herself off.

"I'll be here, day after tomorrow," said Rene' kissing her hand.

"I will too," smiled Lauren, and she called to the dogs.

*   *   *

Life held new appeal for Lauren now that she had a diversion. She was more patient with Madame, more attentive to her duties and above all more carefree. She hummed when she picked up the bedroom, cajoled Madame when she threw a temper tantrum and even carried treats in her apron for Baroness and Duchess.

Eugenie was happier too. On the days Lauren stayed home, she would go out, and the brief escapes lightened her heart. There was a world of news for them to share and Marianne took great joy in seeing her girls so happy.

"Eugenie, what did you do yesterday on your afternoon out?" whispered Lauren as the girls were in the scullery stirring a batch of soap.

"I walked to market. I like the smells from the baker's shop, and the fruit at the grocers stand always looks so pretty in the baskets."

"So you are always alone?" asked Lauren.

"Always."

"Sometimes you take Monsieur's supper to him at the mine. Do the workers ever flirt with you there?"

"No, of course not," Eugenie stated avoiding Lauren's eyes as she stirred the soap in the crucible.

Lauren noticed that whenever she quizzed Eugenie on the topic of boys, the girl froze. This time Lauren decided to press the girl, her youthful curiosity getting the better of her.

"Surely there is someone you like."

"No," said Eugenie flatly.

"Oh come now. You will never tell me anything. There must be someone," said Lauren with a devilish smile. "Have you ever been kissed?"

"I don't want to talk about this," lisped Eugenie. She turned and started for the house.

Lauren followed her into the kitchen and watched her chopping turnips. "I know there is someone, and you are keeping it from me," she teased. "I can feel it. We are best friends and I will not go until I find out."

Suddenly, Eugenie slammed the knife down on the table and barked, "Mind your own business! Now leave me alone!" The girl's voice was shaking and her fists clenched.

Lauren was dumbfounded. Her mouth dropped open and she stammered, "I--I'm sorry Eugenie. I was just teasing."

She reached out to touch her shoulder, but Eugenie jerked back. "Well, don't tease me!" and she left the room.

Fighting back tears, Lauren returned to Madame's boudoir. There was a side to Eugenie she would never understand, and she realized that today she had asked too much of the girl. Lauren would have to accept that there would always be ghosts between them.

*   *   *

All summer long Lauren met Rene' by the river. They would walk hand in hand along the banks of the Kaskaskia whispering confidences and sharing caresses until they found a secluded spot and would drop down into a passionate embrace. Gabriel was unaware of how often the two met and he would have been alarmed had he known the direction their relationship was heading. Lauren's impulsive nature and Rene's ardor were a dangerous combination, and their visits began to take a serious turn.

"I wish we could run away together, Rene'," sighed Lauren as she rolled over onto her back to look at the clouds one fine afternoon. "We could go to Paris or Vienna. It wouldn't matter as long as we were away from here."

A small, red ant crawled up the sleeve of her gown and carefully Rene' picked it off turning his attention to her neck and breasts. He slid his lips along her skin, up to her ear and whispered, "Every night we could sleep side by side and awaken to each other in the morning."

"Oh, that would be wonderful," she murmured.

He kissed her and said, "Let's go Lauren. I mean it, just you and I together. We can marry and take the convoy to New Orleans in the spring and from there to Paris."

"Do you mean it?" Lauren said sitting up, looking into his blue eyes. "Do you really mean it?"

"Yes I mean it, Lauren because I love you." He eased her back and pressed his mouth onto hers as he had a hundred times before, but this time something was different. Lauren felt herself losing control. She would not have the strength to refuse his advances this time. *Why should I ruin the moment? This is the man I will marry. Nothing matters but Rene'.*

Chapter 11

It had been a year since Lauren had arrived in Kaskaskia. She marveled at how quickly the months had gone by and how drastically her life had changed since that stormy day in New Orleans. Rene' had awakened passion in her, and she felt as if she had left all her schoolgirl notions behind. On rare occasions the guilt of the nuns would haunt her, but she would remind herself that it was fine because Rene' was the man she would marry.

By now, her figure had grown to its full maturity. Her limbs were long and graceful and she was slender and willowy. She was now a young woman capable of giving and receiving pleasure, and she began to realize the power she had over men. Simone had been aware of this power long before Lauren, and she had used it to manipulate the hired boys back at the convent. Simone was born knowing these things, thought Lauren, and she marveled at how advanced her sister had been.

Lauren's thoughts were frequently with Simone, and she longed to see her sister again. Many nights she shed tears of loneliness for her twin, struggling to understand why Simone would want to remain buried at the convent when there was a wide world to explore.

Rene' felt as if he knew Simone, Lauren spoke of her so often. He promised to take her to the convent before they left for Paris, and it eased Lauren's mind to know she would see Simone once more.

A year passing also meant another convoy journeyed to New Orleans. For months, the wives and mothers felt the strain of waiting and worrying, but today they could put their fears to rest. The convoy was downriver and had returned safe and complete, every bateaux in attendance. The whole town rejoiced and turned out to greet the men.

"Are you going down to meet the convoy?" asked Madame the afternoon of the arrival.

She sat in her favorite pink armchair twisting a lace handkerchief anxiously.

"No, I have no one to welcome," Lauren replied tucking in the sheets and shaking out the pink bed curtains.

Josephine Aberjon reached over to her nightstand, opened a drawer and pulled out a letter, "Well I do. This is from my son. He is returning home from his studies in Paris, and he will be with the convoy. I need someone to meet him at the docks and escort him home."

Lauren straightened up staring at Madame with surprise, "I didn't know your son was coming home. Why didn't you tell me?"

Madame looked down and said, "My son is not a topic we discuss in this house. Jean-Baptist and Claude do not see eye to eye. They never have, and I did not want Jean Baptiste to know of his return until the last minute."

"I see," said Lauren as she continued to arrange the bed, "You would like me to go now?"

"Yes, please, dear. Go to the stable and talk to Toussaint. He will get the carriage ready for you."

Lauren went down to the kitchen, took off her apron and put on her straw hat. Marianne looked up from her cooking and said, "Madame is sending you out?"

"Yes, I am to pick up her son from the convoy. He has returned from Paris."

The old woman's jaw dropped. "*He* has returned, oh mon Dieu!"

"Why has no one told me about him?" asked Lauren.

"He is not worth talking about," said Marianne, shaking her head. "He is bad for this family. He is bad for us all."

Lauren stood staring at Marianne, unable to comprehend what she was saying.

"You better go quickly. He won't want to be kept waiting," the woman warned.

Toussaint drove the carriage down to the docks, and reluctantly Lauren stepped out into the afternoon sun. It was a lovely autumn day but she did not notice the colorful leaves or the fresh crispness to the air. The noise and confusion of the docks bombarded her instead. Men loaded barrels onto carts, tearful wives embraced their husbands, children darted in and out playing tag and slaves laboriously unloaded the bateaux. There was shouting and crying, and the noise was deafening.

Lauren wrapped her cloak around herself as if it would protect her from harm and stood by Toussaint, trying to stay out of the way.

"Do you know what he looks like?" she shouted to the old man.

The slave nodded. He remembered Claude Aberjon too well. He could never forget his face.

"I'm right here, Toussaint."

Toussaint turned around, and there stood a tall, thin pimply-faced young man with a cane. When Lauren turned around, his eyebrows shot up. "Well, I see father has refined his tastes."

"I am Madame Heathstone," said Lauren. "I am your mother's companion. She has asked me to meet you."

With a sarcastic sweep of the arm, Claude Aberjon indicated that Lauren should step into the carriage first. He climbed in after her. Toussaint climbed onto the driver's seat and snapped the reins, sending the carriage off with a jerk.

Claude sat back and ran his eyes over Lauren's figure saying with a smirk, "Spare me the pretense. You take care of my father, not my mother."

"No," explained Lauren, not understanding his insinuation. "It is your mother who needs the help. Her fits are growing more frequent. She has increased to ten outbursts a day."

Claude studied her for a moment. He could see that she was telling the truth and that his mother's condition had indeed grown worse. He closed his eyes and dropped back onto the seat, moaning. "Oh God, I come home to this. I suppose she will expect me to dance attendance on her, visit her day and night, take my meals with her, play cards with her--and the dogs! Oh, my God the dogs. How tedious," he whined.

There was a moment of silence, then suddenly he leaned forward and said, "But you will be a welcome diversion."

Lauren looked confused. She was unsure how to take this comment, but she did not like his tone. No one had ever talked to her like this before, and she did not know how to respond.

When they returned to the house, Madame was having one of her fits. Lauren ran up the stairs and Claude chuckled, throwing his hat and cloak onto a chair in the drawing room. "Well, well it's good to be home," he said to himself as he opened the liquor cabinet. His eyes ran across the bottles of liquor and Madeira and he picked up a crystal glass.

"What the hell are you doing here?" snarled Monsieur Aberjon coming up behind him, grabbing the glass from his hand. "I told you to stay in Paris."

"And I told *you* that I was out of money," returned the young man. "That paltry allowance was not enough."

"You wasted your time coming back here. I told you, I have nothing more to give you. There are no gaming tables in Kaskaskia, so you might as well return to New Orleans." Jean-Baptist yanked the brandy decanter out of the other hand and put the bottle and glass back in the cabinet.

Claude hated his father. His coarse demeanor and drooping eyelid repulsed him. He sat down flinging his leg over the arm of a chair and began arranging the lace at his wrists. "If you wanted me to stay in school you should have sent more money, Father."

"I cannot afford schooling for you any longer. You'll have to work like everyone else."

"Work! Where? At the lead mine like you?" Claude said with a smirk.

Jean Baptist stepped forward and grabbed his son's throat with one hand. "That *lead mine* fed clothed and kept you in the lap of luxury for twenty one years. You will show some respect."

Claude's eyes grew large as he looked into Jean-Baptist's face. He had dropped his guard and showed his father exactly how much he scorned him. *That mistake must not be made again.* He realized the facade of respect must not drop if he wanted anything out of the old man.

Monsieur Aberjon withdrew his hand and turned away. His chest was heaving as he straightened his waistcoat. "I'll find something for you to do at the mines. Don't think you can lie around here. You'll start tomorrow."

Claude said nothing and stood up, walking to the window. He detested his father. He detested everything about his pedestrian life and his working class demeanor, but he must placate him for a while. *I'll do what the old man wishes until I can get some money again.* Claude looked outside. He saw Lauren taking some rugs off a line and asked, "Is she yours, Father?"

"What?" said Jean Baptist walking over and looking out the window.

"No, she is your mother's companion."

"So I am free to amuse myself?" Claude said.

His father shrugged his shoulders and walked out of the room. Claude could hear him say as he passed into the hall, "I don't give damn what you do. Just stay away from me."

Josephine Aberjon was delighted with her son's return. Even though the visits to her room were few, they sustained her for hours. From the moment Claude was born she doted on the boy, showering him with toys and gifts, deferring to his every whim, giving him the distinct impression that the world revolved around only him. Not until adulthood, when Claude began to make financial demands on his father, did the trouble begin. First, there were the failing grades at the academy in Paris, then there was the drinking and gaming, but what dominated Claude's attention the most was women. His taste in courtesans was expensive so in no time the boy began to drain the financial resources of the family.

Josephine brought a substantial amount of money into the marriage and those funds were the first to go. Initially, Jean-Baptiste was willing to indulge the boy's whims, being grateful he was an ocean away, but as time went by it became apparent that Claude was depleting every resource.

The young man was furious that he had to work. Claude had never lifted a finger to support himself his whole life, and suddenly he had to sit in the stuffy office of the family lead mine and scratch numbers into a moldy ledger all day. He thought the work of merchants was beneath him and he detested his father for being too inadequate to support him properly. All day he would wait for the sun to set so he could slam the office door behind him and ride to the alehouses by the docks. There he found enough drink to sustain him and enough women to satisfy him, at least for a while.

Lauren was grateful Claude was gone all day until late every night. She had seen little of him since his return four months ago, but she locked her bedroom door every night without fail. Lauren did not speak of Claude to Rene' She knew that he would worry and insist upon marrying her immediately, but a wedding in Kaskaskia during the Lenten season was taboo, and she needed time to make preparations.

The couple continued to meet several times a week even though it was the middle of winter. Rene' found a small, abandoned cottage off the Cahokia road which the two cleaned up and set as their trysting place. There were holes in the roof that they patched, and it was small, but with a fire the structure kept the lovers warm and dry.

"I think that we should talk to father," said Rene' one cold March afternoon as he stoked the fire. "I think that it's time to tell him that we are going to marry."

Lauren bit her lip. She liked and respected Gabriel, but she feared his temper.

"What will he say about us leaving Kaskaskia?"

"Neither one of them will like it, but we must make our way together in the world."

The fire snapped and popped as Lauren sat hugging her knees her long auburn hair falling over her shoulders. She turned to him suddenly and said, "We shall be gypsies you and I, Rene'. No place will hold us. I love Kaskaskia, but I ache for something else. It's not--well, its not home."

Rene' didn't hear a word Lauren said. He had stood up and was looking outside through a crack in the wall. "I heard something. Who would be down here this late in the day? It's almost nightfall."

"Never mind, Rene', your father would never find us here."

He sighed and sat back down. "You're right. *You* are what I should be worrying about," and he pushed her down on the deer skin. "Now where were we?" he said and began to kiss her.

Chapter 12

The ox struggled as Gabriel reached deep into the animals mouth. Rene held the animal, but given the size of the beast and the pouring rain it was an impossible task restraining the brute "I can't feel anything. I don't know why he is choking," Gabriel said.

Rene loosened his grip on the massive animal as his father removed his hand from the ox's mouth. "Are we done now, Father?" Rene' asked anxiously.

"Why? Where are you going?"

"Oh, I told Jean Paul I would help him with the shearing," Rene' lied.

Gabriel dismissed him with a wave of his hand and went back to his work. He had known for a long time that Rene' and Lauren had been meeting on a regular basis. Although he knew they were not a good match, he wanted a marriage before Lauren was compromised.

A few days later, the couple came and asked Anne and Gabriel for their blessing, informing them that they would be leaving Kaskaskia after they were married. The Lupone's were not happy about their plans but said nothing.

Lauren had not found the courage to tell Madame Aberjon about her wedding. The matron did not do well with change, and this news would surely send her into frenzy. She continued to wake Lauren at all hours of the night, screaming and crying, calling for Jean-Baptiste or Claude. She always ended face down on the bed sobbing hysterically.

One night after a particularly difficult episode, when Lauren was leaving Madame's room, someone grabbed her from behind knocking the candle to the floor, pinning her against the wall. "You'll like what I have for you," said Claude as he pressed himself against her breasts.

The candle extinguished when it hit the floor, and the hall was dark. Lauren's heart was pounding as she struggled to free herself. "Let go of me," she demanded trying to push him away.

In spite of his drunkenness, Claude was stronger than Lauren and began to pull up her shift. "Calm down. You'll be grateful in a moment," he said hoarsely.

Suddenly, there was a crash, and Madame screamed. Lauren freed herself dashing into the boudoir. There on the floor by the light of the fire was Madame reaching for the nightstand about to pull it over. Claude stopped at the threshold, weaving back and forth.

Madame spotted him and cried, "Oh, Claude! I am so afraid! Help me." Her red hair hung wildly about her face, and her nightgown was drenched in perspiration. She pulled herself over and wrapped her arms around his legs.

"Get away from me, old woman," he said yanking himself free. He turned to Lauren and snarled, "If you are going to live in this house, there are certain things expected of you. You have duties!"

"Stay away from me!" Lauren said. She was only vaguely aware of Madame sobbing.

Claude thrust his finger in Lauren's face and snarled, "Just ask that savage you've befriended. She'll tell you about her duties to my father."

Lauren's jaw dropped. She was speechless.

"My boy, my darling boy, please help me," sobbed Madame as she reached for him.

Claude shrieked, "Stay away from me, you lunatic!" and he kicked his mother in the chest, sending her reeling back onto the floor.

Turning to Lauren he hissed, "You have been warned!

*   *   *

All night long Lauren tossed and turned; cursing Claude for his violence and the vulgar lies he spoke about Eugenie. *Marianne was right. He was bad for this house and from the minute he entered it, a gloom descended upon everyone.*

Madame sank into a deep melancholy, eating nothing and speaking little. Lauren had hoped her mistress would not recall the incident with Claude, but it was apparent she remembered everything. All day long she stayed in bed never opening her eyes or asking for anything. Lauren stayed by her side gently urging her to take some broth or water, but the woman would only turn her head away.

In spite of the outbursts and unpredictable behavior, Lauren had grown to love Madame Aberjon. She learned to look past the tantrums and focus on the helpless person drowning in the illness. She missed their games of *morris* in the morning and *trique-trac* in the afternoon.

Madame's chocolate grew cold on the nightstand day after day. Lauren even stayed in the woman's room at night, curled up with a blanket in an armchair waiting for some glimmer of life from her mistress. The melancholy of Madame went on for days until one night she sat up in bed suddenly and exclaimed, "You never believed me, did you?"

Lauren who was sleeping in the armchair jumped with a start and said, "What?" She rubbed her eyes to examine Madame more closely. "What did you say, Madame?'

"I said that you never believed me, but now I can prove it to you."

A strange prickling crept up Lauren's spine. The moonlight streaked across the bed and onto the floor as Madame pulled off the covers and walked barefoot to the door. Her pale gown glowed in the dim light, and her complexion was a pasty white.

"Come with me," Madame said then suddenly she bolted for the door.

Lauren screamed, "No!"

The madwoman raced down the hall toward Jean Baptiste's room. She stopped outside his bedchamber and announced, "Look! See for yourself!"

Madame Aberjon threw the door open. There on the bed in the firelight was Eugenie with Jean-Baptiste on top of her.

"God damn it! What's going on!" roared Aberjon throwing back the covers and jumping out of bed. He stood in his nightshirt and roared, "Get the hell out of here!"

Lauren stood paralyzed with her eyes riveted to Eugenie.

"I said get out!" said Jean-Baptiste pushing them both out of the room and slamming the door.

Madame burst into hysterical laugher in the hall babbling something about everyone believing her now. Lauren pushed her back to the bedroom, horrified and confused at what she had seen.

It took some time, but she finally settled Madame down and fell into a chair by the bed, stunned and struggling with the tempest inside her. Madame fell into a deep sleep, but rest never came for Lauren. She hated Eugenie. Hated her and all of the lewd, disgusting secrets she had kept from her. Lauren felt betrayed and wondered what other shameful things were hidden behind that placid demeanor. It all made sense now. *Eugenie would never talk about a lover because Monsieur Aberjon was her lover, and that day when Madame threw chocolate all over her, she was trying to tell the world that Eugenie was her husband's whore.*

The next morning Lauren went down to breakfast and said nothing to Eugenie. She couldn't even look at her. She poured herself some cider while Marianne made conversation, but

Lauren kept her answers brief and retreated upstairs as soon as she was done eating.

The next day Eugenie stopped her in the hall. "Lauren, please there is something I must say."

All Lauren could see when she looked at the girl was her naked body in Jean Baptiste's bed, and she turned away, repulsed. "There is nothing you can say to me."

"You don't understand, Lauren."

"Oh I understand alright," she said in a voice heavy with sarcasm.

"No, no," said Eugenie shaking her head as her eyes filled with tears. "You don't understand."

Lauren turned abruptly and walked down the stairs, wanting nothing more than to get away from Eugenie and her pathetic excuses. She whistled to the dogs and was out the gate before Eugenie could stop her. Without looking one way or the other she walked than began to run down to the river. There was a secluded path she had discovered that ran along the bank, and the dogs loped happily along side of her darting in and out of the underbrush.

It took a long time, but Lauren's pace slowed, and her heart finally quit racing. She couldn't wait to get out of the Illinois country. Kaskaskia suffocated her, and it seemed that everywhere she looked there was ugliness and lust, from the lewd advances of Claude to the depraved behavior of Eugenie. This was not her home, and these were not her people. She would never find contentment here.

Suddenly, she heard one of the dogs growl, and she spied a raccoon walking unsteadily up the path toward her. He would fall and stand up, fall and stand up again as if he was sick. The dogs shot past her kicking up mud as they ran. When they reached the raccoon, the animal drew back its lips and lunged. This sent the Danes into frenzy, and they began to bark and snarl at the creature. When Duchess bent down to snap at the animal, the raccoon jumped at the dog's neck sinking its teeth deeply into the dog's flesh. Long, strands of white drool ran out of its mouth as Duchess tried to shake the creature loose but the animal did not let go until Baroness attacked. Lauren screamed a command but the smell of blood filled the dogs with frenzy and they tore repeatedly at the raccoon until the animal was unrecognizable. Duchess' neck wound was deep, and the dog staggered into the underbrush to lie down.

"Oh, *Mon Dieu*!" Lauren cried.

Baroness bolted after Lauren as she ran toward the house. As they approached the gate, Monsieur Aberjon's carriage pulled up and he stepped out. Lauren blurted out, "The dogs tangled with a raccoon and both were bit. Duchess is hurt badly."

"Where is she?" questioned Jean-Baptiste."

"Down by the river but wait," she said grabbing his arm, "The raccoon was rabid."

Monsieur Aberjon looked at her for a moment, turned and walked into the house returning with a pistol. Without hesitation he walked up to Baroness who was lying at Lauren's feet, pointed the gun and pulled the trigger. The animal kicked back from the blast and slammed to the ground with a thud, blood gushing from its head. Lauren stood and stared at the dog as she bled to death at her feet.

Holding the firearm at his side Aberjon demanded, "Take me to Duchess."

Everything was happening so fast that Lauren's head began to spin. "Where is the other dog?" snapped Monsieur.

She hesitated, thinking of Madame Aberjon and then said, "This way."

Chapter 13

For the first time in weeks, Lauren felt optimistic. Claude was in the North Country on business, Madame was eating again, and spring was on its way. Lauren found it hard to believe she had seen two springs in Kaskaskia already. Maybe it was her wedding or the knowledge that she would be leaving the village soon that elated the girl. A convoy was being organized, and Rene' had arranged for them to be on the manifest. Lauren was overjoyed. She longed to see a big city like Paris and live in a place where cows and crops were not important.

All seemed to be going as planned when a crisis developed in the community. There was a ban on all unnecessary travel due to an outbreak of rabies. Lauren's encounter with the raccoon proved not to be an isolated incident. Many villagers witnessed similar attacks, and all stray and domestic animals were under scrutiny. In spite of his cold unfeeling attitude Lauren knew that Monsieur Aberjon had been right to put Madame's dogs down. The only way to check the contagion was to destroy the carriers.

This ban did not stop the trysts between Lauren and Rene' though. The lure of springtime and their own passions caused them to disregard their own safety and meet at the cabin every chance they could get. Although the arrangement with Eugenie and Marianne had crumbled, Lauren stole out many afternoons when Madame took her nap. The couple had the understanding; that if one could not show up, the other would wait an hour, and then return home.

It was a muddy spring afternoon, when Lauren set out to meet Rene' at the trysting place. She laced her stays quickly and slipped her pink gown over her head. After lacing her bodice over a cream-colored stomacher, she arranged a *bergere* smartly on top of her head, tied the ribbons under her chin and was ready to go. This was Lauren's only good gown. Madame had been kind enough give her some of her unused wardrobe, and Lauren reworked the gowns and skirts into very fashionable everyday wear.

She could hear the water running off the roofs of the houses and the snow melting as she stepped out into the sunlight. Finding the ground beneath her feet brown and greasy, Lauren lifted her skirts and jumped over a puddle, almost losing her balance as she slid in the mud.

There was someone playing a fiddle in the distance, and her spirits began to soar. She could hardly contain her excitement at the thought of leaving with the convoy and traveling across the ocean to see new countries. She would never be content to read about these places in books like most girls, she must experience them, taste and feel them.

As she approached the cabin, she realized there was no smoke curling up from the chimney, and her heart sank. Rene' was unable to get away. Nevertheless, Lauren built a fire and sat down in front of the flames to wait in case he was late. Lost in her thoughts time passed quickly, and before she knew it, it was time to return home. She put out the fire and tied her cloak over her shoulders.

As Lauren stepped out the door, she had the unnerving sensation that someone was watching her. She remembered Rene' saying several weeks before that he heard somebody in the woods, and she felt uneasy as she started down the road. It crossed her mind that maybe some diseased animal lay in wait for her, so she quickened her pace.

The melting snow crushed under her feet, and she could hear the water running in a stream not far away. Suddenly, a horse snorted, and there was the sound of hoofs behind her. She jumped to one side as Claude Aberjon rode up the path. He pulled up sharply on the reins as the horse danced around the road splattering her with mud. She knew that he had returned from the North Country that afternoon, but she thought he was with his father.

"So, if it isn't the princess," he sneered.

"What's wrong with you!" Lauren screamed, "You could have killed me!"

"You mealy-mouthed little hypocrite, playing the virgin with me. You've been coming here for weeks whoring with someone."

His eyes ran over her body. Lauren's firm breasts pushed up from her tightly laced bodice, and her auburn hair fell around her shoulders.

"It's my turn, now," he said and started to dismount.

Lauren's anger turned to fear. Claude was in the habit of taking what he wanted, and she knew she had to act quickly. She darted around the back of the horse and broke into a run. In a flash, Claude jumped down and was upon her, grabbing her around the waist. He swung her down into the muddy snow pinning her to the ground.

His grip was like iron, and she struggled for air beneath the weight of his body. She could smell his foul breath and feel his hands begin to pull up her skirt. He pushed her legs apart with his knees, and Lauren knew she was about to be raped. With all her strength, she squirmed out from underneath him and began to crawl along the ground on her belly. His long nails tore at her skin, and she knew that if he seized her this time she would not have the strength to escape.

With a grunt, Claude stretched to his fullest and wrapped his hand around her ankle. Lauren grabbed frantically at the underbrush trying to stop him from pulling her back, but nothing proved stronger than Claude's fury.

Suddenly, something snapped in Lauren. She was no longer scared. She hated this vile creature, and she rolled over, drew up her knee and smashed the heel of her boot into his face.

"You filthy bitch!" he shrieked as he rose up onto his knees. Blood colored the snow. "You've broken my nose!"

Sobbing from terror Lauren pulled herself onto Claude's horse and threw her soaked skirts over the saddle. The last thing she saw as she rode off was Claude Aberjon holding his face in his hands, bright blood sullying his fine silk shirt.

*   *   *

Lauren was surprised when no one commented about Claude's broken nose. No one came to her for an explanation, there was no gossip. Everyone seemed to ignore the fact that Claude had been assaulted. After some initial sympathy even Madame dropped the issue, but Lauren knew Claude would not forget. She knew that he would make her pay someday, and as a result, she was more anxious than ever to leave the Illinois Country.

Eugenie was the only person to see her return on Claude's horse that afternoon and even though tears streamed down Lauren's face and her clothes were wet and muddy, the Indian girl asked no questions. She quietly took the reins and led the beast into the stable as Lauren dashed into the house. She longed to tell Eugenie everything. She needed desperately to unburden herself and share her fears with someone, but she could not. Her pride prevented her from approaching the girl, so she carried on alone and frightened.

Returning to a familiar routine seemed to be the best antidote for the anxiety, so Lauren threw herself back into taking care of Madame Aberjon. They spent long afternoons together playing cribbage and savoring the delectable *petite-fours* Marianne made for them. On several occasions, Madame wound up her music box and watched Lauren dance around the room with an invisible partner. The charade amused them both and helped Lauren to forget her worries. She loved the delicate tune the porcelain box played and she marveled at the graceful little dancer turning round and round on the cover.

"What does he look like?" asked Madame one day as Lauren danced.

"Who?" asked Lauren as she glided around the room.

"Your partner."

"Oh--well he's handsome of course, Madame."

"Of course," was the woman's reply.

"You know, I was a handsome woman in my day," said Madame wistfully, leaning back onto her pink pillows.

Lauren stopped dancing and sat down on the edge of the bed. "Tell me what you were like, Madame."

"Well," she said reaching up to her hair, "my locks were a deep, brilliant red. Not streaked with gray like now, and my figure was fine and full in all the right places. I had dreams like you of parties and romance, and there were many men courting me. Girls who were jealous said that men only wanted my large dowry, but I knew better."

Lauren pulled a pillow into her arms and leaned forward, eager to hear more. "What were they like? Your suitors I mean?" she asked.

"Oh, there were many but none to compare with Jean-Baptist. He was strong and good-looking and took charge of my needs immediately. I knew instantly that I could depend on him the rest of my life."

"Was he," Lauren paused uncomfortably, "kind to you?"

"Oh indeed he was and very sympathetic. He said that he loved me and would marry me in spite of my illness." Suddenly the smile dropped from her face, and she said, "But father didn't like him. He called him a gold-digger and a moneygrubber. Father didn't like any of my beaux."

Lauren agreed with Madame's father about Jean-Baptist, but she said nothing. "Are you happy Madame, I mean, in spite of it all?"

Madame smiled, and for the first time Lauren saw how lovely she must have been as a girl.

Josephine Aberjon looked out at the bare trees against the icy, blue afternoon sky. "Happy? Yes, I suppose I am happy. My mother used to say, 'If we could examine everyone's problems like clothes hanging on a line, we would always choose our problems back again.' "

Madame sighed and slid down under the pink duvet. The afternoon's entertainment had exhausted her and she faded off to sleep, but her words did not fade from Lauren's mind. The girl pondered them and for the first time since the incident with Claude, she found some peace.

The next afternoon as Lauren was about to take Madame's chocolate upstairs there was a knock on the front door. She put the tray on the hall table, pulled the heavy door open, and to her surprise, Gabriel Lupone was standing in front of her. She smiled instantly.

"Hello Lauren. I am here on a matter of business with Monsieur Aberjon."

"He is not here," Lauren said. "He has not been home since this morning."

"That matters not. I have purchased his pistol and come to pick it up."

"Oh," said Lauren stepping back. "Please come in. I'll get it for you."

Lauren had seen Monsieur Aberjon cleaning the piece in the study and after searching several drawers, she found the weapon. It was a lovely lightweight piece with a fleur-de-lis carved onto the ivory handle. She handed it to Gabriel.

"Is that the right pistol?" she asked.

He nodded and said with a sigh, "I can rest now, knowing Anne will be able to protect herself while we are on the convoy."

Lauren brightened instantly. "Any news about how soon we will be leaving?"

"Nothing yet," he said with a faint smile. "Be patient, girl." Gabriel's expression grew somber. "Is there any chance I could talk to you away from the house for a moment?"

Lauren looked up the stairs toward Madame's room and back down at the chocolate which was growing cold on the hall table. Madame was still sleeping, so she nodded and stepped out the door.

There was a funeral procession passing by the house, and the two stopped outside the gate to let it pass. Lauren couldn't look at the sober faced mourners and grotesquely draped hearse. The driver pulled up on the reins to let the two pass, but Gabriel waved his arm to move the funeral on.

"You never want the procession to pause in front your house, Lauren. It's bad luck."

"Really?" she gasped.

"I don't suppose it's true, but that's what everyone says."

They walked down to the river side by side. The wind was strong that afternoon, and it whipped Lauren's skirts wildly about her legs and sent the trees waving back and forth furiously. Whenever Lauren was around Gabriel, she felt like a naughty child, and this time her intuition told her he was very concerned about something. She raised her voice against the wind and asked, "What is it Monsieur? Have I done something wrong?"

"No you have done nothing wrong--yet."

He stopped and rubbed the back of his neck saying, "Lauren please listen to me. It is wrong for you to marry Rene'."

Lauren frowned, and she turned away angrily. She refused to listen and began to walk away. Gabriel caught her arm and said firmly, "Listen to me, child."

She wheeled around, pushed the hair from her face and shouted over the wind, "Monsieur, I am not a child anymore."

"You are acting like one."

Lauren tossed her head.

Because of the wind, Gabriel raised his voice too. "You long for exotic lands and grand adventures. Don't you? You may have these things for a short while if you marry Rene' *but*," he paused and shook his head firmly. "He will always return to Kaskaskia."

Lauren would not look into Gabriel's eyes, but she heard what he said.

"He will bring you here and bury you in this back country--forever."

"That's not true!" she said stamping her foot. "He wants to leave here as much as I do. We will make our home together anywhere but here!"

Gabriel shook his head sadly and took her hand. "My darling Lauren, you are not meant for Rene'. This is his home, not yours. Kaskaskia will never be your home. You must move on and find your place somewhere else. You must find *your* home. That restlessness you feel inside--" and he tapped his chest. "It will plague you relentlessly until you find where you belong."

Hot tears welled up in Lauren's eyes. *Gabriel had no right to tell her how to run her life. She would marry Rene' and prove him wrong. They would live their lives together as gypsies and be wildly happy.*

"Is that all Monsieur?" she asked, pulling her chin up and snatching her hand away.

"Lauren, please believe me. Follow you heart elsewhere. Do not allow yourself to spend eternity in a Kaskaskia graveyard like me."

Lauren's heart was pounding. She was the happiest she had been in months and now it seemed as if Gabriel was trying to steal it away from her. She turned her back on him and walked up to the house. The wind fought her every step of the way, but she was determined to get away from him as soon as possible. Lauren said to herself that she was through with Gabriel and all of his advice. She was sick to death of his meddling, and she was not going to take it anymore. She would marry Rene' and never set eyes on that man again.

That evening after the cows were milked and the barn was cleaned, Gabriel Lupone neatly rolled out a large canvas tarp in front of the cow stalls. After combing his hair and straightening his clothes, he stood in the middle of the tarp, took up Monsieur Aberjon's ivory inlaid pistol and put a bullet into his mouth.

Chapter 14

Every time Lauren closed her eyes she could see herself handing Gabriel the gun. She could only imagine the misery and despair he must have felt when he realized the ox had passed the rabies on to him. When his ox had been mysteriously choking week ago, Gabriel had reached deeply into the beast's mouth to determine the problem. He did not know the open wound on his hand could provide an avenue for the transmission of disease. Later when the erratic behavior started in the ox, he realized it was rabies.

He told the family nothing and waited, alone and anxious, to see if he had indeed contracted the disease. When his throat began to constrict, he knew that the disease was upon him, and a choice had to be made, live for two to three more days and face a violent agonizing death putting his family at risk, or deliberately plan his own demise.

On that last windy morning, Gabriel told Rene' to take his mother and the children to Prairie Du Rocher to visit Anne's sister. He said that Anne needed a diversion, and that he had far too many chores to take her there himself. After the family left, he went to the Aberjon residence to get the gun. Although

Gabriel had a musket, the act was not possible with such a weapon, so he lied to Lauren to obtain Aberjon's pistol. He returned home, put his affairs in order and took his own life. All of these facts were in a letter to Anne. The majority of the testament contained instructions about the estate, but one page was for Anne's eyes only, and this she locked away in her hope chest.

Monsieur Aberjon did not berate Lauren for giving Gabriel the pistol. He did not have to chastise her; Lauren punished herself instead. She paced the floor of her room; turning over the events of that day, chiding herself for handing him the gun, feeling overwhelmed with guilt. She hated herself for saying she never wanting to see him again and believed that she had been too selfish that day to see that the man was suffering.

There was a full moon the night before they buried Gabriel Lupone. It illuminated the front lawn of the Aberjon residence. As if staring at an empty stage, Lauren sat at her bedroom window gazing at the lawn below. She needed solace; she needed Simone, she needed Eugenie. She ached with loneliness. It was a peaceful, quiet night and it lulled her briefly into serenity. As if answering her prayer for companionship, a little brown rabbit hopped across the yard into the moonlight. The little creature stopped to nibble on a blade of grass and looked up at Lauren, its nose twitching. For the first time in days, Lauren smiled. In spite of the ugliness, there was still beauty. Suddenly, a fox dashed out, grabbed the rabbit by the neck and dragged it into the underbrush as it screamed.

"*Mon Dieu*!" gasped Lauren slamming her hands onto the windowsill sending the window crashing down. "Is there no escape?"

She wished the sun would not come up at all. She hated Kaskaskia. She hated the thought of burying Gabriel in a solitary meadow outside of town because he had been banned from consecrated ground.

The next day Lauren walked at the back of the funeral procession carrying Celeste', Gabriel's youngest daughter. The wind snapped the skirts of the women, and the slate gray sky promised rain. The funeral was brief, without benefit of clergy, and after Rene' read a few words from the Bible the simple wooden casket was lowered into the ground. The small procession ended at the Lupone home where a few loyal friends and neighbors gathered to give their condolences. Since taking ones own life was a sin many stayed away, condemning Gabriel for his action.

Filled with shame, Lauren wished she were invisible. She believed everyone was thinking, "There is the foolish girl who handed Gabriel the gun."

Nevertheless, abandoning the Lupones at their time of need was unthinkable. Filled with anxiety, Lauren waited all afternoon for the guests to leave and then approached Anne. The older children were washing dishes while Anne readied the younger ones for bed. She was by the fire arranging Celeste's trundle when Lauren approached.

She swallowed hard and said "Anne, I know you must hate the sight of me, but I must say before I go that am so sorry for giving Gabriel the gun."

Anne straightened up. The woman had dark circles under her eyes and her hair fell in tangles around her face. "What?" she gasped. "You think I hold you responsible? Never, never for a moment!"

Lauren stammered, "Then--then you don't blame me?"

"How could I? He told me everything in the letter. He said that you and Monsieur Aberjon were innocent." Anne clutched her forehead. "Oh Lauren, I have been too absorbed in my own grief to realize you knew nothing of the contents of that letter. He absolved you and Monsieur Aberjon of any responsibility. I should have told you immediately. *I* am the one who should be apologizing."

At this news, tears began to stream down Lauren's face. Anne pulled her into her arms. The Lupone children came running, frightened and confused wrapping themselves around Anne's legs.

"My poor child, you have been torturing yourself these past days," Anne murmured stroking Lauren's head.

One of the little boys reached up his pudgy hand and offered Lauren his dirty hankie. Lauren chuckled and dried her eyes. "I'm better now," she murmured.

"You go home and get some rest," urged Anne, guiding her to the door. "We are all exhausted. Rene' is out doing chores. He'll walk you home."

* * *

The trysts ended with Rene'. He was far too busy doing work on the farm. Lauren broke away from the Aberjon's whenever she could to help Anne, but her opportunities were few. Late one afternoon when she stopped by the house to help feed the Lupone children, Rene' came in from the fields and said, "Lauren, I must speak with you. Let us talk outside."

He led her out to the porch and took her hands. She noticed that his eyes were red rimmed and his face was drawn. He swallowed hard and said, "I'm sorry, Lauren, but we must put off the wedding until this summer. No one is in any mood for a celebration."

"No!" cried Lauren, pulling away from him. "That's not true! We all need something to look forward to. It will brighten everyone's attitude. If we wait until later we will miss the convoy and not be able to leave Kaskaskia."

Rene' shook his head. "I know how anxious you are, but we cannot be married right now, Lauren. There must be a period of mourning. It would not be proper."

She turned and walked to the other side of the porch fighting her anger.

Rene' continued. "I'm only doing what is best for us and what is best for my family. We must stay here--at least until next spring. My mother needs me."

Lauren turned and looked at Rene blinking as if she had seen a ghost. Gabriel's words haunted her. "There must be--" she stammered, "There must be someone who could take care of your mother."

"She is my responsibility, Lauren. Don't ask me to leave her."

This could not be happening. Rene' could not be changing his mind. Could Gabriel have been right? Maybe Rene' would never leave.

Lauren turned and started toward the gate.

"Where are you going?" called Rene', but she did not hear him. Her feet carried her away faster and faster until she broke into a run.

Chapter 15

As time passed, so did Lauren's dreams of leaving Kaskaskia. Someday maybe they would leave the Illinois Country, but it did not appear to be soon. Lauren's hopes were buried along with Gabriel. Spring turned to summer, and Anne suggested the two should be married at last. The time for mourning was over, and she said there should be something hopeful for all of them. A morning in July was set aside for the ceremony, and instantly Lauren felt rejuvenated. Every night she worked diligently on her new gown after Madame went to bed, planning and dreaming about the days to come, but when Madame fell ill everything stopped again.

It began as a mild stomach complaint, but the illness lingered far too long and was growing in intensity. This alarmed Lauren, but what disturbed her most of all was Madame's attitude. Without warning, the woman turned against her husband and son. Almost overnight, she recoiled from the two men stating that they meant to do her harm.

"Don't leave me, Lauren," she pleaded one afternoon. "They'll hurt me."

"What are you talking about?" questioned Lauren. "Who'll hurt you?"

"Jean-Baptiste and Claude. They are planning to kill me!"

"Don't be absurd!" Lauren laughed. "You have always wanted them by your side. Now you want them to stay away? Honestly you *are* unpredictable."

The woman bolted upright, grabbed Lauren by her gown and hissed, "You've got to believe me! You are my only hope! I heard them the other night in the drawing room."

"You were downstairs?"

"Yes, after you went to bed."

"What!" gasped Lauren.

Madame had a wild look in her eye. She drew the girl closer and whispered, "Take heed. One can learn a great deal after dark."

"Madame, you must stay in your room at night! You could get hurt!"

"You must believe me, Lauren--"At that moment, Madame froze. Her eyes focused on something behind Lauren.

Jean-Baptiste stepped over the threshold and asked, "How is Madame today?"

Lauren pulled Madame's fingers from her bodice and straightened up, arranging her gown. "Well, Monsieur, I am concerned. There is increased pain in her stomach, and she eats nothing. Do you suppose we should call for Dr. Guillard?"

"Nonsense," he replied. "The man will come, examine her, and tell us what we already know, that she has simply a stomach complaint. What concerns me is her mental state. This seems to be worsening."

"Yes, Monsieur, her outbursts appear--well appear to have changed." Lauren turned back to look at Madame Aberjon who continued to watch Jean-Baptiste warily.

He shook his head sympathetically, "The illness can manifest itself in many ways. These unfounded fears and delusions are an unfortunate example." He walked over to the bed and said, "I am going into town, Josephine. Is there anything I may purchase for you?"

Madame turned her head away and said nothing. As he bent to kiss her, Lauren noticed Jean-Baptiste's linen shirt appeared threadbare and his boots worn. This was out of character for Monsieur Aberjon, but she thought no more of it.

After he left, Lauren sat down to think over a game of solitaire. She had never been comfortable with Jean-Baptiste, but Madame's accusations were indeed the ravings of a lunatic. It was very unsettling and it may be a sign that her demons were worsening.

Days passed and Madame's stomach problems increased. She grew weaker and could not keep any food down. For Lauren this meant endless days of basins and chamber pots and endless nights of changing the bed. Marianne could see the strain on Lauren and one evening offered to take care of Madame so the girl could get away.

It was sultry summer night, which reminded Lauren of New Orleans. She stepped out into the night air and thought of Simone and the lazy summer evenings of their youth spent by the fountain in the convent courtyard. She remembered the cool mint drinks the nuns taught them to make and wished she had one now.

Candles illuminated the windows in town as Lauren strolled through the streets, fanning herself. It was good to be away from the sickroom breathing fresh air. She enjoyed walking through town and decided to explore a new route to the Lupone home. She turned down a quiet street lined with well-kept homes inhabited by the wealthier residents of town. She enjoyed watching the families through their front windows dining, reading by candlelight or sharing the day's events over a sapinette.

Suddenly, she stopped. There in the candlelight was Jean-Baptiste dining with a lavishly dressed woman of middle age. They were sipping out of aperitif glasses conversing intimately. Lauren stepped back into the shadows as the woman rose, dropping the ties on the damask curtains. Lauren's heart began to pound. The relationship between the couple did not look platonic and a feeling of dread washed over her. Madame's voice echoed in her ear, "Take heed. One can learn a great deal after dark."

She continued down the street. *It was all too unthinkable. Who was this woman? Perhaps a business associate from the lead mine? A relative?* Suddenly, the peaceful evening had taken a dark turn. Monsieur Aberjon's clothing had looked threadbare lately and Claude's monetary demands were indeed extravagant. The thought crossed her mind that maybe Jean-Baptiste needed another "good" marriage to pay some debts. Try as she might Lauren could not dismiss the image of Jean-Baptist in the window with that woman. *Could there be something more sinister at play here than a mere stomach complaint?* It all seemed too absurd yet a tiny voice inside of her screamed "danger".

By the time she reached Rene' she could contain herself no longer and told him everything that she suspected.

"You are becoming as addled as your mistress!" he laughed. Then his smile dropped. "Don't be accusing someone as powerful as Jean-Bapiste Aberjon of murder, Lauren. That is a very dangerous business."

Lauren frowned. "I cannot sit by idly and watch her die!"

"Yes, you can, because there is nothing to be done. It may be her time. This is all ridiculous. However, could they poison her? You and Marianne make all of the meals."

"I know, I know," admitted Lauren covering her face with her hands. "It all seems so absurd. I have been around Madame so long that I am starting to think like her."

"Put it out of your mind immediately," he said drawing her near. But try as she might Lauren's mind was not with Rene' that evening.

Lauren felt compelled to do something about the failing health of her mistress. When Madame fell asleep the next morning she returned to her room, threw her apron on the bed and tied on a cloak. Glancing in the mirror she stopped and looked closer. She did not recognize herself. She had dark rings under her eyes, and her face was pale. She swallowed hard and took a deep breath. For days now she had been fighting the urge to wretch, unable to eat, completely nauseated cleaning up Madame's vomit and flux.

Thunder rumbled as Lauren stepped out the front door. The skies opened, and it began to pour. By the time she reached the doctors home she was soaked to the skin. Lauren stood by the fire dripping on a small, braided rug as the doctor finished packing his medical bag.

In spite of his years the man moved quickly, and his mind was alert. "I have many calls to make, child. I must go."

"But I fear for Madame's life," pleaded Lauren. "She is most ill."

He darted to a cabinet, removed several bottles of tonics and placed them inside of his bag along with some clean bandages. "I must trust Jean-Baptist's judgment in this matter. He has taken care of Josephine for many years now, and he knows what is best for her." Dr. Guillard snapped his bag shut and grabbed Lauren under the chin. "You are a good girl and Josephine is lucky to have you. Now run along."

"Doctor!" blurted Lauren, stepping forward. "There is something you don't know." Her heart began to pound.

The old man drew his gray eyebrows together and said, "Well--what is it?"

He was growing impatient as Lauren wrung her hands in desperation. "Poison!" she cried out. "They are poisoning her!"

"What! Who is poisoning her?" he gasped.

"Jean-Baptist and his son are poisoning Madame Aberjon!"

"This is unbelievable! Do you know what you are saying?"

Lauren looked down at the braided rug and whispered, "I do."

He grabbed her by the arm and barked, "There will be no more talk of this kind! Do you understand?"

"But Madame heard them plotting--"

"*Madame* is a lunatic!" he roared. "Now please. Say nothing of this again. That is a *very* dangerous accusation. You must go."

The doctor pulled open the door and waited for her to leave. Lauren could feel his gaze as she stepped out into the storm.

*   *   *

It was late at night when Eugenie finally emerged from Monsieur Aberjon's room. She lit a taper and started down the hall. No one was awake this time of night, and she started when she met Lauren on the stairs. Their eyes met for an instant, but they said nothing passing each other.

Having second thoughts, Lauren took a deep breath, turned around and said, "Eugenie, may I talk to you?"

Eugenie stopped walking, her back to Lauren. The only sound was the steady ticking of the clock in the hall upstairs. Lauren continued, "I know when you tried to explain things to me I ran away. I--I am sorry." Her hand was perspiring as she grasped the railing waiting for Eugenie to reply.

Finally, the girl said quietly, "We will talk on the *galerie*."

They met outside on the porch. The night air was sultry and close. Lauren was tense as she reached for the post to steady herself. Eugenie stared straight ahead.

"I've missed our talks," Lauren said at last. "I used to tell you everything and--I thought I knew everything about you until--until *that* night."

Eugenie remained aloof.

"Help me to understand why you go to Monsieur Aberjon," continued Lauren.

The girl remained mute.

"Why have you chosen *him*?" Lauren asked.

"Chosen him! Is that what you think?" she said, turning toward Lauren. "Did it ever occur to you that I *have* to go there?"

"But--" stammered Lauren.

"But what? You forget. I am a slave. He owns me and has the right to beat me or sell me. He can do whatever he wants. He could sell me into a life that is even worse!"

Lauren stared at Eugenie then put her hand to her forehead. She walked down the steps and murmured, "Oh. I have been so stupid."

"You'll never know what its like to be a slave," Eugenie said. Her were eyes cold. "You are a white girl. Free to leave here whenever you wish!"

Suddenly someone screamed. It seemed to reverberate through Lauren's bones. The blood drained from her face as she stared at Eugenie. She turned abruptly and took the stairs, two at a time with Eugenie behind her. When the girls burst into the boudoir, they found Madame thrashing and writhing on the bed, her eyes open and glazed. She was biting her swollen tongue and gasping for air through her clenched teeth. The girls watched in horror as the woman convulsed on the bed, rising and falling grotesquely. Suddenly Madame fell back onto the bed and sighed.

Lauren watched in disbelief, too horrified to move. Madame was not moving.

"Is she alright? What's wrong, Lauren?" cried Eugenie.

"Oh my God! Oh my God!" Lauren cried rushing to her side. She pressed her fingers to Madame's neck then frantically shook her. There was no response. Lauren backed away tears filling her eyes. She shook her head. "I am too late. They have won. They have killed her."

Eugenie stared at the lifeless body of Josephine Aberjon. She backed out of the room and murmured, "I'll get Marianne."

Lauren slowly approached Madame once more. The woman lay on her back with her mouth open and her hair plastered her face. She was as thin as a skeleton and an odd metallic odor emanated from her. Lauren had never seen anyone die. The nuns had grown old and sickened, but she had never witnessed their demise. It seemed to her as if Madame had simply shed her skin like a snake and passed on. Reaching over she gently closed her eyes. With a hankie, she wiped the drool from her lips remembering Madame Aberjon's words. "If we could examine everyone's problems like clothes hanging on a line, we would always choose our own problems back again."

Lauren agreed with her. Rather than have Madame's difficulties, she would indeed choose her own problems all over again.

Chapter 16

Lauren sat staring at the fire in her room. She could not sleep. This was her first experience preparing a body for burial and most disturbing. Lauren assisted Marianne washing and clothing Madame in her best gown, and they sprinkled her with holy water and lavender flowers. They moved her to the sitting room in the candlelight with her hands folded. Lauren left the room the instant their work was complete. She could not bear to be with the body and left Marianne to say the prayers.

Although it was not a cold night, Lauren shivered, pulling her shawl around her. She was certain now that Jean-Baptist and Claude had poisoned Madame, and she was not going to keep quiet. Even though these were powerful men and she was a homeless girl from New Orleans, she was determined to expose them.

When dawn broke, she dressed and left the house heading for Fort de Chartres. Lauren knew little about the government here, but she *did* know that a lieutenant by the name of Antoine Brobriant was the supreme authority.

The fort was a half-day walk up the Mississippi, and it was the first time Lauren had ever visited the structure. It was not large, but it was certainly imposing perched on a hill keeping watch over the river. The fortress was made of upright logs set directly into the earth, and in the middle of the parade ground stood a stone powder magazine. Men in blue uniforms leered down at her from their posts as she pulled herself up the hill. Lauren jumped when one of them shouted, "What is your business here?"

She cleared her throat and called back, "I am here to see Lieutenant Brobriant."

The soldier looked at her suspiciously, and then opened the gate leading her across the grounds to a building that looked like headquarters. After running his eyes over her, the man spit tobacco juice and barked, "Wait here!"

The ground beneath Lauren's feet was brown and dry, and the sun baked her skin. It was only morning and already the temperature soared. She could feel drops of perspiration run down her back as she tried to calm herself.

She waited for what seemed to be an eternity before the guard returned saying, "You may go in now."

The temperature dropped instantly as Lauren stepped inside the Lieutenant's office. It was cool and dark, and it took her eyes a minute to adjust to the low light.

"May I help you, Mademoiselle?"

Lauren blinked and discovered a gentleman lounging behind a large desk smoking a white clay pipe. He was a man of middle years wearing a powdered wig and a blue waistcoat. To fight the heat he had removed his jacket and was in his shirtsleeves.

"Mademoiselle?"

Lauren swallowed hard and asked, "If a crime has been committed in Kaskaskia, Monsieur, to whom do I report?"

"To me, I am the First Lieutenant of the King. What crime are you reporting?" he said, taking up his quill.

Lauren hesitated. She was afraid that he would respond like the doctor, but she must find the courage to try once more. If she remained silent then she would be as guilty as Jean-Baptist and Claude. Madame's lifeless body sprang into her mind and she blurted out, "Murder."

"Murder!" the lieutenant exclaimed, sitting up straight. "Did you say murder?"

She nodded.

"Who has been murdered?"

"Josephine Aberjon, wife of Jean-Baptist Aberjon, owner of the Kaskaskia--"

"I know who he is," the lieutenant interrupted. "Who murdered her?"

Lauren felt as if she was going to gag, her throat was so dry. "Jean-Baptist and his son, Claude."

"What!"

"Yes Monsieur, I believe they poisoned her by putting something in her food--"

Lieutenant Briobriant put his hand up and said, "Govern your tongue, girl! Before you say anything more, I want you to realize the serious nature of your allegation. If you have any doubts, any doubts at all, I suggest you walk out that door and never return."

She hesitated a moment then murmured, "I have no doubts, Lieutenant."

He stood up and walked around his desk. His eyes narrowed as he scrutinized her. Lauren did not move as the lieutenant approached her. Like a rock, she stood her ground and boldly looked him in the eye.

"Who are you?"

"My name is Lauren Heathstone."

"Your family?"

"I have one sister in New Orleans."

"What is your business in Kaskaskia?"

"I was engaged as a companion to Josephine Aberjon."

He circled Lauren, looking her up and down.

"Really Mademoiselle--I want the truth! You have been slighted in love by one of Aberjon men and you are here to exact your pound of flesh."

"Lieutenant Brobriant," pleaded Lauren. "I am most sincere. Madame Aberjon overheard them plotting--it was all for money--"

"Go home! You are nothing more than an adventuress, and I am a very busy man."

He sat down at his desk and took up his quill, dismissing her.

Lauren was mortified. This man had been her final hope. She must try once more. Suddenly without thinking, she grabbed the quill from his hand.

He looked up, thunderstruck by her audacity.

"Monsieur, if you do not listen to me I shall be forced to appeal to Father Peron. He will not stand by and let you ignore this crime."

The Lieutenant's eyes narrowed. He did not want that meddlesome priest involved. The Church looked for any excuse to undermine his authority.

Lauren continued, "I believe if you check the personal accounts of these men and the books at the Kaskaskia Lead Mine, you will find that Monsieur Aberjon and his son are in dire need of money; enough money to require a prosperous marriage. You will find that Jean-Baptist has been keeping company with a very wealthy woman who lives on Rue Saint Germaine."

Lieutenant Brobriant wanted nothing more than to throw this brazen wench out on her ear, but he felt compelled to investigate further before she brought in that ambitious priest.

"Damn you!" he barked. "When did she die?"

"Last night."

"Of what nature was her decline and death?"

"She had severe cramping and the flux. She could keep no food down. It ended in a grotesque, uncontrollable spasm on the bed."

He rubbed the back of his neck and heaved a sigh. He was overworked and in no mood for schoolgirl fantasies. "I will be down shortly to talk to Monsieur Aberjon and his son. Say nothing of this to anyone."

Lauren's heart jumped. *Someone was listening to her at last!*

*   *   *

Jean-Baptist looked up and down the hall before closing the door to the drawing room. He grabbed the brandy decanter from the cabinet and filled his glass to the brim, looking over at his son.

Claude was leaning on the harpsichord, with his head on his hand, carelessly plucking the keys of the instrument. In keeping with the latest fashion, he had placed a heart shaped patch at the corner of his mouth. His white face makeup was so thick; one could scrape it off with a fingernail.

"Well, what was so important, Father that you had to see me right away?"

"Lieutenant Briobriant was here to see me after the funeral yesterday. He wants to look at our books."

Claude chuckled. "Really Father, I had no idea you were such a worrier. You simply have no stomach for this. I know you loathe me, but you have to admit I was creative in solving our financial problems."

Jean-Baptist gulped his brandy and stared out the window sullenly. He felt surly today, and he would take great pleasure in pummeling his son's face right now. He hated partnering with him in this unseemly business, but it was inevitable, he was in dire need of money.

"You were right about one thing, that wench from New Orleans became suspicious. But never mind, I have everything taken care of. Our man arrived this morning," said Claude.

Jean-Baptist whirled around. "He's here?"

"Definitely."

"And the arsenic?"

"Where it should be."

"Good! Then it will be today," said Jean-Baptist feeling his spirits rise.

"I told you that I'd hold up my end of the bargain," said Claude, rising from his seat. "Now it's your turn. How soon can you wed?"

"Immediately, I don't give a damn what anybody in this town thinks. They'll have their murderer, that's all they want."

"Bravo, Father, bravo," cooed Claude. "Everything is going as planned."

Chapter 17

Late that afternoon Lauren returned to the Aberjon residence to retrieve the last of her belongings. Eugenie and Marianne were in the kitchen preparing supper when Lauren poked her head in and whispered, "Are they gone?"

"Yes, they are gone. Come in quickly," Marianne said.

"I must run up and get my things right away," Lauren whispered looking down the hall. "Have you heard them say anything about my visit to the lieutenant?"

"Nothing at all," whispered Eugenie, looking out the window. "But they spend a lot of time together in the drawing room with the door closed."

"Come and see me soon at the Lupone's," Lauren said hugging the women. The relationship between Lauren and Eugenie had improved slowly.

"You will be a married lady soon," said Eugenie.

"Not soon enough for me!" said Lauren as she inspected into the hall on her way upstairs.

Once in her room, Lauren cleared out the armoire, threw some gowns over her arm and closed the bedroom door. She started down the hall, but when she passed Madame's room she hesitated. Furtively she turned the knob and opened the boudoir. Nothing had changed. The pink drapes still hung in folds onto the floor. The mauve rug was still in place and the rose-colored bed curtains were neatly tied back. Everything was as usual, but the bed was empty. The room was like a loyal dog waiting for its master to return.

Lauren felt a tightening in her chest. She spied Madame's dainty music box on the nightstand and picked it up turning it over in her hands. It seemed like only yesterday she was dancing right here in this room. She wound the box up and the delicate notes filled the room once more. Lauren could see herself gliding past the bed, sailing around the armchairs and soaring by the divan as Madame clapped her hands in delight.

Suddenly loud voices interrupted her reverie. Noise was coming from the back of the house. Rushing to the back room, she threw the shutters open and leaned out. Two soldiers emerged from the slave quarters. One of them had Eugenie by the arm.

Lauren raced down the stairs as they were throwing Eugenie to the floor clamping an iron mask onto her head. Marianne was screaming and sobbing.

"Be quick about it," one shouted. "She may bite."

"No!" screamed Lauren lunging at them. One of the soldiers straightened up and elbowed her. She fell into a mirror which crashed onto the floor into a thousand pieces.

* * *

Slowly, Lauren pulled herself into a sitting position. She could hear someone crying somewhere but could not focus her eyes. Bruised and confused, Lauren pulled a shard of glass out of her arm. She heard the sobbing again and asked thickly, "Who's there?"

"They've taken my darling," sobbed Marianne. She was sitting on the floor in the hall not far from Lauren, rocking back and forth. "They've my taken Eugenie away."

"Why?" Lauren asked putting her hands to her head.

"They say Eugenie poisoned the mistress! They found arsenic hidden in a vial in her drawer."

Lauren tried to pull herself up onto her feet, but she was too weak and fell back heavily onto the floor. Marianne continued to sob. Even through the fog of injury it was clear to Lauren that the arsenic had been planted. *The plan was obvious. The residents of the Illinois Country hated the Chickasaws and they knew they would condemn the Indian girl swiftly and without conscience.*

Lauren dragged herself to her feet and tried to get Marianne to come to the kitchen, but the woman refused. She was beyond consoling and continued to sit on the hall floor, rocking and moaning. Lauren stepped outside and began to retch. Just as she was wiping her mouth a carriage roared up the drive stopping in front of her. The door flew open and Claude Aberjon leaned forward.

"What a lovely picture you paint," he said with a smirk. "Get in."

Lauren straightened up and turned toward the house.

"I say, get in!" he shouted again.

"Stay away from me!"

"For once in your life, don't be a damned fool. I have an urgent note from Rene' Lupone saying that you should come with me immediately. Here see for yourself," and he thrust it toward her.

Lauren pushed the hair from her eyes and ripped the note from Claude's hand. It was indeed Rene's writing telling her to meet him immediately at the L'hotel Bourges, that it was of extreme importance, and that he would guarantee her safety with Claude Aberjon. She looked suspiciously from the note to Claude and said, "I'm warning you I have my boots on."

"Noted," he stated rubbing the bridge of his nose. "Get in."

The carriage lurched as Lauren threw herself onto the seat, and Claude slammed the door. He watched her with a smirk on his face.

"What is this all about?" she demanded.

"You'll see."

"Is Rene' in any danger?"

"No, in fact, you might say that I have removed him from harms way."

He looked at her soiled gown and disheveled hair and joked, "My, you look alluring this afternoon. Run into some trouble?"

Lauren looked out the window fighting the urge to retch again. Claude reached into a small ebony box, snorted a pinch of snuff, then thrust his white face forward and asked, "Darling, how is my makeup today?"

Lauren had had enough of his charade and hissed, "You'll burn in hell for what you have done."

"Oh, aren't we self righteous? Have you ever thought about your part in all of this, angel? We would never have had to sacrifice your friend if you had just kept your mouth *shut*." With this last word, Claude allowed his hatred for Lauren to flare. He leaned forward and snarled, "I never forgot that day when you broke my nose, you little whore, and today I shall pay you back."

With those words the carriage came to a halt, and Claude jumped out. He stood in the door of L'hotel Bourges leaning on his cane as Lauren stepped out of the carriage. It was a small but respectable establishment down near the docks. With an exaggerated flourish he directed her inside and taking her elbow guided her through the boisterous crowd.

The room was filled with people, mostly men; some were eating, and others taking spirits. A buxom waitress wound her way through the revelers holding a tray over her head. The odor of smoke was thick and overpowering as well as the smell of stale spirits. Loud laughter rang out from different tables and heads turned as Lauren walked by. Rene' was sitting by the fire with two men, and when she reached the table the men stood up.

With a look of triumph, Claude introduced her. "Lauren, you know my father Jean-Baptist. Of course, you know Rene' Lupone and I'm sure you remember Monsieur Adair Heathstone."

*   *   *

There was a jangling of keys and a heavy door scraped open. Eugenie sat up and rubbed her eyes. It was dark, and the guard's torch was bright.

"Get up! There's someone to see you," he barked, kicking her.

Lauren fell to her knees and embraced Eugenie. The hideous muzzle was still on her face. The restraint was a piece of iron covering the girl's mouth with several holes punched in the metal for air. The muzzle was fitted with two sets of straps one set encircling Eugenie's neck and the other set running up on either side of her nose to the back of her head.

"Take this thing off of her right now!" screamed Lauren.

"Can't," said the guard flatly. "Lieutenant's orders. It's for your own good anyway. Them savages bite."

"Are you mad! She would never bite anyone!"

He shrugged and slammed the door, bolting it behind him.

Eugenie pulled herself into a corner and faced the wall. Her clothes were filthy, and she smelled like urine.

"Have they hurt you? Talk to me! Why won't you look at me?"

"Go away. I don't want your pity." mumbled Eugenie. Her words were barely audible from the muzzle.

Lauren sat cross-legged facing Eugenie's back. "Yes, I *am* going away. I have come to say good bye."

Eugenie turned slowly on the straw and looked at her. Lauren stood up and walked across the cell looking outside through the bars. "I pleaded to the lieutenant for your release, but the Aberjons are too powerful." After a few moments she added, "Claude found my husband and I am leaving with him tomorrow."

A heavy silence fell between the girls. The guard snored outside the door.

Finally, Eugenie murmured, "What of Rene'?"

"He has washed his hands of me. His mother assures me one day he will forgive me."

"We will both be leaving tomorrow," Eugenie continued. "They are hanging me in the morning."

Lauren froze. She did not breathe. She did not move. She only stared into Eugenie's eyes struggling for words. Eugenie sighed and turned away. "They told me just moments ago."

Lauren took a deep breath and turned to the window. She stared at the stars but she did not see them. Suddenly, a sob escaped her, and she pressed her eyes shut fighting back the tears and the rage.

After what seemed like a long time Eugenie murmured, "I wonder what it is like to die, Lauren."

Lauren continued to stare at the night sky. "I don't know what it's like to die, Eugenie, but I *do* know that when the sun comes up in the morning, the stars are still in the sky, even if I can't see them." She turned and looked at her friend. "And so it will be, after tomorrow. I know, like the stars in the morning sunshine, you will exist--somewhere--even if I cannot see you.

Chapter 18

The next morning, they informed Lauren that she was leaving Kaskaskia before sunrise with Heathstone. He had been in New Orleans on business. Over cards and cognac, Claude and Adair Heathstone found they had an acquaintance in common and in no time Claude informed Heathstone of his wife's whereabouts. He was delighted to reunite the two.

Lauren never looked back at Kaskaskia as the convoy pulled away an hour before sunrise. Gabriel had been right; she had never belonged here. Her search for a home must continue, and she must put the Illinois Country behind her. Lauren turned her face into the wind once more and resumed her journey.

The small group of bataux seemed to fly down the Mississippi toward New Orleans loaded with several men and a great deal of lead; lead that was bound for the English Colonies. Lauren wondered if the French Government was aware that Monsieur Aberjon sold lead to the English, but she would say nothing. She learned that vengeance from Jean-Baptist was swift and unforgiving.

The current of the Mississippi hurtled them downstream once more toward the city of New Orleans. In only seventeen days the journey was over, in contrast with the upstream journey of several months. Adair Heathstone remained aloof throughout the expedition, just as before. In Kaskaskia, he had taken a separate apartment and on the journey downstream, he had not attempted to converse with her. His French was poor and the language barrier distanced him from them all.

Monsieur Mereness, a middle-aged voyageur who learned English to trade goods with the Fox and the Sauk Indians kept Heathstone informed along the way. He told Lauren that Heathstone had paid him handsomely and that if it were not for his money, they would have left him in the wilderness a long time ago. He detested the man and pitied Lauren because she was married to such a boorish oaf. He offered to help her whenever he could.

When they finally arrived in New Orleans, Mereness asked Heathstone if he would allow the girl to see her sister before their departure to the English Colonies. Heathstone gave his grunt of approval. Mereness smiled at her and instructed the men to put Lauren's traveling bag on the vessel along with the Englishmen's trunk. "You had better hurry. Your husband wants to leave this afternoon. It will only take an hour to load then you'll embark."

Only an hour with Simone, thought Lauren. They had not been together for almost two years. Heathstone ordered a burley seaman to escort her to the convent. It was heaven to be back on the streets of New Orleans even if the troll was guarding her. Everything was as she remembered it. The loud, busy docks were still thrilling; the colorful market fresh and bountiful as before and when she laid eyes on the Ursuline Convent a lump came into her throat. She pulled the rope by the massive wooden door ringing a bell inside. A nun Lauren did not know opened the door and asked her to wait in the foyer while she informed Sister Marie-Bernard, Simone's new name that her sibling was here.

The brute Heathstone had appointed, stood guard outside the door as Lauren waited anxiously inside. The room was dark and one candle burned on the small table in the corner. Its flame casting long shadows on the walls. Lauren's heart jumped when the door opened, and her sister stepped into the room.

"Simone!" Lauren cried and threw her arms around her. Simone stiffened. She was dressed in the austere white habit of the novice Ursuline, but her beauty could not be subdued. The wimple made a perfect frame for her oval face and coral lips. A weak smile flickered around her mouth, and she said flatly, "You've returned."

"Yes," Lauren said, grabbing her hands. "I have so much to tell you and ask you. Oh, I am so excited! "

Simone ran her eyes over her sister.

"I know," Lauren admitted. "I must be a sight."

"You have certainly changed," said Simone.

"But look at *you*!" cried Lauren pointing to the white veil. "Here you are a novice. How soon will you take your final vows?"

"Soon."

"Simone, we can't talk here. Let's go to one of the school rooms."

Simone remained motionless, her hands folded. "Sister Marie-Bernard is my name now, Lauren."

Lauren wrinkled her nose and said, "What's wrong with you? You act as stiff as old Mother Magdalena--"

Simone's eyes flashed. "You will be respectful when you are within these walls."

"Who do you think you're talking to? I am not one of your students and I *will* call you Simone. That name was good enough for the De Beauvilles!"

Simone turned to leave saying, "My time here is done."

"What has happened to you!" cried Lauren. "The good nuns of the Ursuline Academy were never sanctimonious. You didn't learn that self-righteous attitude here."

Not bothering to turn around, Simone stated, "Leave here now please and don't come back."

Sudden pain shot through Lauren. "Simone! What's wrong?"

"I cannot see you."

Lauren grabbed her arm. "You cannot leave like this. There is something wrong."

"Please let me go," Simone demanded, struggling to get free.

"No, not until you tell me what is wrong," said Lauren.

Sudden emotion flooding her face, Simone snapped, "Alright, I'll tell you!" She pushed Lauren away and said, "You look so--worldly. You remind me of everything that I am *not*. You have always had the courage to pursuit life. I—I cannot face the world like you. You have never been afraid of anything. I have always been scared. These walls are the only place I have ever felt safe."

Simone pulled a hankie out of her habit, wiped her eyes and looked at Lauren's belly. "I think the hardest part of taking my vows is knowing that I will never bear children. Seeing you gave me a shock. I suppose I am a little jealous."

"What?" said Lauren. "Jealous of what?"

"Why it's obvious. I am jealous that you are with child."

* * *

The sea sickness and the morning sickness kept Lauren in her cabin the entire voyage to New England. The roll of the waves combined with a queasy stomach had a disastrous outcome. It meant hours of dizziness and retching. Every time she attempted to stand, the floor of her cabin seemed to rise up and hit her in the face.

At first, she thought Simone was mistaken about her condition, but when she undressed in the ship's cabin that first night there was no mistaking it; the reflection in the mirror showed a young woman teaming with child. Lauren had been so busy and fatigued taking care of Madame she had attributed all of her symptoms to worry and exhaustion.

Rene would never know she was carrying his child and to Lauren this was just as well. She had left him a confused and angry young man, and this news would have complicated matters further.

In spite of it all, she had little time to be anxious about anything. She boarded the merchant vessel after seeing her sister, and in a matter of hours; she lay in her cabin, prostrate with illness. Heathstone did not appear to notice Lauren's pregnancy or to care. She kept the door joining their cabins shut, and he entered only one time to find her retching uncontrollably into a bucket.

She gradually lost track of her days on the merchant ship. By the time the vessel entered New York Bay; Lauren had regained some of her strength and was able to stand on deck, the wind reviving her. Tall ships, their white masts snapping in the wind, dotted the harbor and beyond them were two story houses with red tile roofs. There was much confusion on deck when the ship finally dropped anchor in New York. Crates and barrels swung overhead, crewmembers were shouting and seagulls darted everywhere, screeching and crying for food.

Heathstone gestured to her to accompany him to shore. He seemed unusually tense and when Lauren looked at him, he had pursed his lips so tightly that they were white. Taking her bag, he indicated that she should say nothing while he escorted her down the plank.

Suddenly, when she placed her foot on shore, the vertigo returned, and she exclaimed, "*Oh! Mon Dieu!*"

The next thing she knew a soldier stepped over and thrust his face into hers asking her questions in English. When she looked at him blankly, he turned and began to argue with Heathstone. She knew something was wrong when the officer gestured for his men to board the vessel and search it. He turned to Lauren and grabbed her wrists roughly binding them together with a leather thong. Lauren's heart began to thud in her chest as she cried, "*Qu'ai-t-je-fait*!"

Heathstone lunged at the officer, but one of the soldier's pulled him away roughly. Everything was happening so fast that Lauren barely had time to scream, "Monsieur Heathstone! Help me!" but to no avail. Two of the soldiers restrained him as the other soldiers swept her away into the crowd.

Lauren was hustled down the street into a large government building which was flying the flag of Great Britain. She was ushered into a room crammed with books and military maps where a gray haired major sat at a cluttered desk scratching numbers into a ledger. He looked up and grumbled, "Who's this?"

The soldier stepped forward. "This little French tart was on a merchant vessel that just arrived, sir. Your orders were to detain French--"

"I know what my orders are," he interrupted putting his quill down. His eyes ran over Lauren, and he demanded, "Do you speak English?"

Lauren knew the phase well enough to shake her head.

"That's no surprise," he replied in French. "You people would never lower your standards and speak English."

He sighed and picked up his quill continuing in French, "Now, why are you here in the English Colonies?"

"I come here with my husband, Monsieur Adair Heathstone."

"Where is he now?"

"I do not know, perhaps at the wharf."

"Where were you born?"

"New Orleans."

"Where did you board this ship?"

"New Orleans."

"New Orleans! The ship's manifest says they embarked in Charleston." He looked at the regular standing by Lauren and barked, "Find the ship's captain immediately!"

The major's eyes narrowed and he leaned forward scrutinizing Lauren.

"Why have you married a British subject?"

"Because--" stammered Lauren, "because Mother Marie Margarite wished it."

"Oh," the Major groaned sitting back. "Another damned Catholic. You are lucky to be in the Colony of New York. They are far more tolerant here than in the Colony of Massachusetts. In fact, you would be denied entrance in that place based upon your religion alone."

For what seemed like hours, Lauren endured a battery of questions and by the time the Major finished she felt weak and faint. The arduous journey, the stifling office and standing for that long had sapped her strength. She rubbed her forehead and stepped forward to lean on a chair for support.

The Major stated, "I'm through with you. You may go now."

A British regular escorted Lauren out of the office and to the door. When they stepped outside, he muttered something and gave her a swift kick. She tumbled clumsily down the steps, sprawling onto the cobblestone street below. No one offered her assistance or sympathy. Several people stepped around her taking care not to touch her. She pulled herself to her feet and brushed her gown off. After pushing the hair from her face, Lauren searched the street for Heathstone. Surely, he would be looking for her, but every face was that of a stranger. She had no idea what to do or where to find him. It was obvious, she would get no help from the authorities and even if she were to find someone willing to assist her, the language barrier was too great. In fact, it had become apparent that she was not welcome in this part of the world at all.

The sun was starting to set and Lauren realized that she must find Heathstone immediately. She would try the wharf first. The masts of the tall ships were just over the rooftops, so she started in that direction. Everything was so different from the modest wooden structures of New Orleans and the Illinois Country. The structures were made of brick with the gabled ends facing the street. The gables were stair-stepped and decorated with ornate ironwork and instead of a *galerie*; the homes had large front steps with benches on either side of the stoop. She noticed that the front doors were hinged separately into upper and lower portions and that many residents kept the upper door open, possibly for a breeze.

She turned onto a street and was surprised to be walking along a canal busy with barges and small crafts and off in the distance she spied a windmill. The streets were busy with carriages and well-to-do shoppers. Not only English was spoken in New York but many other languages as well Dutch, German, and Danish none of which Lauren could understand.

The clothing of the residents was similar to the French, but the hemlines on the ladies gowns dropped onto the pavement. In her homeland, skirts and gowns stopped at the ankle. Many of the ensembles were gaily colored and quite elaborate.

When she arrived at the wharf, the first thing she did was look for the merchant ship on which she had traveled, but it was gone. There was no trace of any of the crew or of Monsieur Heathstone. She approached one of the dockworkers, but he only shrugged when she gestured to where the ship had been.

At last, Lauren recognized one of the young sailors from the voyage, but when she approached him he turned away pretending that he did not know her. He looked furtively at the British soldiers after Lauren had addressed him then darted down an alley. Suddenly, she recalled Heathstone's lips, white with tension, and she wondered what everyone on board that ship had to hide.

She looked up at the darkening sky, and a bolt of panic shot through her. *Where would she spend the night? Where would she get food?* Her heart started to pound as she looked around desperately. Maybe some kind woman would help, and she turned to search the wharf for a friendly face. She spied a woman of middle years watching several men play draughts on a barrel, and she decided to approach her for help.

"Please Madame," Lauren said in French. "I have just arrived this afternoon. I am without shelter--" The woman narrowed her eyes and without warning spat into Lauren's face. Horrified, she stepped back and gasped as the men broke into fits of laughter. She wiped the spit with her sleeve and stumbled into a doorway to hide. Hatred burned inside her for this new land. *If this was the reception she received in New York, what must it be like in the other English Colonies? Where could she go?* For the first time in her life she was being judged not by her character but by the language she spoke.

Lauren took a deep breath and squared her shoulders. She was not about to be beaten. If she had to sleep under the stars every night from now on she would do it, but she would ask for nothing. Instinctively she knew that she had to get out of the city. She did not know how far she had to walk, but to preserve her own safety, she had to have seclusion. Lauren guessed that just like in the Illinois Country, the farther you walked toward the interior, the sparser the population. Therefore, she set off inland getting as far away from the city as possible.

It was not long before she was on the outskirts of town, and the landscape was becoming rural. The low widespread farmhouses were very different from the upright two story brick houses of the city. They were constructed of wood or fieldstone yet impeccably kept like the houses of town.

It grew late, and she was weary. Windmills dotted the landscape and making sure no one saw her, she slipped inside one of the structures. The large millstone dominated the room, but there was just enough space for her to lie down in one corner. She sat on the floor for a long time with her back against the wall, trying to make sense of the horrors of the day. Fatigue overcame her, and she brushed a spot off on the floor dropping down on her side. Tomorrow she would find a better home but for tonight, she was grateful for the mill and the sheltering arms of the sails above her.

Chapter 19

The next day brought little relief. Hunger nagged at Lauren's stomach. The child in her belly gave her a yearning which she had never known before and she set out from the windmill to find food. Before long, she approached a farmhouse where she spied a pie rack holding two freshly baked meat pies. The aroma almost knocked her over, and she stepped behind a tree watching the back door closely.

Suddenly, a woman stepped out placing another baked good onto the rack to cool. She returned to the house, and Lauren crept silently toward the food. Without a second thought, she reached out and took a warm pie, ducking into the woods nearby to run as far away as possible. When she could go no farther, she slumped down and leaned against a tree catching her breath. The pie was still warm, and she stuffed the chicken, potatoes and crust greedily into her mouth. Never had anything tasted so good. She devoured it without stopping then dragged her sleeve across her mouth looking around furtively. It was easier than she had thought and she was surprised at her lack of remorse. For the first time in her life, Lauren understood the plight of the paupers on the streets of New Orleans and their acts of desperation.

She returned to the city to renew her search for Heathstone. She found it ironic that *she* was now the one in pursuit.

Another day passed yielding nothing. All afternoon long, she walked staring into faces, searching the crowd but with no results. Although the meat pie had sustained her during the day, the baby told her it was again time to eat.

She loitered near a fruit stand on Whitehall and Pearl watching the farmer clean up after a long day at market. When he bent over to put some apples into a crate, she crammed some cherries and a plum into her shift. Turning toward the outskirts of town, Lauren made her way back to the windmill wondering as she walked what was going to happen to her. She wondered if she would spend the rest of her life stealing food and sleeping in barns. She tossed her head refusing to think about the future.

After several days, she gave up looking for Adair Heathstone and wandered the streets of New York lost and lonely. She sat down on a barrel by the canal filled with despair and began to cry. No one paid any attention and continued to hurry on their way. She was just another indigent on the streets of New York. At last, a gentleman in a fine carriage noticed her, calling to his driver to stop. "Madame, may I be of some assistance?"

Lauren looked up. "*Pardon?*"

"You're French?" he continued in her language. "Please allow me," he said as he swung the door to his carriage open. "Don't be afraid. I want to help."

She approached the carriage and noticed that there were packages and boxes piled high on the seat as if the gentleman had just returned from shopping. The only spot open was next to him. She crawled in and sat down. He reached over her swinging the door shut and rapped on the wall. The carriage lurched forward as Lauren looked at the man. He was a rotund red-faced gentleman of middle years sporting a powdered wig and diamond-shaped patch on his face.

"You look very unhappy, Mademoiselle," he said. "Here have some port. Its warmth will revive you." He opened an elegant leather case taking out two small crystal glasses and a flask. Lauren noticed his pudgy fingers as he poured them each a drink. He handed her a glass then held his own up saying, "To the King's health," draining the contents in one gulp.

Lauren took a sip, noticing that the man's leg was resting against her own.

"How long has it been since you've eaten," he said pulling a wad of notes from his pocket."

"A while."

"Well here," he said pushing the notes down her bodice. "This ought to help."

He leaned his huge body over and started to run his tongue along her neck. Lauren pushed him back, but he pressed himself harder against her, slipping his hand down the front of her gown.

"Stop!" she cried.

He mumbled something and Lauren began to squirm. Yanking out of his grasp, she lunged for the door.

The man caught her by the hair yanking her head back. "Not so fast!" he snarled.

With all her strength, Lauren threw herself against the door of the coach and tumbled out onto the pavement below. The carriage stopped, but Lauren dashed down an alley. She bolted up one street and down the other until she had lost her breath and realized that the man was not pursuing her at all.

Panting and holding her side, Lauren sat down in a doorway. Suddenly she realized that the notes were still tucked inside her bodice. Her eyes grew large as she pulled out the wad. She counted the bills then smiled. She threw her head back and laughed. The incident had been to her benefit. It had all turned out well. The risk was a small price to pay for survival. There was enough money here to buy food for a week, she thought.

Even though Lauren was frugal the money was gone in no time, and she was back to stealing food again. She was growing drawn and pale, her clothes were filthy and her hair was matted. She noted other paupers on the street viewing them not as companions but as competitors for food.

After several weeks of struggling to survive, Lauren forgot Heathstone, New Orleans and all of her dreams. Her focus was entirely on food and safety. One day it was too difficult to make the journey out to the countryside, so she slept in a doorway, cold and miserable all night.

The next day Lauren watched a house all morning until the resident stepped out to go to market. Armed with an excuse if someone answered the door, Lauren stepped up to the door and knocked. There was no response. To be sure, she knocked again and still no reply. Looking one way, then the other she opened the door and stepped inside the keeping room. Someone had banked the fire, and the smell of fresh baked bread filled the room. It was a modest home decorated in the Dutch style with colorful tiles inlaid in the stonework of the fireplace and Delft china in the cupboard. Lauren knew these things could bring a good price, but she had no time and wished only for food and bedding.

Quickly she darted about looking for linens and bedding to steal, but she could find no beds. She ran from one end of the house to the other, finally opening a large cupboard. There hiding inside was a bed with a fluffy down mattress and patchwork quilt. She was astounded to see a bed in a cupboard. She yanked the quilt off the bed and went back to the kitchen loading it with breads and meats. Rolling it up, she shoved the bundle under her arm and opened the front door. Looking around cautiously, she stepped into the street and stole away.

That night as Lauren slept in a doorway bundled warmly in her quilt; a soldier found her and told her to move on. She moved several blocks away, and again the same soldier roused her gesturing to move again. Desperate for sleep she wandered to the outskirts of town and found a graveyard. Candlelight flickered in the parsonage, so she went to the far end of the churchyard near the woods to bed for the night. She spread her quilt on the ground between two crooked headstones and lay down staring at the parsonage. It was comforting to watch the light in the home. The warmth of the quilt enveloped her and Lauren dropped off to sleep, sharing the ground with those who would sleep forever.

* * *

For weeks, Lauren slept in the churchyard. She had grown attached to her spot between the two crooked headstones. She had even come to know the souls she slept between, Abigail Von Dorset, called to her maker at the age of eight, and Ephraim James brought home at eighty-two. The phantoms appeared to her often, but particularly on the nights when she was most tired and hungry. Abigail, a wispy sprite would perch herself upon her headstone, hug her knees and listen to Lauren reminisce about her carefree days at the convent. When she needed to unburden worries and cares, Grandpa Ephraim would lean on his cane nodding sympathetically. The specters never criticized or laughed at her. They were always patient and understanding, offering her love and kindness when she returned from a day of humiliation and despair.

As the weeks wore on Lauren became gaunt and frail. It was barely noticeable that a baby grew inside her, and most days she forgot that the child even existed. She had developed a nagging cough, which robbed her of precious sleep. Not much more than a specter herself, she whispered to Grandpa Ephraim one night that she was afraid she would be unable to rise from her bed in the morning to search for food. All night long the rain soaked her blanket, and he stayed by her side leaning on his cane keeping silent vigil.

When the morning sun rose, Lauren's faithful friend had vanished, and she sat up slowly rubbing her eyes. It was late in the day and the sun was already high in the sky as a strange droning sound met her ears. Bewildered and groggy, Lauren shook her head to clear the cobwebs. At last she recognized the sound. It was singing and it was coming from the road. She got up on her knees, and hiding behind Abigail's headstone, she spied a funeral procession headed her way.

Like a wild animal, she grabbed her quilt and dashed into the woods to watch from a safe distance as the group walked up and gathered by an open hole near her sleeping spot. After lowering the coffin, the dominie read from the Bible as the mourners dabbed their eyes and threw flowers onto the coffin. One by one last respects were paid, and the group turned back to town leaving only the gravedigger to finish.

Lauren watched from the woods. The man had a broad back, and the weathered face of someone used to a lifetime of work in the elements. Leaning against a tree, he lit his pipe and watched the procession disappear down the road. When the group rounded the bend, he tapped the ashes out of his pipe and walked back to the open grave. Assuming he would fill the hole in, Lauren was surprised when the man jumped down into the open grave then scrambled out again holding a cord. One end of the rope he left in the hole, the other end of he dropped onto the ground near his feet. Now he picked up his spade and began to fill in the hole. When he was finished, he drove an iron rod into the ground which was about two feet high, attached a bell to it and fastened the cord to the bell. Wiping his hands on his breeches, he sighed and stretched. The job was complete and it was time for payment. After disappearing into the parsonage for a moment, he trudged down the road and out of sight.

Hunger pains forced Lauren to move out of the woods. After hanging her quilt up to dry in the trees, she dragged herself into town. Today she was lucky, the cook at the Hogshead Tavern had burned a turkey, and Lauren was the first to discover its charred remains tossed carelessly into the alley. She picked it up tearing at the burned meat savagely, feeling it's nourishment in her belly.

That night in the graveyard, she was asleep the minute she dropped onto her quilt, but before long a bell ringing awakened her. She bolted upright as it echoed in her ears. Rubbing her eyes, she stood up quickly letting the quilt drop to the ground. The parsonage was dark. Everyone appeared to be asleep. Suddenly, the bell rang again, and Lauren dropped down into a terrified crouch. Her heart pounded furiously as she tried to make sense of what was happening. *Where was the bell? Was this a nightmare?* Suddenly Lauren realized the din was not coming from the church but from the small bell perched above the freshly dug grave.

Panting, she stumbled toward the mound where the smell of fresh earth filled her nostrils. The bell continued ringing frantically. Suddenly, Lauren realized that someone was under the earth, buried alive pulling desperately at the cord. Confusion turned to horror as Lauren began to claw at the earth, trying to free the prisoner below. Dirt flew in every direction, but the effort was fruitless. As abruptly as it began, the bell stopped. Lauren froze. *Had the person suffocated? Had they fallen into a swoon?*

She stood up and looked at the parsonage. The ringing began again. Mustering all her strength, Lauren bounded toward the front door and hammered on it with her fists.

"Answer! Please answer!" she screamed in French. No one stirred as she slammed on the door again. "Someone please! Come quickly! Someone has been buried alive!"

There was still no response. She dashed down the steps out to a shed in search of a shovel. In spite of the clear night, Lauren was not familiar with the parsonage, and she tripped over an uneven paving stone sending her into a sprawl. A man in a nightshirt jerked her to her feet.

"What is the meaning of this!" he barked in Dutch.

"Please Monsieur!" Lauren implored, "I was asleep in the churchyard and there was a bell--".

"What do you want!" he exclaimed again in Dutch, grabbing her arm.

Frustrated, Lauren put her finger to her lips, instructing him listen.

Suddenly, the *dominie's* jaw dropped. He heard the bell. The man turned and bound up the steps of the parsonage shouting to his family. Lauren stood wringing her hands until the dominie and his sons rushed out holding lanterns. After grabbing shovels, they bolted out to the graveyard where they began shoveling furiously. The bell ceased ringing.

Lauren's heart was pounding as she watched the men. It was a macabre sight seeing the three figures digging frantically in the lamplight. The lanterns cast long shadows across the dominie and his sons, contorting their images grotesquely.

The heavy smell of earth churned Lauren's stomach as she listened to the spades scoop and toss, scoop and toss. She began to feel weak and dizzy. Steadying herself on an oak, her mind traveled six feet below to the desperate inhabitant of that coffin. *Was the poor soul still alive or had they been too late? How could there be enough air in that small space to keep anyone alive?* She said a fervent prayer to the Virgin Mary and waited. Suddenly she heard the dull thud of a shovel hitting wood, then shouts from the *dominie*.

Lauren dashed to the edge and held a lantern high. Frantically, the young men cleared the coffin as the *dominie* yanked at the stubborn lid. Suddenly it cracked open and there lying motionless in the box was a young woman, pale and drawn, clothed in a white shroud, covered in perspiration and blood. Her blonde hair was a wet and tangled and her hands were torn and bloodied. Lauren knew she had been clawing at the lid of the casket. All of a sdden, there was a swift intake of air, and she began to cough violently.

"Praise God! She's still alive!" declared the *dominie* as he looked gratefully to the heavens. The men quickly lifted the woman up and carried off to the parsonage, for a second chance at life.

For a long time Lauren stood and watched the flickering lights inside the house She wondered if the woman was still alive. She shuddered to think what would have happened had she not heard the bell and cursed whoever neglected keeping vigil that night. There would be no sleep for a while. Lauren was far too unnerved. With a sigh, she took her quilt and started down the road to find a new place to sleep, forced to abandon her home once more. She turned back to say farewell to Abigail and Ephraim, but they were nowhere to be found; only their silent headstones remained.

Chapter 20

Lauren spent a miserable night lying on her quilt behind a necessary house off Pearl Street. She sat up stiffly the next morning, pushing the matted hair from her face. As much as she needed to rest today, it was essential she move on before someone discovered her. She rolled her filthy quilt into a ball. Once again the quest for food was imperative, but today when she stepped onto the cobblestone street a blinding pain shot through her belly. She doubled over in agony. After several minutes, the torment eased, and she straightened up panting. A few people noticed she was in distress, but they offered no assistance. They wrinkled their noses turning away in disgust from the foul-smelling beggar.

Catching her breath, she moved down the street toward the market to try to find food. The pain was gone and hunger returned. She watched with longing as a barge moved down the canal, laden with colorful fruits and vegetables for market.

Suddenly, a well-dressed man, bored with his repast pitched a half-eaten drumstick onto the street. It landed with a thud at Lauren's feet and rolled. Like a bolt of lightening she plunged for the meat but not before a mangy hound snapped it up. With the ferocity of a wild animal, Lauren dove for the dog and grabbed it by the back of its neck tearing the drumstick from its jaws. The dog lunged at Lauren, baring its teeth, but she kicked it and turned away. Lauren was too absorbed with the drumstick to notice a woman calling to her from a coach.

"Put that down!" the woman called in Dutch.

Finishing the meat, Lauren tossed the bone sway and wiped her greasy hands on her skirt, oblivious to the woman.

"Stop now, I must speak with you!" the woman cried in French.

This time Lauren stopped as if waking from a trance. She realized that someone was calling to her from inside an elegant white coach. Cautiously, Lauren approached the vehicle. The heady scent of gardenias met her nostrils as a woman leaned out the window. There was the rustle of expensive fabric as she held out her gloved hand.

"Please. Come here. You are such a jewel." Dressed in a light blue *palonaise*, the woman smiled approvingly. She took Lauren's chin turning her face back and forth. "There is potential here," she mused. "Much potential."

Lauren looked at the woman. She wore a thick coating of wax and powder and although there was some wrinkling around her blue eyes, she was a handsome woman. Her blond hair was dressed fashionably under a large plumed hat, and her fitted gown revealed a supple figure.

"Oh, but you *are* lovely, child," she cooed. "I can see it, even under all that grime." Turning to the coachman she asked, "What do you think, Nemi?"

The elderly Negro slave leaned over and nodded his head.

Lauren backed away.

"No, please, I mean no harm," the woman implored.

Lauren did not trust her and began to retreat down the street. Suddenly the pain in her belly returned, and she doubled over clutching her mid-section and staggering. Her head began to spin, and she crumpled to the ground.

* * *

Lauren regained consciousness sometime later. She was resting deep in a feather bed covered with a cream-colored duvet. She heard a fire was snapping and popping nearby, but she was too weak to look around.

Lauren drifted back into delirium until a voice urged gently, "Here drink this." It was hard to focus, but she could see a pair of dark hands holding a cup of broth for her. She took several sips and slid back down.

"She will live, Nemi," said a woman standing not far away. "And she will fetch a good price. It is a shame she's not a virgin."

The voices continued on for a few minutes then faded off. Again Lauren drifted off to sleep, but the voices returned once more demanding this time she eat something. When she opened her eyes, she recognized the woman from the coach and her black servant. They left some steaming cabbage soup on the nightstand as Lauren pulled herself up to look around the room. There was only a bed and a nightstand in the room, but everything was tidy and well kept. A tub of water sat in front of the fire with a crock of soft soap, and she remembered the woman had told her to bathe.

Gingerly, she slipped from the covers and cautiously tried to stand. There was a dull ache between her legs, but she managed to pull herself over to the tub slowly. Lauren let her shift drop to the floor and stepped carefully into the warm water. It had been months since she had run soap over her body, and the sensation was delicious. When she finished scrubbing herself, she slid down into the tub to rinse her hair. After drying herself, she eased a clean shift over her head and slid back into bed where she began to detangle her auburn tresses with a comb they had left. The effort was too much, and she sank back down into the feather bead.

"*Tres bien*," murmured a soft voice from the door. Lauren looked up, and there in the candlelight was the Dutch woman again.

"I know you are French. I heard you cry out when you were delivering your brat. My name is Madame Vanoss," and she swept over to Lauren picking up a handful of her hair. "Magnificent!"

The smell of gardenias was overpowering, and Lauren turned her head away choking from the heavy scent.

"I am Dutch, but I speak your language," the woman said. "I ran an establishment on the outskirts of Paris years ago. You are very lucky to be alive." She raised a handful of Lauren's hair to her cheek and said, "I want you to wear your tresses down when customers come for you. It is very lush and beautiful. You are a jewel, a true flower. Maybe I will even keep you for myself."

Lauren stared at the woman. She was confused and weary and wanted to be alone. Suddenly, Madame Vanoss bent down and brushed her lips across Lauren's neck. When she recoiled, the woman simply smiled and swept from the room.

* * *

Slowly Lauren gained strength and weight. Madame Vanoss' slave, Nemi was a kind and diligent nurse insisting that she eat and take his folk medicines regularly. The miscarriage had weakened Lauren severely, but gradually she recovered. She knew the child had died, but she did not allow herself to grieve. There was no room for sorrow, only survival.

Madame Vanoss did not visit often, but when she did, Lauren refused to look at her and kept conversation at a minimum. She hated the woman with her heady perfume and seductive manner. Lauren understood life in this house and what it meant. Many times, she had watched the strumpets of New Orleans soliciting, and she knew that soon it would be her trade too, but as terrifying as the prospects were, returning to starvation seemed worse.

Gradually, Lauren was able to leave her bed and walk around the house. It was a large two storied gabled structure in an unsavory location near the wharf. Madame Vanoss posed as a milliner, and her small sham of shop, bulging with ribbons and fabric, boldly faced Broad Street. No one in the community was fooled about her profession. It was common knowledge she ran a house of pleasure. She employed fifteen girls all of whom were thin and drawn with sallow complexions. In spite of their youth, the girls looked depraved and wanton. They awoke late in the day and retired late at night after the last customer was sated. Lauren watched them lounge and drowse throughout the day on divans in the back of the shop smoking pipes filled with a pungent, brown substance nodding and bobbing their heads lazily.

The girls did not associate with Lauren at all; in fact, they looked upon her as a rival. She did not care to know them either, preferring to stay in her bed, staring at the ceiling. She could hear the girls in the halls at night, giggling as they escorted customers to their rooms, and many nights she heard other sounds, sounds which terrified her.

One evening Madame Vanoss swept into the room looking particularly striking. She was dressed in an azure gown with a white lace stomacher with her heavily powdered hair piled high on top of her head. "You are well now and you are to have your first customers tonight," she said in French, her accent thick with Dutch. She stroked Lauren's cheek.

Pulling on her silk gloves, Madame continued, "We are entertaining some of our finest customers this evening and that is why I am having you come out tonight. I have been saving you for our most esteemed, most lucrative guests."

In an effort to thaw Lauren, Madame Vanoss ran her fingers lightly up and down her arm. "Are you nervous, little one?"

Lauren said nothing.

"Of course you are. Don't worry." She pulled open her drawstring bag and drew out a tin box and pipe. She dropped the articles into Lauren's lap and said, "Here, smoke this. One puff is all you need to feel relaxed. Its quite effective I assure you and it will make your job ever so--painless."

Madame Vanoss waited for a reply then shrugged. "I will have Nemi deliver your gown shortly. I want you to look your best. This is an unusual arrangement, a mother and son together, *but* they are paying dearly for you."

Lauren continued to stare straight ahead.

Madame Vanoss started out of the room but before leaving turned and raised one eyebrow, "Look at me!"

Lauren did not comply.

The woman snapped, "*Look* at me!"

Lauren turned and looked at her. Madame Vanoss' blue eyes were hard and cold. "You will comply with the customers needs and give them the pleasure they seek. If you do not, you will be back on the street by morning. Is that understood?"

Reluctantly, Lauren nodded. Madame Vanoss had spoken.

Chapter 21

The evening progressed at an agonizing pace. Mechanically, Lauren dressed in the immodestly cut teal gown that Nemi delivered and let her copper hair fall about her shoulders per Madame Vanoss' instructions. After finishing her toilette, she sat down rigidly on the bed and waited, struggling with fear but reminding herself that there was a roof over her head and food in her belly. The tin and the pipe remained on the nightstand untouched. Lauren was determined not to use the substance. Joining the other girls in that state of delirium was not an option. She must remain alert.

Suddenly, there were footsteps in the hall and Madame Vanoss swung the door open. She swept in all powder and gardenias and announced, "This is my Lauren. Is she not lovely?"

A stocky older woman stepped into the room with a frown on her face followed by a paunchy effeminate fop sporting a powdered wig and patch.

"Yes, yes," the older woman said impatiently, pulling off her gloves. "I can see that she is lovely. Now that will be all."

The woman dismissed Madame Vanoss abruptly. Madame Vanoss did not seem pleased, but when the woman handed her a wad of notes she curtsied deeply and left the room.

Too terrified to move, Lauren remained motionless reminding herself this would soon be over. Mrs. Neville Bench and her son Cornelius exchanged looks.

"I understand that you speak no English," the woman said to Lauren in French.

"No. I do not," Lauren said refusing to look at either one of them.

"Why are you here in this house?" Mrs. Bench continued.

"Because I have no where else to go."

"Have you done this sort of work before?"

"Never."

The young gentleman threw his cloak down on Lauren's bed. Boots and all he jumped onto the mattress carelessly leaning back onto the headboard with his hands behind his head.

"Come here," he demanded.

Cornelius Bench had Lauren turn around as he ran his eyes up and down her figure. She complied stiffly, her copper hair falling over her neck and down her back. "Drop the shoulders of your gown."

"*Pardon?*" she said startled.

"You heard me."

Swallowing hard she pulled down her gown.

"Lower," he ordered.

Slowly she pulled down her bodice.

"Stop!" he barked as the gown reached the tip of her breasts. Knitting his brows, he leaned forward and inspected her shoulders. "She's clean, Mother," he announced.

"Cornelius," said Mrs. Bench as she sat down heavily into an armchair. "I need a light." She spoke rapidly and addressed everyone as inferiors, including her own son. Opening a thin, gold case, Mrs. Bench withdrew a small brown stick and held it to her lips.

Cornelius sighed and slid off the bed, lighting her tobacco.

"I don't believe a woman should smoke a pipe," she said letting out a puff and looking at Lauren. "It's so pedestrian."

Without waiting for an answer she continued, turning the smoking stick in her hand. "These are called cigarettes, my dear. They are all the rage in London and ever so much more refined than a pipe." Again, she drew a long puff into her lungs then let out the smoke leisurely. "Now dear, where were we?"

There was a knock on the door.

"Answer that," she demanded of her son.

With another sigh, he opened the door and Nemi stood holding a tray with a steaming teapot, three cups and some dainties. He put the tray on the table in front of Mrs. Bench and slipped discreetly from the room. With fingers like plump sausages, the matron stuffed a lemon pastry into her mouth, licked her fingers and demanded of Lauren, "Now, some tea."

Lauren moved stiffly to the tray and poured the tea knowing they were scrutinizing her.

"Is anyone looking for you?" Cornelius asked taking a cup from her.

"No."

"Where is your family?"

"In New France. I have one sister. She is a nun."

Cornelius laughed "My, how very Cain and Abel of you. One a nun and one a--"

"Corny! That is enough!" Mrs. Bench reprimanded. She continued to draw on her cigarette watching Lauren closely. "Have you any schooling?" she asked.

"No--no," stuttered Lauren. "You two are my first customers. Madame Vanoss gave me no special instructions on how to--"

"Not that you little fool," the matron said sharply. "Actual schooling as in books?"

"Yes, I can read," murmured Lauren looking from Mrs. Bench to her son. "I am afraid I don't understand."

"You don't have to *yet*," muttered Cornelius as he moved to a mirror and fussed with his wig.

"Who taught you to read, a parent?" asked Mrs. Bench.

"No, I attended finishing school at the Ursuline Academy for Girls in New Orleans."

Cornelius stopped arranging his wig and looked at his mother.

The woman smiled slowly and said, "Well, well. I think we have all that we need."

Mrs. Neville Bench and her son left the room briefly and returned with a cloak for Lauren. "Here put this on. We must leave immediately."

Cornelius opened the door.

Mrs. Bench demanded, "Quickly now!"

The couple hustled Lauren down the stairs and out into a carriage. The horses blew steam and stomped in the cold night air as the three jostled into their seats. The coachman snapped his reins and with a jolt, they were off. Lauren looked at the Benches for an explanation but was met with only silence so she sank down into her fur lap blanket and waited.

Finally, they arrived at a large brick town house on Duke Street, which Lauren recognized to be a very fashionable section of the city. Oddly, no servants met them at the door, and when they entered the enormous sitting room no warm fire welcomed them. Instead, the room was dark and chilly, littered with the white specters of covered furniture. Immediately, Mrs. Bench barked at Cornelius to get her a brandy.

"Where do you suggest I start looking, Mother?" he said sarcastically.

"Don't be a dolt Cornelius the flask is in my trunk."

"Oh, that narrows it down," he mumbled as he waded through crates, trunks and hatboxes.

"*You* build a fire," she said to Lauren in French.

Mrs. Bench fell heavily into an armchair. The short excursion from carriage to chair had winded her significantly. "Bring my chocolates as well, Corny. They're near the brandy.

Lauren could not make out his reply but she gathered it was less than cordial.

When at last the fire was crackling and popping Mrs. Bench ordered, "Pull the sheet off that chair and sit down, my dear."

Lauren slid onto the edge of a black Windsor waiting for her next command. Cornelius returned with a brandy flask and three crystal glasses tossing a tin of chocolates onto the end table by his mother.

She waited until they all had a drink then began, "I have paid Madame Vanoss dearly for you my child, and if you agree to my terms you shall never have to see that hideous creature again."

Lauren looked from Mrs. Bench to her son.

"We have just arrived from London and leased this townhouse. My husband Neville passed away several months ago leaving Corny and I--well somewhat depleted of resources. So here we are sadly destitute and alone in the New World."

Mrs. Bench touched a hankie to her nose and Cornelius stifled a laugh. He changed it quickly into a cough after his mother seared a look into him.

"I have sold some land in the Hudson River Valley," she continued. "And I intend to invest the proceeds here in New York, but first it is imperative that I make the right acquaintances here in the Colonies. These unsophisticated provincials prefer to invest with God-fearing, so-called respectable people so--" she hesitated. "Well in a word, Corny needs a wife. Not just any wife, one of refinement and breeding."

Lauren looked confused. Everything was moving so fast. Only an hour ago she was selling her body for money, now there was a proposal of marriage.

"Why me?" she asked knitting her brow. "Why do you have to shop at a brothel for a wife? Why can't Cornelius find a wife himself?"

Mrs. Bench looked at Cornelius and raised an eyebrow. "He refuses. You see my son has—has rather unusual tastes in lovers and the thought of courting a woman is abhorrent to him."

Cornelius rolled his eyes, leaning against the mantle. "Mother we have been through this a hundred times. That is not the only reason I will not marry. How am I to attract a woman with moths in my pockets?"

Mrs. Bench ignored him. "You are just the woman we seek. You have manners, breeding and to be honest, you are as desperate as we are."

Just as the proposition was beginning to sound inviting Lauren remembered Heathstone. "I'm sorry Mrs. Bench but I'm afraid this is all impossible."

"Why on earth?"

"I am already married."

"What? Where is your husband?" demanded Cornelius.

"I don't know where he is. He abandoned me months ago."

"Abandoned you?" Cornelius barked. "Why did he abandon you? Are you diseased?"

"No! I am perfectly healthy."

"You haven't been in trouble. I checked you myself. You were clean."

"Clean? What do you mean?"

"My son refers to the Fleur-de-Lis of France," explained Mrs. Bench. "It is a brand used by the French authorities to identify a convicted criminal. They apply it to the shoulder usually. He examined you and found you to be free of such a mark."

"I have committed no crimes, and I am not sick!" said Lauren indignantly. "The fact is I don't know why my husband left me. The authorities questioned me upon my arrival and I never saw him again. He never came to look for me."

"Hmm, unusual," said Mrs. Bench tapping her finger on her lips. "Never mind, is your husband a man of means?"

"I don't really know, perhaps," answered Lauren.

"Someone who is likely to move in circles of refinement and respectability?" she continued.

Lauren thought back to Heathstone's dowdy attire and bad manners then said, "No, I don't believe one would ever see him in polite society."

"Do you know anyone at all in the English Colonies besides your estranged husband?"

Lauren shook her head.

"Well, then we have no problem," shrugged Mrs. Bench. "No one needs to know the truth. We will tell everyone that you and Corny wed several months ago. Actually, now that I think of it, this is all for the best. Marriage to Corny would only complicate things."

"What am I expected to do in this masquerade of a marriage?" asked Lauren.

"Learn English for one thing and as quickly as possible," said Cornelius tossing his drink back.

"Flatter and pursue the right people," instructed Mrs. Bench. "Make the right friends. But above all," she warned. "You must keep quiet. No one must know of our arrangement. Remember you have as much at stake as we do. The streets are a cold place."

"Conjugal obligations?" Lauren asked in a business-like tone.

"Heavens no!" Cornelius winced.

Turning to his mother, he changed his language to English. Lauren could hear the eagerness in his voice and sensed her opportunity. She knew that women of education and breeding were rare in the New World and if she played this couple correctly she could further herself in ways unimaginable.

"How am I to be compensated?" she interrupted.

"You will have your food and lodging," said Mrs. Bench.

"Not enough," stated Lauren flatly. "The wife of Cornelius Bench must have a substantial allowance."

The matron's eyes grew wide then she chuckled knowingly, "Why you little--you are a shrewd one, aren't you?"

Lauren continued to meet the woman's gaze until Mrs. Bench said, "Alright, you shall have it but only because I like your style. I can see you won't crumble at the first stuffed shirt you meet."

"I won't let you down," said Lauren as she thrust her chin into the air. "From this day on I shall be known as Mrs. Cornelius Bench, daughter-in-law of Mrs. Neville Bench Esquire," then holding out her glass to Cornelius she said, "Darling, get me another drink."

Chapter 22

Lauren rose late the next morning to find the townhouse on Duke Street bustling with activity. A new fleet of servants had arrived that morning and were scouring and arranging the house, getting ready to present the Benchs to New York society. The furniture had been unveiled revealing richly brocaded armchairs and divans, delicate tea tables and fireplace screens, hutches filled with porcelain figurines and elegant china for formal occasions.

Lauren was simply astounded. The Aberjons had furnishings of quality back in Kaskaskia but nothing this extravagant. She acted nonchalant, but in reality she was amazed. Although the townhouse was built in the Dutch tradition, the decorating was overwhelmingly British. There remained imbedded in the fireplace, inlaid tiles of quaint Dutch landscapes and several sets of double doors but other than that little remained of Dutch influence. Golden sunlight flooded the sitting room. It bathed the mustard-colored cupboards flanking the fireplace in a sweet, warm glow. A round mahogany table sat in front of the hearth with a breakfast of hard-boiled eggs and toast.

"Good morning," said a voice cheerfully.

Lauren turned just as Mrs. Neville Bench took a seat beside her at the table. The woman had removed her layers of makeup and her wig and for the first time; Lauren was able to view the real Mrs. Neville Bench. She had dull, gray hair swept into a white mobcap, and a voluminous blue dressing gown concealed her thick pear-shaped figure. She stuffed herself into an armchair and began to butter some toast.

"Today we will visit the dressmaker. I have made inquiries and Mr. Benjamin Byrd is considered the finest dressmaker in all of New York City. He will be our source of information on everything about the richest to the most influential citizens of this colony. I've yet to meet a dressmaker who isn't a supreme gossip."

"What shall I say about my past? Surely there will be questions," asked Lauren.

"Leave the talking to me. For now, act shy and demure. You may exploit your charms later."

After four pieces of toast, Mrs. Bench peeled an egg and took a large bite of the white orb. Lauren studied the woman while she ate. She concluded that Mrs. Bench had succeeded in life because of a quick mind and keen intuition, not beauty. Her wits and boldness probably earned her a place in the aristocracy without regard to the feelings of others. Lauren respected her killer instinct but also feared it. She had to be careful how she used this woman.

Suddenly, Heloise Bench's small eyes narrowed, and she burned a look into Lauren. "You think you know me. Don't you? You think you know what drives me?"

She sat back in her chair, arranging her napkin. "Well indeed you do. Put aside the gray hair and bulbous figure, and I am just like you; an opportunistic adventuress who was born in a man's world."

Lauren's eyes opened wide and she blinked several times.

The woman continued, "You would like to take every farthing I have because you need it to survive. I recognize that hungry look. I see it in the mirror everyday. You've slept alone and cold under the stars more nights than you care to count."

Lauren opened her mouth to protest.

The woman continued, "Don't act so surprised. Those who have struggled like you can spot the hunger in others."

Lauren stared at the rug on the floor for a moment, and then she looked up at Mrs. Bench and said, "I admit it. You *are* right. I will take as much as I can from anybody to survive. I will never scour the streets again like a dog. I claim no love, no family and no home. I will take what I need from you and your son to make my life as easy as possible."

"Bravo! My dear," Mrs. Bench cheered. "Bravo! Your honesty is admirable but make no mistake, we are not fools." The matron threw her napkin on her plate and rose from the table. She crossed the sitting room and paused. "One more thing, there are others out there that have suffered similar privation. No matter how fine your manners and attire, they will recognize this blight in you. They know exactly what you fear and they will use it against you."

Mrs. Bench started up the stairs then stopped abruptly. "Well what are you waiting for? Lets began your new life!"

* * *

"I think that fabric is hideous," whined Cornelius. "Lauren has taken enough of our time today. I'm tired and hungry."

Cornelius lounged in a chair with one leg flung over the arm looking at himself in a hand mirror. He sat in the corner of a dressmakers shop surrounded by cream-colored cabinets filled with ribbons, thread and faux flowers. The volumes of linen and silk piled high on shelves muffled his constant complaints.

"I'm bored," he announced again, but no one responded.

"You say that can be done by tomorrow?" pressed Heloise.

"Yes, indeed, Madame," stated Mr. Byrd bowing low. "Our motto here is, 'a gown in a day' and my seamstresses always deliver on time."

The tiny dressmaker darted back to Lauren's side running a length of material across her bust line as the girl frowned. Lauren thought it highly suspicious Mr. Byrd had taken her measurement in that spot three times. "Lovely. Yes, so lovely," he mumbled jotting down some notes hastily. His oily hospitality repulsed her.

Mrs. Bench kept a watchful eye on her new "daughter-in-law." She did not like her attitude toward the dressmaker and was anticipating an altercation. She must move quickly. "Mr. Byrd, you seem to be a man who knows citizens of quality," she asked, flattering him.

"Indeed I may know one or two," he said with false modesty, bowing again.

"Please say nothing of our arrival to anyone. We choose to live quietly here in New York and not be bothered by people calling. My son is newly married and would like to enjoy domestic serenity. I seek simplicity. I have grown weary of court life in London. I want to enjoy the informal lifestyle here in the Colonies."

"Oh, of course, of course, I will be most discreet, Madam Bench," assured the dressmaker. He paused for a moment then asked, "Pardon the intrusion, Madam but you have been presented at court?"

"Of course, I had my first introduction many years ago. Believe me. Over the years it grows tiresome." Heloise Bench leaned forward and said confidentially, "It is not as grand as one might assume."

The dressmakers eyes widened and he stammered, "Oh my! Oh, my! It would be grand for *me*, I am sure, very grand for me."

He darted back to Lauren straightening and smoothing the length of silk over her bust again. The girl's eyes narrowed. "Lovely, lovely," he mumbled, licking his thick lips and looking down her bodice. He started to scribble some notes into a book, but his hands were perspiring so heavily that he dropped his quill.

"Allow me," Lauren murmured in French as she bent down to retrieve the quill. When she straightened up, she drove her elbow deep into Mr. Byrd's groin and the man shrieked in agony.

"*Oh! Mon Dieu!*" Lauren cried and filled the air with apologies in French.

The dressmaker doubled over and danced around the shop on his tiptoes, biting his lip.

Heloise raised an eyebrow at Lauren and said, "You are lucky that we just concluded our final order of business."

Turning to Mr. Byrd, she said sympathetically, "How careless of the girl. I am terribly sorry. Good day." She swept from the shop followed by Lauren and Cornelius.

"Mother, why on earth would you tell the dressmaker that we want to be left alone?"

"Honestly Cornelius," Heloise scoffed. "After all these years you would think some of my wits would have worn off on you. The first thing that gossip of a dressmaker will do is inform everyone that we have arrived in New York, and that I have been presented at court. Next, he will tell them we want to be left alone and that will make us all the more desirable. Knowing human nature, they will be pounding on our door within a week."

After dining at the Cheshire Cheese Tavern on Whitehall the three returned to their town home to meet Lauren's new English tutor. The instant the young man entered the room Cornelius' eyebrows shot up, and he looked at Lauren. This was no ordinary tutor.

As Frederick Brink crossed the room to kiss Mrs. Bench's hand, he caught a glimpse of his own reflection in the mirror. It was brief but Cornelius saw the look of admiration in his eyes. Clearly, this young man was pleased with himself.

"I am honored, Mrs. Bench," he said as he pushed the dark hair away from his face.

"This is my son Cornelius and my daughter-in-law Lauren," she explained. "Lauren will be your student."

As Brink bowed low, Corny saw Lauren blush. "Where do you reside, Mr. Brink?" asked Cornelius.

"At the home of Reverend John Francis, I am tutoring his three children at present."

Heloise interjected, "Do you have any objections to beginning your lessons today, Mr. Brink?"

"None, whatsoever."

"We shall leave you then. Come Corny."

As Heloise and Cornelius left the room, Lauren shifted uncomfortably in her chair waiting for a directive from her teacher. Frederick reached into his leather satchel pulled out several books and a piece of parchment. He held out his hand to Lauren and she joined him at the table by the fire. All afternoon he tutored her in English and the art of admiring his splendid profile. He would turn his green eyes upon her and she would blush like a schoolgirl.

Over the weeks, Mrs. Bench, Cornelius and Lauren settled into a happy routine. They would wake late in the morning, dine at one of the local taverns, shop and return home just in time for Lauren's lesson. The rest of the day was spent refusing callers and declining invitations to suppers and parties hosted by the local aristocracy. Heloise remained aloof knowing this would increase the appetites of the curious. Lauren was in no hurry to change their routine either. She enjoyed her life of leisure. It gave her time to read, study and ponder Mr. Frederick Brink.

Mrs. Bench proved to be a stimulating companion for her as well, taking an interest in Lauren as a protégée. She had Cornelius teach the girl the latest dances, she had her fitted for new garments and wigs, and they spent many hours on the proper application of cosmetics. Their days were full as she schooled Lauren in social graces and the art of intrigue. Heloise taught Lauren how to manipulate a conversation, how to study people, and how to flatter effectively to obtain secrets. She told Lauren that above all the courage to be bold was the most important skill of all. Without it, Heloise said, nothing was possible.

For the most part, Mrs. Bench was pleased with Lauren but concerned about her impulsive tendencies. "We must weigh everything before we act or speak, Lauren. Nothing should be attempted without careful consideration. Assaulting the dressmaker the other day is the sort of rash behavior that cannot be tolerated. If we do not present a genteel impression from the start we will never be admitted into the better circles."

Heloise knew that Lauren was her secret weapon. She would attract men and gain introductions, so she taught her carefully not to make assumptions about other people. "You must never judge anyone by their clothing; some of the wealthiest people dress the shabbiest. Everyone must be considered for possible exploitation."

Lauren's relationship with Cornelius blossomed as well. He joined Lauren in her room every night to discuss the events of the day and have a nightcap. He would visit with her while she undressed behind a screen or removed her makeup at the dressing table. Lauren was completely unconcerned when she paraded around him in her shift and stays. She knew that her feminine allure held no appeal for Corny.

"Lauren, its time to speak English," he said to her one evening in her room. "French is growing tedious and you seem ready for the challenge."

"Alright I will try," she said in English as she sat down to brush her amber tresses. "But you cannot laugh."

"Oh, it sounds delightful! I love a French accent," gushed Cornelius. "Don't ever lose it, darling.'

"I want to lose it. It worries me."

"Why?"

"Because they hate the French in New York."

"Oh don't worry about that!" Corny assured. "The French are *'tres chic'* in high society. Everyone sends their children to be schooled in New Rochelle and New Paltz by the French Huguenots. You have nothing to worry about." He walked over and pinched her cheek.

"You're a fool, Cornelius," she laughed pushing his hand away. Lauren had learned to love Corny. Although he was vain and self-absorbed, she loved his keen wit and good heart. He was a good friend and instinctively knew when she was worried, always laughing her out of a bad temper.

Corny walked to the mantle picked up a porcelain figurine, turned it over then set it down. "Your room is nicer than mine," he said with a pout. "Mother caters way too much to you. You spoiled brat."

"Now you know what its like to have a sister. So move over," she said sticking her tongue out. Cornelius was right. Everything in the girl's room was of the finest quality, from the highly polished cherry bed and highboy to the sumptuous Turkish rugs on the shiny hardwood floors.

"I say, has that pompous pedagogue tumbled you yet?"

"What!" said Lauren, her mouth dropping open. "What a thing to ask!"

Corny had been suspicious of Brink for some time. He tossed a brandy back before continuing. "I'm telling you. That man's motives are not honorable."

"Show me a man whose motives *are* honorable," said Lauren.

"*Me*, for example. How many men could hold a civilized conversation with a woman in her stays?"

"Yes, but you are *unusual*," she countered.

"Uh, huh," Corny mumbled. "So I've heard."

Chapter 23

One afternoon when the cold winds blew off the Hudson, Mrs. Bench announced, "Tonight we accept our first invitation."

"What?" gasped Cornelius sitting up on the divan. "Where are we going?"

"We will attend a supper at the home of Rudolf Ghent, a prominent merchant. General Ambrose Stuart will be the guest of honor. He has just arrived from London and is in residence at the Ghent home." Turning to Lauren she instructed, "The General will be your mark tonight."

Lauren sat up straight. At last, she could put her lessons to the test. She was eager to use her charms on this Ambrose Stuart and if Heloise wanted him, she would deliver.

Rudolf Ghent's town home was not far from the Bench's home on Duke Street. The sturdy brick structure was the epitome of a traditional Dutch home. The stair stepped-gabled end faced the street with a large stoop and split double door. In the low raftered common room, a fire roared in the massive tiled fireplace. The furniture was heavy and dark but studded with decorative brass nails and the walls were adorned with colorful pictures. It was very different from the fashionable drawing rooms of London but nevertheless warm and inviting. Rudolf and Marta Ghent matched their furnishings perfectly. Stout practical good-hearted folks, they met Heloise, Cornelius and Lauren at the door with open arms. "Come in! Do come in!" they boomed.

A black slave took their wraps and The Ghents ushered them into the common room to meet the other guests. There were twelve in all, mostly local merchants with their wives and of course General Stuart. He was tall and well groomed, quite dashing in his red uniform but unfortunately had the face of a horse. His jaw was huge and his face extremely long. Lauren swallowed hard, squared her shoulders and told herself if she was to charm and flatter the gentleman, she must concentrate on his attributes.

It was her turn to be introduced to the general. After he kissed her hand she cooed sweetly, "How enchanting to meet you, General."

He frowned and said brusquely, "You're French."

"Well, I was born—" but she would never finish her explanation. General Stuart turned his back, taking up conversation with another guest. Nonchalantly Lauren smiled, arranged a lock of hair then leveled a look at Heloise and Cornelius. Avoiding her they turned to talk to other guests. She came up behind them and whispered, "So we French are all the rage. How did you put it Corny, *'Tres chic'*?"

Heloise murmured, "It's nothing, only a minor setback."

"Oh yes, English hatred for the French is only a minor setback," said Lauren through her teeth. "For *you*!"

"I'll handle it from here. Don't worry," said Heloise.

"No, *I'll* handle it from here," replied Lauren.

Lauren turned to go in to supper, lifting her chin and yanking her bodice as low as possible. Just as the guests were about to be seated, she jumped in front of the wife of a lumber baron and sat down next to General Stuart. He presented her with his back, engaging the woman on his right in conversation. Lauren was not discouraged. The night was young and there would be an opportunity.

The servants and slaves prepared a bountiful repast of Dutch sausages and cheese, boiled cabbages and soup and for the English guests, a steak and kidney pie. Lauren observed the General pick at his food, clearly unhappy with the pedestrian fare. She made a mental note that he may prefer elegant suppers, served in several courses.

"I understand that you are a newlywed, Mrs. Bench," said Marta Ghent leaning across the table smiling.

Heloise pursed her lips watching Lauren closely.

"Yes I am, Mrs. Ghent."

"You have an accent. Are you French, my dear?"

Lauren knew this may be her only chance and her mind raced. "No, I am not French. I am of English decent raised in New France by my aunt. I was orphaned many years ago. My mother's sister married a French merchant in New Orleans."

General Stuart looked at Lauren. She saw his eyes run from her face, to her bodice and back up again.

"Do you find our ways very different from the French?" Mrs. Ghent continued.

"Oh, in some ways they are very different. For example in New France, women cannot spin their own fabric. They must purchase it from Paris."

"How interesting." replied the hostess. "They feel compelled to create a monopoly."

"Yes, I suppose—"

"That is why we are fighting them here," interrupted General Stuart. "They wish to create a monopoly on everything, including this continent."

"I do not believe they will ever succeed, General," said Lauren.

"And why is that, Madam?"

"Frenchmen lack the courage and strength. They are bred to enjoy food, art, wine and women. Their bravery is merely bravado."

The General chuckled and said, "Undoubtedly true, but I find it surprising that you would defile your own people."

Lauren lifted her chin and said, "If they were my people would I be here tonight?" Then she lowered her voice and said privately to him, "There is one other thing that is distinctively different."

"And what is that?"

"I have found Frenchmen lack the vigor of the English gentlemen."

He smiled slowly and said "Indeed, Madam."

Lauren leaned forward so he could look down her dress and murmured, "Indeed."

*   *   *

In a matter of months, Lauren was the toast of New York. The town home on Duke Street had taken on every aspect of a fashionable salon where the well bred met to discuss politics, art, investments and the possibility of war. General Ambrose Stuart was the first to fall to Lauren's charms. Although he was busy conducting business and military matters, he made every effort to attend teas and suppers at the Bench residence. Lauren's youth and vivacious nature enchanted him, but it was her lean, willowy figure and copper tresses, which drove him to distraction. She seldom wore wigs knowing that he admired her sumptuous hair, and she always chose gowns rich in auburn or gold hues to offset her bronze locks.

The first time the General ran his lips down Lauren's neck and shoulders she slapped him soundly, reminding him that she was a married woman. She swept from the room, slamming the door behind her congratulating herself later on a job well done. As expected, General Stuart returned to Lauren, more eager than ever to have her in his bed. All the time Heloise cultivated a relationship with the man consulting him on matters of business and investment. Lauren never knew what Heloise wanted from

Stuart, and she did not care. She was holding up her end of the bargain and having a wonderful time in the process.

Day in and day out an endless assortment of witty, pretentious snobs paraded through the house on Duke Street, flattering themselves on their friendship with the Benches. Several men believed Lauren loved them, but in reality her favor fell on no one except her English tutor, Frederick Brink.

The lessons ended, but Lauren and Frederick continued to rendezvous several times a week. His station in life prevented him from attending parties and suppers at her residence, so they met at Frederick's flat quenching their passion in secret. Lauren was smitten with the tall, dark haired pedagogue. After keeping company with the clumsy General Stuart, Frederick's beauty captivated Lauren. Blinded by his good looks, she could not see the shallow self-absorbed parasite inside.

Lauren threw herself into her new life completely, ignoring the advice from Heloise about reckless behavior. Her earlier privation caused her to be greedy and self-indulgent, so she indulged every whim and gratified every desire. She found it amusing to play with the hearts of the men that frequented Duke Street and would manipulate one against the other using them to feed her vanity, laughing openly at their declarations of love. She indulged her hedonistic side staying out all night drinking to excess and playing pranks, some of which were dangerous. Cornelius accompanied her on these outings reveling in the merriment, throwing himself into numerous trysts and love affairs as well. Heloise was aware of their wild behavior but said little. Lauren and Cornelius brought the rich and well bred to her doorstep; she would not complain.

One morning Heloise's servant burst into Lauren's bedroom, yanked open the drapes and announced, "Mrs. Bench would like to see you downstairs immediately."

"What?" mumbled Lauren rubbing her eyes.

"The mistress, she will see you now."

"What? What's so important?"

"I wouldn't know, Miss, but she said, 'Now.'"

Lauren sat up clutching her temples. "Oh, God it hurts."

"I'll bring tea right away," the servant said as she left the room.

Lauren felt nauseous and her head was pounding. Gradually, she remembered last night's mischief. She remembered a late supper of oysters and champagne at Henry Hubert's country home, a raucous carriage ride, and then Corny falling into the canal. Her last memory was of retching into a chamber pot before falling into bed.

"Get out and let me sleep!" shrieked Cornelius from the other room. Lauren knew that Heloise had summoned him too.

"A pox on that woman," she uttered as she stood up to get her stays. She wondered how she would ever keep the contents of her stomach down with stays digging into her sides, but she had no choice, convention dictated it. The servant returned with tea just as Lauren finished dressing. After draining her teacup, she tied her hair into a loose knot and started downstairs. Every step she took was agony, every muscle on fire. "I'll never drink again," she uttered.

Lauren walked into the sitting room and immediately saw Frederick. He was standing by the mantle looking dignified in an indigo blue topcoat and dark britches. He held his hands behind his back, never acknowledging her presence.

"Good, you're here," Heloise said in a business like tone. She had stuffed herself in her usual wingback chair and was finishing her breakfast.

Lauren looked at Frederick. "What are you doing here?"

He looked the other way.

"What's going on, Heloise?" she demanded.

"Well, my dear," she said pushing her empty plate aside and wiping her mouth. "It seems your esteemed Mr. Brink is blackmailing me."

"What!" Lauren gasped. Suddenly the nausea returned, and she felt weak. "Is this a joke?" she said sitting down on the edge of a chair.

"I assure you our sly friend is not joking," said Mrs. Bench.

Lauren looked at Frederick for an explanation.

He turned to Mrs. Bench. "I reiterate, Madam. I will say nothing to your son about the affair, if I am satisfied."

"What are you talking about?" questioned Lauren.

"Is it true what he says, Lauren? Was there a liaison between the two of you?"

The blood drained from Lauren's face as the fog of romantic illusion lifted. "Yes, it's true."

"Well then. There is only one thing that can be done," stated Heloise.

Cornelius staggered into the room whining, "For God's sake Mother! What's so damned important that--"

"Shut up, Cornelius and sit down," barked Heloise. "Lauren has been having an affair."

Corny made no reply. He groaned and dropped onto the divan rubbing his head and moaning. Everyone was watching him. When the room grew quiet, Corny looked up, realizing that his mother required an answer. "So?"

Frederick's jaw dropped.

"Mr. Brink, I believe you have your answer," stated Heloise. "Corny, please restate your sentiments about Lauren's love affair."

Corny looked at the young man and said, "*So?*"

Frederick's handsome face flushed and his chest heaved. Mrs. Bench noted the jewelry on his fingers and wondered if he acquired the gems from blackmailing other women.

"You are nothing more than degenerate, depraved--" he cried. Not bothering to finish, Brink grabbed his hat and swept from the room.

With an eyebrow raised, Heloise turned to Lauren and said, "There was no harm done this time, but I suggest that you pick your lovers more carefully in the future."

Corny was about to say, 'I told you so' but stopped when he saw Lauren's face. She sat motionless on the edge of her chair, her back stiff and her eyes on the floor. "Oh God," he exclaimed sitting up. "Darling, you're upset. What you need is a good strong drink. As a matter of fact so do I."

Heloise looked at the tears rolling down Lauren face. She wanted to castrate that charlatan for what he had done to the girl. Pushing herself up from the chair Heloise handed Lauren her hanky. "That fraud's not worth soiling a good handkerchief, my dear but here is one anyway."

Lauren dried her eyes, took a breath and stated, "There will be no more tears," and returned the hankie. She left the room with her chin high and her eyes down. Corny and his mother exchanged looks.

Before the day was out Lauren was back to boisterous suppers and raucous carriage rides. Yet she was fundamentally changed, the carefree flibbertigibbet of Duke Street was gone, replaced by a cold apathetic shadow caring nothing for her own well-being.

Chapter 24

After that day, Lauren remembered very little of the years she spent with the Benches. She continued with her undisciplined existence, caring nothing for her safety or well-being, throwing herself into any situation no matter how perilous. She would go for days without sleep, attending every ball and supper New York had to offer, indulging in every excess and then fall ill only to recover and stagger to her next soiree. Filled with self-loathing, she drowned herself in drink denying what she had become; an insipid, self-serving aristocrat of New York society.

After a while, she forgot Frederick Brink. He meant nothing to her, but she could not rid herself of the nagging doubts about her future. She was approaching twenty-one years of age, and she had not yet found a home. She felt trapped on Duke Street, merely a pawn in their game of society chess, so out of frustration and impotence she drowned herself in revelry. Others could see the toll it was taking on her health, but she listened to no one. Heloise and Cornelius tried to talk with her, but she shut them out reminding them that she was still delivering the wealthy and well bred to their front door.

It was early spring 1753 and hostilities began to escalate with the French. There was grumbling from the colonists that England was about to engage in a war with France, and some of the discussions became heated at the house on Duke Street. Lauren cared nothing for their bickering. She learned just enough to sound informed, nothing more.

"The menu card you wrote looks fine, Rosalie," said Heloise to the cook one afternoon. "Clam chowder, green beans, and lobster--everything is fine except your use of that provincial term, 'Albany beef'. How many times do I have to tell you? It is called sturgeon. Obviously your previous owner was Dutch." Heloise continued to peruse the menu. "Let me see flummery, tarts, and nuts for dessert. Yes, very good, very good."

"Heloise, do you have a lover coming to supper tonight?" teased Lauren. She poured herself a glass of port and looked around the room. "Honestly, the way you are fussing. You are a nervous wreck."

Mrs. Bench had taken great care to set the table in the latest style *a la francaise*. In the middle of the table were three salvers, or footed servers, one heaped with faux jewels and decorations, the next with fruit and nuts, and the last with a richly frosted torte. Her shipment of porcelain dinnerware had just arrived that morning, the very latest creation. She used her best serving pieces, finest linens, and most precious bayberry candles all to create the impression of opulence and good taste. She had been working on the menu for a week and even engaged some musicians for entertainment.

Lauren finished her drink and went upstairs to bathe. Heloise had instructed her to wear her finest gown tonight because there would be a special guest at supper. She did not give a damn who was coming to the house on Duke Street. She was sick to death of the aristocrats and dandies. They were all alike. She stepped out of the tub, dried herself and dabbed some oil of lavender behind her ears. Of all the luxuries Lauren had experienced in the last few years, scent was her favorite. She loved the work of the stillroom and created new perfumes on her own at every opportunity. Many of the recipes she learned from Marianne back in Kaskaskia and every time she distilled a new scent or extracted oil, she remembered working with the gentle old slave woman in the Aberjon kitchen long ago. Sometimes a smell would remind her of Simone or Eugenie and she would search herself for emotion, but all she found was emptiness.

Lauren refilled her glass of port then slipped a gold *sacque* gown over her head. After lacing the bodice over a snow-white shift and lace petticoat, she attached a richly beaded stomacher to the front of the dress and stepped to the mirror.

"My God! You need makeup," observed Corny from behind her.

Lauren jumped, and cried, "Damn it Corny! Announce yourself!"

He leaned close to the mirror. "Look at the rings under your eyes. You look like you haven't slept in a month and your skin. It is so gray."

"Mind your own business!" snapped Lauren. "Look at that your own face. You look like a mummer. That white makeup is hideous."

Ignoring her comment, Corny pulled Lauren to the dressing table. After much arguing, she allowed him to apply a bit of cochineal rouge to her cheeks and brush some lampblack on her lashes. He stepped back to inspect his work. The cosmetics had not helped. Lauren still looked drawn and ill, her complexion gray and lackluster. Corny was worried but said nothing instead suggesting, "How about a little orrisroot to whiten--"

"No! Now I have enough on!"

"Have it your way," he shrugged. "Mother wants us downstairs now. The guests are about to arrive."

"Who is this mystery guest she talks about?" asked Lauren.

"I'm guessing its General Stuart's replacement, General George McAffee. He arrived in New York this week."

The guests were starting to arrive as Lauren came down the stairs to join the party. She was the quintessential hostess, engaging them in witty conversation, offering them refreshments, encouraging them to relax and enjoy themselves. The musicians played in the garden while guests drifted in and out sipping Madeira and port before supper.

The only one who was not entertained was Lauren. As the evening progressed, she turned more and more to drink for amusement. It lessened her contempt for the pompous snobs and their endless prattle. She assumed her mark for the night was General McAffee, so after some easy maneuvers she found herself alone with him in the garden. He was a large, unattractive man with bushy eyebrows and a loud voice. Lauren swallowed hard and approached him. *Why are they always so hideous!*

It was a beautiful evening with a warm breeze carrying the scent of roses throughout the garden. A half moon sailed in the sky as the musicians played a minuet. "I hope you will be a frequent guest of ours, General," gushed Lauren as she swept up to him smiling.

"Oh, I am most grateful, Madame, I will be in New York most of the time, but occasionally I will travel to Albany. In fact I leave in a few days for a visit there."

He is leaving in a few days. I must work quickly, thought Lauren. Heloise was in dire need of investments. "Oh my, you will be going to the interior?" she asked biting her lip. "How that terrifies me, the thought of savages and wild animals." Her vulnerability was nauseating, but it seemed to be working. The general stepped closer.

"Those are things a lady should never have to encounter," he murmured

"Oh, I am so grateful the hostilities are on the frontier and not here in my beloved city," she said. The wine made her unsteady, so she backed up against the trunk of a tree putting her hands demurely behind her back. She knew it would push her breasts upward and with any luck, he would try to kiss her.

"I will leave all the danger to you brave men," she said breathlessly.

Just as General McAffee moved closer, a gravelly voice barked, "You would be surprised at the dangers that lurk right here in the city."

An old gentleman hobbled up to the couple. "Don't you agree?"

The General sighed, clearly aggravated and stepped back from Lauren. "I haven't had the pleasure, sir."

The elderly gentleman apologized. "Pardon my intrusion. My name is Leopold Fitch. I too have just arrived in New York." He was dressed in a white periwig, dark coat and britches. He moved slowly as if his joints were stiff, but his dark eyes were as alert as a hawk.

"Charmed," Lauren mumbled.

Her eyes could no longer focus properly so she was relieved when supper was announced. She hoped that food would help her regain some of her composure. The dining room was magnificent. Bayberry candles bathed the room in a golden glow as chamber music drifted in from the garden. The table glistened with silver and crystal resting on a deep plum tablecloth. The guests were enchanted and praised Heloise for her impeccable taste.

Much to Lauren's surprise, she was not seated next to General McAfee. Her card was in the seat next to Leopold Fitch. Unsure who her mark was for the night she cast a desperate look at Heloise, but the woman was far too busy entertaining to notice.

The supper dragged on endlessly as Mr. Fitch asked tedious questions about Lauren's life in New Orleans. She avoided talk about her past especially when she was intoxicated, so after supper she ditched the old gentleman and convinced several acquaintances to go for a ride.

After Lauren left, Mr. Fitch approached Heloise. "I want to talk to you," he said.

"Not here. Not now," she hissed.

"Yes now!" he demanded under his breath.

"You're upset."

"You're damned right I'm upset! The girl is a mess. What have you been doing to her?" he growled.

Heloise shifted uncomfortably, then trying to disguise her agitation waved to someone across the room calling, "I'll be right there, darling." She turned back to Fitch and declared, "What have *I* been doing! What have *you* been doing? You are over a year late."

"Why don't you ask the authorities where I have been for that year?

Her mouth dropped open. "What! What do you mean? Prison again? How is it that I received orders from you?"

Fitch's eyes darted around the room. "Never mind that now. Listen to me closely. I want you to go upstairs and pack a bag. You are leaving tonight."

"What! What are you talking about? I can't leave!"

"One way or the other you three will be leaving this house tonight, either right now or in the chains of a British regular later."

"Oh, My God!" gasped Heloise. She rubbed her forehead trying to absorb the news. "My furniture, my clothing, my silver--"

"There is no time for that. You, Cornelius and the girl are in grave danger."

"I'll tell Corny right now," gulped Heloise. "But I don't know where Lauren is."

"Don't worry about her. You and Cornelius will leave for Boston tonight. I'll take the girl with me."

The old gentleman turned and shuffled out the door leaving Heloise confused and frightened. She crossed into the dining room, ignoring the guests and approached the walnut sideboard. Taking out a brandy decanter, she poured herself a stiff drink and emptied the contents in one gulp. Taking a deep breath, she started up the stairs. It was going to be a long night.

Chapter 25

It was late at night when Lauren's carriage pulled up to the house on Duke Street. The coachman opened the door and Lauren jumped out crashing into a woman passing by on the street. After exchanging apologies, Lauren saw the woman glance back at her before turning the corner. Not giving it another thought, Lauren arranged her hair as she climbed the stairs of the townhouse.

She fully expected to hear the chinking of crystal and the laughter of guests, all was silent and the front door was standing open. Confused, she walked into the sitting room finding the chamber silent and deserted. Candles were burning and chairs had been overturned. There was broken glassware everywhere.

She stepped carefully around the room shaking her head. She couldn't imagine Heloise tolerating such raucous behavior. She turned toward the dining room. *Something was wrong. Something did not feel right.* Her eyes widened as she discovered the remains of Heloise's elegant supper strewn on the dining room floor. Broken porcelain and shards of crystal were scattered everywhere, and someone had removed the tablecloth, silver and all.

Suddenly. Lauren's heart jumped. *Intoxicated guests had not committed this mayhem; they had been ransacked!*

Anxious to know if Heloise and Cornelius were safe, she grabbed a candle and started upstairs. Her heart was pounding, so furiously she could hear nothing but the blood rushing in her ears.

The first room at the top of the stairs was Heloise's bedchamber. As she entered, Lauren held the candle high, but it illuminated only part of the boudoir throwing the rest into shadows. A few clothes littered the floor, but other than that nothing seemed out of the ordinary.

Her breathing was rapid and shallow as she caught sight of herself in the mirror over the lowboy. Her eyes were wide and her expression strained as the flickering candle cast eerie shadows across her face. Suddenly a strange sensation came over her. She could feel the warmth of someone standing behind her, and a man's face appeared in the mirror. Before she had time to scream he grabbed her around the waist and clapped his hand over her mouth. The more she struggled the tighter her assailant's grip became. The man's grasp was like iron as he dragged her out of the bedroom and into the hall. She thrashed madly, kicking and squirming frantically trying to free herself. Lauren almost swooned from fear.

"Calm down!" someone barked.

The blood pumped in Lauren's ears. She heard nothing.

"Be still girl! He won't hurt you!" someone said stepping in front of her from the shadows. The speaker held a candelabrum up. Lauren instantly recognized Leopold Fitch. Her breathing slowed, and she quit struggling.

Jerking free of the stranger's grip she demanded, "What's going on here! Where are the Benches?"

"Everyone is safe. Don't worry," he replied in his raspy voice.

"Where did they go?" she demanded panting from fear and rage.

"I removed the Benches to a safe place. The British Regulars are responsible for tearing up your townhouse."

"What!" she cried.

"Did anyone see you come in?" he asked.

"No! I mean yes—there was a woman outside on the street."

"A woman saw you?" Fitch questioned. "Then they will return soon."

"Why? What do they want? What's going on here?" she demanded.

"I don't have time for that now. You must come with me. You are in great danger," he said clutching her elbow.

"I'm not going anywhere with anyone!" Lauren cried tearing her arm away. She turned to dash down the stairs, but Fitch's huge friend caught her by the wrist. She winced from pain as his massive hand clamped down upon her arm. He was a giant of a man with wild black hair and a low forehead. He reminded Lauren of an overgrown monkey.

"No, Mr. Groot," Fitch ordered. "Release her."

Fitch withdrew a piece of parchment from his breast pocket and handed it to Lauren. "This will convince you if I cannot."

Glaring at him, she stepped up to the candelabra and read the note.

My dear Lauren,

It has become necessary for Cornelius and I to leave New York and you must leave immediately as well. My business ventures on Duke Street have been of questionable legality, and you are in grave danger. Flee now with Mr. Fitch.

Heloise

Lauren's eyes narrowed as she said, "I don't believe it."

"We have no time to argue," said Fitch. "Go to your room and pack a bag."

The giant dragged Lauren down the hall, pushing her into the bedroom and slamming the door. She stood alone in the room, rubbing her wrist trying to comprehend everything. Flight from New York with this stranger was out of the question; she must escape immediately. Pulling off her evening gown, she reached into the armoire for her green wool skirt and riding jacket. She put them on, swung a cloak over her shoulders and approached the window.

Just outside her bedroom was a large oak tree with a sturdy limb stretching toward the house like an arm. Lauren lifted the sash and swung onto the limb, keeping her weight low. It all came back to her. She began scrambling down the tree nimbly proud of the fact she had not forgotten her old skill. Suddenly, her skirt caught on a branch and she began to tumble. Lauren fell through the tree scraping her face on bark, cracking her arms and legs on limbs. She came to an abrupt halt, still in the tree, tangled in the limbs with her skirt pulled above her waist.

Hanging on desperately to a branch Lauren heard Fitch say, "Just let go, you little fool, and Mr. Groot will catch you."

Angry and humiliated, she tried to free herself but eventually tumbled into the arms of the giant who had been waiting for her. Mr. Groot set her on her feet as she yanked her riding habit back into place.

Fitch hobbled over with two horses saying, "Get on."

Lauren hesitated.

"Get on. Now!" he demanded.

Begrudgingly, she climbed upon the horse.

After the old gentleman was mounted the giant asked, "Will that be all, sir?"

"That will be all, Mr. Groot. I am most grateful."

"God speed, sir."

"To you too," said Mr. Fitch kicking his mare.

The Pride of the King

The city was deserted and the sound of hooves on cobblestones rang through the streets. They dashed through the city with Fitch in the lead, tearing madly through the maze of the city. When the surroundings turned rural they slowed their pace. Trudging along, Lauren spied farmers starting morning chores and housewives coming in from the morning milking.

For the first time in her life she envied rural folk for their slow, simple lives. Her anger boiled once more. She leaned forward in her saddle and said, "I demand to know where we are going."

Fitch did not reply. She repeated her question, but there was still no reply. Lauren sat back in the saddle and waited, watching his white periwig and cloak ahead of her. As the sun rose they left the farmhouses and barns and followed a path into the forest. They traveled deeper and deeper into the woods until an umbrella of trees and dense underbrush surrounded them.

Giving it another try, Lauren called, "Mr. Fitch! Where are we going? I demand an answer!" she screamed.

Fitch turned in his saddle and stated simply, "The interior."

"The interior!" shrieked Lauren. "Only voyageurs and women of bad character go to the interior!"

"Oh, I had forgotten that you are a woman of good character," Fitch mumbled sarcastically.

Suddenly, he jerked up on the reigns of his horse.

"What is it?" she called. "What's wrong?"

"Shut up!" he barked, throwing his leg over the front of his steed and jumping to the ground.

Lauren was shocked that a man of his years could move that quickly. He tore off his cloak and stuffed it in the hollow of a large tree, then yanked off his topcoat and waistcoat stuffing those into the tree as well. Clad only in his linen shirt, breeches and boots he continued to watch the trail as if someone was coming.

"What are you doing?" hissed Lauren, her heart pounding. "What's going on?"

He pulled off his white periwig and much to Lauren's surprise Mr. Fitch was not gray at all. He had long, smoky blonde hair; which was tied back in a leather strap. Next he pulled a handkerchief from his pocket and wiped his face makeup off. Once more Lauren was thunderstruck. Underneath the orrisroot and lampblack was the face of a man much younger in years. Fitch rolled up his sleeves and quickly grabbed a musket. Like a miracle, the stooped, frail old gentleman was gone replaced by a tall robust, man in the prime of his life.

"Get down!" he ordered.

Lauren continued to stare in amazement. Fitch's voice was no longer harsh and raspy but smooth and commanding, and for the first time, she noticed finely defined muscles under his linen shirt. Too impatient to wait for her to collect her wits, he stepped over and yanked her off the horse. As she tumbled to the ground he shook her saying, "Run!"

Grabbing her arm, they tore madly through the woods. Brush tore Lauren's skirt and ripped her skin while branches slapped her in the face. Several times she fell and Fitch yanked her to her feet again. He never loosened his grip on her wrist as they dashed madly through the woods.

Suddenly, a horse and rider burst onto the path followed by two more mounted regulars. The first soldier jumped off his horse, tumbling Lauren to the ground as the other two men grabbed Fitch.

One of them pulled his arms back while the other one punched Fitch repeatedly in the face and torso. They were about to change places when a surprised look came over the sergeant's face. He moved his lips as if trying to speak but could only sputter and gurgle as blood oozed from his mouth. The younger soldier stared at him, dumbfounded. Fitch had found his knife and driven a blade deep into the sergeant's neck.

Fitch stepped back yanking the knife out and turned to confront the younger regular, who dashed into the underbrush. Grabbing the sergeant's musket, Fitch turned toward the large, raw-boned regular who was holding a knife to Lauren's throat.

"Let her go and you live," Fitch ordered, blood trickling from his lip.

"Not a chance," the regular said. "There is more on the way."

"Drop the knife or I'll kill you," Fitch threatened.

Sweat poured off the regular's brow.

Lauren took short little breaths, too terrified to move.

"No one is that accurate with a musket," the soldier gloated. "You'll end up killing the girl."

Fitch sighed, dropping his musket. "You're right," he said.

"You cowardly bastard, Fitch!" Lauren screamed.

The regular started to laugh and backed away dragging Lauren with him. Suddenly there was the report of a firearm and Lauren toppled backward with the British regular. The soldier had been shot through the forehead.

Fitch stepped over and offered his hand to Lauren. After pulling her to her feet he looked at the dead soldier and said, "You're right, my friend. No one is that accurate with a musket. My comrade had a rifle."

"Who--" Lauren gasped. "Who shot him?"

Fitch whistled and a tall, thin man stepped out from the underbrush.

"You knew someone was there all along!"

Fitch bent down to pick up the regular's weapon.

She turned to thank the young man for saving her life but stopped abruptly too startled to speak. The young man had tousled brown hair freckles and fine straight teeth, but he possessed one major flaw which overshadowed these fine qualities: he was without a nose. There in the middle of his face was a dark, gaping hole.

Lauren was too stunned to speak. The young man dropped his eyes. He turned from Lauren saying to Fitch, "We must hurry. They are near."

Each man took an elbow propelling Lauren through the woods again. At times she felt as if she were flying. Their speed and adeptness at running through the brush was phenomenal. They leaped over fallen logs and carried her over tangled roots, avoiding branches and rocks like they were deer. She could hear the British regulars behind them, and several times shots rang out but the soldiers were at a disadvantage; horses did not fare well on this terrain. Nevertheless, when the trio reached a deer path the thunder of hooves grew louder. They were gaining ground.

Lauren saw that Fitch was growing winded, and she heard the young man shout to him, "She's just bit farther!"

Suddenly Fitch dropped to his knees gasping and coughing. When the young man stopped to help him, Fitch gestured for them to go ahead.

The boy hesitated, and Fitch gasped, "Go, Isaac!"

Fitch rolled into the brush as Isaac clutched Lauren's elbow. The two left Fitch and dashed through the woods again, but the regulars were soon upon them. Shots were fired. Just as a regular on horseback was about to seize them, they escaped down a steep embankment toward a river. The area was dense with foliage, and several times Lauren slipped and slid down the incline.

Much to her surprise, there was a ship with men scrambling on the deck unfurling sails ready to set sail. The crew raised rifles and began to fire upon the British regulars. As they tumbled into a small boat, Isaac told Lauren to lay low to avoid shots as he paddled them to the vessel.

In a matter of moments the crew was pulling them on board and Lauren was pushed roughly down onto the deck to avoid gunfire. The volley with the British regulars grew in intensity as Lauren heard Isaac shout, "He said we must go!"

Suddenly the sails began to bulge and the fluyt began to creak as they set sail. They continued to send rounds into the regulars when someone roared, "Look! There he is!"

Lauren jumped up looking over the rail just in time to see Fitch running down the hill, his hair flying behind him, and a musket in hand. Just as he was about to jump into the river a soldier knocked him to the ground. With the swiftness of a cat, Fitch rolled to his feet holding his musket like a club. When the regular lunged at him he took the butt of his weapon, and smashed the soldier in the face. The regular pitched back falling to the ground as three other soldiers started down the riverbank in pursuit.

Fitch plunged into the river and began swimming out to the fluyt. The crew continued to load and fire as he swam to safety. Miraculously the volleys of the regulars missed their mark. Fitch climbed a rope and hit the deck panting. The vessel was set at full sail and moved swiftly down the river leaving the British far behind.

Chapter 26

The crew sailed the fluyt up the Hudson River, and by the end of the day were well north of the city of New York. Fitch offered Lauren his cabin under the quarterdeck where she collapsed into a deep sleep until late afternoon. She had been so exhausted that she had not even noticed her surroundings, caring only for sleep to heal her tired muscles and mend her scrapes and wounds. When she opened her eyes the first thing she saw was a highly polished oak desk covered with charts and maps. Some were rolled up; others lay open as if someone had just been reading them.

Lauren stretched and sat up. She marveled at the luxurious maple paneling covering the walls and the highly polished white pine floors. She did not know captain's quarters were this rich and comfortable. The room smelled of spicy soap and cedar with the unmistakable aura of musk reminding her that this cabin belonged to a man.

Someone had left a small tub in the room, and Lauren wasted no time locking the door and stepping into the tepid water. She took a ladle and let the water drench her auburn tresses and roll down her back. The bath felt delicious. The soap freshened her hair and cleansed her abrasions melting away the stiffness of her joints and the soreness of her muscles. After toweling off, Lauren stepped out of the tub looking for her riding habit. Instead, she found a clean shift and wine-colored gown hanging on the back of the door. Without hesitation, she dressed, pinned up her thick hair and went out on deck.

The snow-white sails of the vessel snapped smartly in the warm breeze as the fluyt cut quickly through the Hudson. The water was as blue as the sky above it and on either side tree-covered banks rose up loftily. Fallen trees, subdued by wind littered the shore; some caught up by the branches of younger, sturdier companions, some clinging tenaciously to land while the rush of water struggled to sweep them away. Mallards rode the current while hawks and gulls soared overhead.

Several crewmembers greeted Lauren when she came on deck then returned to their work polishing brass fittings, coiling rope or scrubbing the deck. The ship was impeccably clean and well maintained, and the crew seemed content.

Lauren was leaning on the railing when a deep voice behind her said, "The Captain would like to see you." She turned and looked up into the kind eyes of Mr. Groot, the giant from the house on Duke Street. Before she could ask him how he had arrived so quickly from the city, he bowed and was gone. The man astonished her. His appearance was that of an overgrown oaf, yet his manner was refined and educated. She found him to be a sort of Goliath sporting a drawing room demeanor.

Fitch's reception was not as cordial. He did not look up when she arrived at the helm. He had bathed since their adventure that morning, and he had tied his smoky blonde hair back in a leather strap. He was clean-shaven and neatly dressed in a crisp linen shirt britches and boots. Gone was the frail aged creature Lauren had met on Duke Street. A vigorous, copper-skinned commander of a vessel had replaced him.

"Thank you for the tub of water and clothing. It was most thoughtful," said Lauren.

"I didn't do it. It was Isaac Burroughs," he replied abruptly.

"Oh. Why did you want to see me?"

"You said yesterday that you wanted to know where you are going. Well, I have come to a decision. You will be living in the interior of the Hudson River Valley and in time you will be working in the north on Lake Champlain."

"What!"

"You will clean up your life. You will no longer be involved in tawdry affairs and meaningless liaisons. There will be no parties with degenerate aristocrats and no more hedonistic adventures. You will breathe fresh air and eat healthy food. You will conduct yourself in a respectable manner and exercise good taste." Fitch looked Lauren up and down then said, "With any luck at all you will regain your looks--but I'm not hopeful."

Her eyes narrowed and her hand tingled with desire to slap him.

"My life and my appearance are none your affair and make no mistake--I will not live in this God forsaken wilderness! Now turn this vessel around!"

"And what will you go back to? You have no home in New York and the authorities are pursuing you."

"If it means swimming back to civilization, I will, Fitch!" she cried.

He chuckled and shook his head.

Furious and afraid, Lauren opened her mouth to stay more but reconsidered. Her eyes were filling with tears, but she would not let this man see her cry. She turned on her heel and started back to her quarters.

"Oh, and by the way," he called after her. "My name is James St. Clare, Captain to you."

*   *   *

Lauren stayed below the rest of the day avoiding Captain St. Clare. Granted, she had grown weary of her lifestyle on Duke Street, but she did not welcome the isolation and loneliness of the frontier. St. Clare had so incensed her that she spent the afternoon pacing below, but by evening she needed to clear her mind and breathe fresh air. She climbed the companionway onto the deck. It felt good to stretch her back and watch the sun set. The crew had dropped anchor and Lauren observed several of them on shore building a fire. Pangs of hunger gnawed at her belly, but she was too proud to ask for anything to eat. Lauren heard a noise behind her and saw what appeared to be only one-half a man smiling up at her.

"My name is Henry Bologne," he said. "I am the ship's purser."

Lauren stopped and ran her eyes over him. The man was without legs and his torso rested on a flat wooden platform on wheels. He propelled himself on this vehicle with his huge, overly developed arms. The ship's purser had thick dark hair and a full beard, and he handed her a plate of food smiling broadly in spite of his missing teeth.

Lauren stammered a thank you and took the plate. She had never seen anyone so misshapen, and she was at a loss for words.

"Hear the fiddle?" he said jerking his head. "Mathias plays every evening when we drop anchor. He's pretty good." She looked toward the stern at the old Negro with a fiddle to his chin, playing a sad tune.

"He *is* good. Who taught him to play?" she asked.

"No one knows, Miss. We probably never will. He is mute. Got his tongue cut out back when he was a slave."

Bologne looked at Lauren's plate. "Your meal's gettin' cold," he said turning to go.

She watched him roll away then looked at the Negro who couldn't speak. Captain St. Clare's crew was most unusual, she mused. Lauren gobbled the food greedily, then brushed the crumbs from her skirt and walked over to the railing to watch the bonfire. The flames bathed her in flickering light as she leaned against the railing, watching the sparks jump high into the night sky.

"I was abrupt with you this afternoon," she heard someone say.

Lauren whirled around and faced St. Clare. She raised an eyebrow and replied, "You are a man used to giving orders. I am a woman unused to following them."

"I dare say you will be my most rebellious crewmember."

Lauren smiled. "I have some questions for you."

"I'm afraid I cannot answer them all."

"Please try."

"First of all, who are you and what sort of trouble are you in?" she asked.

He studied her face for a moment carefully choosing his words. "I am an agent who provides goods to the aristocrats of the Colonies."

"What sort of goods?"

He shrugged. "Many things-- fabrics, perfumes, wine, tea."

"It sounds innocent enough. Tell me then, why they pursue you."

"Because the goods are not from Great Britain."

"Where are they from?"

"France, Spain, The Netherlands, all over."

"So you avoid customs. What about the Benchs? What is their part in all of this?"

The men on shore laughed loudly distracting them for a moment.

St. Clare looked back at her and he continued. "Heloise has been an associate of mine for years and Cornelius too. It is simple. They move into a city, establish themselves with the local aristocracy and bribe government officials to be silent. Once everything is in place, we smuggle goods at a reduced rate to the pretentious snobs of society. Heloise convinced General Ambrose Stuart to look the other way down at New York Harbor and it opened up the entire city to us."

"I see," said Lauren. "And my role was to attract men of wealth and power to this web of deceit."

"Yes and you were good at it. Nevertheless, when General McAffee replaced Stuart, our operation fell. The man cannot be bought. An informant told him of our dealings and he planned on arresting all of you at the dinner party."

"What if they had caught us? What would have happened?"

"You would have been imprisoned," he stated flatly.

Lauren gasped. All those years she had attended parties, consumed champagne and led a carefree existence never knowing the danger. "I appreciate you informing me after the fact," she snapped sarcastically.

"Don't play the innocent with me," he said. "You knew Heloise was up to something."

"I'm through with this business, St. Clare," Lauren said, tossing her head.

"Oh you're done, are you?" he replied. "Where will you go?"

"Back to New York."

"How, pray tell?"

"I'll walk, if I have to."

"Oh, of course! You'll walk!" he repeated smiling. "Do you have any idea how far north you are?"

"Well I won't stay here. It's too primitive." Lauren said. "I--I hate being outdoors."

St. Clare started to laugh. "Outdoors or indoors your job now is to return to full health here in the Hudson River Valley."

"Well, you should attend to your own health. I've seen and heard your fits of coughing."

He looked away. "My living quarters were substandard this past year. I'll mend."

"And what about your crew?" she said.

"What about them?"

"There's no mending them. They're misfits."

His face darkened. "Misfits!" and he nodded his head briskly. "Well then you'll fit right in because you're a broken down old whore."

Lauren gasped and tried to slap him, but he caught her arm in the air with a smack. With a menacing look, he held it for a moment then left.

Ashamed she had scoffed at the crew, Lauren walked to the railing putting her face in her hands.

"Are you alright, Ma'am?" It was the young man who had helped her and the Captain in the woods.

Wiping her eyes on her sleeve, she said, "You're Isaac, aren't you?"

"Aye, the First Mate."

"I'm sorry, Isaac. I am just tired. It's been a day of surprises."

"Me and the crew surprised you a bit. Didn't we Ma'am?"

Lauren started to protest but Isaac stopped her. "Not to worry. We're used to it. We are unusual, all of us, and we are together on this vessel for a reason. Cause we've nowhere else to go." Isaac smiled tenderly at Lauren and said, "You have no where else to go either."

It was the first bit of warmth Lauren had experienced in months, and her eyes filled with tears. She looked away and cleared her throat trying to hide her emotion.

To ease her embarrassment he looked at the shore and explained, "When I was a tot, a pack of dogs attacked me and tore the nose right from my face. My poor mamma was beside herself. I bled a lot, and they thought I would die. After a while, I wished I had died. No one wanted to have anything to do with me. Everywhere I went people thought I looked disgusting, or they were scared of me, until I joined this crew."

Gesturing toward the bonfire he explained, "They are all like me. Claypool there, he is blind. He is our boatswain. Groot's a giant. He spends most of his time a running errands for the Captain. Over there is Robert, one of our hands. He's a natural, to name just a few of us."

Lauren looked quizzically at him. "What is a natural?"

"He is very slow," he explained.

"And Henry Bologne?" she asked.

"Oh, he was deformed at birth."

"But it appears several men have no infirmities," she said looking around the fluyt and on shore.

"There you're wrong. We all are outcasts of some kind, every one of us. England and her colony want no part of us." He took her hand and led her to the railing. He leaned over, pointing to the hull and said, "Read the name of the vessel. The Captain thought this described us well."

Firelight flickered on the letters as Lauren read, *"The Pride of the King."*

"Yes," said Isaac in a voice heavy with sarcasm. "We are indeed the pride of King George. Are we not?"

Chapter 27

Shortly after Lauren joined the crew of *The Pride of the King* they dropped anchor in Albany. Standing on the deck, she stared at the landing longing to run away, run away from this group of misfit sailors and their Captain. She loathed St. Clare and his contemptuous attitude. She detested life on the river where she baked in the sun all-day and shivered at night. In New York City, there had been handsome men, witty conversations and luxurious surroundings, but here on board *The Pride of the King*, there was only drudgery and loneliness.

She hated the small stuffy bedchamber the ship's company had erected for her in the hold of the vessel. She hated the fact that she had to lock her room for safety. She missed the spacious house on Duke Street and longed for the company of Heloise and Cornelius. She missed her friends in Kaskaskia and her mind frequently drifted back to the Academy and Simone. It had been years since she had seen her sister, and she longed for her companionship.

As kind as they were, Lauren wanted no part of this group of sailors. She found herself an outcast among outcasts. Every night she cried herself to sleep, longing for her life of elegance and leisure in the city. In the morning she would awaken to puffy eyes and sore cracked hands from the numerous chores the Captain loaded upon her.

She was furious with her pedestrian image in the glass. Gone were the fancy dresses and her creamy complexion. Now when she looked in the mirror, her skin was burned, and her hair was wind tangled. She ate as much as the crew and gradually she lost her soft curves replacing them with hard muscles toned by heavy labor. Every night she slept a sound, dreamless sleep and even though the dark rings vanished under her eyes, she longed for late night indulgences followed by mornings of indiscriminate leisure.

As much as she longed to run away, Lauren remembered the cruelty of life on the streets of New York. She remembered the nagging hunger and her desperate attempt to survive. She remembered her illness after the baby was born and the decadent girls at Mrs. Vanoss' house of pleasure. Everything was as clear and as terrifying as if it was yesterday. Therefore when the vessel weighed anchor that spring afternoon in Albany, Lauren was back on board the fluyt. She knew that some day she would escape this life of desperation and toil, but until then she must be patient and wait.

For months, they sailed up and down the Hudson delivering supplies to villages and hamlets along the river from the merchants of Albany. Isaac told Lauren that it was unusual for *The Pride of the King* to be transporting legal goods, but General McCaffee's presence in New York City prevented them from sailing out to sea where they could obtain the lucrative contraband from the Spanish or Dutch. The routine was always the same, deliver their cargo by day, then move to a secluded location on the river and spend the night. The next morning they would move to the next village and repeat the process again.

Lauren had seen little of James St. Clare since her arrival several months earlier. Frequently he was on shore conducting business with the patroons of the Hudson. Much to Lauren's surprise, these landed gentry seemed to respect St. Clare and treat him as an equal. She spied him on several occasions walking side by side with the powerful looking men, and she knew that he went to their sprawling estates at night to dine and discuss business. She scoffed at these pseudo-aristocrats of this valley, dismissing them as country bumpkins. *They had to be fools to associate with St. Clare. Couldn't they see that he was a boorish commoner, nothing more than an ambitious profiteer?*

When Lauren was near the Captain, he ignored her. He was too busy barking orders at the crew or pouring over maps with Isaac, but one morning as she scrubbed the deck with her holystone, he approached her to say that she now was in charge of the galley. He informed her that she was to shop for food at market each day and prepare an evening meal each night for the men.

After he left, Lauren rested back on her ankles considering the idea. She had always loathed the bland boiled cooking of the English and if this vocation meant reprieve from menial labor then she was in favor of it.

Every morning after that she would sling a basket over her arm and go to the local village to purchase ingredients for a sumptuous meal. She would walk up and down rows of brightly colored produce, inspecting fruits and vegetables plucked fresh from the vine. She would purchase smooth, creamy butter and loaves of rye bread, juicy red meats and fresh catch from the river, then build a fire on the shore and cook the crew a hearty supper fit for nobility. She remembered the succulent recipes the Ursalines had taught her and introduced the men to delectable sauces and seasoned meats, mouth-watering tarts and savory stews. Night after night, they gobbled down her exceptional fare then applauded her abilities. Each morning they would speculate about her supper menu and nag her relentlessly for samples throughout the day. The meals opened dialogue between Lauren and the men, and she found her loneliness subsiding.

Many days Isaac Burroughs would keep Lauren company as she peeled and chopped, kneaded and baked. He would tell her stories about life at sea and on the river. Robert, the simple-minded lad would run errands for her when she needed help, and Henry Bologne would make her laugh with his gift of humor. Mathias, the runaway slave, always had a kind nod for her and the giant, Ben Groot continued to amaze her with his grand manners and boundless intellect.

The only one Lauren did not like was George Blasco, the ship's carpenter. He was short and stocky with curly black hair covering his head and entire body. It pushed out of the neck of his shirt and ran up and down his bulky arms. He had a pug nose and always smelled of stale spirits. What Lauren hated the most about him though was that he wore two faces, one for the Captain and one for the crew. He ingratiated himself to St. Clare in his presence, but the minute the Captain went ashore he cursed him and assassinated his character to the others.

Lauren knew that Blasco was wanted for murder, and she never doubted for a moment that he was capable of it. She knew that he was a skilled artisan, but still it surprised her that the Captain was gullible enough to give this reprobate shelter.

Nevertheless as long as Blasco did not bother her, it was none of her affair.

The weather had grown sultry by late June and the days had grown long. One afternoon, Isaac lounged under a maple tree chewing on a blade of grass while Lauren bent over a fire stirring bouillabaisse. The crew had just finished unloading barrels of molasses and Isaac was taking a break during the heat of the day. Isaac spent every free moment he had with Lauren. Most of the women he had known recoiled from his disfigured face, but Lauren was different. She was not afraid of him. She did not belittle or reject him because of his appearance; in fact, she seemed to invite his companionship.

Lauren enjoyed their time together as well. She loved Isaac's gentle voice and sensitive manner. Unlike the other crewmembers, he was not afraid to comment on the beauty of things or speak of his true feelings. "Isaac, I have been wanting to ask you something for a long time," Lauren said straightening up from the bouillabaisse, "What do you know about the Captain? Who is he? Where did he come from?"

Isaac looked over at the vessel cautiously then back at Lauren. "He is a very private man," he said rubbing his chin. "It took me several years before I came to know him and even still he is a mystery to me. You see, the Captain has never known his parents."

"What of it?" Lauren replied. "Neither have I."

"No, I mean he doesn't know *anything* about his family or himself. He was abandoned at such a young age he doesn't even remember his own name."

Lauren blinked in disbelief. "He doesn't even remember his name," she reflected a moment then asked, "How can children that young survive all alone?"

Once again, Isaac looked over at the vessel to see if the Captain was around. "I suspect one would become like an animal. Don't you agree?"

Lauren remembered the day she ripped food from the jaws of a dog and nodded slowly. She knew firsthand the misery and desperation of starvation.

"How long was he without a home?"

"Most of his childhood, eventually he was snatched off the street and indentured to a gunsmith in Albany, but they must have been cruel to him because at the age of fifteen he ran back to the streets and was picked up by a press gang."

"What's that?"

"A press gang is a group of thugs hired by King George to press young men into the Royal Navy. Usually it is against their will. It was at that time he chose the name James St. Clare."

"Why that name?" Lauren asked.

Isaac chuckled. "Well, he told me that James was the first name he saw when he opened the Bible and St. Clare was the name stamped on a barrel of brandy at the Albany landing.

Lauren smiled. She pondered it a moment then asked, "If he was so destitute, how did he obtain *The Pride of the King*?"

"Well, she was a broken down old wreck when he found her--sort of an outcast like the rest of us--and with the knowledge he gained at sea, he resurrected the old gal."

Suddenly Isaac spotted the Captain and scrambled to his feet. Tipping his hat he said, "Good day to you, Ma'am," and left.

Lauren stirred her stew, and then turned her attention to St. Clare moving about the vessel. She watched him inspect every detail of the craft. She saw him run his hands over the polished brass fittings and touch the sails with reverence. His concern for the vessel was tantamount, and she believed that he viewed her as an old friend. She observed that he was dressed in evening attire. He had on a dark coat and breeches, burgundy waistcoat and highly polished boots. Lauren liked the fact that, even though he was dressed formally, he did not powder his long, smoky blond hair. She guessed he was dining with one of the local patroons that night.

Suddenly, he began to cough and grabbed the mast for support. Lauren heard him many nights coughing and pacing in his cabin above hers, and many mornings he would emerge looking drawn and tired. She wondered what disease plagued him and how he had contracted it.

She noticed George Blasco leaning against a tree watching her. "He was in prison," he announced in a voice thick with accent. He threw the bit of grass away that he had been chewing and came near her.

Lauren ignored him and went back to her bouillabaisse.

"I know what you was wondering. You was wondering what gave him that cough. It was prison. He was in prison, thirty feet underground in a cavern never seeing the light of day for months. Sumptin' like that puts the rot in a man."

Lauren could hide her interest no longer. "In prison? What for?"

"He got caught running goods. We had to do it by ourselves while he was in prison, and we did a damn sight better job than him too."

Lauren knew Blasco wanted her to question him further about St. Clare, but she refused. She knew it would only encourage the man, and his presence made her uncomfortable. She turned back to look for the Captain, but he was gone.

That evening something unusual happened. For the first time ever, old Mathias played a merry tune on his fiddle. The crew was on shore playing cards when they heard the light-hearted strains, and they began to cheer.

"By Jove! What's gotten into the old man!" cried Henry Bologne.

Isaac bounded up from the hold and bellowed, "Why it sounds like a celebration, Mathias! What's the occasion?"

Mathias nodded at the setting sun then played on. Isaac dashed to the railing and shouted to the men. "What day is it?"

When no one answered, he declared, "Wait! It's Midsummer, the longest day of the year!"

With little urging from Isaac the crew hustled on board clearing an area for dancing, and Mr. Groot disappeared to ask the Captain if the crew could have a celebration. The giant emerged from the hold with a smile on his face and a barrel of rum on his shoulder. "Compliments of the Captain!"

Everyone contributed something to the party. Robert and George put up torches, Isaac and Ben Groot arranged the deck, and Henry Bologne pulled out his tin whistle along with Samuel and his drum. Lauren made rum syllabub and brought sausage and cheese to the festivity. Even Mother Nature blessed them with a clear moonlit night.

For the first time in months Lauren could discard her dirty pinner and change into something soft and feminine. She had obtained fabric from Kingston several weeks earlier to make some everyday gowns, and even though none of the dresses were grand, the indigo muslin with the green stomacher seemed festive. She pinned up her auburn tresses and grabbed her skirts dashing up the companionway two steps at a time. She was not about to miss a single dance. When she reached the top step the men stared at her dumbfounded. Even Mathias stopped playing.

Seeing Lauren blush Isaac roared, "What's wrong with you fools! Ain't you never seen a lady before?

They laughed, and Mr. Claypool started the slip jig, "Kid on the Mountain" on his drum. Mathias followed putting the fiddle to his chin. Finding the right moment, Henry Bologne took up his tin whistle and joined in as well.

Isaac took Lauren by the waist and swung her out onto the makeshift dance floor. Tonight Lauren had no cares. Tonight she would dance and flirt with every man on board *The Pride of the King* and feel pretty once more.

The rum was flowing and after several drinks Isaac jumped on top of a barrel to show the crew his fancy dancing. He struck his boots on the barrel in time with the music and kicked his legs high into the air. He did a handstand on the barrel then jumped down onto the deck with a flourish.

Lauren laughed and clapped her hands with delight. She danced with every one of the crew and flirted outrageously with them all. She could not remember having more fun She danced with Robert who stepped on her feet, with the graceful giant Ben Groot and with Isaac Burroughs three times. She even danced with George Blasco.

At last she turned to the ship's purser saying, "Come along, Mr. Bologne. It's your turn," and held out her hands.

Being without legs Henry Bologne did not think he could dance, and he refused Lauren, but she would not allow him to sit out. She took his large hands and whirled him around and around in circles on his platform. She darted under his arms and out again skipping around him like a gypsy around the fire.

"This is my first dance, my girl!" Henry shouted with glee as she tripped about him. His eyes twinkled merrily as he watched her dart around him like a bird.

The torches burned low as the merriment and music continued into the night. When the men were not dancing with Lauren, they were drinking rum, playing cards or singing their favorite chantey. No one noticed St. Clare come on deck and lean against the rail in the shadows. None of them noticed his dark eyes following Lauren as she danced around and around.

Chapter 28

Without realizing it, Lauren began to change. The fresh air of the Hudson Valley filled her lungs and reddened her blood, returning the lusty color to her cheeks. The dark circles under her eyes disappeared and her posture became erect and strong. Her pirate smile returned and she brandished it eagerly along with a laugh contagious to the entire crew. She brought energy and life to everyone on board *The Pride of the King*, and they grew to love her.

There was a spiritual transformation in Lauren as well. The wilderness nourished her and gave her strength like nothing before. It calmed her uncertainties and soothed her senses. She would stand on the deck of *The Pride of the King* and let the winds cleanse her and the scents of the pine trees purify her. The boundless interior seduced her and beaconed to her to explore its mysteries.

At sunrise one morning late in the summer the Captain announced they were sailing into the upper Hudson River country, north of Albany. Until now Lauren had ridden the vessel from village to village, oblivious to its course, but today she noticed the stretch of the river on which they sailed was more remote, and she noticed the vessel hugged the shore as if in search of something.

Suddenly, St. Clare began barking orders and the crew sprang into action. The fluyt came about hard and in the blink of an eye entered a creek which a moment earlier had been invisible. Instantly the green darkness enveloped the fluyt. The tangled limbs of elms, oaks and maples rose up on either side of the vessel, and Lauren could hear the beating of wings as waterfowl sprang from the water, startled at the swift appearance of the fluyt. Without the benefit of wind or momentum, *The Pride of the King* slowed to a standstill and the crew dropped anchor.

"You there!" shouted the Captain.

Lauren glanced up, and then went back to coiling rope.

"You there!" he barked again, standing by the rail. "Are you daft? I am talking to you, girl."

He signaled to her impatiently and Lauren moved to the railing.

"Where are we going?" she asked, looking at the dense underbrush.

"Upstream. Now get in."

The Captain threw a rope over the side of the vessel and lowered himself into a canoe that Robert had retrieved for him. The craft was hidden in some bushes on shore. Lauren leaned over and looked at the rope dangling down the side of the fluyt, opened her mouth to protest and thought better of it. Swallowing hard, she took it in her hand throwing one leg over the railing and then the other. Dangling helplessly on the side of the ship, she started to slide down the rope, but yelped as it burned the palms of her hands.

"Oh, for the love of God!" moaned the Captain. "I should have known! Mr. Burroughs!" he shouted.

After a moment, Isaac leaned over the side of the vessel and said, "Aye, sir?"

"Lower her."

Smiling, the young man eased Lauren down into the canoe while she mumbled profanities in French.

"That will be all," St. Clare said to Isaac. "As for you," he said to Lauren, "Take an oar and start paddling."

Frowning, Lauren took up a paddle as the Captain sat down in the rear of the canoe. They pulled away from the fluyt and traveled up the creek in silence slicing the water like butter. For most of the day, they traveled deeper and deeper into the interior. The tree limbs joined overhead, forming a tunnel for them to glide through, and the air was thick with moisture. Lauren could feel the watchful eyes of wildlife all around them, as they drifted through the backwoods, and occasionally she spied an otter slide into the creek or a fish jump. She saw no sign of human habitation until a landing came into view with several canoes and two bateaux.

"Pull up here," St. Clair ordered and jumped out, pulling the canoe to shore. He did not offer his hand to help her out of the craft or wait for her to come on shore. He instead walked up the embankment out of sight into the woods. Lauren muttered and slogged through the water to shore by herself. Picking up her wet skirts, she climbed up the path to the top of the hill and stopped abruptly amazed at what lay before her. There in the middle of the wilderness was an encampment bustling with activity and life.

"Surprised?" St. Clare said stepping up beside her.

"A village this far in the interior?"

"Yes. You lived far to the north on the Mississippi. This is no different."

Before Lauren could ask him how he knew about Kaskaskia, St. Clare gestured for her to follow. The workers looked up as they approached the community but said nothing to them only nodded a greeting to St. Clare. They all appeared to be tradesmen; blacksmiths, woodworkers all at work in shops.

"Welcome back, Captain!" someone called. A tall man with thin gray hair stepped away from one of the forges and approached St Clare. He wore a leather apron, and his sleeves were pushed up. Smiling broadly, he said holding out his hand, "You had us worried, sir. It's been a while."

"Mr. Griffith. How goes it?" said the Captain shaking his hand.

"I am well," Mr. Griffith said, and then he looked at Lauren, "Welcome to you too, Ma'am."

"We will be staying one night only," said St. Clare.

The two men left Lauren standing alone. She looked after them for a moment, puzzled. St. Clare appeared to be in a position of authority here as well.

Unsure what to do, Lauren walked over to watch the blacksmiths at work. The men invited no conversation but did steal looks at her out of the corner of their eyes. She watched a burley smith slam his hammer savagely against pieces of metal sending white sparks flying while his sooty apprentice labored at the bellows. The boy paused for a moment to nod at Lauren through the murky smoke. As she strolled farther along she saw a smith was working on a rifle. Then in one of the woodworker's shops, she saw an artisan run a plane back and forth over some oak; shaving fine curls off something that looked like the stock of a gun.

Finished with Nathaniel Griffith, the Captain walked into the shop where Lauren was standing and picked up a musket. He checked the sight for accuracy, and then replaced it, giving his nod of approval.

"The sun is dropping," he said to Lauren. "We had better eat before it gets too late. I have much to share with you and it is best done over a meal."

The evening was sultry, and St. Clare told the cook they would eat on the porch of one of the cabins. As they sat at a small table, a breeze cooled Lauren and lifted her auburn hair lightly. St. Clare leaned back in his chair, putting his boots on the railing of the porch lighting tobacco. Lauren noticed that he smoked the same kind of rolled tobacco stick Heloise had on Duke Street.

He blew out the smoke and said, "You must understand. Every man here has a role to play in this operation. Every man here understands the nature of my work and benefits from it. If you cooperate and play your role properly, you too shall prosper."

"Why are these men making firearms, secluded back here in the woods?" asked Lauren.

"They are not *making* firearms. They are repairing them. You will find few men making firearms in this part of the world. If you want a new rifle or musket, you must buy it from England. His Majesty has the arms monopoly here in New England. It brings in revenue for the mother country, and she can monitor how many weapons come into the colony. "

"So you are repairing guns?"

"Yes, and selling them. I refurbish some firearms and others I acquire brand new just off the ship."

"I imagine you obtain all of these guns at an extraordinarily low price," Lauren stated pursing her lips, implying he was a pirate.

"Yes," he said, flipping some ashes from his tobacco. "It may surprise you that in my youth I was apprenticed to a gunsmith. However, I am in quite another business now. And because of this business the firearms are frequently free."

Lauren knew he was alluding to piracy but chose not to comment. She watched some of the men loading rifles and muskets onto a cart. "Does the landowner know you are here?"

"Of course. The landowner is Cornelius Bench. Together we own this property, but it is in his name only. His mother and I have been colleagues many years."

A pang of hurt shot through Lauren, there was so much Heloise and Cornelius had not told her. All she remembered was Heloise saying they owned property in the Hudson Valley but nothing more than that, especially about this James St. Clare. Lauren was beginning to realize the Benchs had many ties to St. Clare.

"Where are Heloise and Cornelius now?"

"Scouting new prospects, marketing our luxuries elsewhere. I cannot share their whereabouts at this time. There are many facets to our operation. Delivering luxuries to the aristocrats in the cities is their specialty; gunrunning is here, shot and powder too. In fact, gunpowder is more in demand than anything is right now. The Crown restricts and forbids its manufacture here in the New World. I offer all these things to the locals at a much lower price," he said with a shrug.

"Still," stated Lauren suspiciously, "it seems like excessive secrecy for merely selling arms and ammunition to the Colonists."

"Ah, but you are an astute girl," he said with a smirk.

Lauren narrowed her eyes. "Monsieur, we are extraordinarily close to New France and war is imminent. What are your intentions with these weapons?"

St. Clare inhaled his tobacco and looked thoughtfully at the setting sun. Blowing out the smoke, he dropped his boots from the railing, turned and looked coolly into Lauren's eyes. He did not have to say anything. Lauren had her answer.

Changing the subject, St. Clare said, "The men are pleased with your cooking. You have a talent for it. My health has returned and I owe it to the fresh air of the Hudson and in part to your food."

"I do not hear you cough anymore," Lauren observed.

"It is over and I am grateful. I prefer to forget the past few years. Oh, look," he said. "Here is Mr. Harrigan with our repast."

A large man in an apron with a red beard and bald head set a plate of food before Lauren. She smelled the pheasant and new potatoes swimming in brown sauce and suddenly had an appetite.

"I will return with ale shortly," said the cook. "May I ask after the health of your wife, Captain?"

Lauren looked up suddenly at St. Clare.

"I've had word recently," the Captain said putting his napkin in his lap and looking up at the cook. "She is in good health, Mr. Harrigan. Thank you."

"Very good, sir," he said, bowing and stepping away.

St. Clare's eyes fell on Lauren for a moment, but she had started on her meal. She found it surprising that any female would find this man remotely attractive, but it only proved what she believed about the women of the English Colonies; they were obtuse.

"How long have you been married?" she asked.

"Several years now. We are frequently apart, but it is the way of it."

"It seems a most unusual arrangement," Lauren observed slicing her meat.

St. Clare wiped his mouth and sat back looking at her. He waited while the cook poured his ale then said, "Oh, and your marriage is not unusual?"

"My marriage is none of your affair," snapped Lauren. "And by the way how do you know about my life in Kaskaskia?"

"Heloise informed me of it. Heloise informed me of everything. I had a right to know who was spending my money in New York City."

"I earned that money," stated Lauren.

"Oh, and indeed you did, my dear. You were known for enjoying your profession a little too much."

"What's that supposed to mean?" asked Lauren frowning.

"Nothing," he said, taking a drink of ale.

Lauren suddenly lost her appetite. The impertinence of St. Clare was grinding on her. The sun was setting and cast long, red rays across the porch where they dined. The craftsmen's shops had grown silent, and candlelight appeared in some of the cabin windows. Lauren sat stiffly watching the lights flicker. It brought back memories of that night long ago in Kaskaskia when she had walked after dark in town and witnessed Monsieur Aberjon with his new conquest. Lauren had that same feeling again of apprehension and dread.

St. Clare continued, "Heloise wrote me a great deal about you. You were talented with the aristocracy of New York. The rich and powerful were taken with your charms in spite of your French background, so I am certain you would be even more successful with your own people."

He had her attention. "For this reason I am assigning you to Fort St. Frederic on Lake Champlain to be our liaison. I need someone to open doors, to make connections for me with the officers at the fort, so we can market our goods and services to the French."

"Oh," said Lauren her eyes flashing. "Oh, because you flatter me I should be eager to take this assignment? How stupid do you think I am? We are at war!"

"Not officially, but I admit relations are a bit strained between England and France."

"Strained. Oh yes, strained and I could strain my neck in a noose, St. Clare!"

He pushed his plate away and stated, "The way I see it, your choices are few."

Lauren clenched her teeth. How dare this man put her in harms way once more. She watched him light his tobacco. How careless he was with her life. At least on Duke Street she was ignorant of the risks, but here in this wilderness during a time of war the stakes were much higher.

Suddenly, something occurred to her. "How foolish I have been. It just occurred to me. I am the only French person you know," she exclaimed. "Yes, that's it. Why, I imagine you need me quite desperately." She chuckled and began to examine her nails. "I will sell myself for you, St. Clare, but I come at a high price."

The Captain sat back in his chair and blew out his smoke. "You are an adventuress to the core, Madame."

The way he said 'Madame' was most unflattering to Lauren. When she looked into his eyes, she saw something disturbing yet familiar.

"If I refuse?" she asked raising her eyebrows.

"You may return to the streets of New York."

Lauren's smile dropped, and her heart began to thud. How could he have known about her life on the streets? She remembered what Heloise had told her that first day on Duke Street. She had said, *"There are others out there who have suffered similar privation. No matter how fine your manners and attire, they will recognize this blight in you. They know exactly what you fear and they will use it against you."*

Lauren knew he saw the blight in her. She hated St. Clare. She hated him because he knew her every weakness, every frailty, every fear. They were of the same blood, cut of the same cloth.

In a heartbeat Lauren considered everything; the dangerous proposition, her lack of prospects and her need to survive. She stiffened her back, meeting St. Clare's gaze straight on. She would not allow him to bully her. She had spotted the blight in him too, so she repeated with even more conviction, "Captain, I will sell my services for you, but they *must and will* come at a high price. That price will be a home for me, a parcel of your land."

Chapter 29

Mathias came to the encampment at sunrise for Lauren, and she returned to *The Pride of the King* with him that morning. She did not see St. Clare for many weeks after their conversation and for this Lauren was grateful.

The Pride of the King spent much of the autumn sailing south on the Hudson without the Captain, delivering shipments of firearms to the English colonists. Lauren resumed her position as cook once more, saying nothing to the crew about her discussion with St. Clare. Her daily talks with Isaac began again and she engaged in cheerful banter with the crew all over again. They teased her at every opportunity, and she loved it. As her comfort level increased, so did her wit. She flirted and cajoled, winked and laughed, tossing her head and using her talents from Duke Street to charm them all.

She had almost forgotten about St. Clare when he appeared one afternoon in October. It was a bright, autumn day, and Lauren had gone ashore in Kingston to market. The village was filled with fresh country faces buying and selling harvest bounty. Giggling children darted around the stalls with cheeks as bright as the autumn foliage, reminding Lauren of her days in Kaskaskia with Renee'. The banks of the Hudson River were splashed with reds, oranges and yellows, and the air was cool and crisp.

Stepping from the fluyt, Lauren pulled her shawl close, longing for the sultry days of New Orleans. It was hard to believe only five years ago she was living with Simone at the convent. It felt like she had been searching for a home forever.

She was walking past the vendors of Kingston handling the produce and scrutinizing the catch of the day when a voice said, "If the fish smells like fish, you don't want it."

Startled, she stepped back abruptly and sent a tray of bass teetering. St. Clare jumped, catching it before it crashed to the ground.

"You scared me!" she cried clutching her chest.

He looked at her and smiled. He ran his dark eyes over every feature of her face as if he was memorizing it and then he stepped back as if embarrassed. "I just wanted to show off my limited knowledge of cooking," he joked awkwardly. "I didn't mean to scare you."

He was dressed in a white linen shirt, tan coat and dark britches. A leather strap crossed his breast and a cravat was tied loosely around his neck. His dusky, blonde hair was pulled back with a leather strap and he held a tricorn hat in his hand.

"You're back," Lauren stated flatly. She was not happy to see him, and it was apparent on her face. Suddenly her carefree autumn on board *The Pride of the King* was a distant memory. She looked down at the ground.

Seeing her frosty reception, his smile dropped. His demeanor changed suddenly from light-hearted to strictly business. He straightened up and said, "Come with me. We have some conditions to discuss before we embark."

Lauren followed him down the busy streets of Kingston to a tavern named, "The Red Lion" not far from the landing. It was a small, dark establishment patronized by many of the locals, but that afternoon only two elderly gentlemen sat on high-backed benches smoking pipes by the fireplace. Pewter plates lined the mantle, and the floor creaked loudly as Lauren and St. Clare walked to the bar. A maid with a baby on her hip emerged from the hams, tongues and bacon suspended from the ceiling and drew them pints of ale as St. Clare chose a table by the window overlooking the landing. The innkeeper retired to the back of the pub with her child again as soon as Lauren and St. Clare sat down.

Pulling a pistol from his belt, St. Clare set his firearm on the oak table, taking a long drink from his tankard. Lauren sat opposite him, with her hands in her lap, stone faced.

"I have considered your demands and spoken with Heloise," he said.

Lauren's eyes grew wide and she gasped, "You saw them? Are they well?"

"Yes, they are well."

"Tell me about them. How does Corny look?"

"I don't have time for that now. Listen to me," he demanded.

Lauren frowned and sat back in her chair with a pout.

"Heloise and I are prepared to give you a parcel of land which overlooks the Hudson River. It is not large, but it has a stream for your water and some tillable land. If you choose to live there, it would be a good site to set up a home. This is in exchange for a successful contact with the French."

Lauren blinked in disbelief. They had accepted her terms. *She would be a landholder. She may even build a modest home someday. It all seemed too good to be true*!

She stared at St. Clare, speechless.

"You realize," he continued with a cautionary tone, "that as long as your husband is alive he can lay claim to this land."

Lauren shrugged. "That does not concern me." She wanted to jump up and down with joy, but she continued to sit primly.

"We will draw up the papers when the contact with the French is secure and only when it is secure," he demanded.

Lauren wasn't listening. She was staring out the window thinking about the land she would own. It would be a place all of her own with a garden, a hearth and a large oak bed with a cream-colored duvet.

St. Clare leaned forward and hissed, "Are you fully aware of the dangers involved here, girl? This is not a game, Lauren."

Shaken from her reverie she blinked at St. Clare, struggling to remember what he had said. He had used her name. It was unnerving to hear him say her name, and his familiarity made her uncomfortable. To steady herself, Lauren took a pull on her ale.

"Now listen to me," he continued, leaning forward and lowering his voice, "I have several ideas on how you can make contacts at Fort St. Frederic. First of all you must--"

"No," interrupted Lauren.

"What?"

"Heloise and Cornelius neglected to tell you that *I* work alone. You will leave everything to me or there will be no assignment," she stated flatly.

St. Clare's eyebrows shot up and he chuckled, "Well, well, I have underestimated the princess." He crossed his arms and sat back with an amused look on his face. "Go on."

Lauren stood up and looked out the window deep in thought, "I want the names and ranks of the officers and their marital status. I need to know their interests and dislikes. Are their wives with them? Do they have children? Do they live in the fort or a settlement outside the fort? Are they religious? Are you getting all of this?" she said suddenly looking down at him.

Startled, St. Clare sat up and said, "Yes, yes. I will get the information for you, but who will you be? Who will you say you are?" he asked.

Lauren sighed and rubbed her brow. She paced in front of the window thinking and muttering. The two elderly men by the fire glanced at her momentarily and went back to their conversation. St. Clare heard her mumble something about needing more information before deciding.

At last she stopped, tossing her hands into the air declaring, "The old ways are always the best ways." She turned to St. Clare and said, "Heloise told me to be myself whenever possible and if I have to be someone else, I must believe wholeheartedly the lie or I shall most certainly fail."

"So you will be?"

"Me. Lauren De Beauville Heathstone, homeless French girl from New Orleans searching for a place to live. I am running away from the English Colonies and everyone I know here longing for everything French once more."

St. Clare sat back in his Windsor chair studying her as she looked out the window. He asked, "Is the part about running away from here the truth?"

Lauren considered his question. "That remains to be seen," she murmured, and looked away.

* * *

Late that afternoon, James St. Clare took Lauren up onto the bluffs overlooking the Hudson to give her a lesson in using a rifle. It was of the utmost importance that she be familiar with firearms for her own protection and also to market the goods properly.

They found an open area just beyond the tree-lined bluffs that looked down on Kingston landing. They could see *The Pride of the King* waiting patiently for them on the river below. The sun was dropping low in the sky illuminating the brilliant colors of the trees, and the wind had died down.

It was a tedious process loading and firing the flintlock, and Lauren seriously doubted her ability to perform it correctly under pressure. Even now under St. Clare's watchful eye, her hands shook and her palms perspired.

"You must practice it until it becomes second nature," he advised. "You must be able to be watching and thinking about your mark as you load. A cool head is of the utmost importance."

She tried it several more times until St. Clare noticed her arms were shaking. "Starting tomorrow, I want you to help Blasco and Price load cargo to strengthen your arms. These weapons are exceedingly heavy and you must keep them steady for accuracy."

Looking at the weapon she asked, "Can you tell by sight where this musket was manufactured?"

"Yes," he replied. "This is English. I have French weapons as well. Those of course will go to Fort St. Frederick, but in reality the demand will be higher for powder and shot. As you can imagine, consumable goods are always in the highest demand." Then glancing up he stated. "It is dusk already. That will be all for tonight."

Lauren took a deep breath and stretched. Her arms were sore and her mind weary. St. Clare walked to the edge of the embankment and gazed down at the river. The sun had set and the sky was darkening into a deep blue. A large orange harvest moon shone down on the Hudson as the fluyt bobbed on the water. Lauren walked over beside him.

"Are you afraid?" he asked, looking out at the river valley.

Lauren was startled. It had been months since anyone had spoken to her intimately. She knew that he was referring to Fort St. Frederic.

She hesitated and then replied, "I don't know. I can't feel anything anymore."

St. Clare made no reply. He gathered up the guns and powder horns, slinging them over his shoulders. Lauren followed him down the path to the fluyt, which was illuminated by the full golden moon. They were trudging down the hill through the trees in silence when suddenly he stopped and faced her.

St. Clare searched her face for a moment and said, "When I was a boy in New York. I fell into one of the canals in the winter. The water was so frigid; I knew that I was most certainly going to die. I gasped for air and floundered. Then suddenly above me in the light, I saw hands. There were hands everywhere reaching down to me. When I grasped these hands, they pulled me to the surface and saved me from drowning. These were people I didn't know. People I had never seen before or since," he said shaking his head. "Strangers that valued a small boy's life enough to extend a helping hand."

He looked down for a moment, then up into Lauren's eyes, "If you start to drown, I will always reach for you."

* * *

Within two weeks, St. Clare was ready to take Lauren to Fort St. Frederic. He knew they must move quickly and have her established at the fort before the snows came. She must spend the winter making contacts and gaining the trust of the French. He sat at the desk of his cabin making final preparations when Isaac knocked, entering the cabin. The Captain had sent for him.

Isaac knew what the Captain was about to say. He had lost sleep worrying about it and dark circles lined his eyes.

"We are leaving tomorrow. It is all written here." He stood up and handed Isaac a piece of paper. "You will find delivery locations for the firearms, fabrics, wines, perfumes and your contacts as well. Everything has been taken care of. They are expecting you. You will be in command of the "The Pride" once more, Isaac. When the river becomes impassable, this winter I will meet you in Albany at the usual location. The girl is ready and her identity is determined."

Isaac looked down at the floor and shifted his weight from one foot to the other. St. Clare continued arranging papers on his desk, oblivious to the boy's anxiety. Isaac swallowed hard and asked, "Will she be in danger, sir?"

St. Clare looked up suddenly. He studied the young man's face then said, "What's wrong with you? Why do you ask a question like that?"

"I don't know, sir," Isaac said staring at the floor.

The Captain sighed, then turned to a cabinet behind his desk and took out two crystal glasses and a decanter of brandy, pouring a drink for Isaac and one for himself. Handing Isaac a glass he said, "You have never met anyone like this woman from New Orleans, have you? She knows and has experienced far more than you can fathom, Isaac. She is a survivor to the core. She can take care of herself, don't worry."

Isaac looked at the Captain, squared his shoulders as if at attention and stated, "I cannot allow you to put her in harms way, sir."

St. Clare's eyes grew large. He looked hard at the young man for several minutes, then sighed and tossed his drink back. He knew Isaac had known few females. Many times the Captain had seen girls in town recoil at the gaping hole in his face or cruelly mock him when he turned his back. Lauren was the only female to converse ever with him, flirt with him, and St. Clare knew Isaac was madly in love with her.

He would not punish him further. "You have feelings for this woman, don't you?"

Isaac said nothing.

"You know she is married," St. Clare warned, looking at Isaac out of the corner of his eye.

"He abandoned her," Isaac replied defiantly.

The Captain chuckled and walked back to the liquor cabinet filling his glass one more. Isaac's face was flushed and he twisted his hat in his hands longing to be dismissed before he lost his temper.

St. Clare was not finished. "Heloise schooled her for many years. She taught the girl how to entice a man, how to entertain a man, how to tease a man. Heloise made her a consummate professional. Quite simply, this woman from New Orleans is a whore."

Fire flashed in Isaac's eyes, and he raised his fist to smash the Captain's face, but quick as lightening the Captain caught his arm and lowered it gently saying quietly, "No, Isaac."

When the young man's breathing slowed, St. Clare continued, "She is dangerous. Do not pine for her. She may never return. This woman is French and an adventuress to the core who will never be satisfied anywhere."

St. Clare tipped his head back, tossing the other brandy down his throat. "I am sorry to be so blunt, but as you know, we must not allow our emotions to cloud our judgment here on *The Pride of the King*.

He reached out and put his hand on Isaac's shoulder. "Sleep now. Review the information I have given you, and I will make clarifications in the morning. You are dismissed. Good night."

That night Isaac lay on his bed with eyes open, feeling like there was a tight band around his chest. His mouth was dry and his muscles tense. For the first time in his life, he hated the Captain. He knew Lauren was different from all the others, and he hated the Captain for demeaning her. He also knew that somewhere on the vessel she lay near him for the last time in many months, maybe forever.

St. Clare retired shortly after the discussion as well. He lay on his back in the darkness, staring at the ceiling of his cabin too, feeling unsettled and anxious. He did not understand why this operation felt different. Was it because of the threat of war with the French, the English, and all of their Indian allies? Or perhaps the coming of winter in a land filled with danger. Either way he was filled with a sense of dread which he had never felt before. He had misgivings about the prudence of the mission.

When sleep came, it was fitful and restless. The same dream haunted him that night over and over, robbing him of his rest and peace of mind. It was a dream of hands reaching out to him desperately in the darkness, hands which he could not reach.

Chapter 30

The crew of *The Pride of the King* sailed on the Hudson as far to the north as the river would allow then dropped anchor, bidding farewell to Lauren and Captain James St. Clare. The two would make the remainder of their journey on foot crossing overland at the Great Carrying Place, then canoe up Lake George to Fort St. Frederic on Lake Champlain.

Lauren dreaded saying goodbye to the crew on the morning of their departure; she squared her shoulders and climbed the companionway from her cabin to find them lined up with hats in hand, ready to bid her farewell. She shook their hands one after the other carefully avoiding eye contact, tears filling her eyes. She hated the finality of the English, "goodbye," so she used the French phrase, "*Au revoir*," hoping they would understand its meaning which was, in fact, "until we meet again".

At the last minute, Lauren realized Isaac was not among those on deck, and she turned suddenly to ask Mr. Groot his whereabouts. The giant mumbled something indistinguishable and cast his eyes down. Lauren looked everywhere, but Isaac was not to be seen. She was confused and hurt. When she approached Henry Bologne for an explanation he advised her with, "Let him be, Ma'am."

Reluctantly, Lauren climbed into the canoe and began to paddle to shore with St. Clare. As she stepped onto shore, she searched the deck once more, but the young man never appeared to say farewell. She turned away, disappointed and hurt and began her walk deep into the interior with the Captain.

A slate gray November sky lingered ominously over James St. Clare and Lauren as they traveled through the woods to Lake George. The wind grew cold, and Lauren pulled her hood up and her woolen cloak closely around her. She trudged behind St. Clare who said nothing only led the way in silence, carrying his rifle on his shoulder. She watched his long hair, tied back in a pigtail, trailing down his collar and his dusty three-cornered hat pushed back on his head. Occasionally the wind would carry his scent to her, a mixture of tallow soap, spice and tobacco. As much as she disliked the man, she knew she needed to stay close to him. His ability to survive gave her peace of mind as they ventured farther and farther into the wilds of the continent.

Late that afternoon they rendezvoused with a fur trader who allowed them to sleep in his greasy cabin on Lake George. He also agreed to sell them a canoe. They would start out in the morning. Several Indians and voyageurs St. Clare knew camped nearby, setting Lauren on edge. She saw the men ogling her, and she stuffed her hair deeply under a cap putting her hood up and her eyes down.

That evening as the two built a campfire; St. Clare informed Lauren they would canoe the length of Lake George and stay the next night at a fur trading post called Warren's Landing. At that point, they would be close to Lake Champlain and only a few hours away from Fort St. Frederic.

"At Warren's Landing I will introduce you to Phillipe Cozen," he said. "He trades furs with the English and the French. He knows both worlds and may be aware of positions at the fort for servant girls."

"He deals with both the French *and* the English?" asked Lauren suspiciously.

"Yes, and you are right to question everyone's motives here. Boundaries are blurred in this part of the world. The French and the English, the Mohawk, the Abenaki, and the Iroquois all mingle and spill each other's blood in this place. There is no more dangerous part of the continent. No man can claim dominion here and no corner is safe. Forty some years ago, France and England declared a boundary at Split Rock. New France was to stay to the north and New England to the south. Here is where the important waters converge, and whoever gains control here rules the New World."

The fire crackled and popped sending sparks high into the sky as Lauren looked into St. Clare's eyes. Cold fear suddenly washed over her and her palms began to sweat. She realized at once the danger surrounding her, and that Fort St. Frederic was indeed the heart of the beast.

Lauren stood up and paced trying to rub the cold from her arms. She longed for the safety of the Ursaline convent, the lush surroundings of Duke Street, or even the humble loft of the Lupones. She had been wrapped in safety, swaddled in security at those places, but now she was standing in the middle of a tempest of war.

Lauren's sleep was fitful that night, and when St. Clare woke her hours before dawn, her muscles ached from fatigue and fear. The stale smell of animal fat and human urine from the trapper's cabin lingered on her clothing. She longed to slide into a tub of warm water to bathe and rest her muscles, but when they pushed the canoe onto Lake George the crack of the November wind awakened her mind and heightened her senses.

St. Clare insisted on changing their plans, and they left well before the sun rose. All day long, they paddled on Lake George the north wind pushing against them. Occasionally flakes of snow drifted down from the sky, and at these times Lauren could feel the tension in St. Clare. He was abrupt and short tempered at every turn. He allowed few breaks, driving them to press on at an unendurable pace.

By late afternoon, they saw a break in the pine trees which he identified as the trading post of Warren's Landing. As they steered the canoe toward the small timbered stockade the skies opened up driving large wet flakes into their eyes blinding their approach. Lauren's fingers were numb and her cheeks were burning. To hasten their voyage, Lauren drove the paddles deep into the water while James strained to see the landing, paddling madly as well. Through the veil of white the timbered walls of the structure became discernable, and in a moments time the shoreline was upon them. They jumped out and hastily pulled the canoe up on the sand and rocks.

As Lauren yanked a pack out of the craft, St. Clare shouted, "Leave it!" and grasped her wrist, yanking her under some pine trees. It was quiet and dry under the blanket of green. They stood on a thick cushion of needles as Lauren wiped the wet hair from her face and rubbed the moisture from her eyes. St. Clare stood panting with his eyes riveted on the trading post, water dripping from his face and his hair plastered to his skin. His body was taut.

"What is it? What's wrong?" she asked.

He ignored her, continuing to survey the post and its environs. He grasped Lauren's wrist like an iron shackle and whispered, "We must approach everything here with the caution of a cat."

At last the wind died and the snow began to drift lazily to the ground. The trading post on the hill became visible and they looked up. There on top of the small stockade were three men seated at all corners keeping watch. They were dressed in buckskin and fur overcoats with hats pulled low and collars pulled up to protect themselves from the elements. One spare young man was sitting up at strict attention facing the lake with a musket on his lap. Another had his back to them guarding a path in the woods, and the last man faced them. He had dropped off to sleep his bearded jaw resting on his chest.

Lauren shuddered. The snow was turning to ice on her volumes of hair. "Come, we must get warm. The snow is melting all over me," and she took a step toward the clearing.

"No!" hissed St. Clare, yanking her back. He pointed at the post and said, "Look you little fool. The snow is not melting on *them*!"

To Lauren's horror the snow that had gathered on the guard's shoulders had not melted or been brushed off because the men had not moved.

"This is a trap!" he barked. "They're dead. We must get back to the canoe. No one is here yet or we would be dead already."

St. Clare turned toward the canoe then stopped abruptly. "Look!"

There on the lake was a canoe carrying three passengers heading toward the trading post. The snow intensified and the travelers were lost from view.

"Quickly, we must pull the canoe out of sight," he ordered.

Lauren picked up her soaked skirts dashing behind him. They dragged the canoe filled with packs onto shore behind a pile of wood cut for the upcoming winter. The snow was blinding as they ran to the shelter of the fur post. Rifle in hand, St. Clare passed through the courtyard, kicked open the door of the post and stepped in scanning the room for danger. It had obviously been ransacked. Empty crates and barrels were scattered everywhere, a fur press had been smashed to pieces, and some dried blood was spattered on the wall. Lauren followed behind him carrying a rifle too. She followed him up the ladder onto the lookouts where the dead held vigil.

"This is an old trick. They use dead bodies as decoys to lure traders with goods to the post," James said. "Go over there and strip that one of his clothing. Then push his body to the ground inside the walls of the post."

Lauren was speechless. She blinked several times and walked toward the corpse. The boy looked to have been only Lauren's age. He had red hair with freckles, and his wide vacant eyes resembled the milky eyes of old fish. Bile rose in her throat, but she squelched the urge to wretch and bent over undressing the corpse.

First she must pull a long stake from the jacket. The stake had held the dead boy upright, feigning guard duty. The buckskin jacket and pants were next. They were stiff and frozen as Lauren struggled, ripping the drawstrings open, pulling the pants off and yanking the shirt from a body that was stiff from death and frigid temperatures. When the corpse was reduced to only small clothes, Lauren straightened up and looked over at St. Clare. He was pushing his corpse off the wall.

"Do it!" he shouted. "Do it now!"

Lauren scrambled and sat down between the cadaver and the timbered wall, drew up her knees then pushed the body with her feet over the edge of the battlement. Before she had time to stand up and look over the edge, St. Clare was down the ladder and into the yard pulling the two bodies out of sight hiding the muskets as well.

"Now dress in his clothing quickly and sit as he was sitting!" he barked dashing up the ladder to his post.

Lauren obeyed, dreading what she was about to do. She pulled on the stiff clothing. It skinned her knuckles and scratched her arms, but as the heat from her skin melted the ice on the fabric, the clothing gradually conformed to her body.

St. Clare finished dressing in the clothing of the bearded trader and leaned forward straining his eyes through the blizzard. He could make out the canoe coming ashore. Crawling on his hands and knees to Lauren, he pulled a pistol from his belt.

"Hold your rifle in your lap and stay still. Put this pistol in your belt. You will know when it is time to kill."

Lauren watched him crawl back to his corner, her heart pounding. Her eyes widened as he rolled forward onto the sharpened timbers, motionless. He needed to hide his face and the fact that he was clean-shaven. Suddenly, she heard voices and quickly pulled the dead boy's cap low over her head, stuffing her long hair into the buckskin coat. With the rifle on her lap and pistol in her belt, Lauren sat upright barely breathing staring straight ahead.

A huge Mohawk man got out of the canoe first and started up the hill followed by a white fur trader. The Indian wore the traditional stiff crest of hair, or roach as it was called, along the middle of his head with a long fur coat and leggings. He carried a rifle and looked around furtively as if suspecting trouble. The European backwoodsman followed close behind him carrying a musket. He was of average height but appeared dwarfed next to the gigantic Indian. He stared up at Lauren and James. They remained motionless on the lookouts.

The last to step from the canoe was a young Indian woman who dropped her fur hood staring at the decoys as well. Her long dark hair was in a braid and her eyes sharp and clear. "The bearded one has fallen," she said in her native tongue, pointing to St. Clare.

The Mohawk pointed down to the ground. "Someone has passed here." His dark eyes darted around the trees and swept over the post.

The backwoodsman said nothing passing under the decoys into the yard. Lauren strained to hear his steps on the ladder, but the wind roared loudly in her ears. She saw the Mohawk enter the post as well. The Indian girl remained in front watching the woods and the lake.

There was a vibration on the floor as the men climbed the ladder. The blood rushed so madly in Lauren's ears she thought her head would explode. Her palms were drenched and her throat was dry.

"Straighten him," demanded the backwoodsman of the Indian.

The Mohawk put his rifle down and started toward St. Clare just as a strong gust of wind swept across the lookouts. The wind was so strong it lifted the cap from Lauren's head sending it soaring into the air. Her voluminous hair blew around her head, encircling her face and escaping from her jacket. The cap landed on the ground by the Indian girl, and she looked up. Her eyes widened and she yelled to the men.

In two steps the backwoodsman was upon Lauren yanking her to her feet. Her rifle misfired. Her heart pounding, she yanked the pistol from her belt, looked deeply into the man's watery eyes and pulled the trigger. Lauren saw his face explode into blood and mangled tissue. He staggered back, impaling himself on the sharpened timbers of the outpost, his musket dropping onto the ground below. Before she could take a step, the gigantic Indian was upon her, grabbing her by the neck with his bear-sized hand. She stared into his black eyes as he began to lift her from the ground. She felt her backbone stretch and she struggled madly as he choked her. Trying to free herself, she clawed at his face, tearing at his hair. Then there was a bang and the Indian fell against Lauren. James St. Clare was standing behind him holding a smoking rifle.

Still alive, the Mohawk straightened up pulling a buck knife out of his legging. He lunged at St. Clare, slashing his thigh. James jumped back, arms outstretched, facing the Indian. The Mohawk towered over him. They circled each other as Lauren pulled herself to her feet. She could see the blood oozing onto St. Clare's pant leg. As skilled as he was, she knew James was no match for a man of this size. She saw the Mohawk backing toward his rifle. Searching madly for a weapon, Lauren spotted the stake she had pulled earlier from the jacket of the corpse.

Lauren screamed, "St. Clare!" tossing him the stake. He caught it, took two steps forward and with both hands drove the stake into the Indian. Blood spattered onto his face and arms. The Indian roared and staggered again, grabbing him by the jacket, toppling them both over the edge of the lookout onto the ground below.

Lauren cried out and started to run to the edge of the lookout but was stopped abruptly by a sudden burning in her shoulder. She stumbled and fell against the timber fortifications, stunned. Looking up she saw the Mohawk girl holding a smoking musket. Blood stain oozed onto Lauren's jacket as the Indian girl began reloading.

Lauren looked about frantically for a weapon. Her heart drummed as the Indian girl withdrew the ramrod from the muzzle of her musket. So it would all end here, thought Lauren, after all she had endured, everything she had overcome, killed at an ugly outpost wearing the clothing of a corpse.

Enraged, she dashed over and said, "Not yet!" and with one swift motion pushed the girl over the wall of the outpost, musket and all.

Blood gushing from her shoulder, Lauren dropped to her knees and began to crawl toward the ladder. She must find James. She knew if she could reach him, they would find a way out of this. Then everything began to spin, and she fell to the floor losing consciousness.

The fall from the lookout killed the Mohawk and stunned St. Clare. Pushing the hair from his face, he dragged himself to his feet, clutching his thigh. He pulled himself up the ladder where he found Lauren unconscious and bleeding. She was alone, and he scooped her into his arms starting down the ladder. Bearing weight was excruciating, but he carefully eased her to the ground.

Concerned there may be others coming, James elected to tend Lauren's injuries away from Warren's Landing. He threw all the rifles and muskets into the canoe and pushed off. Not until he was away from shore did he notice the Indian girl waking from her stupor on the side of the outpost. They would be long gone by the time she could raise the alarm, and he turned the canoe out into the lake.

Moving them to a safe location, he rested the paddles in the canoe and bent over Lauren. She was ghostly pale, and her lips were white. He tore open one of the packs and pulled out a shirt soaking it in the lake to clean her gunshot wound. He then applied a salve of comfrey and oil he kept on hand. Even when he touched the wound Lauren did not move her swoon was so deep. He wound a bandage made from torn small clothes then around her shoulder and eased her back onto the bottom of the canoe.

Completely drained, St. Clare slumped back panting. He was exhausted and worried. His own injuries demanded attention, so he pulled himself up again. With much discomfort, he yanked the cloth from his thigh that he had applied earlier and inspected his wound. The blood had dried underneath the dirty rag, adhering bits of fabric to the wound. He winced removing the threads one by one. After dabbing his laceration with salve, he bandaged the injury and slumped back once more. He could only rest for a moment because the sun had dropped in the sky and already the air felt frigid. Throwing several blankets over Lauren, he picked up the paddles and moved on. Where they would spend the night was a mystery to him, but he was sure of one thing; he would return Lauren to the Hudson River Valley and bring her back to full health.

Chapter 31

The fire popped and Lauren's eyelids fluttered. She opened her eyes and stared at the flames for a moment and then fell back to sleep. James looked up from the table of maps where he was standing and sighed. He was still not convinced she would live. He walked to the window and looked outside. The sun had set, but it was not evening yet. In a few weeks it would be the shortest day of the year. Lauren had been ill for a month, and it was not until the last few days that she had shown any improvement. On occasion she would open her eyes or mumble but nothing that lasted.

James yanked his topcoat from a peg. Taking his powder horn and rifle, he left the cabin to find food. The dwelling where Lauren slept was the hideaway of James St. Clare. It lay deep in the interior on Popple Creek which flowed into the mighty Hudson highway. Lauren was its first guest and it sheltered her from the raging snow and winds of December. St. Clare used the cabin to collect his thoughts and formulate new plans. Here he could rest and think clearly being free of intrigue and tension.

The cottage was furnished simply but had a quality of complete security and warmth. There were several braided rugs on the pine floor woven in warm rich colors and a bed warmer rested against the hearth near the trivets, kettles and pots. A small corner hutch was by the fireplace with several painted plates and cups that appeared to be Dutch, and two Windsor chairs sat on either side of a homemade table by the window with a candle on it. St. Clare's bed was pulled in front of the fireplace for Lauren. She was buried in clean white goose down blankets and pillows. A bedroll lay on the floor where St. Clare slept.

What was singular about this dwelling was its camouflage. St. Clare had constructed it partially into a hill and the face of the cottage was completely covered in vines, so when the house was not in use, the front of the cabin could be covered easily with brush and leaves and hidden from view. It was a refuge for James and a corner of the world all his own. A world he had shared with no one until now.

Lauren opened her eyes again and looked around the room. She could not get her bearings. The last time she had this experience she was in the house of Madame Vanoss, and this certainly was not that dwelling.

The door swung open and in stepped James St. Clare. After stamping the snow from his feet, he put his overcoat on a peg and walked to the fireplace to put his rifle on the rack. Suddenly, he stopped and turned around. Lauren had been staring at him. She looked into his dark eyes and smiled. He laughed and said, "My God, girl. I thought you were going to leave us."

Before he could say anything else Lauren drifted off again.

* * *

The next morning, James helped Lauren sit up and gave her some broth from the stew he made. It steamed as he fed it to her, and the warm liquid cleared her throat enough for her to ask him questions. He told her that he had canoed all night that first night, thanks to a full moon getting them to safety. Then at a fur post he bought supplies and hired two boys to portage his canoe back to the Hudson, leaving it at the mouth of Popple Creek. He dragged her on a litter over the Great Carrying Place, and then canoed up Popple Creek to this cottage.

As sick as she was, Lauren understood the magnitude of this undertaking and whispered, "Thank you."

"Here, eat more," he demanded. "I'm tired of taking care of you."

The following day, Lauren sat up taking solid foods and steadily making progress everyday thereafter until she was able to walk small distances.

One evening St. Clare announced, "The crucible of hot water for your bath is ready. I am going to pour it in the wooden tub here by the fire. I will help you in."

Lauren blanched. "I think not," she said.

"I think so," he stated firmly. "You may leave your shift on but you must wash. It is time to thoroughly wash the stench of disease and death off of you."

Lauren remembered wearing the clothing of the corpse and nodded her head.

He stood up and ladled buckets of hot water into the tub. After getting the crock of soap and towel, he rolled up his sleeves. Lauren could not help noticing the muscles in his forearms and his tan skin. She felt unsettled as she watched him stoke the fire.

He looked outside and said, "It is snowing again. You know that it will be Christmas soon. You have slept a long time."

He bent over the bed looking into her amber eyes and pulled the covers back. Sliding one arm under her back and the other under her knees, he picked her up and held her for a moment. Lauren had never been this close to him before. She felt his warm skin and his breath on her face. It seemed effortless for him to lift her.

James lowered her into the warm water and Lauren felt herself melt. It felt delicious and relaxing in the bath by the fire. Her thin shift did little to hide her figure, but it was enough to satisfy her modesty. She picked up the soft soap and began to lather her arms while James knelt by the tub, unwinding her braid. She did not see him holding the auburn tresses in his hands, pulling handfuls up in the flickering light. He washed her hair by the fire, running his fingers over her scalp, lathering her tresses, pouring water down her hair and over her body. It had been months since anyone had touched her, and Lauren felt confused. Only a few weeks ago this man had treated her with disdain, now he took care of her.

James lifted her out of the tub, water running down his clothing. Her shift hugged her skin and he ran his eyes down her figure, then up again, stopping at her lips. The firelight danced over them and for a moment Lauren lost herself. Fear, loneliness and desire all clouded her judgment, and she opened her lips to kiss him. James leaned toward her and then as if embarrassed, he set her down on her feet abruptly. He mumbled something about her catching cold and handed her a towel with a clean shift.

Lauren felt foolish and awkward. She looked at the floor and folded her arms in front of herself. St. Clare put on his coat and went out standing for a long time outside the door and staring straight ahead. Then he walked briskly down to the creek.

Putting on a dry shift, Lauren slid into bed. She hated him. He had made a fool of her, and that would not happen again. It was nothing more than a moment of desperation. The last man for whom she had felt passion was Frederic Brink, and that had ended in disaster. No man would toy with her again. St. Clare was married and that was the end of it.

When James returned, his arms were filled with firewood. Without a word, he threw some logs on the fire and snuffed the candles by her bed. Lauren pretended to be asleep, but she saw him walk to the cupboard and pour a drink. He did not sit down. He stood there tipped his head back and poured the drink down his throat and then repeated it again. He went at last to the Windsor chair by the window and sat down to smoke. She did not know how long he sat there but in the morning he was gone.

*   *   *

On Christmas Eve, Lauren felt strong enough to go outside. James had left early that morning to hunt, so she stepped outside the cottage door and looked around. The air was cold, but she tied her cloak around her shoulders and stepped out. It was a clear afternoon, and she watched a brilliant red cardinal and his mate pick seeds from an evergreen. She could make out James' footprints crossing the frozen creek and trailing out under the trees. She wished he would not come back. She wanted to get as far away from him as possible, but she needed him. She longed to go back to New York or even to Fort St. Frederic, but now in the middle of winter that was impossible.

The wind picked up reminding Lauren of her task. Gingerly, she took steps to a pine tree near the house cutting several boughs and putting them into a basket. It was difficult for her to raise her arm, but she knew she must work the muscles to loosen the painful, stiff joint.

Returning to the cottage, she arranged the branches on the mantle and placed some over the window. The birds had left a few red berries on a bush outside the door and she scattered those among the greenery for color. She smiled when she remembered the angry chickadee scolding her as she plucked them from the branch.

Tired but satisfied, she sat back in a chair to observe her work. It pleased her to see a bit of cheer this time of year. She missed life in New France. New Englanders were so austere and serious. The nuns had always made the season so joyful, and she remembered her days in Kaskaskia; the Christmas Eve Gabriel danced with Anne, the snowball fight with Rene when he kissed her, and playing cards with Madame Aberjon on Christmas day. They had made themselves sick on chocolate and *petite fours*, laughing until they cried. They were all gone from her now, many dead and gone forever, and Lauren suddenly felt cold.

The door opened with a burst of wind and James came in holding up his trophies. "I've shot some pheasants for our Christmas supper tonight."

"Good. I'm hungry!" Lauren said standing up. "I'll help you dress them."

"I see you have been busy too," he said looking around the room at the boughs and berries. He smelled of fresh air and good nature.

Lauren was glad it was Christmas. The holiday tasks warmed her. They worked side-by-side preparing the meal well into the evening. They were limited with ingredients, but with Lauren's skills, the two were able to put a suitable bill of fare together.

James worked on the poultry and dressing while Lauren made biscuits, roast turnips, venison pasty and a pie out of their store of dried apples. James brought in more pine boughs and cones, arranging the branches in the middle of the table where he would set the pheasant.

After he pushed Lauren's bed to the side of the room and the table up to the hearth, he put a bottle on the table and said, "Here. It's a bottle of French wine I purchased at Fort Lyman over a month ago. I thought you might enjoy it."

"Oh, thank you," she said, picking it up and smiling. "So this bottle was not smuggled in?"

"If it was smuggled in, it was not smuggled by me," he laughed, taking it from her and uncorking it.

They sat down to eat, and James waited for Lauren as she said grace in French then he poured her a glass of wine. "Taste it," he said watching her.

She put it to her lips, and for a moment, she was back on Duke Street. The aroma was divine and the flavor delectable. James held up his glass to the fire, looking at the color. He tested the aroma and sipped it as well. "It is good. I do miss these little luxuries when I am here in the interior."

He didn't realize Lauren was watching him. He was a mystery to her. He had no family, no formal schooling or guidance, yet he had all the manners and breeding of an educated man.

"I have a question," Lauren said suddenly.

"Ask anything," he announced, lifting his glass. "I am feeling magnanimous tonight."

Lauren did not know what that large, English word meant, but she continued, "Isaac told me of your background. How did you learn the ways of the aristocracy?"

He shrugged. "I listened, I watched, and I made the right connections."

"Was Heloise your teacher?"

"No, I met Heloise many years later. I had been introduced to several teachers by that time."

Lauren pursed her lips. She knew he was alluding to women. St. Clare was usually reticent in talking about himself, so Lauren took this rare opportunity to press him further. She poured another glass of wine. "How did you learn to read?"

James leaned back into his chair and smiled wistfully. "A young girl taught me to read. She was only thirteen or fourteen years of age. I can still see that freckled face. Oh, the hours she spent with me and how I struggled. She was the daughter of the gunsmith to which I was apprenticed." He chuckled and shook his head. "Pass the wine. You are drinking it all."

"You are a most unusual man, Captain St. Clare," Lauren said pouring him a glass. "How does one who has come from so little, have so much?"

His eyebrows shot up. "You have been listening to gossip?"

"A little," Lauren said.

"I will tell you once and for all if you will let me enjoy my supper afterward."

He put his fork down and sat back in his chair, looking at the fire. "I don't remember my parents. I don't know if I was abandoned or lost or if they died. I don't even know what my given name is or where I came from. Was I born here or in Europe? I will never know. So I merely survived. I was dirty. I was uncouth, but most of all I was alone. When you are a child, you think of nothing but eating, drinking, and staying safe. This is what I did. I slept wherever I found a dry spot. I ate what I could steal or find; garbage, small animals, even rats. I lived by my fists and my wits."

Dragging his eyes away from the fire, he looked at Lauren and shrugged, "Whatever we have to do to survive. Isn't that right?"

Lauren did not like his familiar tone but said nothing.

"I was apprenticed to a gunsmith," he continued. "Who took great pleasure in beating me and another lad. I knew one day I would find my revenge on that pug-nosed bastard, but it was not for many years. While I was running an errand one afternoon for him, I was snatched by a press gang. As a result, I spent several years at sea, but when I returned I remembered that gunsmith. One night I crawled through his window and took what he owed me in rifles, muskets, and powder. Then I went to the docks and sold the firearms to everyone I knew making a fancy profit. From then on, I have been involved in illegal endeavors. I moved quickly from petty theft, to crimes against the Crown without a hint of remorse or regret."

He sighed and looked back at Lauren, "Anyway, that is my life in a few words."

They remained silent for a while then St. Clare said, "It all came from hard work. I was diligent and forged my education-- unlike you."

Lauren straightened up and said, "How dare you. You know nothing of me."

"Heloise told me of your Ursaline girl's school, how you were bred to be a great lady. I know much more about your life than you think," he said, going back to his meal.

Lauren grabbed the bottle of wine, poured another glass and then drained it in several gulps.

James watched her and shook his head. "That wine will go to your head," he warned. "You have been sick."

"I don't care," she declared and hiccupped. "You infuriate me."

St. Clare laughed, "You *amuse* me. In fact you amuse me more than any woman I have ever met."

"Oh, I see. It is humorous to see how far the privileged child has fallen," she sneered.

"Quit being so combative. I meant it as a compliment. You do the damnedest things. I will never forget the first day I saw you, leaning against that tree in Heloise's courtyard trying to seduce that old man. Or that night when you were trying to escape and you tangled your skirts in the oak tree." He chuckled again and said, "But what I loved the most was when you were hanging on that rope off the side of the fluyt last summer."

"So," said Lauren cocking her head. "Have you had a good laugh with your wife about me?"

The smile dropped from St. Clare's face. "That is not a subject I wish to discuss."

"Well I do," she demanded. "I have a few more questions for you, Captain St. Clare. Where is this wife of yours? Why don't you live with her?"

"My work does not allow us to be together."

"Why? Is she of high birth?" Lauren sneered.

"She is," he replied with a cross look.

Lauren had not expected that answer and was stunned. It had not occurred to her that his wife might actually be well bred. She could feel the blood pulsing in her cheeks. Even if the wine was loosening her lips, she was glad. She was tired of the secrecy and ready to clear the air.

"I see," Lauren said pursing her lips. "Your wife is too precious to be discussed with a broken-down courtesan from New France?"

James threw his napkin on the table and stood up. "Alright. What do you what to know?" He walked to the window and looked out, his fists clenched.

"Do you love her?"

There was a moment's hesitation and he said quietly, "That is none of your business. Nevertheless, I will tell you. It is a marriage of convenience."

"You didn't answer my question," she said.

In two steps, he was upon her lifting her to her feet, holding her by the arms and looking down at her.

Lauren was stunned.

"Why?" he demanded, giving her a shake. "Why do you care if I love her? Would you like to have me? To make another conquest? Another scalp for your belt? Is that it?"

Lauren was breathless. His hands felt hot upon her arms, and she struggled to free herself, but his grip was too tight. He continued, "If I had wanted you, I would have taken you a long time ago."

Their eyes locked in an angry stand off.

"But you don't interest me," he growled and pushed her away.

Her heart pounding, Lauren straightened her gown and pushed the hair from her face. The minute she heard the door slam, hot tears filled her eyes. She took her Christmas dinner and pitched it in the fire.

* * *

Later that night when Lauren was asleep, James returned to the cottage. She had cleaned up everything from the meal, banked the fire and gone to bed. He lit a candle and leaned over some maps, stealing a look at Lauren. He shuffled some more papers around, scribbling some calculations on parchment and looked up once more at her.

Sighing, he started toward the bed and then changed his mind walking the window. After watching the snow, he at last approached the bed and leaned over her. Lauren had forgotten to braid her hair and her tresses tumbled over the pillow in copper waves. He reached out tentatively and touched it. Something disturbed her slumber and she turned onto her back, her lips parted. James bent over Lauren so closely he almost brushed her lips and whispered, "I didn't know how to say this," he said studying her face. "But yes, I do love my wife."

Chapter 32

The winter seemed endless for Lauren. Most of January she spent gaining back her strength. Her shoulder continued to be stiff and painful, but she was diligent about completing her household tasks to increase her flexibility and endurance. On many occasions, she thanked Anne Lupone for teaching her skills necessary to survive and make life more comfortable on the frontier. She mended clothing, cooked, scrubbed the cabin, did laundry, and on occasion did the work of the stillroom. James spent most days hunting for game or chopping wood and in the evenings poured over maps and plans, inventories and records. He discussed little with Lauren about his business ventures, and for that, she was grateful. If it did not involve her directly she was not interested and she knew from her days on Duke Street that remaining ignorant was a safeguard against danger.

When Lauren did have some free time, she took the opportunity to do some needlework or slept. She tired easily, but as the days passed and her strength grew, she became restless and bored. Sometimes she had nightmares of the mangled face of the man she killed at the outpost and she would awaken with a start. Rest would not come easily after that, but it was comforting to know St. Clare was nearby. James conversed little with Lauren and she did not encourage it. Their encounters had always ended badly, so she kept silent longing to put distance between them. She hated herself for stealing looks at him when he was over his maps or watching the muscles in his back when he was chopping wood. She attributed it to isolation and loneliness, but when he was gone, she found herself watching for him out the window. What she did not know was that he was watching her as well, watching her take her hair down at night or studying her face while she slept in front of the fire.

A thaw came in late February, and James told Lauren he would be gone all day visiting the family of George Blasco.

Lauren's eyebrows shot up. "There are people up here?"

"Yes, the snow has melted enough for me to get through. I will be back tonight," he said as he put on his coat and took his rifle. "I have business to discuss."

She followed him to the door and asked, "These people are related to that carpenter from the fluyt?"

"Yes, they are gypsies. They are called *Melungeons*."

"Sounds like *mélange*," she repeated. "In my language that means mixed."

"It's close. They are a mix of many peoples. They have a hatred of the Crown as we do on *The Pride of the King*. They are outcasts and lead a gypsy existence traveling the Hudson in the warmer months, but in the winter they stay here in the backcountry.

He opened the door and said, "Keep your rifle close. I'll be back late tonight."

The next day, he left again and the day after that and everyday for a week until the snows returned. By that time, Lauren was happy to see the blizzard. It meant an end to her loneliness even if James was her only company. He came back late just as the blizzard was starting. She was bending over the fire, removing a kettle for tea. She looked up and smiled.

"Oh, the fire looks good," James said shaking his coat off and stepping over to the hearth rubbing his hands together. "I thought I was going to lose my way. The snow is blinding."

Lauren poured some tea into a pewter mug, added rum and molasses, and handed it to James. He stood by the fire and took a long drink. "Grog," he said with a sigh. "This always gets the chill out. I haven't had it since I was a boy at sea. Where did you learn to make it?"

"Isaac taught me," Lauren replied as she fussed with the trammel getting St. Clare's supper ready.

He looked down at his cup then said, "You know that boy's in love with you."

Lauren said sarcastically, "Oh really? Contrary to what you may think, men and women can be friends."

"You are blind, Lauren," he said shaking his head. "He is in great pain."

"Oh I see," she said straightening up and putting her hands on her hips. "Here is where you make some base reference to scalps on a belt."

"The men on the fluyt are starved for the love of a woman, and you sharpen your fangs on them."

Lauren gasped, "Do you really believe that I am so calculating?"

James shrugged and looked away, dismissing her.

*   *   *

Spring was on its way, and James traveled to see the Blasco family several times a week. One foggy morning, he announced to Lauren that she would be accompanying him. Lauren jumped at the possibility of going on an outing.

"It's time you meet them. These are the people who will be taking you to Fort St. Frederic."

"Are they familiar with the French?" she asked putting on her cloak.

"Yes, a bit. They move freely between cultures. They are of Portuguese, Indian, and African blood," James said shutting the door behind them.

They started down a path on the creek. The snow had melted leaving the trail greasy with mud, and ice chunks floated swiftly along Popple Creek.

"Shouldn't these *Melungions* be your contacts instead of me?" Lauren asked.

"No one trusts them," he explained. "They are not welcome anywhere because of their mixed blood, so they remain aloof to all. They have been successful though, trading guns with the

Huron and Abenaki, and this is one of the things that brought them into The Pride of the King.

"So, they sometimes travel on the fluyt too?"

James stopped and looked at her curiously. "What are you talking about? Has no one told you?"

"Told me what?" said Lauren.

"The Pride of the King is not just a vessel. It is a network, an entire organization reaching far beyond the crew of the fluyt. It encompasses scores of outcasts throughout all of New England working together in many commercial ventures."

Lauren was flabbergasted. "And all of this was started by you?"

He shrugged and said, "Well yes." and turned back onto the path.

Lauren followed St. Clare, observing him much differently. Here was a man dressed in a tattered shirt, leather vest, and topcoat. Aside from his leather boots and fine features, he appeared to be of no particular status or wealth, nothing more than an ordinary gunsmith or merchant captain, yet he was probably one of the most powerful men in all of the English colonies.

Lauren followed him for what seemed like a long time until the tree line ended, and they stepped into a clearing. Several men were standing outside a small outbuilding which Lauren recognized as a sugarhouse for cooking maple syrup. A large crucible was bubbling on an open fire by a cabin. Several pony carts covered for the winter with animal skins were off by the woodpile as well as a large enclosed wooden wagon.

"*Ola` again, Capitao!*" boomed a tall dark haired man who reminded Lauren of George Blasco. Two other men stepped forward as well. One had a long black mustache with dark skin and curly hair and the other had high cheekbones and a straight ponytail resembling that of an Indian. "So this is the day we meet her," the first man said looking at Lauren. "My name is Vincent Blasco, and these are my brothers, Gaspar and Davi. My mother is inside with my sister Fatima. Welcome. We will be taking you to Fort St. Frederic."

Before he could go on an older woman came down the steps of the cabin, wiping her hands on her apron and smiling. She was a tiny woman and had dark features like her sons. She took Lauren by the hand and escorted her inside talking in another language Lauren was stunned when she stepped into the small cabin. She had expected a table and some chairs in front of a hearth, maybe a braided rug and a bed, but instead the room was crammed with racks of clothing, wigs, bolts of material, feathers and musical instruments. There was a fiddle, a horn, and some large drums in a corner and a small dressing table with an open box of makeup. Lauren had never seen anything like it. Every way she turned there were splashes of color, glittering beads and the smell of heavy spices and perfume.

Mrs. Blasco encouraged her to look at everything. The woman proudly showed her a gown for a wizard with a long white beard and a costume for a pixie and a highland kilt. Lauren sighed and ran her hands along a red velvet cape made for a gentleman in a medieval play. Just as she was about to pick up a cap studded with glass beads, a girl emerged from a rack of costumes holding a swath of silk, needle and thread.

"Welcome to our home. I am Fatima," she said with a brilliant smile. Lauren was stunned at the exotic beauty of the young woman. Her skin was the color of cinnamon and thick lashes framed her deep blue eyes. Her wavy black hair was short and curling just above her ears, and her full lips were as red as her cheeks.

"Thank you. I am glad you speak English," Lauren said. "Do you speak French as well?"

"A little," the girl said. "But my oldest brother is much better."

Fatima was dressed like Lauren, in a shift and bodice with a homespun skirt, but beside her Lauren felt like a common sparrow.

"You are from France, Madame?" the girl asked.

"New France, by the Mississippi River," explained Lauren.

"I have heard of this river. You are far from home."

Lauren nodded her head. Mrs. Blasco pushed some ribbons and lace off the table so Lauren could have a seat for tea. After pouring, the old woman and her daughter pulled long pieces of material onto their laps, sat down and began to sew. Their fingers moved quickly and deftly, but they were oblivious to their work as they visited with Lauren.

They spent the afternoon conversing in English and French, Fatima translating much of it into Portuguese for her mother.

Lauren learned that in the warmer months, the family toured villages up and down the Hudson with their wagons, entertaining with music dance and theater. Sometimes they would join with other troupes and put on small festivals celebrating midsummer or the harvest. The Blascos would entertain all the while making contacts and new customers for The Pride of the King. Lauren noticed whenever the girl spoke of James, her eyes dropped demurely to the floor as if she were embarrassed.

Looking at Lauren's copper tresses Fatima apologized for her short hair. "I must keep it this way to wear wigs. Sometimes I must play a boy on stage as well."

Lauren looked at Fatima's figure and thought the role of a boy would not be very convincing.

"Do you get lonely out here all winter?" she asked

"Oh Madame, there are ten or twelve more cabins not far from here," gestured Fatima. "There are aunts and uncles, cousins, and many more of our people. Vincent and Gaspar have wives and children too. My Father died several years ago, so it is Mamma, Davi, and me here in this cabin."

Leaning forward, Lauren addressed Mrs. Blasco and said, "I was on *The Pride of the King* with your son, George."

The elderly woman looked at Fatima who translated her words. Madame Blasco shook her head and looked down. "She misses my brother very much," Fatima said. "We are all very grateful to Captain St. Clare for his help sheltering him."

"He is an excellent ship's carpenter," Lauren offered.

Fatima put her needle down and sighed, "Yes, he is a good carpenter, but George has been in trouble many times. Many times he has disappointed my mother, yet he remains her favorite child."

Late in the afternoon, a chill came into the air and Fatima and her mother brought the fire up to warm the cabin and make supper. They made spicy soup of fish, dried tomatoes and peppers that Lauren found delectable paired with herb bread.

Lauren saw nothing of the men all day. They stayed by the sugarhouse watching the sap boil and making plans for the upcoming season of trade for *The Pride of the King*.

When it was time to leave, Lauren thanked the women. Just as she stepped to the door, Fatima touched her gently on the arm to say something, but when she opened her mouth no words came.

"Mademoiselle Blasco," said Lauren. "What is it?"

"Oh--" the girl hesitated. "Oh, its nothing, but--you are not what I thought. You are very nice. I did not want to like the Captain's wife."

Lauren raised her eyebrows and laughed. "No, Mademoiselle. I am not his wife. I simply work for the Captain."

The girl looked surprised, and her mouth dropped open.

"No, not like that!" exclaimed Lauren, realizing the girl thought her relationship with St. Clare was carnal. "I am hired only to find contacts at Fort St. Frederic."

Fatima translated for her mother, but neither one looked convinced as Lauren pulled her cloak over her shoulders. She was sick to death of everyone doubting her virtue and St. Clare was the most condemning of them all.

As they were leaving, Lauren saw Fatima trying to catch the eye of the captain but he showed no interest in the girl. It was obvious the young woman was madly in love with him, but he remained aloof as always. Lauren wondered what qualities St. Clare's wife possessed to bewitch him into such devotion to her. Foolish women thought Lauren, putting her hood up and starting down the trail.

Chapter 33

When they returned to the cabin, Lauren was tired and wanted nothing more than to drop her soggy skirt, unlace her bodice, and go to sleep, but James lit several tapers and told her to sit down. "Can't it wait until tomorrow?"

"No, tomorrow we start preparations for our journey to St. Frederic. The Blasco brothers have just returned from the area. They were conducting business with the Abenaki, and they obtained the information you requested."

Lauren slumped into a chair. "And?" she said.

"There is an established settlement just outside the Fort. A number of settlers reside there, some of them are farmers and some are in trades. The French are encouraging growth. They have a windmill and a sawmill. The population is much higher than I realized. These colonists need supplies and are dependent upon the mother country for a number of things. France has a monopoly on certain articles and forbids the settlers from producing some of their own necessities."

"Yes, I remember," agreed Lauren, rubbing her forehead.

James continued, "A settlement beside the fort opens up many new opportunities to us; fabrics, spirits, spices and of course weapons. The war is escalating, and there will be a confrontation here soon. Many weapons and supplies will be needed. If the British cut off Fort Frederic from Montreal, the demands may be staggering. But, beware. It will be dangerous."

She straightened up, now interested and asked, "How many officers?"

"Several."

"Married?" asked Lauren.

"All," was his reply.

Lauren sighed.

"But," St. Clare added, there is an aristocrat visiting for the season from Montreal who is unattached."

Lauren looked at James, and one corner of her mouth curled up. "I'm guessing he finds the peasant fare at the fort ghastly. He may want a cook."

"What if food is not important to him?" St. Clare cautioned.

"There are two things important to a Frenchman and food is just one of them," she replied.

James stood up and started stacking some parchment. Lauren did not notice the scowl on his face. He continued, "We will say that you befriended Miss Blasco when the family was performing in the Hudson valley, and that you are paying them everything you have to help you escape to French soil."

"Yes," agreed Lauren. "Running away from my husband."

"Yes, that's it," he said curtly.

There was a pause and he said sharply, "We are done now. If you don't mind, I have work to do."

Lauren sat for a long time absorbing this news. It was all starting to happen, and it was thrilling. She stepped behind the wooden screen, dropping her soggy clothes and putting on a clean shift for bed. She was too excited to notice St. Clare leave the cabin, slamming the door behind him.

* * *

The next day supplies were gathered and packs placed in canoes. James took a lantern and in the small hours of the morning set off for the Melungion settlement. He told Lauren to be ready by sunrise, and they would meet her at the shores of Popple Creek.

The air was cold and filled with moisture as Lauren trudged down to the water at sunrise. The sun struggled to show through the gray clouds hanging low in the sky. She saw two canoes gliding toward her silently. Gaspar and Davi were in the first canoe followed by Vincent and stranger just behind. "You are in this canoe," ordered the stranger.

She realized the stranger was James. He was dressed as one of the Blasco brothers. They had darkened his skin with makeup, and given him a woolen Monmouth cap. Lauren did not have time to ask questions. She sat down in the middle of the canoe and they pushed off.

The group paddled deep into the backwoods portaging the canoes over the Carrying Place to Lake George by afternoon. They camped that night outside the same fur post where Lauren and James had slept the autumn before. Lauren discovered a fire pit with a wooden tripod some trapper had erected and started supper. Gaspar built a fire for her while she assembled the scant cooking supplies and ingredients they had packed. Once the stew was prepared she straightened up and stretched her back, hands on her hips looking at the men of the group. They were an unusual assortment of characters. Vincent was the oldest brother, huge, strong as an ox and good-natured; Gaspar thoughtful and kind, willing to help anyone and Davi, humorless, thin and wiry. Lauren did not trust him.

The men stoked the fire after supper as the light faded and the temperature dropped. The flames soared high into the sky.

Lauren asked James about his disguise.

"Fatima is a master of makeup and costume," he explained. "She is the one who assisted me this morning. Thanks to her I have passed undetected a hundred times under the most dangerous circumstances, such as the night on Duke Street when I met you. Heloise didn't recognize me at first or Corny, but he was too drunk to see anyone."

"Why a disguise this time?"

"I want to blend with the Blascos."

"You weren't in a disguise the first time we came up here,' she said.

"I should have been. I was careless," he admitted kicking a log in the fire. "It was almost fatal for both of us. I believe someone recognized me here at the fur post and set the trap for us at Warren's Landing."

"Why?" asked Lauren.

"Ransom may be one reason. My organization is not entirely a secret. Maybe someone wants to take over The Pride of the King and start a smuggling operation of their own up here."

Lauren's palms began to sweat. The thrill of adventure she felt yesterday seemed foolish and immature to her now. "Why did you come up here? The Blascos could have brought me to the fort."

"We have other business to conduct up here," he replied. He turned to Vincent after that, and they began talking in hushed tones which made Lauren uncomfortable. She knew that there was more going on here than they were telling her.

Even though she was exhausted, Lauren's sleep was fitful. When they finally pushed out into the lake at sunrise, she was relieved. She wanted nothing more than to put this trip behind her and settle at the fort in a new position. All day they paddled up Lake George, the air frosty and the wind raw. Lauren cheeks were red and chapped and her body weary. It reminded her of being on the convoy in the Illinois Country, but here a heavy sense of doom clouded everything. By late afternoon, they portaged around a series of small waterfalls and joined a larger body of water James told her was Lake Champlain. He signaled to the men and said, "We will stop here."

They guided their canoes toward a clearing and Lauren crawled out of the craft to collect firewood for supper as the men pulled their packs out for the night. Lauren noticed James standing for a long time on the shore watching the lake, his dark eyes scanning the woods and water. Finally, he sighed and turned around. She was standing behind him and he looked down at her. "What is it?" he asked irritably.

"Something is troubling you," she said.

He shook his head and mumbled, "Nothing."

Lauren could tell from the pinched look on his face that he was uneasy. He had been quiet all day, constantly surveying the lake. Tired of the disguise, James took off his cap and pulled his shirt off over his head. He would put on his disguise again in the morning. Lauren stole a look at him as he bent down on one knee lathering and splashing his face and chest. She saw the well-defined muscles in his back and arms and wondered how his wife felt when he held her. She looked away. Tomorrow he would be gone, and maybe she would never see him again.

The sun went down as Lauren finished cleaning up from supper. She hung her towel on a branch and James took her arm leading her to the shoreline. The moon was full casting a white glow on them as they faced one another. "This is our last night," he began. "And you will be gone for months. Are you familiar with everything?"

"Yes, I know how to do my job," Lauren said rolling her eyes.

"No, I mean have you committed to memory, the types of weapons, powder, quantities, types of luxuries we have, fabrics--"

"We have been over this a hundred times. Yes, I know everything," she said, nodding. "Why are you acting like this? Don't you trust me?"

He continued, "When you have made information go to the highest point on the windmill and shine a lantern. Someone will be watching on the first day of the every week. Meet them at the base of the windmill, and tell them what you know."

Lauren was looking down at her nails, concerned because they were broken and jagged.

"Are you listening to me!" he barked.

"Yes, I am! Why are so cross?" she complained.

"Because this is important," he continued. "Tomorrow is the day we will take you--"

Suddenly, there was the crack of a musket. Gaspar was dashing from the bonfire screaming, his clothing and hair ablaze. He tore to the water, flames reaching into the sky, and threw himself into the lake shrieking and writhing in agony. Vincent was struggling with the Indian who had hurtled his brother into the fire.

James tore up the hill, pulling a buck knife out of his belt. He yanked the Indian's head back and drove a blade into his neck. He dragged it savagely across the throat, spraying Vincent with blood. As he threw the body to the ground another Indian dropped to one knee taking aim at him. James dove to one side as the gun went off.

Davi was dodging the buck knife of a brawny Huron who was backing him closer and closer to the bonfire. A wounded

Vincent staggered over to help his brother, but a Huron jumped in front of him, and with one swift stroke smashed Vincent's face with a hatchet.

Lauren watched as the Huron kicked the body out of the way and turned toward James. In a flash, she picked up her skirts and dashed up the hill. As quick as lightening, she grabbed a flaming branch from the bonfire and swung it at the Indian. The Huron jumped to one side and crouched down, growling and smiling at her. Lauren was stunned when she realized he was a European dressed as a Huron. He was about to lunge at her when St. Clare smashed his head with the butt of his rifle.

Panting, James reached down and with one hand yanked Lauren to her feet. Davi ran over to them, blood trickling from his lip. They swung around in readiness for another assault. The three listened and waited, but it was over. The only sound was their heavy breathing and the crackling of the fire.

James took a deep breath and murmured, "There may be more. We must move quickly."

Davi nodded and bent over the dead body of Vincent, gently closing his eyes. Next, he pulled the lifeless body of Gaspar from the water, placing him next to his brother on shore while Lauren and James scooped up rifles and supplies. The three survivors pushed off, looking back one last time at the two brothers at rest, side by side in the moonlight. They paddled swiftly in silence for what seemed like hours when finally James directed them to shore and whispered, "We are near the fort now."

They jumped from the canoes, crouching down in the brush by shore. St. Clare spoke to Davi for a moment, and the young man nodded. Lauren watched him take her pack out of the canoe and go into the trees across from them.

"James, who were those men back there?" she whispered. "They weren't Huron."

He shook his head and said, "No, they were not Indians. Whoever they are were they did not want to be recognized. From here you will go the rest of the way with Davi," he stated.

"What!" she gasped, standing up. James clapped his hand over her mouth and pulled her into a pine grove. She struggled and kicked trying to break free.

"Be still!" he demanded.

Finally, she settled down and he released her. Her chest heaving Lauren demanded, "Why aren't you taking me the rest of the way?"

"I must go back. I cannot endanger you any longer," he whispered.

A chill went through her. Suddenly she realized that she was on her own again. James would be gone and she would be all alone. The wind blew, making the pines overhead sigh and creak.

"Where will you go?" she asked searching his face in the half-light of the moon.

"I am not sure yet."

"I must know," she insisted wringing her hands. "I must know where to find you."

James swallowed hard and looked away exasperated. "I don't know,' he whispered. "I wish I could tell you, but I just don't know."

"Just say it. Tell me the truth. You will return to your wife!"

"Not this again," he said, shaking his head. "You don't understand."

Lauren jerked from his grasp and started toward Davi. "Not yet," he said yanking her into his arms.

She felt his arms tighten around her and felt his breath on her face. He ran his lips over her skin and down her neck, and her heart began to pound. His arms seemed to crush her as he pressed his mouth down onto her lips. She returned his kisses then suddenly remembered his wife and her spine stiffened. Pushing him away she said, "Is this how you kiss *her*?"

James stopped, looked down at her in the moonlight then pulled her into his arms once more, bending her head back parting her lips. She felt the heat from his hands as he ran them up and down her back, tangling her hair in his fingers. His breathing quickened and she pushed her breasts up against his shirt wrapping her arms around his neck. He held her face running his lips over her cheeks, forehead and the tip of her nose.

Lauren thought she heard him whisper, "Don't go."

"What did you say?"

James stepped back, swallowed hard and replied, "I said you must go."

Chapter 34

"Madame, Madame!" cried the little boy from a branch high in a chestnut tree. "Look how high I can go!"

Lauren looked up and laughed, "High enough. You have won, Xavier. You are better at tree climbing than me." Swinging her legs and chewing on a blade of grass, Lauren was sitting several branches below her new friend, Xavier Moreau. She was looking down on Fort St. Frederic and Lake Champlain. It was a beautiful afternoon in May and Lauren was thinking about the convent and wondering about her sister, Simone. She pictured her kneeling with a rosary in her hands, cloistered in a dark sanctuary that smelled of candle wax and incense, petitioning to save Lauren's soul.

"Look Madame, a boat!" the boy cried.

Lauren eagerly scanned the lake for *The Pride of the King*. It was only a French sloop. She felt silly hoping to see the fluyt. *It would never appear here. It was not only dangerous but also impossible to navigate all the way to Fort Frederic through French territory.*

She shook her head and sighed. Since returning to New France, everyone associated with New England and *The Pride of the King* seemed like a dream to her, almost as if she had never left Kaskaskia at all. It was wonderful having everything familiar here at the fort; the French-speaking people, the customs, the attitudes, but it did not feel home and her loneliness returned. Night after night, she dreamed she was on the *"Pride"* again, the sun baking her skin and the breezes combing through her hair.

Lauren looked up at Xavier and called, "We must return. Your mother will be wondering where you are."

"Only a moment longer, Madame Heathstone," the boy pleaded.

"Yes, yes a moment," sighed Lauren. She looked out at the massive lake and leaned her head on a branch. It was the first warm week of spring and the ground was drying up from months of snow. It was beautiful here at St. Frederic; the scenery, the quaint settlement, the graceful windmill, but she felt unsettled. She liked the community, and they welcomed her, but she was not one of them. The authorities did not seem suspicious, in fact they applauded her determination to return to her homeland and escape the cruelties of New England, but everything seemed lackluster.

It all was too easy. She made negative comments about the English colonies, and the French commended her. She condemned the rigid puritanical Protestants, and they applauded her. In short, they admired her. There was no challenge.

Lauren found her thoughts returning often to *Pride of the King* as if it had been a dream. Everything about James St. Clare and the crew seemed unreal to her. She blanched when she thought of that night by the lake when she kissed St. Clare. Obviously, danger had been clouding her judgment. He was nothing more than an arrogant scoundrel taking advantage of her.

She drifted back to when she first came to St. Frederic. So much had happened since that night on the shores of Lake Champlain. It seemed longer than two months ago when Davi delivered her to the Moreau family in the settlement. He introduced Lauren as an acquaintance from the Hudson River Valley, an acquaintance who paid him dearly to help her escape to New France.

The Moreaus were overjoyed to have Lauren. The hardy big-boned dairy farmers were good honest people married and childless for many years. Suddenly, they were blessed with several children one after another, the youngest being five when Lauren came to them. They were delighted with the blessing of children, but they also found it overwhelming this late in life. Lauren came along just in time to help with chores and childcare. In exchange, they gave her a room in the loft and food.

As time passed, Lauren met the residents of St. Frederic and made a point of telling them that she had experience cooking for families of quality and distinction. She baked pastries for the officer's wives gifting them her specialty from New Orleans, bread pudding with caramel sauce. She hoped to gain an introduction to the few single gentlemen at the settlement, one being Julien Gautier. He was a visiting businessman from Montreal, the gentleman James mentioned earlier to Lauren, and she learned that this merchant had gained wealth and success in the fur trade.

One afternoon as Lauren was beating rugs outside the Moreaus, a bride of one of the officers stopped with a question.

Lauren noticed the basket of pastel flowers she carried matched perfectly with her pink complexion and flaxen hair.

"Excuse me, Madame Heathstone," she said. "My name is Ariel Devereaux. I know you are busy, but I am having Major Boyer and his wife and Monsieur Gautier to supper and I am very unsure of myself in the kitchen. If you could spare some time, would you help me with some of the cooking and serving tonight? I would be ever so grateful," the girl said the color rising in her cheeks.

"Certainly," replied Lauren, pulling the kerchief off her head.

Lauren smiled to herself as the girl continued down the road. At last, her opportunity had come to meet this Monsieur Gautier. Lauren marveled at how easy it was to befriend these people. After the suspicious snobs of Duke Street, everything here seemed effortless.

That afternoon Lauren menu planned and shopped. She taught Ariel Devereaux table setting and some basic cooking techniques including a *meuniere* sauce for her fish and a *gateau sirop* for her dessert. To impress the guests, Lauren included an *amusee` bouche'* to begin the meal.

The Devereaux had one of the finest homes in the settlement with a sitting room, a dining room, two bedchambers, a stillroom and a kitchen. Although it was a far cry from the townhouses on Duke Street, the dwelling was comfortable by Fort Frederic standards.

"Go now and enjoy yourself, Madame Devereaux," ordered Lauren. She had just completed the meal in the young bride's kitchen and the guests were arriving. She put her hand on Ariel's elbow and gently guided the girl to the dining room door.

"Everything looks wonderful. Thank you, Madame Heathstone," the girl said.

"Oh, and here," Lauren said arranging Ariel's hair. "Allow some strands to fall around your face. It looks softer."

When the girl left the kitchen, Lauren ducked down to glimpse her own image in a small, cracked mirror on the wall. She pulled off her mob cap, put on a clean apron and put her hair in a knot, letting a few strands frame her face too. After peeking outside the door, Lauren stepped back to the mirror and pulled out a tiny pot of color, applying a hint of red to her cheeks and lips. Then lacing her bodice tightly, she yanked her shift down underneath her dress to reveal the tops of her breasts.

Grabbing a tray of food, she stepped out into the dining room quickly surveying the table to make sure everything was in its place. The fine china was arranged meticulously, the napkins looked crisp, and the vase of pink flowers looked charming. Lieutenant Devereaux, a gangly pock-faced youth was at the head of the table looking uncomfortable. Ariel was at the other end wringing her hands in her lap while Major Boyer and his wife joked with Julien Gautier.

Lauren served the elderly couple first. They were dressed in modest evening attire and sported poorly fitted white wigs. They congratulated Madame Devereaux on the lovely appearance and aroma of the food. While she was serving the first course, Lauren looked up and locked eyes with Julian Gautier. He took her breath away.

He was a tall, broad shouldered man, in the prime of his life, with jet black hair light skin and piercing black eyes. He wore his hair tied back in the fashion of the day wore a blue woolen frock coat, and matching waistcoat. His crisp, white linen shirt had just a hint of lace at the neck and wrists.

Lauren placed Gautier's plate in front of him. As she stepped back she caught the scent of his cologne and felt her stomach jump. The rest of the meal, Gautier watched Lauren as she moved around the table, discreetly trying to catch her eye. When Lauren raised her eyes to meet his own she felt the color rise in her cheeks and a smile flicker on her lips. He was so unexpectedly dashing that she felt aflutter.

At the end of the meal as Lauren was retrieving the dessert plates, young Madame Devereaux said, "It would be unfair if I took credit for the exceptional fare tonight. Madame Heathstone is responsible for this remarkable repast."

Lauren looked down modestly.

"My dear," said Madame Boyer putting a monocle to her eye. "Where ever did you obtain your skills?"

"The good sisters of the Ursaline Order in New Orleans," Lauren said quietly with a curtsy.

There were murmurs of approval, and Julien Gautier asked, "Certainly you have served in this capacity before?"

Ariel answered before Lauren had a chance. "She has, Monsieur Gautier, but not here., in the English Colonies. She is new to our settlement and works as a nursemaid for Monsieur Moreau. It is a shame to waste such talent. Is it not?"

"Indeed it is," agreed Julien Gautier burning a look into Lauren.

* * *

Lauren's thoughts returned to the present. Sliding off the branch she called, "Come along, Xavier. We are late."

She brushed her skirt off and reached up helping the little boy down from the tree. Giving him a squeeze before putting him down, Lauren remembered the little girls at the convent and how she had loved to hold them. It felt good to have a child near her again.

"We shall race, Xavier. Are you ready?" she exclaimed.

"I am ready, Madame!" the boy said, crouching down with one cubby leg thrust forward.

"Go!" cried Lauren.

Off they dashed, through the meadow, down the hill toward the settlement, Lauren holding her skirts up, staying two strides behind little Xavier.

When they reached the door of the Moreau residence, Lauren scooped Xavier up in her arms and burst through the door. Two of the children ran over and hugged her legs.

"I won, Mamma! I won again!" the boy cried with glee, his cheeks glowing.

Gray haired Madame Moreau looked up from the hearth and smiled at her son. "How is it you win everyday, my pet? You are most amazing!"

Lauren laughed as she set Xavier down, her eyes sparkling and her hair tumbling everywhere.

Grabbing her shawl from the peg she said goodbye and started out the door. Walking briskly down the road, she reached up and twisted her hair into knot. The sun warmed her skin, and she took a deep breath of the afternoon air thick with the smell of rich soil and pine needles.

Lauren looked up at Fort St. Frederic. It was much larger than Fort de Chartres in the Illinois country. The limestone walls were massive and a drawbridge spanned a dry ditch which encircled the entire fort. Most impressive was the redoubt or citadel, a tall building within the confines of the fort, four stories high which housed a bakery, a powder magazine, and officer's quarters. Lauren thought it resembled the castles of old with the French colors flying overhead.

Passing the fort she headed toward the lake toward the home of Monsieur Gautier. Even after several weeks of employment, Lauren was still amazed at the elegance of Monsieur Gautier's residence. It was a cottage near the windmill overlooking the Lake Champlain. The back of the home was hidden from view by trees, but the front of the residence had been cleared for an expansive view of the lake. Windows were extremely rare in the settlement, and Gautier had two installed in the cottage to look out over the water. Lauren suspected he put these in not only for the view but to set himself apart from the ordinary villager.

Julien told Lauren that the first few years he came to St. Frederic he had stayed in the citadel, but when it became necessary that he must return every summer he had the cottage built for privacy.

She found his cozy cottage utterly charming. It was small but the design was exceptional. The plaster walls in the sitting room were painted a golden hue to compliment the browns and blues of a lush oriental rug on the hard wood floor. Two high-backed upholstered chairs sat in front of the hearth with intricately carved legs and one wall of the sitting room had a mural of the French countryside. However, what amused Lauren was an end table sporting a 'trick of the eye' on its surface. When she first saw the table she thought a deck of playing cards rested on the tabletop but was in reality only a painting, an optical illusion, or *trompe-l'oeil*, a hugely popular art form in Paris.

The kitchen had every modern convenience, and Gautier's bedchamber reflected the taste of a man used to fine things including a large maple wardrobe, curtained bedstead with an indigo blue duvet and an inlaid washstand from Paris.

Lauren loved coming here to cook and keep house and was pleased about the progress she was making with Gautier. Initially he was very reserved, speaking mostly about daily affairs at the fort, but lately he was complimenting her on her personal appearance. His manner was always respectful, but as each day passed Lauren could see he was becoming increasingly infatuated with her. She found him to be a refreshing change from St. Clare who was surly and argumentative, eternally poised for a fight.

Julien explained to Lauren that he came to the fort from Montreal every spring after the first thaw to meet with the voyageurs and buy furs. Coming inland allowed him first choice of furs before they reached the larger centers like Montreal and Quebec. Then when the voyageurs returned to the interior in the fall, he returned to Montreal. His company shipped these furs to France where they were made into hats and garments. He returned to Montreal in the fall to conduct his affairs from there.

Julien expected an orderly home and supper waiting for him every evening when he returned from his appointments at the fort, and he paid Lauren handsomely to complete these tasks for him daily. The routine had been the same for several weeks until one day she had been instructed to set another place for supper. She heard the front door open and looked out from the kitchen noticing the door to Monsieur Gautier's bedchamber was closed. Nothing seemed out of the ordinary. His habit was to return from a day of work, wash before supper, change his clothing and then read until supper.

Lauren put the finishing touches on his meal and peeked out in the sitting room to see if the guest had arrived yet. He was still sitting alone reading.

Julien looked up at her and said quietly, "Madame, I hope you do not mind. You are the guest this evening." He put his book down and stood up. With a playful bow he said, "Would you do me the honor of joining me this evening?"

Lauren smiled and nodded. Her heart skipping, she returned to the kitchen, unpinned her apron and removed her cap letting her auburn tresses trail down the front of her burgundy dress. She picked up the tray of food and went out to the table. Gautier stood up and took the tray from her and said, "It is apparent you have been on both sides of the serving tray, Madame. Tonight you shall be served."

"Each has its privileges and drawbacks," she replied taking a chair.

He smiled at her. The atmosphere seemed charged with excitement. Gautier brought Lauren her plate of food, took his own and sat down. She thought he looked handsome tonight. He was dressed casually in a brown waistcoat, white shirt and dark britches, but even in this simple attire Gautier looked elegant and well bred. His dark eyes distracted her, and on several occasions she had to look away from his intense gaze.

They talked of many things, Julien leaning forward listening to Lauren, eager to learn about her. Lauren asked questions too, wanting to know more about this mysterious aristocrat from Montreal and why he was here in the backwoods of New France.

"I must apologize if I am intrusive," he said, taking a sip of red wine. "But where is your husband? The man would have to be mad to let you go."

Lauren looked down at her plate and sighed, "Monsieur, it is most tragic. He disappeared on the streets of New York City shortly after we were married."

Julien looked at Lauren sympathetically and said, "I am sorry. You think he is perhaps--dead?"

"Or imprisoned," she added. "Although I searched everywhere in that city, he was no where to be found. It has been difficult," she lied, touching a napkin to the corner of her eye. "But one must go on."

Finishing his meal, Gautier wiped his mouth and rose from the table. He walked over to Lauren and held out his hand. "Come let us walk by the lake and enjoy this beautiful evening."

Lauren stood up and brushed closely to him but instead of stepping back, he pulled her close. Lauren met his gaze for a moment then looked down. He raised his hand, stroked her cheek then let go of her. They walked along the shores of the lake in the moonlight. Loons were calling in the darkness and they could hear the lake splashing gently against the shore.

Under the shadow of the windmill, Julien lifted Lauren's face and kissed her lightly just one time. Lauren was swept away by the restraint he showed and the respectful distance he kept. His slow approach and light touch teased her intensely and left her filled with passion, wanting more. Rene' had been her only experience with men from New France, but he had been young and clumsy. This time a grown man wanted her in his bed, a Frenchman experienced in love and the art of seduction

Julien pulled Lauren close and kissed her again but this time with more urgency. Suddenly, she remembered it was Sunday and there was a sentry stationed in the woods from The Pride of the King. It could be St. Clare himself watching her kissing Julien, and she pushed the Frenchman back abruptly.

"What is it?' he said breathlessly.

"I am afraid someone will see us," murmured Lauren.

Gautier began to laugh. "Oh, my little one," he whispered scooping her into his arms. "If it's privacy you want, then we shall go inside."

Chapter 35

The month of June Lauren spent in the arms of Julien Gautier. Gone were the stiff and formal suppers in the evening; now the dining was intimate, in the cottage bedchamber where Lauren and Julien would feast on fresh summer berries, cheeses and wine. Julien treated her like his princess, lavishing her with gifts and surprises at every turn. It was always something new, trinkets and ribbons, fabrics and perfumes to pamper and please her.

"Oh, Julien, this scent is divine," Lauren cooed one evening putting her wrist under his nose. "It must have cost a fortune."

Pulling her onto his lap, he said, "Luxuries are indeed expensive here on the frontier, but you are worth it, my little one."

Lauren blossomed under his care. She felt like a woman again and took long baths, smoothing oils on her skin and combing different scents through her hair. Everyday she would attend morning Mass, spend the day with the Moreau children, then late in the afternoon walk to Julien's cottage, prepare an evening of culinary delights then fuss with her appearance until he arrived.

She told him how brilliant he was in business and feigned fascination while listening to him explain the fur trade. Gautier was arrogant and Lauren knew exactly how to play to his vanity, although the praise and flattery were not entirely insincere. Lauren was truly attracted to the aristocratic Frenchman. His long, dark hair, intense black eyes and haughty attitude appealed to Lauren, and she felt lucky to be sexually attracted to her mark. It was a pleasing change after the elderly gentlemen, fops and dandies of Duke Street.

During the long days of midsummer, Julien and Lauren would picnic by the lake or sit on the *galerie* dining and watching the sun go down. Lauren was constantly near him, sitting on his lap or in a passionate embrace. She had never known a lover so skillful yet so demanding.

Sometimes James St. Clare would come into her mind and Lauren would push his memory aside, choosing the familiarity of this man from her own world. Lauren was satisfied with herself. She felt confident that Gautier was infatuated with her, and it was time to set the hook and convince him there were good easy profits to be made selling smuggled goods to the residents of Fort Frederic. She was pleased with herself thus far even though it had not been much a challenge.

It was time to introduce him to the financial advantages of smuggling. Lauren decided to make all of his favorite foods one evening, clean the cottage thoroughly and polish his best boots. She dressed in his favorite gown, put fresh flowers on the table and had his favorite dish bubbling in a pot. She even made a fancy apple dainty placing it on a footed cake plate. When she put the feast before him she expected delight, instead he raised his eyebrows and chuckled.

"What is it?" asked Lauren her eyes wide. "What's wrong with it?"

"Well," he said.

"Did I do something wrong?" she questioned.

Julien pushed away from the table, picked up the dish and took her hand leading her into the kitchen.

"My Darling." he sighed. "I know you try, but you have forgotten again. I prefer beef in this dish, not mutton. No harm has been done, dearest but--" he bent over and scooped the food into the swine jar. "Please make it over."

Lauren stammered, "I--I am sorry, Julien. I thought--"

He placed two fingers on her lips and shook his head. "No need to apologize, little one. Simply make it over correctly. I understand these things can be difficult for you."

Lauren blinked in disbelief but said nothing.

"I'll just finish up some paperwork while you correct it," he said and left the kitchen.

Lauren put her apron back on, rolled up her sleeves and remade the dish with beef, cursing Gautier under her breath the entire time. They did not dine together that night, and Lauren returned to the Moreaus early.

Everything about the evening shook her confidence. She tossed and turned all night wondering if she had been too smug, too self-assured and too careless. She had not even begun to groom him as a contact for The Pride of the King, and he was finding fault with her. Lauren vowed to get back into his good graces immediately, and the next time he spoke of the war escalating with England she would suggest the need to make a liaison with a smuggling operation.

The opportunity arose several nights later when Julien explained that business was always bolstered by war. Lauren asked him if Fort St. Frederic could ever be cut off from the supplies of Montreal. He said that it was a possibility. "We will see serious bloodshed here before the year is out. The French and the British are posturing for formal war declarations." They were lying on his bed, arms and legs entwined and he reached out, tracing the lines in her brow. "Don't worry about it. These things should not concern a female."

"I hope we never have to the live austere, plain lives of the British subjects."

"What?" Gautier said pulling back from kissing her neck.

"The King restricts and taxes everything in New England. It is so different from in New France. Those self-righteous Protestants, they frown on all luxuries, forbidding what we take for granted. So the average person is forced to buy from smugglers. It is a way of life down there. In fact, the family who helped me get here has ties to smugglers."

"Yes," Julien chuckled. "Those gypsies, it wouldn't surprise me."

He wrapped his arms back around her and said, "If it becomes necessary, I too would deal in the black market, especially if we were cut off from Montreal. There is no disputing English powder is superior. I have heard there is money to be made in such traffic, especially weapons. It is good to know if there is a blockade we can still maintain our way of life here at the fort."

"Oh yes," she murmured, snuggling next to him. "It is comforting to know we can find the right people if the time comes."

*   *   *

The following night, Lauren lay awake, waiting until all sounds of movement died down at the Moreaus, and then she laced her stays, pulled on her gown and crept down the stairs of the loft. With a lantern in her hand, she searched the road, but all was quiet. She started toward the windmill looking up at the dark giant keeping vigil for the French at Fort St. Frederic. Shortly after she had joined the community, Lauren learned the windmill housed six swivel canons which served as the first line of defense for those at the Fort. It had two purposes as it stood over the lake; to grind flour and grain for the residents and to guard one of the greatest forts in New France.

Lauren shivered as she stepped inside the door of the mill. Her lantern cast long, swinging shadows into the room and she fully expected someone to jump at her from the darkness. Instead, memories assaulted her. The last time she had been in a windmill, she had been wandering the countryside in the colony of New York alone and with child. She had been homeless, starving and near death.

Taking a deep breath, Lauren squared her shoulders and climbed the stairs, holding the lantern before her. When she reached the top floor, she stood by the window, held the lantern up and waited. Straining her eyes in the darkness, she saw nothing but the vast emptiness of the lake and the woods around it. She continued to hold the light to the window for a few more moments, then dropped her arm and went down the steps and out the door to wait.

It was not long before a figure darted out from the trees and dashed toward Lauren. She felt her heart pounding as the man approached and yanked her roughly into the windmill. She held up her lantern to see the messenger. Davi Blasco pulled his cap off and asked breathlessly, "What information do you have?"

"Davi!" she exclaimed. Lauren had not expected to see a familiar face. Memories of that violent night by the campfire flashed before her eyes. He looked drawn and fatigued. She had no doubts that he grieved for his brothers.

"There have been many taking turns watching for your light," he explained.

"I have a contact," she whispered.

"Good. Who?"

"He is a visiting merchant from Montreal. He has a large business in the fur trade."

"His name?"

"Julien Gautier," she responded. "And I will have him ready soon to strike a bargain."

"Very good," Davi responded. "Anything else?"

"That is all," Lauren said. "Your mother and sister, are they well?"

"They are."

Lauren felt her palms perspire and she asked, "And Captain St. Clare. How does he fare?"

"He is well and in Albany, on business with a woman there."

Lauren's stomach tightened. "What sort of business?"

"He tells me nothing. I must go," he replied pulling his cap on and putting his hand on the door.

"Is there anything you need?" he offered.

Lauren whispered, "No," and he was gone.

*   *   *

The rest of the night Lauren tossed and turned. She cursed herself for asking about St. Clare, yet repeatedly her thoughts returned to him. She remembered the way he ran his fingers through her hair, the urgency of his kisses, but most of all she remembered how safe she felt in his arms.

Lauren doubled her efforts to please Julien. She felt she was getting close to making her final move. The next step would be to introduce him to a representative of The Pride of the King.

Then they would begin to place and receive orders. Large amounts of money would be exchanged and Julien's greed would prevail. She knew money was more important to Gautier than anything else, and once he realized there were great profits in illegal traffic, he would become an eager customer.

Julien had been attentive and affectionate toward Lauren again for weeks without incident until one afternoon he came home early, greeted her with a kiss and slipped his hand inside the material of her gown, pulling out her pocket searching the contents.

"What are you doing?" said Lauren pushing him back. "What are you looking for?"

Gautier did not respond, dropping her pocket and turning to lift the lid of a Dutch oven in which Lauren was baking a pie. "Did you miss me today?" he asked as he was bending over smelling the pastry.

"Of course I missed you," she said with a scowl, tucking the pocket back into the slit of her gown.

Julien turned and smiled at Lauren searching her eyes. "You know, I adore you." He took her hand and led her to the bedchamber, and this time when they embraced Lauren felt as if Julien was punishing her, not caressing her.

Everything began to change after that. Lauren did not understand what was happening, but she did know that Gautier's grip began to tighten on her, and it was frightening. At first she thought he was simply being possessive and it was flattering, but as time passed, Gautier seemed to be watching her movements. He would come home early or stop by the Moreaus asking

Madame her whereabouts. He knew nothing of her relationship to The Pride of the King, yet this sudden possessiveness could pose a threat if Lauren needed to send a signal from the windmill.

Other things changed as well. Gautier seemed to find fault in Lauren more and more, pointing out flaws in her cooking and criticizing her housekeeping skills, but what infuriated the most were his disparaging remarks regarding her appearance. Frequently he asked her to change her gown or fix her hair differently, chuckling and calling her tastes in fashion pedestrian. At first, the comments hurt Lauren, then after several weeks she grew resentful burying her loathing under an exterior of compliance and docile acceptance.

Now more than ever Lauren needed to introduce Gautier to the contraband trade in case the relationship soured. She endured it all in silence, smiling sweetly yet watching and hoping the right time would arrive soon, and she could finish up. He expressed interest in meeting with her contacts, but insisted he do business first with the proprietor. This indicated to Lauren that he was indeed interested in a large-scale trade agreement, but it would be difficult to get word to James in time. The summer was waning and Lauren had no idea if St. Clare was still in Albany or moved out to sea. She knew she must work quickly before Julien returned to Montreal for the winter. Success was essential this fall, so she could return to the Hudson Valley to claim her land.

Thoughts of her property were what sustained Lauren now. Late at night she would lay on her bed in the loft, arms behind her head and speculate about her future home; what it would look like, what curtains to have, flowers and vegetables in the garden and what sort of view there would be from the front door. Sometimes she even thought about owning some chickens, a horse or a dog.

The days went by at a snail's pace. She could not rush things. Acting too early could be disastrous and dangerous. Her carefree days of summer were gone, and she found it fatiguing and nerve wracking maintaining the charade of adoration for Gautier. The relationship that had started so carefree now had become draining and exhausting. In just a few months, she had gone from sincere passion for Gautier to complete disdain. She finally began to understand, to a small degree, the degradation Eugenie must have felt at the hands of Jean-Baptiste Aberjon.

Not everything was painful and tedious though. Lauren enjoyed the good-natured company of Madame Moreau, and sometimes the women would share breakfast or sit and sew. One afternoon, the good woman invited Lauren to attend confession with her at the chapel in the fort.

"At long last, Father Piermont has some help," Madame Moreau, explained. "He has taken in an old priest who hears confessions for him. The man is a deaf mute and somewhat addled, but kind. He suffers from apoplexy."

Lauren put her sewing down and said, "Oh, what a shame."

Madame Moreau covered her mouth and giggled, "Being almost deaf makes him a perfect priest to hear confessions don't you think?"

"Madame!" Lauren gasped then giggled too.

Several afternoons a week, the women would walk to the fort, cross the drawbridge and go to the chapel to say their confessions. One afternoon after they emerged from the chapel,

Lauren told Madame Moreau to return home without her because she had a pastry to bring to Julien. Lauren climbed the steps of the citadel to the officer's quarters where Julien did his business. The door was cracked but just as she was about to knock she overheard Gautier say, "St. Clare is nothing more than--"

Lauren stepped back, startled. She put her hand to her chest. *Gautier was speaking of St. Clare!* She held her breath and listened.

"Has anyone seen him since he left Albany?" asked Gautier.

"No sir."

Goosebumps rose on her arms. Her heart thumped so hard she was terrified they may hear it.

"Damn! We were so close to eliminating him at Warren's Landing and here on the lake earlier this spring."

Someone was shuffling parchment.

"We must flush him out immediately," Gautier ordered. "If I am to obtain the arms and luxury monopoly I deserve. He is not to infiltrate here before me. Now search the waters and the woods."

"The woman can tell you nothing of his whereabouts?"

"No, I tried to set up a meeting through her, but she doesn't know where he is. I had hoped she could lure him here."

"If you expressed an interest in trade with his organization would he come?"

"No, I believe he would only send representatives. I have obtained the information I need from her. She is of no use to me anymore."

Stepping quickly but quietly down the wooden stairs, Lauren departed. She stopped at the entrance to the parade ground and looked around. There were soldiers everywhere and Indians loading carts. She knew if she ran, she would attract attention so she steadied herself, thrust her chin into the air and forced herself to walk casually to the gate.

When she was out of the sight of the sentries she broke into a run for the tree line. Holding her skirts high above her knees, she struggled through the brush, branches and nettles finally stopping at the base of a huge white pine exhausted and terrified. Her chest was heaving and her heart felt as if it would burst. She told herself to calm down and make an escape plan quickly. It all was clear now. Julien was the one making attempts on St. Clare's life. He wanted the lucrative smuggling venture here. She could not have entangled herself with someone worse. She cursed herself for being so careless and naive.

Lauren examined all of her options. Traveling on the lake was impossible; she had no boat. Walking overland was feasible only with a guide, her only chance was to wait until dark, take a lantern to the windmill, and hope someone from The Pride of the King would be watching. Even if it were not the appointed night, maybe Davi or someone would be there. It was her only hope. She must warn St. Clare and all those in The Pride of the King of the danger.

Lauren waited in the woods until the sun went down. She thought she would lose her mind fighting the flies and the bugs. She sat on the pine needles in her shift covering her head with her gown. When the moon finally came up, it was merely a crescent, and Lauren was grateful. It shed just enough light for her to steal out of the woods and down the path to the Moreaus.

It was late when she arrived at their home and she knew they would be asleep, so she eased open the door and slipped into the sitting room. She heard snoring from Madame and Monsieur Moreau's bedchamber and in the dim light saw bundles on the beds by the fireplace. She knew these were the children. Lauren bent over the fire, lit a candle and placed it in a lantern. She took a towel to pass in front of the lantern to send her distress signal and slipped out, darting down the road to the windmill. It loomed large in front of her and her hands were shaking as she threw open the door and raced to the top of the stairs. She started toward the window and stopped. The hair raised on her arms. She felt it. She was not alone. Suddenly, someone threw her against the wall. Her lantern crashed to the floor shattering.

Pinned against the wall and gasping for air, Lauren heard Julien say, "You thought I was stupid!" Gautier put his hands on her throat. He tightened his grip and she started to gag. "You little whore. The only way you'll leave me is in a coffin."

Struggling for air, she reached up, grabbed his hair and yanked his head back with all her might. With the swiftness of a cat, she dragged her nails across his eyes, feeling his flesh tear. He let out a roar. Slipping from his grasp, Lauren dashed for the stairs, but in the darkness lost her footing. She stumbled once, found a step but the momentum from running was too great. She lost her balance tumbling wildly down the stairwell. Sprawled at the base of the steps, dazed and injured, Lauren tried to stand but slumped back onto the floor, losing consciousness. When she woke up, she was bound and gagged, lying in a prison cell at Fort St. Frederic.

Chapter 36

Repeatedly Lauren would dream of Eugenie. The girl was hanging from the gallows, her muscles twitching in the final moments of death, her face covered in the hideous leather mask. Lauren would awaken with a start, covered in perspiration and sit up in the tiny prison cell hitting her head on the ceiling of the vault. Desperately she would grope her face and neck, then drop back down onto the soggy straw. There was no leather restraint covering her skin and no noose was around her neck yet.

Lauren's prison cell was nothing more than a wooden box, smaller than a coffin and she could only lay in the enclosure with her knees drawn up to her chest, languishing on soiled straw, delirious and injured. A soldier shoved food and water through the bars, but it was of no consequence she ate nothing and drank little.

"It's only a matter of time for you. You English cunt," the guard snarled. "They're making gallows special just for you."

He bombarded Lauren with insults throughout the day, but she did not respond. On most occasions, she was unaware of his comments, being too weak and too tired to be aware anything. After the third day, it became difficult for her to distinguish illusion from reality. Her perception of time became confused;

one moment she believed she had been in jail for months, the next for only for a few hours.

One morning she heard a jangling of keys, the grinding of a lock and the door was yanked open. Reaching in, the guard yanked Lauren up out of the cell to set her on her feet. She crumbled to the floor, her legs too weak and numb to stand.

"Bring a cart!" he demanded of another soldier. "Jesus Christ, she stinks," he said, turning his face away in disgust.

They dropped Lauren onto a pony cart and wheeled her across the parade ground into a room on the first floor of the citadel. It was the headquarters of the commanding officer of Fort Frederic, Paul Louis Dazemard de Lusignan. Lauren opened her eyes as they placed her on a chair in the middle of the room, a room filled with men in blue uniforms. An older gentleman in a powdered wig presided at the desk while several officers stood at attention behind him. Gautier was among them, a bandage over one eye. The room was small and crowded, filled with the musky odor of men in unwashed woolen uniforms.

Lauren struggled to hold her head up, but she was too weak her chin dropped down onto her chest, her hair hanging in matted tangles around her face. The trial was quick, a mere formality for the officers of Fort St. Frederic. In their eyes, the girl was guilty of treason well before the hearing. Gautier accused her of being a spy for the British, and they convicted her without question. Lauren heard the words treason and punishment, and then someone leaned close to her ear and roared, "I said, 'Do you want a priest!'"

With great difficulty, she raised her head and whispered, "Yes."

The officer straightened up and ordered, "Get him over here!"

Lauren's mind drifted to the Ursalines. Once more she heard their soft voices and whispered prayers. She was back in New Orleans, young again and filled with hope and promise. Sister Gertrude smiled down at her brushing the hair from her face. Lauren could feel the touch of the young nun's hand as she lifted her chin.

Opening her eyes, she realized that it was Father Reynard, the old deaf priest, who had heard her confessions at the fort. He placed a small piece of parchment into her hand, closed her fingers on the note, and then teetered back to a corner. Lauren tried to read the parchment, but her eyes would not focus. One of the officers grabbed it from her roughly. He squinted at the note and exclaimed, "It doesn't make sense."

"Just read it out loud," barked the commanding officer from his desk.

The officer looked down at the note and announced, 'If you start to drown. I will always reach for you.' " He shrugged handing the paper to the commanding officer.

Dazemard muttered impatiently, "Must be from the Bible. The old fool."

Lauren opened her eyes blinking several times as if waking from a dream. She recognized those words but could not place them. *Where had she heard them before? They sounded so familiar.* Then in a rush, she remembered. James St. Clare had spoken those words to her last autumn on the banks of the Hudson River, when he told her about falling through the ice as a child. Lauren lifted her head and looked for the priest. He was standing quietly in the corner. It took a moment for her vision to adjust, and then she recognized him. The eyes were unmistakable. Father Reynard was none other than James St. Clare.

*   *   *

"I want every inch of the fort watched, the settlement, the lake and the woods!" demanded Gautier pacing anxiously. "St. Clare will come for her tonight. I know it."

"Yes, Monsieur," replied an officer, who bowed briskly and left the room.

Everyone had left headquarters except Commander Dazemard de Lusignan and Gautier. The commander was lounging behind his desk, packing a pipe as Gautier paced back and forth dressed in dark blue breeches and waistcoat, an expensive white wig arranged on his head. His left eye was covered in a bandage and three red gouges ran up his forehead as if he were wearing a plumed mask for Carnival.

"You've told me little about this St. Clare," said Dazemard putting his feet on the desk and lighting his tobacco.

"There is little to tell," said Julien, placing a hand on his hip. "He is an adventurer from the English Colonies, a smuggler and profiteer who masquerades as a gentleman."

Stroking his chin, Dazemard studied Gautier. "Why is he a threat to you?"

Julien shrugged, "He is of little consequence to me. Although, I think the interests of the Crown may be at risk."

The commanding officer smiled. "Oh, of course you have the best interests of the Crown at heart," he said in a voice heavy with sarcasm. "But this St. Clare may interfere with your business ventures as well."

Gautier said nothing.

The commander continued, "You and your brothers have always dominated the merchant shipping industry in New France. Is it possible this man may prove to be more daring and successful than you?"

Ignoring the comment, Gautier looked out the door at Lauren as she was being pushed back to her cell. The soldiers were returning her to the stockade where she would await hanging the next morning

"What does that woman know about you?" Dazemard de Lusignan asked after looking at Lauren.

Gautier shrugged. "I told her I was a fur trader from Montreal, nothing more. The women I tumble don't need to know anything about me."

"Yes, it really is unnecessary. Isn't it?" agreed the commanding officer. "They find out soon enough what a ruthless bastard you are anyway."

* * *

It was growing late and only a few torches lit the dark parade ground. The soldiers on guard duty leaned carelessly on the battlements and two officers played cards outside the door of the citadel. They leaned back in their chairs, their boots on a barrel examining their cards, talking quietly while three Huron Indians stooped near a fire smoking in silence. Most had retired for the night.

Everything was still until Father Reynard banged the chapel door, stepping out into the courtyard, holding a leather bag in his hand. He nodded a greeting to a Mohawk slave woman pulling a fertilizer cart and continued slowly across the parade ground toward the stockade acknowledging no one else. At the sight of the wagon, the Huron scattered aromatic herbs on the fire. They knew the *honey cart* was filled with human feces used as fertilizer for the fields.

Suddenly a gust of wind swept across the courtyard whipping the cassock of the priest and blowing a hat off an officer playing cards. Everyone looked to the sky. Clouds were sailing across the moon and a rumble of thunder could be heard in the distance. The officers grumbled, threw their cards down and retreated inside the citadel to avoid the rain as the sentries on the bastions pulled up their collars. Only the Hurons ignored the threat remaining outside.

Father Reynard hobbled up the steps and into the stockade. It was a small timbered structure, holding six cells for prisoners. It had a stone floor and the enclosure smelled musty and damp.

"What do you want?" barked a guard at the old priest. Father Reynard continued past him without a word. "Hey! Just what do you think you are doing?" The guard hopped to his feet in a huff then stopped abruptly remembering the old man was deaf and dumb. He was too feeble to present any kind of a threat, so the soldier waved his hand in disgust and sat back down.

Father Reynard approached Lauren's cell bending down stiffly onto one knee, opened his pouch and drew out a crucifix, then some bottles containing holy water and oil used for the sacrament of Extreme Unction. Seeing this, the guard relaxed. He sat back in his chair crossing his arms in front of his chest.

Father Reynard made the sign of the cross and put oil on his finger reaching through the bars to anoint Lauren. He bowed his head in prayer as the guard's eyelids grew heavy.

Suddenly a bell clanged outside the door of the stockade. With a start, the guard sat up, cleared his throat and shouted, "Alright God damn it, just a minute!"

Grumbling profanities, he got up stiffly, and went to the door. The same Mohawk woman Reynard had greeted earlier waited outside with the honey wagon. She was dressed in a traditional buckskin shift, her black hair hanging in a neat braid down her back. She had come to collect excrement from the stockade.

"Well, well," the guard said running his bloodshot eyes over the girl's cinnamon colored skin. "I don't remember you."

She smiled and cast her eyes down modestly. In the dim light, he could see the curve of her full breasts under her supple, leather shift. Licking his lips, he moved closer to get a better look. There was the sound of a crack, and he stumbled forward abruptly with a grunt. His eyes bugged out as he staggered, then tumbled to the ground, hitting his head on the stone floor like a melon.

Fatima, masquerading as the Mohawk, jumped back to avoid the sentry's fall. James threw aside the chair he had smashed over the guard's head and smiled down at her. Fatima felt a thrill go through her body. In spite of the disguise of an old man, Fatima could still feel the youth and vigor emanate from St. Clare.

He bent down to make sure the Frenchman was unconscious as she scanned the parade ground. They grabbed the guard's feet and tossed him into the honey wagon. Although it was empty the stench was overwhelming, and they turned away in disgust.

Next St. Clare unlocked Lauren's cell, rolled her in a blanket and placed her carefully in the wagon as well. He was glad she was unaware of the pungent smell as he covered the vehicle with a tarp and signaled for Fatima to take the reigns.

"Is Davi waiting on the road?"

"No, his leg is broken. George is here instead."

St. Clare scowled. George had a temper, and he did not want trouble. Still dressed as Father Reynard, James pulled up the hood of his cassock and hobbled back across the parade ground toward the chapel. There was a crack of thunder and it began to pour. The wind began to blow the rain in horizontal sheets and the sound was deafening. Water ran down Fatima's forehead and into her eyes plastering the hair to her face. St. Clare watched the girl approach the gate. She pulled up on the reigns until a sentry jerked his thumb toward the road directing her to cross the drawbridge. Nothing appeared out of the ordinary, enslaved Mohawks transported excrement to the fields every night.

St. Clare knew that the gatekeeper would never ask to see the contents of a honey wagon and with the rain; it was even more unlikely he would climb down from his post to investigate.

Fatima passed out of sight unmolested to meet her brother, George Blasco, who was waiting down the road in the bushes. The plan was to toss the unconscious guard into a ditch, and carry Lauren to the safety of a canoe on Lake Champlain where Isaac waited ready to take Lauren back to the Hudson Valley.

Father Reynard approached the gate shortly thereafter. The old cleric was known to minister to the sick at all hours of the night in the village, so when he teetered by, nothing seemed unusual either.

The rain pummeled St. Clare's back and soaked his robe as he hobbled across the drawbridge. The material was heavy with moisture and weighed him down considerably. He longed to break into a run, but knew that he was still in plain view of the fort. Finally, by an abandoned cabin, he ducked into an outhouse where Fatima had hidden dry clothing and a rifle. Shedding the wet, woolen robe, James yanked on his breeches, shirt and boots and loaded his firearm. Using his soaked garment, he rubbed his face clean of makeup, then stepped cautiously out into the night.

Dashing into the woods, he ran down an overgrown path, holding his rifle out at his side, jumping over branches and tearing through underbrush. He must move quickly before his powder became damp. Emerging from the trees, he arrived at Gautier's cottage.

He took several long strides to the threshold and kicked the door open. Pointing his rifle, he stepped in cautiously scanning the sitting room and kitchen. It was dark except for a few embers in the grate. They shed enough light for St. Clare to see the remains of supper scattered on the table. He heard a woman giggle behind a closed door. Without hesitation he lifted his boot, and smashed the door open. There on the bed was Gautier naked, his pale skin covered in perspiration and a woman with blonde hair straddling him. The bug eyed female screamed and leaped off Julien, dashing out of the room.

St. Clare dropped his rifle, reached down and pulled Gautier to his feet, ramming him into the wall before he had a chance to move. A mirror crashed to the floor and a small end table toppled, smashing a crystal decanter. Julien whimpered and squirmed as St. Clare choked him.

"Tables have turned," hissed St. Clare. "Now you are the woman struggling."

He ripped the bandage from Gautier's face revealing a scarred and disfigured eye. "I see she left her calling card, that's my girl."

St. Clare itched to kill this dandy, but chose a warning instead. "Know this," he snarled. "If you ever harm my family again I will ruin you and your little cartel. Killing you is too merciful. Instead, I will see you lose everything. You will be reduced to a dog on the street. Mark my words, Gautier. I will find you."

With that, St. Clare dropped the Frenchman, and he fell to the floor gasping for air, his naked body a ghostly gray. James picked up his rifle, put one leg on the bedroom sill, and hoisted his body through the window just as regulars rushed though the front door of the cottage. He slipped down the steep hill to the lakeshore, the embankment slick with fallen trees and brush. The rain had ceased, but the descent was slippery. Just as he reached the shoreline, the clouds passed from the moon illuminating two canoes waiting out in the lake.

James plunged into the black water and swam out to the craft where he caught the outstretched hand of George Blasco. After pulling his Captain to safety, he paddled furiously to where Isaac and Fatima waited with Lauren. Shots rang out from the French, but it was too late. The members of The Pride of the King were underway for the Colonies of New England.

Chapter 37

They canoed down Lake Champlain the night of the escape unmolested, then across Lake George and moved Lauren overland, joining *The Pride of the King* after several days. There were fatigued but joyful. With diligence and care, the ship's company brought Lauren back to full health in a matter of days.

The fluyt resumed sailing on the Hudson leaving St. Clare in Albany to attend to business at Fort Orange and Fatima in Rhinebeck to join her mother. Once recovered, Lauren returned to her duties as cook feeling as if she had never left *The Pride of the King*. She was at peace here, and the current of the Hudson animated her body as if it was lifeblood.

Although there was a routine, the days were never monotonous. Lauren would rise before the sun, shop for food on shore in town, feed the crew breakfast, then bake and cook all afternoon preparing an evening meal. The crew slipped back into their old routines as well. Henry Bologne joked with Lauren again, Robert and Mr. Groot ran errands, and even George Blasco conversed with her on occasion. Her distaste for the man lessened considerably after she had witnessed his loyalty to his family, yet she would never be entirely comfortable with him.

Everyone reverted to the old ways again except Isaac. Always courteous, never rude, the young man avoided Lauren, and she avoided him. He did not invite conversation and Lauren did not encourage it. She did not press him and stayed at a respectful distance. Reluctantly she admitted St. Clare had been right; Isaac had cared for her beyond friendship. She did not try to ease her guilt by making amends with him, but carried on in silence.

She was also silent about the absence of Captain St. Clare and her longing to see him again. It had been easy to push the man from her mind in New France. She was infatuated with Julien and life at the fort was a novel distraction, but now back on *The Pride of the King* she was reminded of him constantly. His imprint was on every aspect of the ship, his memory a constant.

On one occasion she stole into his cabin in the quarterdeck and stood as if hypnotized, memorizing every detail of his room and his belongings. It appeared as if James had just stepped out. Maps and parchments were scattered on his desk, he had left his chair pushed back and his berth was rumpled and unmade. The cabin was small but warm and inviting.

An old barrel, gray and rusty with age, caught Lauren's attention. It appeared to be serving as a nightstand by the bed with a half consumed glass of brandy sitting on top of it. Barely visible on the side of the cask were the words, '*Châteaux St Clare, Provence.*" Lauren gasped, realizing that this was the barrel from which he had obtained his surname. She ran her hands along the coarse wood, smiling at his sentimentality.

Then impulsive as always, she stepped over and pressed one of his shirts to her to nose, taking in his scent once more. Suddenly, tears filled her eyes, and she brushed at her face frantically, fearing discovery. Lauren left the room abruptly, vowing never to return.

The days grew shorter as autumn arrived in the Hudson River Valley. *The Pride of the King* returned to Albany and Lauren felt the excitement in her grow. She did not care if St. Clare had been with his wife or any woman for that matter; she just wanted to lay eyes on him once more. She told herself she needed to thank him for his daring rescue, but in reality, she just wanted to be near him.

The first day in Albany she waited patiently, and he did not return to the fluyt. The second day, Lauren found herself bored and irritable as the crew went on shore for leave. She cleaned her room and the galley from top to bottom, collected slush from the barrels, shined pots and pans did her laundry, and then when the warm autumn sun beckoned, she went ashore to shop and amuse herself. When she returned, Henry Bologne handed her a note from Captain St. Clare. Lauren's heart jumped. At last, he had contacted her. He requested her presence at the 'Red Lion Tavern' at sunset for an urgent meeting.

For Henry's benefit, she showed no emotion, but he spied her racing down the companionway to her room. She pulled off clothes and stepped into a hipbath, lathering and rinsing her skin and hair. She put on a clean shift, laced her stays tightly, and chose a gown the color of amber to match her eyes. She piled her hair on top her head and looked at herself in the mirror. A little voice reminded her St. Clare was a married man, and she muttered to the mirror, "I don't care!"

Lauren placed a wide-brimmed, straw hat over her cap, tied the cream-colored ribbons under her chin and started down to the 'Red Lion'. When she arrived, the tavern was filled with men, smoking and drinking and talking loudly. It was dark in the establishment, the wood floors and paneling absorbing every bit of light. Lauren was hesitant to enter the tavern without an escort and looked in the door, biting her lip. Finally, she stepped over the threshold, waiting for her eyes to adjust.

"Are you looking for Captain St. Clare?" a woman called to her. It was the female innkeeper Lauren had seen a year ago. The woman leaned over the bar, her face drawn and tired with a new baby on her hip. She was trying to retain her good humor in spite of the drunken customers seeking her attention.

"Yes," replied Lauren.

"The Captain sends his regrets," she shouted over the din. "He can't join you tonight."

The blood rushed to Lauren's face, and she clenched her fists.

"I'm sorry, Miss," the innkeeper said turning back to her work.

Lauren stepped out of the inn grinding her teeth. The sign of an angry red lion swung over her head mirroring her own expression. In a fury, she pulled off her straw hat and stomped on it. It was only an hour ago St. Clare had demanded her presence, now he had other plans. It was unthinkable. "How could I have ever been so stupid," she muttered tossing her head. "I am nothing more than a business associate to him."

Furious and hurt, Lauren traversed the streets of Albany, returning to the fluyt. The sun had dropped low in the sky and already the streets were teeming with raucous workmen and prostitutes. On several occasions, Lauren had to break free from the clutches of an amorous sailor, hurling curses at him like a fishwife.

Finally reaching the fluyt, she stepped onto the deck pulling her cap off and yanking the pins from her hair, her tresses tumbling down. She marched toward her room.

"Why are you retiring so soon?" someone said.

Lauren whirled around. In the dimmest of light, she could see James St. Clare, smoking his tobacco.

"I thought--" she uttered.

"You thought you would go to bed after Henry and I went to all this trouble?"

St. Clare casually pulled a flake of tobacco from his tongue, then stepped back revealing a table set for two on the deck. A small seaman's lantern sat in the center illuminating the seating area, leaving the rest of the vessel enveloped in darkness. She heard Mathias playing his fiddle from the stern of the ship.

"I wanted to thank you for a job well done at Fort Frederic," he said.

"I-I don't understand," she stammered. "Why weren't you at the tavern?"

"I was here onboard, getting your supper ready. The rendezvous at the 'Lion' was only a ruse to lure you away from the fluyt temporarily."

She searched St. Clare's eyes for answers. Only moments ago, she had vowed never to trust this man again, but now this gesture of gratitude warmed her heart. She walked to the table, running her fingers over the white tablecloth, her anger melting away.

"You must be hungry. Please sit down," he suggested. St. Clare was wearing clothes he ordinarily reserved for evenings with the Dutch gentry of the Hudson River Valley. He wore a fine white linen shirt and cravat with an indigo blue vest, dark britches and his best boots.

Lauren swallowed hard, trying to absorb everything, and sat down sweeping her gown under the table. She scanned the place setting for two with sparkling wine goblets and then looked up at the sky. The moist night air was blurring the stars slightly and across the harbor, candles winked in the windows of Albany. She could hear the waves gently slapping the hull of the fluyt, and when she looked across the table, St. Clare was studying her face. He opened his mouth to say something but suddenly changed his mind.

Instead, he looked out at the city lights and said, "I have been on business in Albany recently. This is why I asked you here tonight."

Any illusion of romance vanished the minute St Clare brought up Albany and business. She remembered his wife. She pursed her lips and snapped her napkin open. "I see. What is it you wish to discuss?"

"Well, our attempt at a contact in New France failed," he said.

Lauren was about to say something, but before she could speak, James held his hand up to silence her. "But without you I never would have known that it was Gautier who was trying to kill me.

She frowned and shifted in her chair, wishing he had allowed her to go to her cabin instead dine her in the moonlight. Luckily, Henry Bologne broke the tension, rolling up with a tray of food, wearing his best smock and a gold earring in one ear. He avoided eye contact, handing them each a plate of food and bowing deeply. He had instructions to be on his best behavior tonight.

"You deceived me earlier today with that note, Mr. Bologne," Lauren said with a smirk.

"That I did, Ma'am," he said, a smile flickering on his lips. He continued to look down arranging serving pieces. "But I had to get you off the vessel so we could prepare everything here."

"I see," she said raising her eyebrows. "We shall discuss it later."

"As you wish, Madame," he replied, with a wink, then left.

The smell of supper reached Lauren, and she realized that she was ravenous. Everything looked delicious; there were chops in wine sauce, buttered carrots, pickled beets and sally lunn bread.

Begrudgingly she said, "It has been a long time since anyone has cooked for me. Thank you.'

St. Clare shrugged and poured Lauren a glass of wine.

"Most of it was Bologne. You know he thinks the world of you. He missed you when you were in New France--we all missed you." Lauren looked up as he said, "Some of us were in a closer proximity than others."

"Yes," she smiled. "Some were in the neighborhood chapel."

They both laughed, easing some of the awkwardness. The food was delectable, and when Lauren was finished she sat back and sighed.

The fluyt rolled lightly and a breeze blew her hair. "So what was the business you wished to discuss?" she asked.

James wiped his mouth and said, "We had a bargain, you and I. You would identify a contact for me in New France and I would give you land. Even though you were unsuccessful, I believe you have done me a much greater service."

"How so?"

"You saved my life."

"Oh," she chuckled, shaking her head.

"You saved mine," she returned.

"You are to receive payment. There will be no more discussion. The papers have been drawn up for your land."

Lauren sat back in her chair, thunderstruck.

St. Clare said, "If you want to make the Hudson your home, it is yours. "

Tears filled Lauren's eyes. All her life she had searched for a place to belong and at last she had found a home.

Seeing her struggle to maintain her composure, James looked away.

Wiping her eyes, Lauren sat up straight and whispered, "Of course this will be my home." Maybe it was her imagination, but Lauren thought she saw relief pass over his face. "But what of Heathstone?" she asked. "What if he should find me? The land would be his to take."

James shook his head. "My dear Lauren, you are a landowner in the outermost reaches of the English Colonies. Do not give that man a second thought."

He stood up, lighting two torches then went aft. When he returned, Mathias was playing dance music.

"Come now," he demanded holding his hands out. "Tonight is a celebration and you have never danced with me. It is time."

"No, James really," Lauren protested putting up her hands. "I couldn't. I am not in the mood."

"Nonsense," he said. "You have danced with everyone on, *The Pride of the King* except the Captain. You owe this to me."

She smiled and reluctantly stood up. He took her hands and they started to dance. They twirled and parted, linked arms and swung around in circles. At first, Lauren's dancing was stilted and restrained, but St. Clare took charge of her every movement and gradually she lost her inhibitions. Each time he brushed near her, she felt a shiver run up her spine. His breath on her shoulders felt delicious, and she felt her face grow warm under his gaze. Never in all the years she had been on Duke Street had a dance partner taken her breath away like this man.

Mathias finished his tune but struck up another immediately, and they danced again but this time more intimately. James drew Lauren closer, pressing his body against hers more firmly. They danced around the deck and each time Lauren was near James he would pull her firmly to his chest looking down into her face as if he was about to kiss her.

This time when the music stopped, he did not let go of her. He pulled her close and kissed her, running his hands up and down her back and over her arms.

"I can't breathe," she gasped.

"Tell me to release you and I will," he murmured, burying his face in her hair. Lauren's legs felt weak. His hands held her upright as his kisses grew more urgent. He bent her head back and ran his lips down her neck lingering where her breasts met her gown. His firm thighs pressed against her legs.

"Did you love Gautier," he asked. "I must know."

"No, James. I never loved him. How could I?"

He stopped and looked into her eyes, then scooped her into his arms carrying her to his cabin.

After a while, the music stopped, and old Mathias went to bed. The torches burned low, and Henry Bologne rolled out on his platform to clear away the dishes. He pulled himself up and snuffed the torches, then turned to look at the shoreline. He remembered a girl he had known a long time ago in Albany and wondered if she ever thought of him. She had kissed him on an autumn night like this one. He chuckled and shrugged his shoulders, jumping back down onto his platform. He glanced at the Captain's cabin and smiled, congratulating himself on a job well done.

Chapter 38

Lauren wound through the streets of Albany the next day, a basket on her hip, shopping for fresh meat and produce and pretending as if nothing had changed. She could see from shore the crew of the fluyt hanging on the side of the hull, making repairs and attending to their duties. It was the same as every other morning, but in Lauren's world everything was different.

She reached up and touched her face. It was hot and sore, burning from James' kisses. Although clean shaven, he had run his lips and whiskers over her so many times he had chaffed her skin. They were up before sunrise, dressing without words, but before he stepped out the cabin door, he pulled Lauren into his arms telling her to come back to him that night.

When she climbed back on board *The Pride of the King* that afternoon he caught her eye, holding her gaze only for a moment before returning to his work. When he looked at her it warmed her as if she were standing in the summer sun after a long winter.

He remained aloof and detached, in keeping with his role as master of a merchant vessel, but he did acknowledge Lauren with small gestures. He would give her the faintest of smiles at mealtime assign her with duties on deck to be near him or grab her wrist for a moment as she passed by. She delighted in these quiet acts of affection, and they sustained her until the evening when they could be alone. She knew she had moments with him that no one else would ever share, and those intimacies were gifts which set them apart from every other soul on earth.

"Mr. Bologne," said the Captain as they finished their duties one evening. "I would like a moment of privacy." He nodded toward the stern of the fluyt where Lauren was standing. Immediately Henry stationed himself as a buffer between the crew and the Captain as he walked toward Lauren.

"You are watching the sunset?" he said leaning on rail beside her.

"James, the crew will see us," Lauren warned looking behind her.

"No one will see us. Henry is standing guard, but we must talk about this, Lauren.

The two had been meeting every night for weeks, but the secrecy was putting a strain on them.

"Even though our relationship is of no surprise to the crew, you and I have agreed not to flaunt it in front of them. We are to remain in our roles as members of *The Pride of the King* by day, but by night we must break away and be ourselves. When we have free time we cannot deny our need for intimacy. I would like to take you ashore tonight. There can be no hiding that from the ship's company."

"It will be awkward."

"Yes, at first but Lauren, I am the supreme authority on this vessel. The crew must accept my choices."

She cocked her head. "Does that go for me too?"

"Yes," he replied softly, looking at her face as if he were memorizing it. "Now get your hat or cloak or whatever it is you women wear in the night air. We are going for a walk."

James took Lauren on shore, and they followed a path along the river. It was one of the last warm nights before the autumn turned cool and the trees skeletal. The leaves seemed to capture the low light of sunset, making the colors more brilliant than ever. The couple did not speak until they reached a clearing where James told Lauren they would build a fire.

Bonfires dotted the shoreline up and down the Hudson; occasionally a voice could be heard across the water or a dog barking in the distance. Their fire reached to the sky, sparks soaring into the night. James sat down on the ground, his arms resting on his knees and pulled Lauren next to him.

"We used to build fires even bigger than this when I was young," he said. "The boys and I would wrestle and dance around them like goblins."

Lauren looked at him as he watched the light, the flames reflecting in his eyes. "I wonder what happened to them all?" he mused. "I wonder if they still live."

"They were without homes too?" she asked.

He nodded. "I still see their faces on the street to this day. Once you have lived on the street you see them everywhere."

"Yes, they are everywhere," Lauren agreed. "In doorways, behind necessaries, hiding in cemeteries." She felt his eyes on her. For some reason she felt he had already known these things.

"You have a sister, do you not?" he asked.

"I do. She is my twin, but we do not resemble each other."

"Do you miss her?"

Lauren took a deep breath and shook her head. "No, if Simone were to see me today, she would think me coarse and depraved. She has taken vows with the Ursalines and is living a life of seclusion and safety in a convent in New Orleans."

The fire snapped and popped, filling the silence as they stared at the golden light. In spite of the flames, the air felt damp rolling off the river, and Lauren crossed her arms.

"We weigh anchor day after tomorrow," James announced.

"Where are we going?"

"We shall resume our normal route on the Hudson, but we will be sailing past your land."

"We are?" she gasped sitting up straight.

James grinned, and touched her cheek. "Does that make you happy?"

Lauren's face was beaming. "That makes me very happy!"

"We shall walk it together tomorrow," he said.

*   *   *

Preparations for departure started the next morning, but Lauren noticed Isaac was absent. She had not seen him for a long time, and it was highly unusual for the first mate to be gone the day before a departure.

As the evening came to a close, Lauren approached Samuel Claypool, the boatswain. Although the man was blind, he used his keen sense of touch and frequently had Robert at his side to be his eyes, checking rigging and inspecting lines. He coordinated and supervised many duties on the vessel, and Lauren knew he would be the one to ask. "He's been gone for near four days now, Ma'am. The Captain had us searchin' everywhere--taverns, pleasure houses, even the alms house. He's nowhere to be found." Samuel took off his cap and scratched his bald head, his white eyeballs rolling.

"Did he say where he was going, Mr. Claypool?"

"No, Ma'am, he went drinkin' and whorin' with the rest of us that first night, and we lost track of the lad."

Lauren sighed and thanked Samuel. When she spoke with James that evening in his cabin, he could add nothing more. "It will be hard to go without him. I couldn't ask for a better first mate, but I am confident he will turn up by the time we return," James said.

His words were optimistic, but Lauren saw him pour several fingers of brandy and toss it back quickly. As infatuated as Lauren was with James, there was a side to him she could not penetrate. He was guarded and reserved in almost every way.

They spent their first weeks together quelling their passion, but as time passed Lauren longed for more intimacy, an intimacy that can only come with the knowledge of another's heart. They spoke of many things, taking their discoveries as far as they were able, but there was an emotional reluctance in James she could not breach. He seemed unable to give of himself fully, always holding something back. She sensed an undercurrent of mystery in the man which she thought may stem from his untamed youth, but there was another possibility which she did not want to admit. It was the possibility that James still loved his wife.

The Pride of the King weighed anchor the next day in a rain shower. Clouds rolled overhead all day, drenching the crew, and then the sun would break through long enough for another shower to gather. Lauren stayed below most of time taking inventory with Henry and organizing food in the hold and in the galley. Once again there were large crates of firearms to work around, but Lauren knew it would only be a short duration before the cargo was gone. The *"Pride"* never carried weapons or powder too long in case a customs inspector boarded her.

Midday Ben Groot called down the companionway for Lauren. She was to see the Captain. She brushed her hands on her apron, lifted her skirts and climbed up on deck. It had stopped raining, but the sky was still cloudy and the deck wet. St. Clare was at the helm. He lifted his chin in the direction of the shore and said, "Stand by. We are almost there."

Lauren looked starboard at the thick mass of trees on a point, then jumped off the poop deck, picked up her skirts and ran to the bow of the fluyt. Leaning forward, she held onto the rigging and waited. She could hear the rush of water as the fluyt sliced through the river. The sails snapped smartly in the wind, and the

Pride groaned as she rounded the bend. Suddenly, the sun broke through the clouds illuminating a brilliantly colored riverbank running steeply upward into a cliff.

"There she is!" James shouted.

As Lauren's eyes traveled up the slope her lips parted and she gasped. Several of the crewmembers stopped their work hypnotized by the sun splashing the riverbank thick with yellow, red and orange leaves.

"For the love of God," one of them uttered looking at the sight.

In summer the bluff would have been majestic, but in autumn the cliffs were breathtaking. The entire precipice was a wall of colors from the maple, birch and sumac. The jagged rocks interrupted the leaves with their sharp protrusions and a small water fall tumbled and trickled off the bluff. Shadows from the fast-moving clouds sailed across the treetops like a cutter in a tempest.

She did not hear James call to the crew to drop anchor. Lauren heard nothing. She was completely mesmerized. It wasn't until Robert told her the Captain was ready to take her to shore that she realized the fluyt was at a standstill. St. Clare rowed the two of them to shore and hopped out, reaching for Lauren's hand. Holding her skirts high, she jumped from the boat onto shore and they started up the bluff on a deer path. The ground was wet and greasy from the rain, and Lauren's hem was soaked, but she didn't notice. She was far too enthusiastic about seeing her land.

The terrain was steep and on several occasions James had to pull Lauren up, but they made it to the top stopping by the waterfall. "This is your water source," he explained. "There is a stream that runs through your property."

They walked along the bluff until they found a clearing which gave them an unobstructed view of the Hudson and the fluyt waiting below.

"I had no idea it was going to be like this," said Lauren.

"True, it is remote," St. Clare admitted.

"I am not talking about that," said Lauren. "It is by far the most beautiful place I have ever seen."

James was obviously pleased. "Down that way is Edith Quill's place. She runs *The Boar's Head*. It's the only tavern around here. She is a tough old bird but loveable."

"So there is a road nearby?"

"Yes, it sits back from the bluff, running from Newbury to Hampsted. We could get supplies in for you that way or build you a quay on the river."

Lauren gasped. It was daunting to think of hauling supplies up that bluff.

"When we get back I would like to see the deed for my land," she said.

"We will have to get from the Benchs."

Lauren's eyes opened wide with surprise, and James chuckled.

"It is in Cornelius' name. They do this for most of my properties. I pay them for their trouble. This way they appear wealthy and I remain anonymous."

The sound of thunder rolled through the valley. The clouds were forming quickly, and James took Lauren's arm. "Come we must hurry. It is dangerous up here."

He stopped before they started down and said, "We will discuss your deed shortly with Heloise because our next stop is at the Van den Berg manor to see the Bench's.

Chapter 39

"I have instructed Heloise to have a dressmaker to the house. Of course you will look like a pauper to them," James announced before leaving the cabin the next morning. "I will drop you off and return in one week."

Lauren was beside herself with excitement. A coach was waiting for her at the landing, and it took her on the post road to the Van den Berg Manor. The house overlooked the river and reminded Lauren of the homes of Kaskaskia, but on a much grander scale. It was a two story stone residence with access to the main level by two stairways in the front of the house. A *galerie* wrapped around the home just like the residences of the Illinois country and several outbuildings dotted the landscape, including a tavern farther down the post road.

Several hounds met the coach broadcasting the arrival of Lauren to the inhabitants of the manor. A black servant stepped out of the house opening the door of the coach and pulling down the steps. It amused Lauren to see grand manners and gestures once more. It was reminiscent of Duke Street, and she knew that only an estate of this magnitude would suit Heloise and Cornelius.

The servant escorted Lauren up the wooden staircase and through the front door. She reached up to pull the pins from her straw hat and looked around. The front door opened onto a long hall, with rooms lining either side of the foyer and a grand staircase leading to the second floor. The wood floor was polished to a high shine and several small end tables lined the walls with mirrors and fresh flowers.

Lauren untied the ribbons under her chin and was removing her hat as Cornelius came around the corner. "My God, Darling! What has happened to you!" he exclaimed, arms outstretched as he approached her.

"Lovely to see you too, Corny," Lauren laughed, kissing him on both cheeks.

He stepped back holding her hands out, looking her up and down. "Oh don't mind me. Aside from your sunburned skin, you look adorable," and he turned her around. "How I've missed you!"

Corny had changed little; aside from some extra weight, he remained the same lovable dandy. He was attired in the latest fashion, his suit was of the finest silk, and Lauren noted his shoes were of fine leather.

"You look prosperous, Cornelius," Lauren observed.

"Well we *have* earned our money. Mother will tell you more."

"Where is she?" asked Lauren.

"In the sitting room, heaven forbid she gets up from her chair to greet you," complained Corny.

"I will take your things upstairs, Miss," said the servant. "Madame Bench will see you now."

"What did I tell you?" Corny said, hooking arms with Lauren. "She has granted us an audience."

When Lauren entered the sitting room, the first thing she saw was Heloise sitting in an armchair, a table pulled up over her lap, sipping tea and eating toast. Lauren smiled. Nothing had changed.

"Well, well, if it isn't the darling of Duke Street," declared Heloise. "Come over here child and give me a kiss." Lauren obliged, pulling a chair over to sit near the matron.

Heloise reached out and stroked Lauren's hair, looking into her eyes. "You are my little darling," she said gently. "There," the woman said, withdrawing her hand. "That's enough of that. I had to do that for Corny's benefit. He believes I am cold as ice."

Corny did not comment. He was inspecting a blemish in the mirror.

Lauren looked around the sitting room. It was small but meticulously decorated. There was blue painted wainscoting on the walls and around the fireplace, new oak furniture, and many volumes of books on shelves alongside elegant, porcelain figurines. "Who lives here, Heloise?" asked Lauren.

"The Van den Bergs, they're a merchant family from New York City. He inherited this tract of land some years ago. They have ten children, all grown now."

"Where are they?"

"Heralding the arrival of their eighteenth grandchild in the city. They were devastated they could not be here during our visit, but graciously offered their home to Corny and I."

"You aren't considering moving here, are you? Surely the population is too small for you to establish yourselves," Lauren observed.

Corny walked over and slumped into a chair. "Oh dear me, no, we tarry not."

"We are here for you, dear," Heloise explained. "We are signing off on the deed to your land. James summoned me some months ago. We hide numerous pieces of property for him in our names. Everyone benefits. Appearing to be landholders adds credibility to Corny and I when we sweep into a new city, and James' assets remain undercover."

"Captain St. Clare has turned his liability of being without a name into an asset," chuckled Cornelius.

"But mind you, the Van den Bergs know nothing of The Pride of the King. They are customers of James, not confidants," cautioned Heloise.

She ran her eyes over Lauren and said, "The dressmaker is coming this afternoon."

"The poor child needs help, Mother," added Corny.

Lauren stood up and walked over to look at the porcelain figurines.

"Where did you go after Duke Street?" she asked.

"Oh dear Lord, where didn't we go," Heloise replied.

"Boston was a disaster," commented Cornelius."

He turned to Heloise and asked, "Mother is it too early in the day for a drink?"

Lauren smiled, same old Corny.

"We finally settled on Newport," Heloise said, ignoring him. "Boston was far too prudish. Corny didn't fit among all those Puritans."

Corny started to laugh, looking at his nails.

"We made several good contacts there, and it seems Corny has stepped into your position as bait."

Lauren looked at him with surprise. He lifted his eyebrows and cocked his head coquettishly.

"He is quite talented," Heloise continued. "In his avant guard way. And what about you, my dear?" said Heloise. "I see you have recovered from your hatred of--Leopold Fitch or dare I say his true name, Captain St. Clare."

Corny looked up at Lauren. Lauren smiled and shrugged.

"Oh, secretive are we?" said Heloise.

"We have days and ways to get information out of her, Mother," Corny said.

* * *

It pleased Lauren beyond measure to be back with her old friends. They had several days to catch up, and then Heloise had to get down to business and mix with the local patrons. By week's end they were back to afternoon teas and evening fetes.

"These people are small customers, darling," she whispered one night at a supper given by neighboring gentry. "I wish James would make up his mind where we can be of most use. This damned war is upsetting everything. As you know he even talks of going back out to sea."

Lauren looked at Heloise. "What?"

Heloise eyes grew large and she turned quickly to the guest next to her.

That night, in the coach on the way back to the manor, Lauren said, "Heloise, what was that you said at supper tonight about James going to sea?"

Even though the coach was dark, Lauren could see Cornelius turn and look out the window, fearing a confrontation.

"Just that," said Heloise curtly. "He mentioned that he may have to seek new ventures away from this part of the world."

"Why?" snapped Lauren.

"Because--," fumbled Heloise. "Well, because of failures in other arenas."

Lauren's heart jumped. "What arena would that be, New France?"

"I will not discuss it further. He will have to tell you more himself."

"Oh yes!" cried Lauren. "He can tell me during one of those frequent heart-to-heart conversations we have!"

The coach was silent for a long time. All that could be heard was the beating of the horse's hooves and the crunch of the wheels. Lauren stared out the window at the dark landscape, sick at heart. Heloise and Cornelius sat back in their blankets, tense and tight-lipped.

At last, Heloise shifted in her seat, fumbling for her tinder box and rolled tobacco. "Help me with this, Corny," she demanded. After Corny helped his mother light her tobacco, Heloise took a puff, blew out the smoke and said, "I have known James since he was a very young man. You must understand, he too has an encumbrance, just like Isaac, Samuel Claypool and Henry Bologne. The difference is James bears his limitations on the inside."

Lauren continued to look out the window, the carriage jostling her gently.

"I know he does not always talk with you. Experiencing human emotion is very difficult for him. In his quest for survival as a child he was so preoccupied with food and safety he never had a chance to be close to anyone. You and I have had years to understand ourselves and our feelings. He is just beginning. It does not surprise me that he has not told you about going to out to sea. There are many things he holds in secret. Few know his plans. Aside from me there is only one other person in the world who really knows what comes next."

Heloise leaned forward and patted her hand, "You have chosen a very difficult man my dear, but he is ever so worthy."

"That other person who knows everything about him," Lauren said between her teeth. "Would that be his wife? Does *she* know everything about him or does he keep secrets from her too? Am I one of those secrets?"

Heloise sighed, and sat back in her seat and resumed smoking in silence.

*   *   *

The next day when Lauren came down to breakfast a servant told her that the Benchs were taking refreshment on the lawn with a gentleman who had called that morning. Lauren went to the window and saw Cornelius and Heloise lounging on chairs in the sun. They were sipping tea with a tray of sweetbreads on a table between them. No gentleman was around.

Lauren looked in the entry mirror to adjust her hair, picked up her skirts and started out onto the lawn. It was a long, manicured expanse which ran to the river bank. Since the estate was elevated well above the river a view of the water was impossible, but nevertheless the vista was sweeping and exceptional. There was a barn, stable and small mill made of stone not far from the main house and several peacocks strolled leisurely out on the front lawn They scattered when Lauren swept by, headed for Heloise and Cornelius.

"Good morning Dear," said Heloise. "How did you sleep?"

"Not well," Lauren said, stuffing some bread into her mouth without sitting down.

Cornelius chimed in, "Now darling. It is a brand new day. The sun is delightful. Let's not speak of anything unpleasant today. You know how I adore that sassy, 'Nobody is going to walk all over me' pout of yours but perhaps another day. How about--"

"Who is that over there?" interrupted Lauren.

Cornelius exchanged a look with Heloise.

"Is that St. Clare?"

"Now Lauren," warned Heloise.

"Oh look," said Lauren in a voice heavy with sarcasm. "He is coming this way."

St. Clare walked up the lawn, leading a chestnut-colored mare. He had been riding and perspiration soaked his shirt to his skin.

His smile dropped when Lauren burned a look into him, but he ignored it and said to the Benchs, "I have been thinking about buying this mare. Just look at her. She is over fourteen hands, simply amazing." The mare tossed her head and pranced around nervously. "She's a beauty? Isn't she?" he continued. "But she is a hard ride. She needs a little taming."

Cornelius started to laugh, and then covered his indiscretion with a cough.

Heloise looked at Corny and pursed her lips. Turning to James she asked, "James, what on earth do you need a horse for?"

"You're right of course, old girl, but it's fun to dream," replied St. Clare. "I better take her back to the stable now. I just wanted you to see her."

Holding the reigns, he started for the stable, and said casually over his shoulder, "Lauren, would you walk with me, please?"

Avoiding his eyes, Lauren accompanied James to the stable.

"I am happy to see you, Lauren but it is obvious you are not happy to see me. Now what is the problem?"

"When were you going to tell me you were putting out to sea?"

"When I knew that it was certain. Not before. Heloise must have told you."

"Yes." Lauren stopped and looked at him. "Why don't you include me in your plans?" she asked.

"Because, what goes on in every facet of The Pride of the King does not concern you."

"Alright," said Lauren putting her hands up. "I agree. I do not have to know all the details, but when something concerns *you* I want to know. Am I not a part of your life?"

He stepped forward and pulled her into his arms. "The biggest part," he said touching her cheek.

"Then talk to me. I want to know who you are. There seems to be a whole side of you I don't know."

He let go of her and they started walking again, James holding the reins and the mare trailing behind them. "I am not like you," St. Clare said. "Words bubble freely to your lips. It comes easy for you."

He stopped as if he would tell her something, and then changed his mind. He gave the mare to a stable boy, and they walked out onto a stone bridge by the mill.

"The first time I saw you at Heloise's dinner party on Duke Street I was mesmerized," he explained. "You were quick witted and outgoing with that disarming smile of a pirate. I was completely enchanted with you. You were fast to anger and fast to laugh, with a joy for living I wanted to capture for my own. You are everything I am not, Lauren. Soon I will tell you more. But for now I must ask you to wait--"

"Wait for what?" Lauren said, her eyes flashing. "For you to tire of me and return to your wife? I won't do it James. It's different with you. I can have business liaisons with others but I cannot--I cannot be *your* whore."

St. Clare ran his hand through his hair exasperated. "You just don't understand."

Lauren searched his eyes but found no answers. The wind blew her skirt and leaves skittered out onto the water, swept away by the current.

He is right. I do not understand. She blinked suddenly as if waking from a dream. She realized at that moment that she had been deluding herself all along. She had rushed head long into his arms without thinking, impulsive as always, just as she had with Rene' Lupone and that insipid tutor on Duke Street, even Julien Gautier.

"Gabriel told me once I was restless," she said.

"Gabriel?" asked James.

"It was a day like today," she mused. "But the wind was icy then."

Lauren brought her eyes back to St. Clare's face and said, "I *am* restless. He was right. I am restless and I will not wait for you, James. One day I will leave you, and that is something *you* do not understand."

*   *   *

Lauren heard someone calling her name. She rolled over and propped herself up in bed squinting from the light which was being held in her face. The maid hovered over the bed, holding a candle.

"Please, Miss, you are wanted in the sitting room right away."

The servant girl stepped back, letting the bed curtains fall. Lauren sat up, rubbed her eyes and slid out from the bed as the maid lit more candles. She handed Lauren a dressing gown and left the room.

She took a deep breath, ran her fingers through her hair and started down the stairs holding a candle. She grabbed the railing to steady herself. It was late; the house was dark and she could hear the sound of voices in the sitting room. When Lauren walked through the door, she saw Heloise sitting on the edge of a chair, a candle next to her on a stand. It illuminated her rumpled dressing gown and night cap. Her eyes were like saucers.

St. Clare stepped up from the shadows, his expression like stone. He was dressed in a cloak and he was holding a tricorn hat in his hand. "Lauren, I have news." He paused a moment, looked down at the floor then up into her eyes. "Isaac Burroughs is dead."

Lauren stared at him and her jaw dropped.

James swallowed hard and continued, "He turned up in Kingston two nights ago at a tavern. The customers didn't like the way he looked, so without giving it a second thought, they dragged him in back and beat him to death."

Chapter 40

Lauren spent hours in the garden at the Van den Berg manor watching leaves scatter in the autumn wind. Thin and dry as parchment, they tumbled over her feet or flew up into the cold, grey sky. Sometimes a maelstrom would sweep them up, sending them sailing in circles until the wind died down, and they dropped listlessly to the brown earth.

Not until Isaac was gone, did Lauren realize that she was part of a family, an unorthodox mix of souls struggling to survive in a world that utterly loathed them. Until now, she had held herself apart from the crew, not wanting to admit she was part of the group, but now with Isaac's death, Lauren realized their struggle and was proud to be among them.

Along with this realization came the intense shame of betrayal. Lauren believed she had betrayed everyone and contributed to Isaac's death, reproaching herself severely. She believed her romantic involvement with St. Clare drove Isaac away from *The Pride of the King* and if she had been more sensitive, she would have realized her relationship with the Captain was detrimental to the young man. Eager to gratify her own desires, she felt she had plunged headlong into the liaison, succumbing to her impulsive nature once more.

James' reaction to the tragedy was even more severe. He drew into himself, refusing to speak of the matter to anyone, throwing himself feverishly into work all day and solitude all night. He was aloof to Lauren, and she in turn avoided him. Their last conversation had been on the bridge by the mill, and it had ended in a silence that endured. Heloise noted the couple's separation and remained detached, encouraging Cornelius to do the same.

The morale of the crew also worried St. Clare. The night they had learned of Isaac's death, George Blasco and another sailor, Demetrius Miskowic disappeared. Everyone knew the men traveled to Kingston to find those responsible for Isaac's beating and as anticipated, it ended badly. The authorities contacted Captain St. Clare several days later looking for the two, reporting that they had assaulted three men in Kingston and murdered another. St. Clare told them he knew nothing. Blasco and Miskowic never returned to the fluyt, and Lauren suspected they were hiding north of Albany in the *Melungion* community.

The situation remained static for weeks until Heloise received word one day that the Van den Bergs were returning home before the snows of late autumn. Suddenly, they must prepare for either social contact with the Van den Bergs or departure. They chose departure.

Before Lauren could make any plans, St. Clare called a meeting at the tavern near the manor. Although the main room of the public house was quiet, St. Clare asked for a room at the back for complete privacy. When Lauren walked into the tavern she recognized several farmers indentured to the Van den Berg estates playing cards near a window. They nodded respectfully to her as she passed, and two seamen talked quietly by the hearth. The room at the back was a makeshift dining room, consisting of a table and chairs in a dark storage area filled with casks of wine and beer as well as hams dangling from the ceiling.

"Good evening, Lauren," St. Clare said standing up and offering her a chair. Corny bent over Lauren's hand briefly and sat back down. Heloise tight-lipped and sober faced was silent, smoke from her cigarette curling around her head. St. Clare offered Lauren something to drink, but she declined.

"I will come right to the point," he said sitting down. "There is no time to lose. We must depart tonight. The actions of Blasco and Miskowic have drawn attention to *The Pride of the King* and we must embark before a discovery is made."

"They are asking questions?" said Cornelius.

"Many questions. Today the officials requested our log. They are very suspicious, especially now during the conflict with the French. We must make haste."

St. Clare rubbed his forehead then said, "Everything has changed so quickly since Isaac's death. Tomorrow we sail for Pennsylvania, where I will inquire about a man I have in mind for first mate. He is a Prussian, with whom I sailed many years ago. He is a trusted and loyal friend. They transported him here for acts of piracy, and I believe I can buy his servitude."

At any rate--" and he turned to Heloise, "You and Cornelius will accompany the '*Pride*' up to Providence. I have a mark for you there and possibly some lucrative ventures. You will remain at that city until further notice. The crew and I will put out to sea."

James looked at Lauren. She sat erect in her chair, her face like stone, ready for an assignment. "Lauren--" he started.

"I know I cannot go to sea. I understand this," she interrupted. "But why am I not going to Providence?"

"There are many reasons," he said shaking his head. "I have made arrangements for you to stay on the Hudson and work at the 'Boar's Head' with Mrs. Quill."

Lauren gasped, "So, I am being put out to pasture!"

Not wanting to lose his temper, St. Clare said through his teeth, "It is the inn I spoke of a while ago near your land. The woman is getting on in years and is in need of another hand. You can live there until your cottage is built."

"Oh, I see," said Lauren nodding her head. "You have made arrangements for my cottage as well? So I am to be the new mistress. What is it you English say? Oh, yes, now I remember, 'A woman in every port.' "

James slammed his hand down on the table. "I will not tolerate insubordination! You are still a member of The Pride of the King, and if I say you stay in the valley, you will stay in the valley!"

There was a long silence while Heloise and Cornelius held their breath. Lauren did not flinch. She continued to look into St. Clare's eyes, her chin held high. Suddenly she stood up and swept from the room, slamming the door behind her.

*   *   *

"What would you have him do, darling?" said Cornelius that evening in his dressing room. Lauren paced back and forth her fists clenched and her eyes red. He lifted a powdered wig off his head and placed it carefully on a wig stand. "You would be furious with him if he used you to lure men in Providence," he said. "And he cannot risk taking you to sea. Now admit it. He has no choice but to have you stay here."

Lauren stopped pacing and said impatiently. "But it seems as if I am being left behind just to wait for him."

"You are angry that you cannot go with him," said Corny.

Lauren sighed and slumped down on the divan her lips in a pout. "You are right."

Corny began remove his makeup. He sat at a dressing table in front of an ornate gold mirror. Bottles and hairbrushes littered the tabletop.

"I don't want him to leave, Corny. It scares me."

Corny turned and looked at her. "You must realize this is the life he leads."

Suddenly she sat up. "I must apologize to him."

"What, now?"

Picking up her wrap, Lauren rushed to the door. "Do you know where he is? Is he down on the '*Pride*'?"

Corny opened his mouth then stuttered, "I--I don't know. I mean he had a meeting somewhere else. I think."

Lauren stopped in her tracks, her hand on the door latch. "Who is he meeting?"

"I--I don't know."

Her eyes narrowed. "Don't lie to me!" she snapped.

Cornelius blanched.

"His wife? Is that who he is meeting?"

"No, no!" he cried rushing over to her and taking her hands. "Not his wife. Good gracious, no. Do not go bursting in there. It is a private affair. Come sit with me, darling. We'll have a brandy." Corny leaned out into the hall and called loudly, "Mother! Come here!"

Lauren yanked her hands away, "Where is the meeting?"

"Dearest, I beg of you sit down."

"Tell me!"

Corny was mute.

*   *   *

The ground felt hard under Lauren's feet as she marched down the road toward the tavern. Flakes of snow whirled around her lantern. The flakes dusted the brittle vegetation and frozen earth along the path. Her heart was pounding. At last she would see the woman who so captivated St. Clare's heart. For months she had agonized over her rival; contemplating her beauty, her disposition, her station in life. She suspected the woman had money and was responsible for funding The Pride of the King, but it was all guesswork. St. Clare had given so few clues and guarded her identity so jealously, that she knew little. She believed that he protected his wife from the philistines of The Pride of the King as if she were some precious porcelain figurine too fragile and valuable to share.

Even though the hour was late, there was a light flickering in the tavern. It was obvious the innkeeper still had guests in the main room and had not yet banked the fire and gone to bed. The wind blew strong and Lauren pulled up her hood. Two horses waited under the tavern sign as she stepped onto the threshold putting her lantern on a bench by the entrance. As she lifted the latch of the door, a burst of wind pushed her into the main room abruptly.

The first thing she saw was St. Clare seated by the fire. Because of her hood, he had not recognized her and he returned to his conversation.

"How can I be of service, Madam?" inquired the innkeeper behind the bar.

Lauren said nothing, hanging her cloak on a peg. The tavern was empty except for St. Clare sitting by the fire with another person, a high backed chair concealing his companion's face. James was leaning forward resting his forearms on his knees, engaged in conversation. The innkeeper loaded a tray with steaming bowls of soup, a loaf of bread and a bottle of wine.

Lauren ran her fingers through her hair briefly then stepped forward, smiling sweetly. "Please allow me to take this over. I want to surprise them." Before the innkeeper could protest, Lauren pulled the tray over. It was heavy and she took a deep breath, steadying herself as she started across the dark dining room. The blood rushed in her ears and her heart thumped in her chest so strongly that she thought she would faint. The fire cast long shadows across the room, and flickered on St. Clare's face. He watched his companion intensely.

At last, she reached the couple. Breathless with anxiety, Lauren stepped up to look at St. Clare's wife. The individual in the high-backed chair turned and looked at her. The blood drained from Lauren's face. The tray slid to the floor with a crash.

"What the hell!" James said, jumping to his feet. Lauren took several steps back as Monsieur Heathstone stood up from his chair. She gasped in horror.

The innkeeper rushed over to clean up the tray, and St. Clare barked, "Leave us!"

For what seemed like an eternity, Lauren stared at Heathstone. The only sound was the fire crackling in the room.

James stepped forward and reached for her. "Don't touch me," she warned, her eyes never leaving Heathstone.

Stepping back cautiously, James said, "Adair, you had better leave."

Bowing to Lauren, Adair Heathstone picked up his hat and cloak, and left the tavern. The moment the door closed Lauren turned to James and gasped, "He has found me!"

"No, Lauren. It is not as it seems--"

Consumed with panic, Lauren bolted for the back door.

"No!" exclaimed James, lunging for her. He caught her and yanked her into his arms. "You are safe from him now. You are here with me."

"No! Let go!" she screamed.

Like an animal, she began to kick and tear at him as he tried to restrain her.

"Listen to me, Lauren! Stop this!" he roared.

"Let go! I am his wife. He will take me away! He will take my land!"

"No, Lauren!" With all of his strength, St. Clare pushed her against the wall, pressing his body against her, holding her face and making her look at him. "You are not his wife!"

Still she did not hear him. Lauren kicked his shins and clawed his arms.

"Listen to me. You are not his wife!"

Mad with panic, she continued to struggle furiously, flinging curses at him in French.

"Stop it, now!" James demanded. "You are not his wife!"

Exhausted at last and panting, Lauren blinked, trying to read St. Clare's eyes. At last she listened to him. "What? What did you say?"

"You are not his wife, Lauren. You are *my* wife!"

Chapter 41

Lauren stared at James, trying to comprehend his words. "I am *your* wife. Are you mad?" She tried to wrench free again and James tightened his grip.

"Listen to me. That was *not* Heathstone you married in New Orleans. That was me." Lauren tossed her head trying to clear the hair from her eyes and said, "Well, then you are better at masquerade than I realized."

"You little fool. It was a marriage by *proxy*."

"What?"

"Proxy, stand in. Heathstone was my stand in. Think back Lauren, the ceremony was in English. You did not understand a single word. I approached the Mother Superior asking for the hand of a French orphan girl and by the time you were of age, I was in a British prison. Heathstone went in my place."

Lauren's eyes grew large with astonishment. "Then the marriage is not real?"

"Oh, it is most certainly real and legal. The royals have done marriage by proxy for centuries."

Lauren blinked as if waking from a dream and pushed the hair from her face. James loosened his grip and stepped back.

She pulled at her gown, straightening her bodice and skirt, her eyes never leaving St. Clare's face. "Why?" she asked suspiciously. "Why did you want to marry *me*?"

James did not answer at first, searching for the right words. Finally he said, "I needed someone who could introduce The Pride of the King to New France. I needed someone who knew the language and the way of life, so we could infiltrate the French colony. I could find no one suitable in New England, no one at all, so I contacted the Ursalines to ask for the hand of an orphan girl."

Lauren said nothing. She was too overwhelmed to speak. She thought of all the times she had cried herself to sleep thinking she was married to an old man, how she had fled New France and lived on the streets of New York terrified and hungry and how James had held her in his arms over and over again never admitting the truth about their marriage.

Suddenly the frenzy of betrayal ignited within her. Her eyes narrowed and she said, "All this time you played me for a fool!"

Before he could stop her, she slapped him squarely across the face and said, "I hate you!" and bolted out the door.

* * *

Moments later, Lauren threw open the entrance of the Van den Berg manor with a crash and shouted, "I want to talk to both of you!"

Heloise and Cornelius stood frozen at the top of stairs. They were dressed in traveling clothes, their eyes like saucers. "We must make haste, dear," Heloise said uncertainly to Lauren. "Corny and I are to leave for Providence tonight."

"No one goes anywhere until I get some answers," Lauren ordered, slamming the door behind her. She swept up the stairs and Heloise and Cornelius stepped back as if she was about to strike them.

"How long have you known?" Lauren hissed leaning close to Heloise.

The feather in Heloise's hat quivered nervously. "About what, dear?"

"You know what I am talking about. How long!"

Heloise swallowed hard and stuttered, "Since-well, since before the brothel. We knew long before we met you at Madame Vanoss' establishment."

Lauren gasped. "You knew who I was before you approached me at that whore house?"

"Yes-yes we did. Vanoss had been looking for you for months. The moment she found you, she notified us. We came immediately to interview you to make sure you were the girl from the Ursaline convent."

Lauren studied Heloise's face.

"She--" Lauren struggled to understand. "She worked for the *'Pride'* too?"

"No," said Heloise. "But she has known Captain St. Clare for years."

Lauren turned away, running her hands through her hair. Cornelius stepped up to steady her, easing her down onto a hall chair.

"I hated knowing everything and not telling you, darling," he said. You must believe me. Mother and I could say nothing. We did not like deceiving you."

Heloise nodded. "I advised James repeatedly to explain everything to you, but he chose to remain mute on the subject. He is a most unusual man, my dear."

It seemed to Lauren as if James St. Clare had orchestrated her entire life. Through his people, he had watched her every move and had heard her every word. It seemed as if he had manipulated every facet of her existence. She rubbed her eyes and dragged her hands down her face. She felt utterly weary and overwhelmed. She asked breathlessly, "And what about the ship Heathstone and I sailed on to New England? That too was part of The Pride of the King?"

Heloise nodded again. "That vessel was smuggling lead from the Kaskaskia lead mines, bound for the Hudson to be made into shot and firearms. That is why the crew disappeared when the customs officers boarded the vessel."

Lauren nodded. "Leaving a French girl in New York all alone."

"Captain St. Clare was furious," said Cornelius. "Twice Heathstone let you slip away."

"The first time was during the hurricane," said Heloise. "We thought you were dead, washed away in the fury but several years later you were found again."

"How did you find me on the Mississippi?"

"That was an accident. The Kaskaskia lead mines are known for doing business with everyone, not only the French, but also the Dutch and even the English. The Captain sent Heathstone there to purchase lead for shot."

"Oh, Mon Dieu!" Lauren gasped her heart pounding. "Are the mine owners part of the organization too?"

"Goodness no, my dear. The Pride of the King is far reaching, but it does not go beyond New England. That is why we obtained you as a contact; to infiltrate New France."

Lauren sighed, and slumped back in her chair. The thought of Jean-Baptist and Claude being a part of The Pride of the King was indeed terrifying.

Heloise she sat down by Lauren. "Damn St. Clare," she grumbled. "Leaving me with this unsavory business." She sighed and continued, "He wanted to infiltrate New France. There was simply no one in New England of French background who would be suitable for the position. As you know dear, seldom do our two worlds mix. I happened to think of the Ursalines in New Orleans. They are of course known the world over for turning out girls of exceptional breeding, and since James was unmarried, it seemed the perfect solution. We wrote to the Sisters asking them if they had any young women of age without prospects and they recommended you. Unfortunately, James went to prison a few months later, but as you know his power is far reaching and he managed to direct, The Pride of the King from his confinement. He sent Adair Heathstone to marry you in his place. The plan was to bring you to New York, teach you English, explain everything to you and set you to work as a connection with New France but--" and she paused, "the hurricane changed everything."

"I ended up in Kaskaskia," whispered Lauren.

"Yes, we found you only to lose you again on the streets of New York where Madame Vanoss had been watching for you."

"I cannot believe that creature knew everything," groaned Lauren. "It seems everyone knew I was married to St. Clare, but me."

"No, darling, none of the crew knew," explained Corny. "No one else in 'The Pride of the King' knows your circumstances."

Lauren's tear stained eyes suddenly grew wide again. It occurred to her that the land in the Hudson River Valley had been hers all along because of this marriage. She had gone to Fort Frederick and sold herself to a French aristocrat to buy land that was rightfully hers. "This is indeed the final insult. St. Clare paid me with my own property!" she gasped.

The dogs started to bark as horses thundered up the driveway to the front door. Lauren was too engrossed in her own thoughts to notice Heloise and Cornelius gather their bags, and start down the stairs. She looked up only when Ben Groot burst through the front door as thunder cracked.

"We have no time," he bellowed in his deep bass voice. "Everyone must go!"

James pushed past the giant and took the stairs two at a time up to Lauren. "Get your things. We have locked customs officers in the hold of the fluyt. They found our contraband."

"My God, James!" Heloise called up the stairs. "You have kidnapped customs officers! I fear you have gone too far this time."

James laughed. "I believe I have this time, old girl, isn't it wonderful? We shall drop our new friends in Pennsylvania free of charge."

The Benchs scurried out the front door, and the moment they climbed into the carriage, Ben Groot jumped into the driver's seat and cracked his whip, sending the horses bolting down the driveway.

"We must leave now," James urged, taking Lauren's arm. "We have much to discuss but there is no time. We are in great peril."

"No, *you* are in great peril," Lauren replied. "I am no longer a part of The Pride of the King."

Picking up a candle, she turned mechanically and walked to her bedchamber. Without a word, she began to stuff personal items into a bag.

James followed her to the door. "What the hell are you doing? You are surrounded by wilderness and there is a war going on in the north with the French."

"You forget that I survived on the streets of New York all alone. I can do it on the frontier as well."

"You fool."

She pushed past him down the stairs and out into the pouring rain. He followed her into the deluge, and grabbed her wrist. Shouting over the downpour he said, "If you don't come with me now, you will most certainly die."

Something in his voice made Lauren stop and listen. The rain poured down upon them.

"No," he said. "That's not true. If you do not come with me, *I* will most certainly die."

Lauren was stunned. Never had his words held more emotion. Never had his face shown more distress. She wanted to run into his arms, but she jumped back and pulled a pistol from the pocket of her gown.

Startled, he looked at the weapon and then up at her face. She saw the hurt in his eyes and he murmured, "Why?"

"I warned you some day I would leave you. You are a liar and a cheat," she said holding her arm over the weapon to keep the powder dry. "You have deceived me on every count from matrimony to my own property. I should kill you, but I would be pursued for it. From now on, I will find my own way and try to erase the shame of being married to a man that never deserved a name."

There was a long silence as they stared at each other, the rain drenching them. Lauren watched the struggle on St. Clare's face, then without a word, he mounted his horse and rode away into the storm.

Chapter 42

All night Lauren sat with the pistol on her lap in her bedchamber. She shook with emotion for the first few hours then dozed fitfully the rest of the night in front of the fire, too anxious to sleep soundly. At the first light of day she took her bag and crept down the stairs to the dining room of the Van den Berg manor. She could hear the servants in the kitchen as she filled her bag with bread, cheese and sausages.

Lauren chose not to wait for a vessel to stop at the Van den Berg estate. There was no time to lose. She knew before the day was over the authorities would be questioning everyone at the home about *The Pride of the King*. The post road was a safer alternative.

The cold morning air swept the cobwebs from her head as she walked briskly down the path heading south. It was quiet this time of year when the Hudson was still open and free of ice. During the milder months, the road was not used because the river was a more efficient form of transportation but very soon, when the ice made passage impossible on the Hudson, the post road would become a very busy thoroughfare.

Lauren pulled her cloak closely around her shoulders and touched the pistol in her waistband. It had been months since James had given her shooting lessons, but she knew what she lacked in skill she made up for in resolve. Without realizing it, Lauren had returned to her survival instincts and a cold calm enveloped her. She remembered St. Clare speaking of a woman by the name of Quill who needed help at a tavern near Hampsted. She knew it could only be a temporary position because it would be the first place St. Clare would search for her, but for now he was gone and the frozen days of winter were arriving inhibiting transportation. Hampsted would be unreachable.

It took her two days to walk to the settlement. She spent the first bitter night in a barn and the second night in the burned out remains of an old cabin. She met few people along the post road and when she did encounter someone she remained aloof, hugging her pistol closely. By the afternoon of the second day she reached the outskirts of Hampsted. Lauren wondered if she was in fact passing near her own property. At first the thought elated her, but it was quickly replaced by bitter disappointment when she remembered that it was indeed and always had been St. Clare's land.

The road took her down a hill and into a clearing where a fieldstone structure sat with smoke curling out a chimney. It was a large, square building with green shutters and sign swinging over the front door saying, "The Boar's Head".

A tall, boney woman with a horse face was in the yard strewing feed to chickens. She stopped abruptly and put a hand on her hip when she spied Lauren. "I don't give hand outs here," the woman cried, pursing her lips.

Lauren slowed her pace realizing her appearance must seem shabby. Her clothing was soiled and her hair tousled. She smoothed her skirt and ran her fingers through her hair. "I beg your pardon, Madame. My name is Lauren De Beauville."

The woman's eyes grew large in her long, drawn face, and she gasped.

Lauren said, "Please do not be alarmed."

The woman's back stiffened and she replied, "I most certainly am not alarmed. I have not been alarmed by anyone since the year of our Lord, seventeen thirty nine. What is your business here, you-you French woman!"

She swallowed hard, cleared her throat and said, "I have been sent by Captain James St. Clare. Are you Mrs. Quill? He told me you have work."

"Not for you. You bold faced thing!" she said.

The elderly proprietress turned on her heel and went into the tavern, slamming the door behind her. Lauren growled and clenched her fists, approaching the door. She licked her lips, took a deep breath and knocked. Almost immediately the door flew open and Mrs. Quill stood in front of her with a musket.

"Well?" the woman barked.

Lauren looked inside the tavern. "You have not yet cleaned up from last night, Madame?" Lauren asked.

"That is no concern of yours."

"It is almost supper time again. Why are you not ready?"

Mrs. Quill did not reply. She studied Lauren for a moment then said, "You're a Papist, aren't you? I don't serve Papists."

"I am not asking to be a guest," Lauren replied.

She hesitated a moment, gathered her courage then stepped around Mrs. Quill into the common room. The hearth was cold, the room damp and dark. Four or five tables were placed near the fireplace and a long, empty room yawned off to the left with a bar, several more tables and another stone fireplace. Dishes had not been cleared from the night before, the straw on the floor was dirty and the room smelled of stale beer.

"I can have this cleaned and a meal ready by tonight," Lauren announced.

The woman's eyes narrowed and she said, "You are very sure of yourself."

Lauren raised one eyebrow and stated, "I am accustomed to entertaining."

"That," Mrs. Quill said sarcastically, "is obvious. You're nothing more than a tart."

Lauren ignored the insult and walked around the room, examining the cooking implements and blowing dust off the mantle. Mrs. Quill watched her then growled, "I admit, my health has prevented me from keeping the tavern in tip-top shape lately, but I am not ready for the bone yard yet. I have no money to pay you."

"You will eventually if you hire me," said Lauren. "For now I am only interested in a roof over my head for the winter."

"There will be no Papist practices here," the woman warned, shaking her finger.

Lauren chuckled as she pulled off her gloves. "Do not worry, Madame." she said in a voice heavy with sarcasm. "I lost my rosary years ago."

*   *   *

Lauren threw herself into resurrecting The Boar's Head Tavern to a thriving establishment. She told herself it was to gain the trust of Mrs. Quill, but in truth it was to keep her thoughts from James and the betrayal she felt toward The Pride of the King.

The first afternoon she arrived at the tavern, she shed her filthy traveling clothes, put on a fresh mob cap, gown and pinner and began to scrub the floors. Mrs. Quill worked alongside her grumbling all the time. Lauren dusted and cleaned, hauled wood, mended fences and tended the animals. Afflicted by a bad back Mrs. Quill, prepared ale and took care of the sewing and bedding. She was slow to trust Lauren watching her suspiciously and mumbling, "Papist" regularly under her breath, yet she allowed her to stay.

The first part of December the temperature dropped and the snows began. For the first time in her life, Lauren was grateful for winter. She knew *The Pride of the King* could no longer sail up the Hudson, and her privacy was now secure. Late every night after cleaning up from supper and the tavern crowd, Lauren would climb the creaky stairs to her room at the back of the tavern and drop onto her feather bed falling asleep instantly, never allowing herself to think of the Benchs or James.

The betrayal and loneliness began to erode her well being and a nagging pain developed in her stomach. It plagued her from the moment she woke up in the morning until the time she fell into bed at night. It prevented her from eating properly and she grew thin and drawn. Mrs. Quill could not help but notice Lauren's decline.

"How come you are not with your French people?" she asked one day as Lauren stoked a fire outside. She did not reply at first, stuffing laundry into a crucible with a stick. Wiping her hands on her apron she said, "I was taken away many years ago as a bride and brought to this land. I had little choice in the matter."

Holding a basket of clothes Mrs. Quill sat down stiffly on a stump. She looked around at the landscape of thick pines and maples. "It was the same for me. Mr. Quill brought me to this back country thirty years ago. I came from a good family in England, a family of means, the Adams of Portsmouth. The Hudson seemed like the other end of the earth. He dragged me here, and then had the audacity to die three years later."

"Why didn't you go back to your homeland?" asked Lauren,

"Why didn't *you* go back?" the old woman echoed.

Lauren looked down. "Just like you. There was no reason to return. It is the way of it. I have no regrets."

The two were quiet for a moment, lost in their thoughts.

"I have been thinking," said the matron. "The winters are brutal here in the valley, and I can use another hand on a regular basis. I must be in my dotage, but you may stay if you wish."

Lauren smiled mischievously, looked up and made the sign of the cross.

Mrs. Quill barked, "But there will be none of that!"

Chapter 43

Initially the customers at the Boar's Head Tavern were suspicious of Lauren. In spite of their diverse backgrounds, her French upbringing was difficult for the residents of Hampsted to tolerate. The conflict between the countries consumed the Colonies and every evening the conversation inevitably turned to politics. On several occasions, disparaging remarks were directed at Lauren, but immediately Mrs. Quill squashed them, demanding respect for her employee. Eventually the townspeople relaxed their attitudes and learned to like Lauren. They found her culinary skills above reproach, and when they teased her they found her saucy French attitude engaging. They even defended her when the occasional out of town guest maligned her.

Lauren learned to enjoy the banter as well. It sharpened her wits and her mastery of the English language. The repartee amused the men especially, and the flirtation gave them a welcome diversion during the cold winter months in the valley. The conversation also brought more business to the Boar's Head and for this Mrs. Quill was grateful.

Yet Lauren found as her new life grew more predictable, she felt more unsettled. The diversion of a new home and position distracted her initially, but over time the restlessness returned. She struggled to keep thoughts of James from her mind, but he found his way into everything she did. Now as she looked back on her past she could see his hand in everything. For the first time in her life she was without him and she felt quite alone.

At night she would think back to her days in Kaskaskia as a young woman and her infatuation with Rene Lupone. She blushed at her silly schoolgirl attitudes and was ashamed that she had ever been so shallow. Gabriel had called her foolish, head strong and impulsive, and he had indeed been right. She knew nothing then of deep emotion and was ignorant of the kind of yearning that nags at one's belly like a cancer. Now she realized Gabriel understood these things profoundly and pondered them deeply before he took his own life.

She missed her friendship with Eugenie as well and chastised herself for never appreciating the suffering the young girl had endured. She struggled to remember her conversations with Isaac and the heartfelt laughter of Henry Bologne. She even revisited her ethereal companions Abigail and Ephraim from the churchyard in the city, still unsure whether they were fancy or heavenly companions.

But the individual who robbed her peace of mind most completely was James St. Clair. He stirred something within her that was almost primal as elemental to her existence as lifeblood and from this sensation sprang supreme loneliness and yearning.

Mrs. Quill did not know exactly what plagued Lauren but had the wisdom to know it was a lost love and that she was impotent to help. She remembered her own pain when her husband died, and she knew that it would never subside, only dull over the years. She developed a genuine affection for Lauren, and their companionship helped quell the dark loneliness they endured together.

Fear now also accompanied their loneliness. There had been reports from travelers that tribes had been swooping down from Canada launching assaults on settlers to the north, and it put Lauren and Mrs. Quill on edge. Lauren tried not to be afraid, but it was unnerving to complete her chores outside. She tried not to turn her back to the woods and kept a wary eye out whenever her employer ventured to feed the chickens or milk the cows. On several occasions Lauren spent the day mending fences returning to the tavern at sunset more exhausted from tension than actual labor. For the first time she actually feared for her life. She had almost been killed in a hurricane, almost died in childbirth and hanged in New France but now the thought of dieing terrified her.

"You don't seem afraid at all," she said one day to Mrs. Quill as they entered the tavern hanging their cloaks on pegs by the door.

Mrs. Quill walked stiffly over to the fire and threw another log onto the grate. "I am not afraid anymore. I have lived out my days. I will die a woman contented with her life." She sat down and watched Lauren as she stared into the fire. "You, my dear are not content. You still have a life to live. That is why you fear losing it."

"But I never cared before. I don't understand. I never cared until now," Lauren replied.

The matron picked up her sewing and began to stitch. "Perhaps for the first time there is someone that needs you to live," Mrs. Quill suggested.

*   *   *

While Lauren made her life in Hampsted, *The Pride of the King* put out to sea. They left the customs officers along the coast, Heloise and Cornelius in Providence then headed to warmer waters to seek firearms. All winter long they acquired contraband then returned to the Hudson River Valley in the springtime successful and bulging with munitions, eager to supply the British or the French with low cost weaponry.

General McAffee's replacement in New York City, General Barnhill, welcomed bribes, so the fluyt had little trouble sailing past the city and on up the Hudson. They navigated far to the north to the secluded creek, and then canoed munitions up the water to the remote gunsmith operation Lauren had visited two years earlier. There the guns were refurbished and stored until buyers were obtained.

Everyone who knew Captain St. Clare noted a change in him since he left the Van den Berg manor. He had never been a demonstrative man, but now more than ever, he retreated within himself. He spent hours alone in his cabin examining charts and maps and pouring over plans. He was short with the crew and impatient with his business associates. Occasionally he went ashore to visit patroons on business and could be seen dining with some of the more distinguished women of Albany, but he never visited the same one twice. He always returned to the fluyt sullen and out of sorts as if dissatisfied and frustrated.

The crew had changed as well. The loss of Isaac then Lauren drained the joy from the men and laughter was seldom heard anymore. The work of sailing the fluyt, once a pleasure and a satisfaction now turned to drudgery. The crew merely went through the motions of sailing her.

In spite of it all the organization prospered. The war between the English, French and their Indian allies fueled the growth of the operation, and James St. Clare seized every opportunity to expand. At last he had found several contacts in New France who were willing to initiate trade with the *Pride*, and the expansion of troops on Lake Champlain and Lake George provided ample opportunities to supply arms to both sides, including the Indians.

It was for this reason that Captain St. Clare left the fluyt and traveled first to his gunsmith community, then to the north to his cabin and the *Melungion* settlement on Popple Creek.

"*Ola` Capitao!*" called George Blasco as St. Clare stepped off the path late one afternoon into the clearing of the Melungion community. In three long strides the ship's carpenter was upon him shaking his hand vigorously.

"Welcome back!" George said.

"I am glad to see you are well after you run in with the authorities," said St. Clare. "And how does Mr. Misckowic fare?"

"He left, Captain, when the roads became passable. He didn't say where he was going."

St Clare scanned the settlement. "I see new cabins."

"Two couples have just wed," explained Blasco. "My cousin is expecting their first child. Family is good. No?"

St. Clare smiled and nodded. He knew in spite of the upcoming birth, a void was strongly felt in the community after the loss of Vincent and Gaspar. The men shouted greetings and put down their work gathering around the Captain eager for news as the women stood in the back straining to hear what was being said. Captain St. Clare informed them of the successful acquisition of guns and new contacts, and then the Melungion men informed St. Clare of troop movements, French and English.

"Is it true the Hurons and Abenaki have been conducting raids?" St. Clare asked.

"Yes, but it is the white soldiers we fear above all," they replied.

Davi looked around as if searching for someone, "You have come alone this time? No Madame?"

"No, no Madame," St. Clare said flatly. Any reference to Lauren made his throat tighten.

Suddenly, a woman demanded in Portuguese, "Step aside, you oafs! Move out of the way!"

The men parted and there stood the tiny, aged matron Madame Blasco. "Come, come!" the wizened old woman barked, taking St. Clare by the hand. "You are hungry." She lead him to a long table placed under a large oak tree, gave him some ale, bread and cheese and hobbled back to her cabin to prepare supper.

Fatima, delighted to see James, visited with him for a moment before she too disappeared into the kitchen with the rest of the women. St. Clare could not understand why her face was so flushed and why she was so tongue tied.

Several more tables were set up and everyone gathered for supper just as the sun was about to go down. After a hearty meal of venison, root vegetables and pie, the men gathered around a large bonfire for an evening of drinking and taking tobacco. As James walked over he noticed several Indians sitting off in the shadows. There were three of them, two men and a woman. They were of a tribe he did not recognize. The men's heads were shaved except for a single scalp lock and they wore colorful tunics over their buckskin pants.

"They work for you, Capitao," Davi explained. He introduced St. Clare to the two men who told him in English that they had traveled a long way from the lands of their people and that they were of the Chickasaw nation far to the west. St. Clare remembered that several years back he had hired interpreters for the organization, but he had never met them. He employed in all eight Chickasaw individuals who were strategically placed across the northern colonies. When a confidential message needed to be sent it would be dictated to a Chickasaw interpreter. The interpreter carried the message to its destination, often over great distances and under great peril. Being of a separate Indian nation and speaking the Muskegon language the Chickasaw was considered neutral in the war posing no threat to either side.

"I hold your skills in high esteem, gentleman," said James. "Thank you. It is an honor to have you serve with us."

As he was about to turn away Davi took his arm and nodded in the direction of a woman, "There is another you have forgotten and is probably the most learned of the eight Chickasaws."

A petite woman stepped forward. She wore a buckskin shift and her black was hair tied on top of her head with decorative beads. St. Clare noticed her face was scarred. He nodded a greeting and said, "I am told you have exceptional skills. What languages do you speak?"

"English, French, my people's language and now Portuguese. I was a slave for many years, Captain St. Clare and forced to learn the words of the white man."

"Where were you enslaved?"

"On the great river called the Mississippi in a town named Kaskaskia," she said.

James stared at her a moment then took Davi by the arm, turning away from the girl. He whispered, "Is this the woman Adair Heathstone purchased from the French years ago?"

"Yes," Davi said. "She was about to be hanged. Do you know her?"

St. Clare did not reply but approached the young woman once more.

He put his fist to his lips for a moment deep in thought then said, "You left Kaskaskia on a convoy several years ago after being emancipated by an Englishman. Is that correct?" She nodded and James continued, "With the understanding you would serve as an interpreter for The Pride of the King for a set period of time."

"Yes," she said quietly, her brow furrowed.

Every muscle in his body pulled tight as he searched her face. "Please think back to when you were in the town of Kaskaskia. Did you ever meet a girl by the name of De Beauville?"

The young woman frowned, and she shook her head slowly.

"Are you certain?" he urged.

He studied her face. Again she shook her head. St. Clare sighed and rubbed the back of his neck. Just as he was about to turn away he realized his mistake. "No," he exclaimed, correcting himself. "No, it was not De Beauville. It would have been Heathstone! Lauren Heathstone!"

The young Chickasaw's eyes widened, and she nodded. She began to chatter excitedly in French.

St. Clare grasped her arms and cried, "No, in English. Please!"

"Yes! Lauren was my friend there. My only friend," she said thickly, her excitement and scarred lips slurring her speech.

"What is your name?"

"At that time, I was called Eugenie," she replied. "I lived at the Aberjon household with her."

St. Clare ran his eyes over Eugenie. Just being near someone who had been close to Lauren gave him joy. For the first time in months, he smiled and said, "Yes, she spoke of that place and she told me that she had a friend there."

"Is she near?" she asked.

"Yes. I believe she lives somewhere on the Hudson River. Please sit with me," he said gesturing politely for her to sit down by the fire. "We must speak of many things."

Chapter 44

The winter had been long and exceptionally cold in the Hudson River country. When the sun finally strengthened and began to stir the inhabitants of the valley, Lauren was beyond restless. Something erupted within her that was akin to panic as she watched for the signs of spring. Mother Nature played its usual tricks melting the snow one day and sending an icy blast the next, teasing everyone especially Lauren into a frenzy of frustration. She was anxious to be as far away from the Boar's Head Tavern as possible, gone from the river valley. She knew that in no time the white sails of, *The Pride of the King* would billow on the waterway, and she was determined never to see its Captain again.

"This is impulsive foolishness. You are nothing more than an immature flibbertigibbet!" barked Mrs. Quill when Lauren informed her she was leaving with the first thaw.

"You have nothing to worry about," Lauren said. "You have two new barmaids starting soon. They will help you."

The matron trotted behind Lauren as she carried a load of wood into the kitchen one dark morning. She dumped the pile by the hearth and bent over to feed the fire, ignoring the woman's badgering. Mrs. Quill made several more comments then scooped up her little dog Ogden and placed him on the canine turnspit to run the treadmill which turned the meat.

"How do you think you will live? How are you going to feed yourself?" she pressed.

Lauren tossed Ogden a bit of fat ignoring Mrs. Quill's challenge.

"Who are you running away from?" the woman continued.

Lauren stood up straight and said, "If that had been your business, I would have told you a long time ago."

"It has something to do with that St. Clare man doesn't it?"

"St. Clare?" Lauren said shrugging. "I hardly know him."

"Know him! No one knows him. That is part of his damned allure."

Lauren swung around with a look of surprise at Mrs. Quill.

"Oh come now," the matron said. "I may be a horse faced old woman, but I can still appreciate a fascinating man."

Lauren had to agree, he was an enigma, but she was no longer interested in his riddle. At the first opportunity she would put a great distance between them.

Mrs. Quill looked at Lauren out of the corner of her eye and remarked, "The townspeople say that he is your husband."

Lauren stopped prodding the fire. She clenched her teeth then said, "The residents of Hampsted enjoy speculation."

"Word travels fast up and down the Hudson especially among servants and workmen. They have big ears," Mrs. Quill said smugly.

"And even bigger mouths," Lauren replied. She wiped her hands on her apron and passed into the empty common room.

Mrs. Quill followed her, continuing to talk while Lauren lowered the wooden chandelier lighting several candles. "I think you are in love with your husband."

"And I think you are on a flight of fancy, Mrs. Quill. No one marries for love. You know that marriage is nothing more than a business agreement."

"Yes, but on rare occasions spouses fall in love with each other after they are married."

Lauren stopped what she was doing and looked at the matron. "I believe you fell in love with your husband."

Mrs. Quill thrust her chin into the air and answered, "I may have, but he died. So there is nothing more to say on the matter. *Your* husband is still alive. Don't wait until it is too late."

*   *   *

The women did not speak again about marriage, love or parting. Their attention turned to matters of war. As the snow melted, reports of Indian raids increased, and the residents of Hampsted became terrified. They seldom left their homes and even fewer travelers were on the post road. Business was slow at the Boars Head which added to Lauren's impatience. She needed diversion to keep her mind from racing and the endless monotony of waiting for customers grated on her nerves. The ice was almost out of the Hudson, and she looked forward to being on the first craft headed to the north. She knew it was dangerous near the lakes, but she needed to be among the French again if she ever hoped to be away from the English Colonies and return to New Orleans. She had no concrete plan in mind, but she was certain an opportunity would arise.

The sun was sinking low in the sky one April afternoon as Lauren walked briskly up the post road from Hampsted. She had avoided leaving the inn of late but on this day it was imperative she get salve for the open sore on Mrs. Quill Adam's leg. What started out as a minor scrape now had become swollen and bright red.

She carried a rifle but she knew it would be of little use as the sunlight faded. The night was growing cold, and she increased her pace. She hated the dense forest that lined either side of the post road. The impenetrable darkness unnerved her, and she constantly had to push back stories she remembered of settlers brutalized by Indians. By the last turn she startled a herd of deer, and her heart jumped into her throat. It took several minutes for her to calm herself again, and she breathed a sigh of relief when she saw the flickering candlelight of the Boars Head Tavern. She chided herself for her foolishness, remembering after all she had endured far greater dangers at Fort Frederic and on the streets of New York.

Suddenly a dark form stepped into her path. She froze in her tracks, flooded with cold fear. In a heartbeat she could tell that the shadowy figure was an Indian. Lauren turned on her heel and burst into a full run away from the man. Another Indian jumped into her path that direction as well. Consumed with panic Lauren threw her rifle and dashed into the thick underbrush of the woods, clawing madly at the branches and brush. In no time the two men were upon her, stifling her screams and dragging her back out onto the path. She thrashed about wildly, but she was helpless against them.

They carried her with lightening speed into the stable of the Boar's Head Tavern where someone waited with a lantern. They pulled the doors shut and put Lauren roughly onto her feet, still grasping her tightly and covering her mouth. One of them held her head, forcing her to look straight ahead. Lauren tried to wrench herself free but could not move the grip was so rigid. Gradually her eyes focused, and she saw a petite Indian girl standing in front of her. The girl did not move a muscle; her dark eyes watched Lauren intently. Lauren stopped struggling and looked back at the young woman. There was something about the girl that seemed familiar, but she was confused.

"I am still of this earth, my friend," the girl said gently. "You knew me once as Eugenie."

Lauren started. The man tightened his grip, but he had such a firm grasp on Lauren that she could not breathe. She started to gasp for air. As her mind tried to absorb Eugenie's words, her body reacted with shock, and she began to swoon. Eugenie jumped forward releasing her from the man before she fainted. The men eased Lauren down onto the floor of the stable, and she began to regain to her sensibilities. Her hair lay in tangles all over her face, and Eugenie pushed the mass of curls back to examine her eyes.

Lauren gazed at her and whispered, "I dream."

Eugenie shook her head as her eyes filled with tears, "You do not."

"How can this be? How is it you have been delivered to me?" Lauren asked still not believing the reality.

"Captain St. Clare," Eugenie murmured.

Lauren sat up and grabbed Eugenie, kissing her hair and holding her face in her hands, tears streaming down her face. She touched her cheek and repeated, "You are alive. You are alive. How can this be?"

"An Englishman bought my freedom the morning I was to hang. He brought me here, and I have been here working with the organization, The Pride of the King ever since."

Lauren looked at the two men and Eugenie explained, "There are eight of us from the Chickasaw nation employed here. This is how I met my husband."

Eugenie stood up, pulling Lauren to her feet, helping to steady her for a moment. Taking one of the men by the arm, Eugenie introduced him as her husband. Lauren looked from one man to the other. They appeared identical in every way.

Eugenie smiled and said, "You are correct, Lauren. They are twins."

Lauren rubbed her forehead. She felt overwhelmed and unsteady. It all seemed so fantastic and unbelievable. "How did you ever find me?"

"Captain St. Clare thought you might be here. I met him a short time ago near Popple Creek."

"So all these years you have been near me, alive and living so close," Lauren murmured in disbelief. Then she said suspiciously, "Did St. Clare know this?"

Eugenie shook her head. "The first time we met was at Popple Creek a few weeks ago. The moment he realized our connection, he sent me to you."

Just as Lauren was about to say something, Eugenie's husband stepped forward and spoke in his native tongue. Eugenie nodded and turned to Lauren explaining, "They are going back to the river where we are staying tonight. You and I only have tonight. It is dangerous here for us. There are few places in this part of the world where we are welcome."

Lauren nodded, "I understand. I too am an outcast."

Eugenie was just like every other member of The Pride of the King an outcast, a Chickasaw in Iroquois country sheltered and hidden by an organization of pariahs.

Walking to the stable door, Lauren stole a look at the tavern and whispered, "The innkeeper will be watching for me. I must return to the tavern for a short time until she retires. Then I will come to you."

Slipping out of the stable, Lauren took the salve to Mrs. Quill, helped the woman to bed then stole back to see Eugenie. They talked until the sun rose, holding hands, sharing their journeys, exchanging memories, and trying to in vain to fill the years of separation.

"As much as I hated the Aberjons, my life was familiar to me in Kaskaskia," Eugenie explained. "And I was afraid to leave the Illinois Country. I did not want to be a part of this world. The

English terrified me. It was not until I met my husband that I could find peace at last. In him I have found contentment and one who I will gladly follow the rest of my life. I have also come back to my Chickasaw roots as well. I am a free woman now, and I have taken back the name my father gave me. It is Isi."

"Isi" Lauren repeated nodding slowly. "It is not the name of a slave."

Lauren saw that Isi was no longer a shy, withdrawn girl. She had grown into a confident young woman who had found her place in the world. The dress of her people suited her perfectly, not the shoddy French peasant clothing she was given as a slave in Kaskaskia. Lauren was glad also to see that her fine mind and heart were appreciated by those around her.

"And tell me Lauren. Who is special for you?"

Lauren smiled wistfully and shook her head. "There is no one."

"Do you still think of Rene'?"

Lauren smiled. "Once in a while with fondness."

"You are restless still," Isi said. "I can feel it."

"I am," Lauren admitted. "I am older now and learning that I may never find that special place. Perhaps drifting is what I do best."

"You are like a leaf on the river, carried forever on the current," Isi said. Suddenly she grew serious. "Lauren, it is time for me to go."

A sob escaped Lauren. She quickly covered her mouth, her eyes filling with tears. She nodded her head as Isi turned toward the door.

The young woman stopped and said, "I will be in the north. There are those with organization who know where to find me. We will never be apart again, Lauren. I promise you."

They held each other for a moment then Isi was gone. Lauren watched her slip noiselessly into the woods disappearing into the darkness. The sky was beginning to lighten as Lauren filled her arms with firewood. It was time to feed the animals and start breakfast. It was another day alone in the Hudson River Valley.

Chapter 45

At the end of April, Martin Willem the cooper's apprentice in Hampsted, approached Mrs. Quill to host his upcoming marriage to Maggie Sutton. It was to be the first week of May, and Mrs. Quill was delighted. Business had been bad all spring and a wedding would bring revenue and a welcome diversion from the fear and anxiety of war.

"Life must go on. In spite of everything," she said joyfully to Lauren that afternoon. "I will be making a menu shortly, and I expect you to cook your best--"

"No, no," Lauren interrupted, shaking her head. "The new barmaids have started, and they are quite capable of helping you. I have told you countless times that I am leaving the first week of May. In fact, the water traffic is frequent enough for me to have left last week. I only stay because your wound needs attention for a few more days."

"You ungrateful girl!" barked Mrs. Quill straightening up in her chair. "How dare you forget that I took you in last autumn when you had no home. I even indulged you in your Papist practices. This is how you thank me!"

Lauren turned away clutching her belly. She hadn't the energy to fight anymore. The clutching pain in her stomach had increased, plaguing her day and night. She stepped into the larder and took a deep breath to try to calm herself. Ever since Isi had left, Lauren had slept little and eaten even less. She was confused and disgusted at her reaction. She told herself that she should be overjoyed at the girls return, but instead she felt lonely and full of despair. She hated herself for her weakness and jealousy. Isi seemed so satisfied and at peace. Her happiness seemed to magnify Lauren's emptiness. Isi had overcome so many obstacles and found her way, why couldn't she complete her own journey.

At night, she paced in her room, terrified about her future and uncertain about her direction. In the past, the thought of an adventure exhilarated her, but now it only frightened her. She avoided the river completely. It only reminded her of her lack of direction and of her recurring dream of white sails on the waterway.

She never allowed thoughts of James to enter her mind anymore. She felt only the mildest gratitude to him for sending Isi to her. She believed firmly all of his actions were merely to benefit The Pride of the King and nothing more; true human emotion was unknown to him. Heloise had warned her many years ago about this failing and Lauren had to admit she was right and wished she had listened to the woman.

She threw herself into running the inn and training the new help while Mrs. Quill recuperated. She told herself she would stay at the Boar's Head only a few more days, but now the wedding gave her another excuse to avoid departure. She knew what she was doing and berated herself for being cowardly, delaying her return to New France.

"How many times have I told you Polly to heap the ashes evenly on the lid or the pudding will cook too fast on one side!" barked Lauren at the new girl.

"I am sorry, Miss, but I was distracted chasing Ogden. He hides every time I begin to fuss with the treadmill."

"I told you, give him fat and cracklings. He'll not perform without them." Lauren picked up a knife and chopped vegetables impatiently. After a few moments, she began to feel guilty. She had been short with the new girls lately and, she hated herself for it. The nuns had been so kind at the convent teaching kitchen duties to her years ago. Why couldn't she offer the same gift to these girls. Lauren reached up and with her sleeve rubbed the perspiration from her brow. She couldn't help but smile watching Polly get Ogden onto the treadmill.

Polly Quackenboss was a stocky flaxen-haired girl of Dutch ancestry with plump rosy cheeks and eyes that disappeared into slits whenever she grinned. Lauren admired her good nature and knew with a bit of training she would serve Mrs. Quill well.

Lauren asked, "I haven't seen that young man of yours lately, Polly. Where has he been?"

"Oh, never far, Miss. My Pim has been busy helping Martin get the cottage ready for Margaret once they wed."

"Yes, we are all getting ready," Lauren agreed. "Tomorrow is the big day, and I must say it will be a miracle if we get it all done. I still have two more cakes to make, we must shell some more nuts and there is chowder to finish. When will Lizzie be back with more molasses?"

"Anytime now, I would think, Miss." Polly replied. "I must go and check on Mrs. Quill before she walks and aggravates her foot again."

Lauren finished late that night rising the next morning at four to make final preparations for the festivities. Like all weddings, the ceremony was first thing in the morning at the church. Amid much celebration and merry making, the bride and groom would climb onto their flower-covered wagon and make their way to the Boar's Head Tavern for feasting and drinking afterwards. Everything had to be in order well before midday, and Lauren was aware that many things could not be done until the last minute.

"I told you it would all get done," observed Mrs. Quill as she entered the common room hobbling unsteadily with a cane. Lauren was standing on a chair draping a garland as Lizzie passed more greens and flowers to her. They continued working, talking to each other, commenting on the appearance of the decorations.

"What I mean to say is," the matron continued in a louder voice. "Thank you."

Lauren turned toward Mrs. Quill. They looked at each other for a moment with unspoken affection.

"I think it will go well, Mrs. Quill," Lauren replied and went back to work.

Lauren was truly fond of her and she knew it would be hard to leave the crusty old innkeeper. In spite of their constant bickering, there was an understanding between the women which sprang from their mutual loneliness and isolation on the boundaries of the frontier.

Lauren heard music outside. The fiddlers had struck up a tune signaling the approach of the bride and groom in their wagon. She heard cheers too and in no time, the common room was flooded with guests, laughter and music.

The time flew for after that. Lauren was busy cooking and serving food, running in and out of the common room, flirting and exchanging cheerful banter with the men as they grew more and more intoxicated and amorous. Dancing moved from the green into the common room after dark, continuing late into the night.

Around midnight Lauren finished washing the last dish, wiped her hands and took off her apron. Putting her hands on her back she stretched for a moment then walked out to the common room to watch the merriment. Mrs. Quill sat near the fire, her foot elevated, laughing and heckling the dancers. Polly and Lizzie whirled and hopped past, dancing with their beaux. In spite of the late hour, the inn was full and the stable still crowded with horses. Lauren danced two contra dances and jig but had to decline her fourth invitation.

"Your legs are giving out on you, aren't they?" Mrs. Quill teased.

Lauren laughed and nodded as Polly came up to join them. "I hope my wedding is every bit as merry as this!" the girl gushed breathlessly. "Pim wants to have it here, Mrs. Quill."

"We'll see," the matron grumbled, not relishing the work of another large celebration so soon.

"I never asked you, Polly," shouted Lauren over the music. "How did you meet Pim?"

Polly thought a moment then said, "Why Miss as long as I can remember he has been in my life. He kept popping up over the years. He just wouldn't give up. At first, I found it annoying and told him to leave me alone. Nevertheless, I got used to seeing his face, and I guess I just couldn't live without him. Not really romantic or anything, but he *is* the boy for me."

Polly started when she looked at Lauren. "Miss Lauren? Are you alright?"

Lauren did not respond.

"Are you feeling sick?"

Lauren shook her head and turned away. The room seemed to be pulling away from her, and she clutched the chair to steady herself. She had to get outside for air. Pulling the door open, she stumbled out into the darkness. She needed to think. What was it Polly had said that had so disturbed her? Fresh air filled her lungs, and Lauren squeezed her eyes shut for a moment trying to remember. It was something about her sweetheart. Then she remembered. Polly had said he had always been there, her whole life.

Lauren declined the offers of help from guests standing outside. Going directly to her room, she fell back onto the bed, staring at the ceiling. Barely aware of the horses snorting and the wagons grinding into the distance as guests went home, Lauren continued to stare into the darkness, until the sun rose.

For the first time in days, the house was quiet at dawn. Since sleep would not come, so Lauren decided to rise and do some tilling in the vegetable plot near the river bluff. She put on her mobcap, straw sun hat and stepped out into the warm spring day.

Squinting in the sunshine, she walked to the vegetable garden, rolled up her sleeves and began to hoe. When her arms tired, she would pause and look at squirrels scurrying in the trees or shade her eyes and watch eagles circling the river.

She continued to work the soil late into the morning, cutting long straight rows for seed. The routine and monotony of the labor were soothing for her and gave her a chance to reflect on Polly's words. Over and over, they repeated in her head, "As long as I can remember he has been in my life."

Lauren would drag the hoe across the soil, pick it up and drag it back again repeating, "As long as I can remember he has been in my life." Soon it was not Polly's voice she was listening to but her own. *As long as I can remember he has been in my life.*

Suddenly, she realized what she had been repeating over and over. For almost as long as she could remember, James had been in *her* life, James St. Clare, her constant companion, not always visible but ever enduring. He had always been there, waiting for her, watching over her. It had been him all along. James, the one constant in her lonely world holding the keys to the only home she had ever sought *The Pride of the King.*

She reached up, wiped tears from her eyes and walked under an oak tree, dropping down underneath it. As the tears drained the poison out of her, the pain in her belly disappeared. Lauren began to shake her head and laugh. *How could she have been so stupid? At last, she had her direction.* Suddenly, there was no more fear and anxiety. For the first time in her life, she knew where to find her home, and she could chart her course.

Lauren sat under the tree for what seemed like hours, lost in thought, reveling in her epiphany until she heard Mrs. Quill calling for her. Picking up her skirts, she ran back to the inn feeling as light and as happy as she had ever felt. After helping to situate guests for the night she returned to the garden to till once again until the sun set.

She was pulling the hoe back and forth rhythmically lost in the work, when suddenly she remembered the river. It had been months since she had gazed on the waterway, and the sunset promised to be beautiful that evening. Yet it was growing late. Dismissing the idea, she went back to her work, this time stopping for only a moment to push back her tangled hair and adjust her hat.

After a short time, she looked again at the trees and shrubbery that concealed the Hudson. The river seemed to beckon to her. She resumed her hoeing until she heard dogs barking in the distance. She wondered what roused them. The river pulled at her once more, and she tossed her hoe to the ground walking over to the bluff.

Deer had trampled a path down the embankment and Lauren stepped in, pushing back branches and thorny vines. The thick brush pulled at her skirt and tore at her hair, but she fought back determined to see the river. Flooded with anticipation, her heart began to pound, and she walked faster and faster. Soon she began to run, stumbling on roots, madly pushing back branches and foliage. She could see a break in the trees and burst out of the woods. There was the river valley opening at her feet. She could breathe at last, and the fresh river air filled her lungs. The sunlight was blinding and the blue of the water stunning as she stood on the bluff panting, absorbing the beauty of the expanse. She reached up to shade her eyes looking upriver and spied something glimmering on the water. Her stomach jumped. It was the full, white sails of a vessel, its rigging straining in the breeze. Impatiently Lauren pushed the hair from her eyes to get a better look. Her heart lurched. It was *The Pride of the King*!

"Oh!" she cried. "Oh! Up here!" she called, waving madly.

She began to slide and stumble down the path along the bluff, calling and gesturing. The ground was uneven and several times, she tumbled and slid onto her backside, springing up again waving wildly with delight. "Hello! Up here!"

The fluyt glided on in silence until one of the crew on the masthead spotted Lauren's frenzied display and shouted, "Ahoy there!"

St. Clare looked up from the stern toward the riverbank. In a flash, he ran to the bow. Grasping a line in one hand, he thrust the other hand high into the air calling, "Hello!" In his joy and elation, he called to her again without realizing his words. "Lauren! Lauren St. Clare!"

The crew burst into action, a flurry of excitement guiding the vessel toward shore. Lauren continued to scurry and slide down the embankment until she reached the shoreline, where she danced about waving and laughing.

Before the fluyt had even reached the Boar's Head landing, St. Clare was overboard wading waist deep in the water to Lauren. She too, ran into the river where they met and embraced with such fervor it almost toppled them over. James kissed Lauren and swung her around overcome with joy. Scooping her up, he waded to shore pushing the hair from her face, running his lips over her forehead, cheeks and neck. Lauren was breathless with happiness. Her search was over. At last, she was where she belonged. She had found her home.

Chapter 46

That night he whispered words to her in the darkness, spoken softly as he brushed near her ear. James told Lauren that he loved her. These words did not come easily for him but were born of true devotion and tenderness. When she returned the words of love, he experienced at last the most supremely joyful and fulfilling of human experiences.

With *her* love, Lauren found contentment. She could rest knowing that she was at last home. After searching for years, sleeping in windmills, churchyards, bordellos and townhouses, Lauren found her home. In the end it was a vessel, a home without roots, with one person that never settled anywhere. The fluyt and the man who piloted her never stopped moving. They were eternal gypsies like her, changing course and forever seeking new horizons. The home and the man suited her completely.

The crew was elated seeing Lauren again and delighted to hear of the marriage. They gathered around her as family gathers around a loved one that has been too long from the fold, bombarding her with questions, teasing her like schoolboys, vying for her attention.

James indulged them for a while then announced, "It is time for supper, Mr. Bologne. Can you and Robert cook something better than dried peas and biscuits?"

"That I can, Cap'n! Be more 'an happy to!" Henry boomed.

Ben Groot stepped forward bending over Lauren's hand, offering best wishes. It never ceased to amaze her that someone of such gigantic and cumbersome proportions could be so delicate and genteel.

Then for the first time, Lauren saw the new first mate, Josef Duerr. James had known the man for many years and spoke highly of him as a sailor and a person. Lauren watched them talk on deck. Duerr was a man of later years, thick necked with short grey hair and leathery skin. When he tipped his hat to Lauren, she noticed one of his arms hanging limply at his side, shriveled and small. No further explanation was needed why he was part of *The Pride of the King*.

She heard James say, "Mr. Duerr we will only be here for supper. Tonight we take the post road to Hooksett. The *"Pride"* should join us there in three days."

Lauren looked at James and smiled. It pleased her that he had set aside time for the two of them.

After supper, they went to the Boar's Head to gather Lauren's belongings and to speak with Mrs. Quill.

"So you are up and leaving me!" the matron barked. "After all I have done for you!" Mrs. Quill acted slighted, muttering and complaining, but it was all a ruse, she was truly happy for the girl.

As James saddled two mares for the journey, Lauren and Mrs. Quill faced each other for the last time. The matron pursed her lips then said begrudgingly, "Papist or not, you will always have a home here."

"I will be back, Mrs. Quill. I'm sure that I forgot something," Lauren murmured. She reached out and embraced the woman then crossed the threshold out into the twilight. Mrs. Quill watched them as they mounted and rode off in the dim light of sunset on the post road.

"Yet another person disappearing from the Boar's Head," she grumbled to Ogden. Sighing, she climbed the stairs to the inn. Mrs. Quill felt suddenly very tired and went straight to her chair by the fire. As she sat down, she noticed something hanging from the wooden mantle. Leaning to get a closer look, the matron smiled broadly at Lauren's final joke. Taking the rosary from the mantle, she chuckled and said, "Damned Papist."

* * *

Lauren and James devoted three days to finally living as one. They understood that the intimacy they had known in the past had been fraught with secrets and dishonesty, but now they could start fresh and explore one another completely.

Lauren told James everything. She talked of her friendship with Cornelius, her love for Isi and her sincere affection for the crew of the *Pride of the King*. Curiosity about her past consumed him, and he would listen to her reminisce endlessly. They would sit for hours in the common room of the inn by the fire talking.

Elbows on his knees, James would ask Lauren about her home in New Orleans, her life in Kaskaskia and her escapades on Duke Street. He devoured every word she said, trying to make up for their lost time together.

James was more reticent to speak of himself, but he did try. Lauren knew that he would give as much to her as he could, but asking him to drop his reserve and reveal everything was unrealistic and unkind. He frequently did not understand his own feelings and actions, so it seemed pointless and cruel to press him. He seldom spoke of his own experiences but when he did share, Lauren carefully disguised her keen interest with casual questions then quiet reflection. She was grateful for any little thing that he revealed to her and satisfied just knowing that he loved her.

"*I* am an exception to a rule, James," Lauren announced rather abruptly one evening over supper.

He looked up from his meal, still chewing. "Why?"

"I am a wife that has fallen in love with her husband."

He studied her eyes with the hint of a smile on his lips. "It is a most agreeable business arrangement. Is it not?"

After a moments reflection he went on, "For your safety, I do not want our marriage to be a public affair, Lauren. I know the crew is aware of it, but I would prefer that no one else in the organization know."

Lauren nodded and murmured, "I understand."

The three-day holiday was like a dream for them both. They went for long walks along the river; they slept late in the morning and lay together in the afternoon. They dined alone in the evening by the fire, and held each other close throughout the night. In those few days of intimacy, they forged a bond of love that would last a lifetime.

On the third night at supper, Lauren slumped back in her chair and said, "I don't want to go back tomorrow."

James sighed and put his fork down slowly. He had been quiet over supper, and Lauren assumed that he too was disappointed their holiday was ending. He sighed and said, "I didn't want to tell you this, but I am afraid we must leave the inn after we dine tonight."

"What! Why?" Lauren cried.

"Ben Groot was here earlier with a message for me. There has been an incident in the Melungion community to the north."

"The Blascos?"

James looked down. "Yes, and others."

"What happened?"

He signaled the innkeeper to bring another glass of rum, which he tossed back in one swallow. Grimacing he said, "The British cleaned out the camp three nights ago. There are many dead, many injured and many have scattered into the woods. They are defenseless and alone in a land under siege. We must find them."

Lauren stared at James, "When do we go?"

"No, you will not be going, Lauren."

"What! You know that I will be at your side from now on."

"Do not argue with me on this," he warned. "I cannot take you up there. You will stay here with Mrs. Quill."

Lauren leaned in and said, "So we have come full circle, have we? We are back to where we were before you put out to sea. I survived all these years alone. I stand a much better chance of surviving if you are near me."

"A very convincing argument but the answer is still, no."

"When you depart I will simply set off to the north on my own."

St. Clare's jaw tightened, but Lauren was determined.

She continued. "I cannot and will not forget that the Blascos risked their lives for me at Fort St. Frederic and that two of them died by my side on Lake Champlain. I am a member of The Pride of the King as well." She nodded her head vigorously. "I will go, James St. Clare whether I have your blessing or not!"

He sat back in his chair and was silent while Lauren waited for an answer. The air was thick with tension. "Alright," he said. "Pack your things. We must make haste."

*   *   *

St. Clare met briefly with his first mate familiarizing the man with last minute details before he left him in command. At a post outside Albany, Lauren made a trade for a buckskin shift and plaited her hair down her back. Practicality and speed were of the utmost importance and heavy skirts with tight bodices would encumber her on an overland trek.

The fluyt got underway quickly that morning and dropped anchor at the mouth of the creek, which flowed to the gunsmith community. Hidden on the bank was their canoe. Immediately Lauren and James waded through the water, pulled it out from its hiding place and started paddling up the creek. The air was thick and stale as they canoed all day back to the remote locale, bugs buzzing around their heads and stinging them relentlessly. Occasionally James would hand Lauren some dried meat encouraging her to eat while they paddled. It was exhausting and difficult ignoring her weary arms as they paddled deeper and deeper into the interior at breakneck speed.

She knew that it was approaching midday by the way sunlight filtered through the boughs overhead and she wished they would break and rest, but James drove them forward. Whenever she wavered, she reminded herself of the Blascos and all their kin, dead or homeless and her resolve strengthened.

Farther and farther back they paddled until at sunset, James steered the canoe toward shore. The journey seemed interminable, and they climbed stiffly out of the canoe wasting no time pulling the boat onto shore and into the underbrush.

Without saying a word, James took Lauren's hand and pulled her up the hill quickly toward the encampment. Suddenly someone grabbed St. Clare from behind and there was a flash of steel. A gigantic man with matted hair, held a knife to James' throat, and a boy stepped into Lauren's path aiming a rifle at her chest. Her heart jumped into her throat as she locked eyes with this grubby young man about the age of fourteen. His hat and his clothing hung on him like a scarecrow.

Without moving a muscle James murmured, "It is Captain St. Clare, Mr. Magneson."

It took a moment then the man announced in a loud Swedish accent. "Why it's the Captain, Gunnar!" With a push, he released St. Clare and said, "Ya, I should have known!" Magneson signaled to the boy to take the rifle off Lauren and began to brush the Captain off and straighten his coat. "I am sorry but one can never be too sure, Captain."

"No, no," James replied. "Excellent work. Now more than ever we need your diligence."

"Ya, tank you, Captain. I try," the big Swede replied.

Lauren studied Mr. Magneson. The man made no eye contact with the Captain, staring straight ahead without blinking. Surely, Lauren thought, they would not have a man who was blind patrol these woods, but as she studied him she realized he was indeed without sight.

"Gunnar," James said to the boy, "You have grown up. I am pleased to see you are helping your father." The boy shuffled his feet and mumbled something indistinguishable. Then turning to Mr. Magneson, St. Clare said, "I wish to meet with Mr. Griffith right away so I will not keep you. Thank you both."

Mr. Magneson tipped his hat and elbowed his boy to do the same. "Ya Captain, tank you too, Captain."

St. Clare started up the path toward the outpost. Lauren ran alongside him and asked, "Was that man blind?"

"Yes."

"How can he patrol these woods?"

"His lack of sight is not a problem. In fact, it is an asset. The fact that he is blind makes his skill superior to that of a man with sight," explained St. Clare. "His hearing is so acute that he can even identify an Indian out here in this wilderness. On the other side of the outpost, I have a sentry who is deaf. His eyesight is so keen that he can see the slightest of movements, like a bird of prey. He too is an exceptional guard."

When they arrived at the gunsmith community, St. Clare greeted the artisans cordially but wasted no time on small talk looking for Mr. Griffith. The village was as it had been the last time Lauren had visited, bustling and efficient, yet so far from civilization. Sounds of hammers hitting metal rang through the air as smoke pumped out from numerous forges. Lauren heard smiths shouting instructions to apprentices as workmen pushed planes back and forth blanketing the floors with sawdust. Several times, she had to jump aside as carts carrying firearms roared past her on the road.

A tall, lanky gray-haired man in a smith's apron emerged from a workshop shaking St. Clare's hand and Lauren recognized him at once as Mr. Griffith, the foreman of the outpost. They walked to the cabin where Lauren and James had dined several years earlier, but this time they sought privacy and sat inside the dwelling rather than on the porch. There were several long tables with benches and they sat in the back corner near the fireplace.

Griffith sighed and shook his head. "It was a terrible thing, Captain. Many were butchered in their sleep, many fled to the interior. If they lose their way, it could be--"

The door of the cook shanty opened suddenly. It was George Blasco. His nose was bandaged and his face was swollen and purple. When he greeted them, Lauren noticed several of his front teeth were missing.

He sat down stiffly at the table and looked at James. "They slaughtered my family, *Capitao*," he said.

James said nothing searching his face.

"They came in the night," he continued, his voice cracking. "Breaking the doors down, British regulars and some Mohawks. They pulled everyone out and those that resisted they shot. They left some of the family in the cabins then burned them to the ground. Many women and children tried to run to the woods, but many did not make it, their throats were cut or they were scalped. I fought my best but was knocked out. When I woke up, no one was left."

St. Clare asked, "Did anyone else survive?"

"I had word from Davi. He said some have fled into the woods." Blasco's eyes filled with tears and he murmured, "They even killed my little Mama."

Lauren squeezed her eyes shut, fighting tears.

George continued, "Davi sent word a short time ago. Two British regulars are holding Fatima hostage at the burned out remains of our village. God knows what they are doing to her."

Griffith was studying St. Clare. He asked, "What is it Captain?"

James stated, "If any of these butchers still remain, they are deserters. Are the Mohawks still there, Mr. Blasco?"

George shook his head. "Davi said only two regulars."

"We will eat, rest for a few hours then leave under cover of darkness for the settlement," stated St. Clare. He looked at Lauren and asked, "Are you able?"

She nodded.

"Certainly she may stay with us, Captain," Griffith offered. "I believe it would be safer--"

"She stays with me."

The Captain stood up and ordered the foreman to gather a group to search for the Melungions who fled into the woods. He wanted them to set out immediately.

Lauren was awake most of the night. She would occasionally turn and look at James who lay awake as well. He would reach out and run his hand along her cheek then turn back to staring at the ceiling. She watched his silhouette in the darkness, the line of his jaw, his hair spilling down the pillow and his arms behind his head. After several hours, they rose, rendezvoused with George Blasco and set out for the remains of the Melungion settlement.

Springtime was new to the colony and the night air still carried a chill. Lauren had goose bumps at first but eventually the brisk pace warmed her blood. Several times, they upset deer and sent owls into flight, their wings flapping heavily. They forged ahead at breakneck speed, determined to make the settlement before sunrise. Lauren found it difficult to keep up with the long legs of the men, but she did not falter vowing not to slow them down.

The sun was just beginning to rise when they drew near the community. Their first clue was a charred smell. When they spotted the settlement, James signaled for them to drop down into a crouch.

"Davi said to meet him near the creek, by the privies," whispered George.

In the dim light, only shadows were visible of the skeletal remains of the Melungion homes. With horror, Lauren imagined how the village must have looked several nights earlier when it was engulfed in flames and how the screams of agony must have resounded. James pulled her arm, and they moved around the periphery of the settlement. There was only one cabin remaining and Lauren guessed this was where they held Fatima hostage. Keeping low, the three moved through the underbrush until they reached the privies by Popple Creek.

Without a sound, Davi emerged the brush and into the clearing on the shore. Lauren would have known him anywhere; tall and lithe with hair like a black sheet hanging down his back. George jumped forward and hugged him. Lauren found it curious that Davi's arms were hanging limply at his sides as his brother embraced him.

Without warning, he pushed away from George and swung his rifle up taking aim at St. Clare. James froze in his tracks. Lauren did not move.

"Drop your firearms," Davi demanded of them all. The rising sun shone on his rigid face. His eyes were black and lifeless, his expression flat. They dropped their rifles.

"My brother, what has come over you!" gasped George. "Where is our sister?"

"Dead," stated Davi. "There is no one left but me."

George pleaded, "But why? Why do you do this thing--?"

"Shut up!"

Never taking his eyes off St. Clare, Davi snarled, "You were lucky that morning on Lake Champlain at Warrens Landing and again at your campsite when Gaspar and Vincent were killed. My plans failed at Fort Frederick as well. I broke my leg and could not warn Gautier to you were in hiding there as a priest."

James did not move a muscle. Lauren's chest heaved with fear and panic. They were all stunned by Davi's admission of guilt.

"But at last, here and now it will happen. Move away from them, St. Clare," Davi demanded jerking his head to the side.

James moved away from Lauren.

"St. Clare," Davi said. "Here is a calling card from Monsieur Gautier." With those words, his swung his rifle around aiming at Lauren.

James yelled, "No!" and dove at Davi, but it was too late. George had thrown Lauren to safety and instead of hitting Lauren Davi shot his own brother through the head.

Chapter 47

Davi dashed into the woods as James scrambled over to Lauren. George Blasco lay on his back, his lifeless eyes staring at the sky. Lauren cried out struggling with James trying to get to George, but he pulled her into the underbrush.

He shook her demanding, "You must run!"

James pulled onto her feet and they tore through the woods, running down a deer path at a feverish pace. On and on they dashed, fearful Davi would jump out at any moment. Perspiration ran down her back and drenched her forehead. Lauren thought her lungs would explode but she wanted nothing more than to put distance between her and the carnage at the settlement. To avoid discovery, they zigzagged through the woods crossing Popple Creek on several occasions, climbing down ravines and cutting through meadows taking any path rather than the one they had traveled earlier.

It was not until James stopped and began yanking brush back, did Lauren realize they had come to his hideaway. At last, she could catch her breath and feel safe. They collapsed onto the floor, panting.

Lauren asked breathlessly, "Does Davi know about this place?"

James shook his head and pulled himself up. He yanked the top off his powder horn with his teeth, primed and loaded his flintlock then did the same for Lauren. Standing up, she walked to the cupboard and pulled the cork out of a bottle of brandy, putting it to her lips. She relished the warm glow the liquor brought to her body and offered some to James. Taking a long pull, he set it on the table, wiping his mouth on his sleeve.

Collapsing onto a chair Lauren said, "I'm scared, James."

He sighed and sat down heavily. "I knew something was wrong, but I just could not see it. What is wrong with me! I almost got you killed."

"I don't understand how Davi was involved in any of this," Lauren said. "What was he talking about? Was he one of the men by the lake the night before we went to Warren's Landing?"

"Yes, he was among the group that camped nearby when we slept in the trapper's cabin. You had not met him yet, but I spoke to him there briefly. Even then, my instincts told me something was wrong. Do you remember? I changed our plans and we left in the middle of the night, arriving at Warren's landing just before the Indians. It was our good fortune to be able to surprise *them*, not the other way around."

James continued, "Those Indians were not Mohawks at Warren's Outpost that morning and now I know it was not British soldiers massacring the *Melungions* several nights ago. They were French masquerading as British and Mohawks. It served two purposes, to slaughter members of the Pride and to bolster hatred for the British.

Lauren said suddenly, "Davi accompanied us to Fort St. Frederic!"

"Yes, he informed Gautier of all of our movements."

Lauren's jaw dropped. "So, Gautier knew all along! He knew why I came to Fort St. Frederic from the first because of Davi. Gautier turned out to be the one playing me!"

"Gautier must have paid him handsomely." He took another pull off the brandy and ran his hands through his hair. "I must think, I must think."

After a moment he said, "We will rest for a few hours then at nightfall we will journey again."

*   *   *

James awakened with a start, soaked with perspiration. He sat up in bed rubbing his eyes and panting. His jolt roused Lauren, and she pushed herself up on one elbow. The two were fully clothed with flintlocks by their sides. Utterly exhausted they slept through the daylight hours, and it was twilight.

"We must go, "he ordered jumping off the bed.

Asking no questions, Lauren rubbed her eyes. Her muscles shot pain through her body as she slid off the bed. Fear of discovery prevented them from lighting a fire, and the room was frigid. After eating some bread and cheese from their packs they stepped out of the hideaway, powder horns, belts and packs strapped to their bodies and rifles in hand. Lauren ached all over, her body and mind under assault. They started their journey at a swift and steady pace, but before long, James urged them into a full run again. Lauren followed him closely as he dashed madly, bounding through brush, pulling branches aside, leaping over fallen trees. He would stop and let her rest for only a moment before he resumed their pace again too anxious to wait for long. Several times, branches whipped her in the face, but she did not falter, she raced on behind him feeling his urgency and his panic.

Suddenly, the charred smoke of the *Melungion* settlement filled her lungs again. She wondered why James had brought them here once more, back to this scene of ruin and carnage. He stopped abruptly at the clearing and dropped down into a squat. When she reached his side, he yanked her swiftly to the ground as well. Confused and exhausted, she struggled to understand why they were here. Finally, when the clouds passed from the full moon, she understood. She could see that they were not at the *Melungion* settlement at all but at the smoking remains of the gunsmith community. The French had destroyed this settlement as well.

James rolled onto his stomach, rifle in hand. "Watch our backs, Lauren."

In a flash she too rolled over and turned her firearm behind them, scanning the woods by the light of the moon. It cast long shadows through the trees with an eerie glow. She held her breath; there was no movement, no sound. Even the creatures of the forest had fled. Minutes seemed like hours as they waited and watched, straining in the semidarkness to see or hear anything.

"They are gone. No one remains," St. Clare whispered finally.

"When did this happen, James?"

"It must have been within hours of our departure for the *Melungion* settlement. Davi knew we that we would be much easier to confront up there at the settlement, rather than here with help all around us."

"All this pain and butchery. Gautier already has a lucrative business. Why go to this much trouble?" asked Lauren.

"This is what confuses me. There is more to this than Gautier eliminating his competition," James said cryptically.

Like the Melungion community, only a few charred walls stood, alongside blackened stone fireplaces and forges. Lauren's stomach churned at the thought of the gruesome human remains that lie within. She turned her head away from the stench, nauseated.

"These men were outnumbered here," he said. "God knows they had access to weapons. We can only hope some escaped."

"To the interior like the *Melungions*?"

"No. Cavendish Ferry. That is where we are to meet if there is a raid. I tried to convince the Melungions to have such a plan, but they insisted on remaining apart from the rest of us. They said that they would take care of their own."

When at last the clouds drifted back over the moon, James and Lauren slipped cautiously to Popple Creek for their canoe. They found it undisturbed in the brush where they had left it a few days before. All night long they paddled down the creek in the pouring rain thankful for the deluge which covered the slosh of paddles in the water. Lauren knew James was taut with worry and fear. She tried to quell her own anxiety by sorting through all that had happened over the past few days. Her mind kept returning to what James had said earlier about members of The Pride of the King gathering at Cavendish Ferry. *How many would be there? Would they be waiting for instructions? Would the Pride of the King dissolve?* All night she agonized over these questions, and by morning when they arrived at the Hudson, she had made a decision.

It was here, at the confluence of Popple Creek and the Hudson River where they would conceal their canoe and start their journey overland to the south to the fluyt to make plans. She avoided looking at James as he stepped out of the craft pulling it toward shore.

The rain had stopped and the sunrise bathed the Hudson in a golden light. St. Clare strapped on his soaked pack and with a sigh started down the path toward Albany. When he did not hear Lauren's footsteps behind him, he turned around and asked, "What's wrong?"

Lauren took a deep breath, squared her shoulders and said, "I have been thinking all night. There is no one to salvage what remains of organization here in the north. I have decided that *I* will go to Cavendish Ferry and try to find the missing and reorganize. After a lifetime of searching, James I have at last found my home and my people. I will not lose them without a fight."

Their eyes locked. Lauren was unsure whether he was surprised or furious. Swallowing hard she continued, "And you James, must fly to the crew of the fluyt alone. They may be next."

He took a deep breath and turned his back. His shirt was drenched, and his hair was hanging in a wet ponytail. He drew his hands into fists and began pace on the riverbank. Finally, he stopped and looked at the river as flowed by catching the golden sunlight. "I've had you such a short time," he murmured.

Lauren's eyes filled with tears and she stepped up beside him. "And you will have me again."

James draped his arm over her as they watched the river in silence. Finally, he said to her, "I can still see those hands reaching out to me from above, those hands that saved me from drowning. I know now one of them was yours."

Chapter 48

They parted that morning by the river, James heading south in search of the fluyt, Lauren to the north to Cavendish Ferry. Reluctantly, St. Clare let her go. Every instinct to protect his wife was under siege, yet in his heart he knew that he must safeguard everyone in The Pride of the King not just Lauren. He told himself that she was like him, a survivor to the core, but it was small consolation when he watched her figure grow small in the distance.

Lauren did not look back. She would not allow herself to falter for one moment. She feared that one gesture from him would send her flying back into his arms, and her resolve would be lost. She had not told him all of her reasons for going to Cavendish Ferry, the most significant being a feeling of dread. Her instincts told her there was something more to the destruction of The Pride of the King than Julien Gautier's wounded pride, and she had to uncover the truth before any of them could be safe again.

After sitting in the canoe most of the night it felt good to stretch her legs, and Lauren moved swiftly along the banks of the Hudson. She punctuated running with walking along the deer path, staying close to the river in the warm sunshine. Occasionally she would observe a British military vessel sailing north filled with regulars, evidence of the escalating war with the French, but she gave it little attention. Her only thought was Cavendish Ferry.

Just as James had instructed, by late morning she came around a bend in the river and saw a cluster of buildings and a fort in the distance under construction. Stumps and brush were everywhere from construction. The small settlement in front of it was Cavendish Ferry. The most prominent structure of the hamlet was a tavern made of fieldstone and dark wood, a flatboat and a bateau bobbed on the river with a mill and several small cabins clustered along the water. A gangly looking young man in a cap pulled over his eyes stepped out of the tavern toting a bucket, headed for the pigpens. Chickens scattered, clucking and scolding around his feet as he made for the swine.

"Good day to you," Lauren called.

There was no reply.

She came closer and repeated her greeting. "Good day, young man."

When the boy turned to look, Lauren recognized him immediately as the son of the blind guard at the gunsmith outpost. "Oh!" she said with surprise. "We have met. I was with Captain St. Clare at the outpost."

He looked at her in a dazed way then dumped the slops into the trough, the sharp wind snapping his jacket.

"I am so glad to see you are well after everything," Lauren said pushing the hair from her face. "Is your father inside?"

Gunnar hesitated then mumbled, "No." He shook the bucket several times, buried his face in his jacket and trudged back to the inn.

Lauren stood frozen in place, horrified by her insensitivity. She realized by the boy's reaction that Mr. Magneson may be dead. She had been in such a hurry that she had not remembered the refugees seeking shelter at Cavendish Ferry were probably grief stricken. She remembered Fatima and George Blasco and a sickening feeling washed over her. Taking a deep breath she started up the steps of the tavern, reminding herself that everyone must and will be accounted for and that The Pride of the King will endure.

As she walked up the stairs, her head began to spin. Stopping a moment, she steadied herself. Lauren knew the strain of the past few days had been severe. Anxiety had reduced her appetite to nothing, and the hours of physical exertion had been extreme. She ran her hand over her forehead. Her skin was clammy. She stumbled into the front room of the tavern, leaning heavily upon the door. A man in a white apron looked up from his sweeping. His skin was the color of strawberries, and his face appeared as if it had been melted, his features running together like candle wax.

Startled, she reminded herself that she was feeling ill, and it was her mind playing tricks on her. "*Pardon, Monsieur,*" she mumbled. Lauren leaned on a table for support, but it was no help, she began to reel.

The man dropped his broom and ran to her side easing her onto a chair. "Georgiana! Come quickly!" he called.

Lauren heard footsteps.

"She seems ill. That's French isn't it? What is she saying?" the innkeeper asked anxiously.

"Something idiotic, something about a music box and clothes on a line," she heard a woman reply.

"What?"

"It makes no sense."

The innkeeper dabbed a wet towel on Lauren's face, and her eyes gradually refocused. She had not been mistaken earlier, the innkeeper did indeed have skin the color of strawberries, and it was drawn taut over the bones of his face. He had no chin and his features melted from his lips down into his shoulders as if he had a pink flour sack pulled over his head and gathered at the neck. Lauren stared at him in disbelief, lost for words. As if ashamed, he suddenly lowered his eyes.

"Look here! You scared her, Cavendish!" the woman snapped. "How would you like to wake up and see you!"

Lauren looked up at the woman. She had beautiful blue eyes, a full sensual mouth and volumes of golden hair tied behind her head. She was a beautiful woman in the prime of her life, but there were open sores along her lips and under her eyes, tiny red bumps peppered her forearms as well.

"What is it you want?" she said testily to Lauren.

"I am looking for John Cavendish," she mumbled.

"I am Cavendish," the man said.

Lauren started to say something then looked at the woman hesitantly.

He stated, "It's alright. You may speak freely. She is my wife. There is no one else here."

"I am here on behalf of The Pride of the King."

His eyes widened. "You have escaped from the north?" Mr. Cavendish said eagerly.

"I was with Captain St. Clare until this morning," said Lauren. "He headed south to the fluyt, and I came here to help search for survivors."

Georgiana Cavendish chuckled and said "Good luck," sarcastically. She turned on her heel and left the taproom.

John Cavendish looked at Lauren apologetically. "I am sorry, Madame but there is practically no one left from The Pride."

"No one?" said Lauren.

"Most were lost. Two smiths survived from the outpost and made their way here. They left this morning for Albany. The boy, Gunnar Magneson is the only one who remains here now and the two Indians."

"Chickasaw messengers?" Lauren asked anxiously. "Is there a woman?"

The innkeeper nodded. "She is staying not far from here. I will send Gunnar for her if you wish." Lauren had been anxious about Isi from the start although James assured her that she was near Lake Champlain.

John Cavendish continued, "She arrived yesterday completely ignorant of what had been happening. Her man works here at the Ferry as a translator. He sent runners out immediately across the north country putting everyone that survives in the Pride on high alert."

"Is there anyone who can carry this information to Captain St. Clare?" she asked. "He must be informed that almost no one remains from the outpost."

"The smiths who left today will be contacting him as soon as they reach Albany."

Lauren nodded then sighed. She put her face in her hands then rubbed her eyes.

"You are weary, Madame," said Mr. Cavendish. "May I suggest a hearty meal and some sleep?"

"Thank you indeed that would be most welcome."

Lauren did not realize how hungry she was until John Cavendish brought out a plate crammed with hot turkey in gravy, dark bread slathered with butter and two wedges of thick sharp cheese. She thought she would faint from the aroma when he set it in front of her. After gobbling the meal, she pulled herself up the stairs, bathed and fell onto a bed in a backroom where she slept through the afternoon and into the evening.

Late at night, raucous laughter and singing awakened her. Judging by the noise, Lauren could tell the tavern was of a much different character than Mrs. Quill's inn near Hampsted. A drunken couple burst through her door, landing with a crash on the floor as Lauren bolted upright. They started to roar with laughter.

"Beggin' your pardon, Miss," slurred the man with an Irish accent. He dragged himself to his feet and bowed sarcastically. "Didn't mean to give ya a start. This room was empty last night."

The woman stayed on the floor, laughed and said, "Just go back to sleep, darlin'. We'll be real quiet, and if I know Lieutenant Cartwright, it'll be quick too."

They roared with laughter once more, and Lauren snapped the covers off her bed. She stood up and said, "Don't bother. The room is yours."

She gathered her things and slammed the door just as Gunnar Magneson raced up the stairs. "I meant to catch them, but I couldn't get through the crowd in time!"

Lauren pushed the tousled hair from her eyes and mumbled. "Don't worry, Gunnar. I slept long enough."

Gunnar averted his eyes respectfully when he saw Lauren in her chemise and barefoot. She chuckled. "Oh I am sorry. Can you help me find a place to dress?"

"Well I'll be damned!" a voice boomed. "Look at that!"

Lauren spotted a burley sailor staggering up the stairs toward her, wearing a lecherous grin. Gunnar pushed her quickly into a chamber bolting the door behind them. "This is no place for a lady, Miss."

Lauren smiled wistfully. He was far too young to be this responsible. He should be swimming in streams and shooting squirrels.

"I must leave here tonight to find someone," she said urgently. "But I cannot risk going out among those men. Is there a back staircase?"

"No, Miss."

"I need to disguise myself," she said, thinking out loud. "What about some of your clothes? May I borrow them?"

"Yes."

"I must see the Chickasaw translators immediately. Do you know where they are?"

He nodded his head and unbolted the door. "I will be back with clothes, and I will take you to them. Mr. Cavendish gave me orders to watch out for you."

Gunnar returned moments later with a coarse linen smock, breeches and a large felt hat for Lauren. She pulled the clothes on then stuffed her hair into the hat.

"We must tell Mr. Cavendish where we are going first," said Gunnar as they walked down the stairs into the main room of the tavern.

Lauren made no eye contact as she passed through the room of drunken soldiers, farmers and sailors. There was a circle of men shooting dice in the corner and others played cards by the fire. Most of the patrons bellowed tavern songs at the top of their lungs sloshing beer and rum down the ample bodices of the blousy whores on their laps. Two men almost knocked Lauren's hat off as they pushed each other arguing about money.

She felt Gunnar grab her wrist and drag her over to the bar where John Cavendish was drawing beer for customers. Gunnar tried to talk to the innkeeper, but he did not seem to be listening. He was watching his wife Georgiana talk with an attractive young Major. The woman took a deep breath and leaned onto the bar allowing the soldier to look down her bodice, then pouted her lips moving closer. The Major ran his eyes over her breasts then up to her mouth where he saw the sores. He jumped back and exclaimed, "Not on your life!"

The smile dropped from Georgiana's face and her eyes narrowed. Before the woman could act, Cavendish called, "Georgiana my beauty. There is a table that's been asking for you all night. I have a tray for you to take to them."

Angrily she pulled the tray into her arms then spotted Lauren. Georgiana set her jaw and turned away. Lauren had seen that expression before on Duke Street. Women frequently saw her as a rival for male attention, and Georgiana Cavendish was no exception. In the past men had fallen in line to bed her, but now because of her pox their ardor had grown cold.

Lauren followed Gunnar out the door into the night. He pulled on his floppy hat, looked both ways, and then set out with Lauren behind him. The hour was late, but the hamlet was alive with activity. Drunken soldiers and sailors were everywhere, sporting with women near the river, smoking by the docks, staggering down the road toward the fort. Lauren was grateful she had an escort and a disguise, which made her resemble a teenage boy. They walked in silence down a path into the woods and soon the sounds of the tavern were indistinguishable. Gunnar carried a lantern as Lauren followed him along the trail, which led them to a clearing and a cabin on the river.

Suddenly a large dog sprang into their path, standing stiff legged and snarling. Lauren froze as Gunnar put his fingers to his lips and whistled loudly. She heard a whistle in return from shore, and the dog relaxed. He trotted back in the direction of a dying campfire.

Isi and her husband stepped out of the shadows. Lauren pulled off her hat letting her hair tumble down and the two women embraced. "You are safe," Isi said.

Lauren sighed, "Most have not been so lucky. We must talk, my friend. I have so much to ask you."

She nodded, and they walked down to the campfire. Isi's husband threw several logs onto the embers, sending sparks flying. Lauren could see Isi's eyes in the firelight, and she read fear in them.

"Tell me who is left," Lauren said.

"I only found out yesterday about the slaughter," Isi murmured. "Few are left. Some members survived near Lake Champlain, but everyone else is gone. All that is left of The Pride of the King is in the south."

"James is headed for the fluyt now."

"Good. There are the three vessels and members all the way down to a place called Providence."

James had shared little about his operation in the south with Lauren. There was still so much to learn about the man. A tug of loneliness pulled at her.

"Surely Gautier cannot reach that far into the English Colonies," Lauren speculated.

"Lauren, I think these white men are capable of anything."

"You are right. We must know more. I believe Gautier and his men will not be happy until The Pride of the King lay completely in ruins. I must gain access to those close to Gautier to understand what is going on."

Isi's eyes grew large. "You are not going back to Fort St. Frederic," she said.

"No," said Lauren chewing on a nail, deep in thought. "That would be suicide. There must be another way."

Late the next morning, Lauren came downstairs, stiff and sore but rested at last. She pressed several coins into John Cavendish's hand insisting Captain St. Clair would want him to take compensation for her food and lodging. She took her breakfast outside on the front step of the tavern. Morning sunshine, rest and sustenance gave her new resolve.

She stood up, emptied the dregs of her tea onto the ground, and walked down to the water. Yet another journey lay of her ahead of her, and she felt uncertain and exhausted. She did not know where to go or how to begin this undertaking, and if she was not careful, she could lose her life.

Lauren did not hear Georgiana Cavendish walk up behind her. Feeling her presence at last, she jumped and turned around. The woman did not apologize, but instead looked boldly at Lauren then ran her eyes over her figure. Instantly Heloise's words echoed in Lauren's ears, *"No matter how fine your manners and attire. They will recognize the blight in you."*

Lauren raised her chin and said, "What is it you want?"

"I know you. I know your kind," said Georgiana. "Years ago I belonged to Captain St. Clare."

A look of disgust passed over Lauren's face and she turned away. She disliked this woman and knew that she could only mean trouble. She started up the hill toward the tavern. The woman grabbed her arm and said, "Listen to me you stupid slut. I can help you."

"I think not," Lauren replied and turned away again.

Georgiana called after her, "I don't give a damn about you but I do about St. Clare. I have what you need to put everything right."

Reluctantly, Lauren turned around.

"Someone wants to destroy The Pride of the King, but it is more than that. I believe they want to ruin St. Clare, to rob him of everything he values and loves."

Lauren remembered when Davi tried to kill her instead of James. It was apparent they wanted revenge not just elimination.

"With your French background you need to go up there and find out who is doing this and what they intend to do next."

Lauren said sarcastically, "Really? That never occurred to me."

Grabbing Lauren by the wrist, Georgiana hissed, "I'm not finished yet. For many years, I was a *sutler* following the British and sometimes the French armies all over the North Country. I had a pony cart and sold wares to the troops--liquor, tobacco and sometimes entertainment. There is knowledge to be had as a sutler. You are in the heart of everything."

"So you are suggesting I become a sutler and a spy," Lauren said.

"Yes, but if you are not careful you will get your neck stretched. It is very dangerous."

"How do I become a sutler?"

"Take my place, cart and all. I have only just returned. Get that trashy Chickasaw to go with you."

"If you care so much about the Captain why don't *you* go?" asked Lauren.

"I would but I'm too damned sick. It turns my stomach to think that I have sleep night after night next to that creature Cavendish, but I have nowhere else to go."

Lauren studied Georgiana a moment then asked, "What happened to him?"

"Cavendish? Oh, that was years ago. I had a little too much rum one night and set the bed on fire. Damned fool dragged me out. His clothes caught on fire."

Lauren stared at Georgiana.

"I wish to hell we would have just burned up." She turned and walked toward the tavern her hips swaying from side to side. She called over her shoulder, "The cart, donkey and supplies are in the barn. Take everything and get out. I don't want to see you or that cart ever again."

Chapter 49

Lauren accepted Georgiana's offer of the pony cart and supplies almost immediately, and after finalizing plans with John Cavendish, Lauren Isi and Gunnar set off for Lake Champlain. After many hours of travel they stopped at the home of an elderly couple. John Cavendish instructed Gunnar to stay with them to operate as a courier for Lauren and Isi while they gathered information on Lake Champlain and to help them with their farm.

"Remember, my indigo skirt on the clothes line, Gunnar. It is the signal that we have news," said Lauren. "*Bon chance and au revoir, mon ami.*"

The boy looked up from under his hat and nodded. Isi snapped the reins and the donkey snorted, pulling them away from the cabin. Lauren turned back to look at the farm. The smoke looked cozy curling up from the field stone chimney. The elderly couple Dutch and Lena Claus had immigrated to the Lake Champlain area from Prussia over twenty years ago. She wondered how the couple endured this life of isolation and grueling labor back in the dark interior. With the war escalating these simple people could expect not only privation but violence as well. It was not surprising that the couple was overjoyed to have Gunnar for the summer to help with chores and protection during raids.

Lauren and Isi rode in silence winding their way through the woods nearing Lake Champlain. They had been traveling for many days now, and they were road weary. The fog was thick that morning leaving a fine layer of mist on their skin and clothing. Lauren was sick to death of watching the rolling rump of the donkey as he obediently pulled the cart along the bumpy trail heading north. Her neck grew stiff and she rotated her head several times to loosen the muscles. Isi was quiet as usual, and when Lauren glanced at her profile the girl's face was taut and her eyes were bloodshot.

Isi asked, "How often will Gunnar come to look for a signal?"

"Once a week on the Sabbath, if he finds the indigo skirt hanging out he will come to us under the guise of delivering supplies. Gunnar will run information to your husband who will in turn run it to Cavendish."

The women could now speak freely in French. For many days Lauren had to remain mute carefully guarding her accent from the British patriots and soldiers they met along the road, but now they had at last entered French occupied territory, and Lauren could speak freely. She touched her bodice to make sure the letter of introduction from Georgiana Cavendish was still there. Georgiana had instructed them to report to the French commanding officer and present this letter of reference when they found the encampment. Georgiana was well acquainted with those in charge at Lake Champlain, and she assured them there would be little hesitation to employ the women as sutlers once they read the letter of guarantee from her.

Isi straightened up cocking her head and listening. "What is that?"

"What?" questioned Lauren.

"I hear something--chopping, I think."

In the distance were voices and they heard a cracking sound followed by a dull thud. The donkey jerked his head, startled at the vibration on the ground.

"Sounds like they are felling trees," said Lauren. They observed stumps and brush along the trail and gradually the voices grew louder.

Suddenly around a bend two young sentries jumped out of the mist and into their path. One grabbed the donkey's bridle while the other pointed a musket at them. "Present yourselves!" the young French soldier barked. He wore the blue uniform of a French officer.

"I am Madame de Beauville," said Lauren. "And this is my Chickasaw slave, Isi. We are here to see your commanding officer."

"About?" he demanded stepping alongside the cart running his eyes over the canvas covering.

"We are sutlers," said Lauren.

The young *bas officier* jerked his head at the sentry. The regular, a boney youth with stringy hair, dropped the donkey's bridle and went to the back of cart throwing back the canvas to examine the contents of their wagon. After pushing some barrels and jamming his musket into to some clothing he gave a nod of approval to the *bas officier*.

"Follow me," he said.

With one sentry in front and the other in back, Lauren and Isi guided the wagon toward the French encampment. The soldiers escorted them into a huge clearing littered with brush and debris from fallen trees. A breeze picked up lifting the fog to reveal a panoramic view of Lake Champlain. The area was alive with men at work as they toiled on a sloping hillside not far from a clear rushing stream. There was a thick smell of sawdust and pine tar punctuated by fresh lake breezes. Everywhere French regulars moved like ants, chopping and dragging logs and brush, digging trenches, mixing mud and stacking logs while officers barked orders at crews.

"They build a fort?" Lauren asked the bas officier as they wound past the workmen.

"They do. It is Fort Carillion."

"It is large," Lauren said running her eyes over the spectacle. Then turning to Isi, she dropped her voice and murmured, "This is hard work. They will need much alcohol and tobacco at the end of the day."

Isi raised her eyebrows and nodded.

The sentries took them to a large canvas tent, and the young officer disappeared inside. After a few moments he threw back the flap, poked his head out and said to Lauren, "He will see you now." The women exchanged looks as Lauren climbed down off the cart.

The first thing she saw as she entered the tent was a large desk littered with parchment and maps. In the shadows was a tall man in a powdered wig and uniform standing with his back turned. He had thrown his grey top coat onto a chair, and his shirt sleeves were rolled up at the elbows revealing graying hair on his arms. The room smelled of stale tobacco and perspiration. He turned around to address Lauren, and she felt her throat constrict.

"I am Lieutenant Brobriant. What is your business here, Madame?"

Lauren recognized the man, but she struggled to remember where she had seen him.

He sighed impatiently and said, "I am a busy man. What is it?"

Suddenly it came back to her in a rush. Brobriant was the commanding officer of Fort de Chartres in Kaskaskia many years ago. This was the man to whom she had reported the suspicious nature of Madame Aberjon's demise a long time ago. It was apparent that he did not recognize her.

Lauren babbled, "Lieutenant, I apologize. The journey has been arduous and I am slow to speak." She reached inside her bodice and withdrew the letter of introduction from Georgiana.

Brobriant took it, noting that it was still warm from the skin on her breast. He ran his eyes over her figure, broke the seal on the letter and read it. "You have a wagon?" he asked.

"Yes."

"What do you bring?"

"Tobacco, wine," she shrugged. "Some rum, brandy, pipes, food."

He sighed and turned away.

Lauren felt her palms start to perspire.

"Well," he warned pursing his lips. "I will not tolerate you gouging my men with high prices."

"We will only ask fair market value, Lieutenant."

"We? Who is we?" he said his brow furrowing.

"My slave woman and I."

He sighed again and circled around his desk leaning on the front of it. "My men need diversion. They work hard. Do you sell your services as well?"

"No sir. We do not."

There was a pause and he said, "That is just as well. It causes problems."

Lauren felt her stomach jump; he seemed to be considering the offer. The sooner he consented, the sooner she could go before he remembered her. "That Cavendish woman used to obtain her supplies from a smuggler in the English Colonies by the name of--" he rubbed his brow. "His name escapes me."

"If you are thinking of the organization called The Pride of the King, they exist no longer."

"I don't want to know where you obtain your supplies or who brings them, just get them here promptly and don't bother me with anything," he said handing the letter back to her.

"Very good, Lieutenant," Lauren said with a curtsy.

"You may use the abandoned shack by the stream. If you cause any problems you will be out on your ear. Do you understand?"

"Yes sir, Thank you, sir," said Lauren leaving the tent.

*   *   *

Business was brisk for the new sutlers at the French encampment. The women cleaned and repaired the abandoned shack and white washed the interior. Using her charms Lauren approached several of the soldiers to cut a large window in the shack so the women could erect a counter and sell their wares. This shop window could be bolted tightly with shutters at night since they would also sleep there. Their quarters were Spartan and cramped with wooden crates and barrels, but Lauren and Isi slept soundly working furiously throughout the day to fill orders.

The French regulars and the officers were anxious for alcohol and tobacco and consumed large quantities returning regularly to the sutler shack when they were off duty. Initially they assumed Lauren and Isi were whores but the women soon established boundaries rebuffing their overtures. Nevertheless, females were a novelty on Lake Champlain, and the men returned to the store regularly for the female companionship.

Lauren was in her element once more, encouraging snappy repartee and good natured flirtation. She worked the men as if she was a courtesan of the Sun King, flattering and teasing, laughing and cajoling each one of them. Then gradually, without their knowledge, she manipulated the conversation to local politics and gossip to gather information about the French officers and local inhabitants of New France.

Isi had her own strategy for obtaining information. The young woman used her status as a slave to eavesdrop on the soldiers as she sold them alcohol and tobacco silently mixing among them, listening to gossip. They believed her incapable of understanding the white man's language, and even if she did speak French they cared little what she heard. They believed women, especially Indian females, were either too stupid or too lazy to be a threat.

Weeks passed and the timber walls of the fort were starting to outline a massive fortress. It was approaching mid summer and the troops now turned their attention to erecting barracks, officer's quarters, storehouses and a powder magazine as well. The spring had been extraordinarily dry and because of the lack of rain great progress had been made on the construction. The hot, dry winds of summer gave the men a great thirst and drove them back continually to the sutlers for libation.

Lauren was growing impatient, and she was beginning to wonder if it had been prudent to come to Lake Champlain after all. It was already the end of June, and they had gathered no information of importance. She missed James terribly and felt cheated. They had only just found each other and now were driven apart once more. She was angry that she may have traveled from the warmth and security of his love on a futile mission fraught with danger. Nevertheless a nagging suspicion held her there.

Over the weeks, the heat and humidity became oppressive and the men grew short tempered and irritable. Lauren scoffed at them. Summer in the north was nothing compared to June in New Orleans and she wearied of their incessant complaining.

"The men are surly and unpredictable, Lauren," Isi said one evening after a regular had grabbed her wrist in a rage when she had dropped his bottle of brandy.

"Yes," nodded Lauren her lips pursed. "Beware; it is good weather for raping."

Her lips softened into a smile as a red haired, sunburned regular approached the cottage. Isi marveled at Lauren's ability to shed her skin like a snake transforming herself from a cool, calculating business woman into a sassy, seductive coquette the troops adored.

"Oh, my little friend, your eye, it is bruised," she said pulling her lips down into a pout. "How did it happen?"

The boy scowled. "It was Maintenon. He turned suddenly and hit me with the log he had on his shoulder. I was the one who was hurt and Lieutenant Brobriant cursed *me* for being careless. I need something strong to kill the pain."

Isi wiped her hands on her apron and turned to find the boy some brandy.

"Brobriant was actually out of his quarters?" quizzed Lauren. She had been reticent until now to ask about the Lieutenant. She did want anyone to suspect that she knew him, but she was curious why he was so far from Kaskaskia.

"Yes. It is not often we see him. He buries himself in his tent, longing for his fat cow of a wife back in the Illinois Country."

"He did not ask for this assignment?"

"No, he was transferred. Everyone knows it is because he accused a powerful man of murdering his wife."

Isi dropped the bottle of brandy.

Lauren covered with a reprimand. "That is two broken bottles now! You clumsy fool. Pick it up."

The women exchanged looks as they bent down to retrieve the shards of green glass.

"Murder is a very serious accusation," said Lauren to the young man. She remembered Brobriant saying those same words to her a long time ago.

"Especially when you accuse, an Aberjon of *two* murders. Brobriant ignored the death of Aberjon's first wife, but when his second wife died suddenly, he began to ask questions."

Isi replaced the bottle, and the young regular picked it up.

Before he left Lauren asked, "How do you know these things my young friend?"

"I am from *Pays des Illinois*, Madame. I was born in the town of Cahokia near Kaskaskia."

*   *   *

"I must talk with him," said Lauren as she bolted the shutters in place for the night.

"It is in the past, Lauren. It can serve no purpose." Isi touched her face remembering the muzzle. The memory was still red hot.

"You heard what that boy said. Brobriant finally believed me," Lauren argued.

"We are not here to bring Aberjon to justice. It can only end badly. You are losing sight of our purpose. Erase it from your mind, Lauren and get some sleep."

Isi continued with their bedtime routine. The women would straighten their inventory, shed their heavy outer garments, kill mosquitoes and drop onto their cots, sleeping heavily until morning, but that night Lauren did not rest well. She confused dreams with reality. She thought she was back in Kaskaskia, sleeping in the Aberjon household then she thought she was in the captain's quarters on *The Pride of the King,* but with each dream came a growing anxiety which woke her with a start before dawn.

Sitting bolt upright in bed, Lauren pushed the damp locks from her face and pulled the drenched shift away from her body. She looked over at Isi who continued to sleep soundly. Lauren unbolted the shutters of the shack for a breath of fresh air and leaned on the counter looking out at the vast lake. Her constant worries prevented her from appreciating the placid beauty of the water outlined with deep, green pines. She did notice the sun's orange and gold rays on the glassy surface of the water and a loon gliding gracefully past. Lauren sighed and rubbed her forehead. She was weary and confused.

Then suddenly out of the corner of her eye she saw someone move toward shore. It appeared to be one of the officers enjoying the sunrise. She watched the man walk slowly by the lake, stopping to sit on a boulder, one arm on his knee. When he turned his profile to Lauren, she realized it was Lieutenant Brobriant.

Dropping a gown over her shift, Lauren tied her hair into a knot and quietly stepped outside. Biting her lip, she took a deep breath and started down to shore. When he heard her footsteps, Brobriant stood up. "Good morning, Madame," he said cordially. "I was just enjoying the sunrise."

"Indeed, Lieutenant. It is most beautiful."

They said nothing for a moment, standing side by side watching the loon dive for his breakfast. Lauren said finally, "It is quiet and peaceful, but it does not have the majesty and power of the Mississippi."

The lieutenant turned and looked at her. "You know of this river?"

"Yes, I was raised on it," Lauren replied still looking out at the lake.

"I too, Madame. Where were you born?"

"In New Orleans but I lived several years in the Illinois country in the town of Kaskaskia."

"*Mon Dieu*! I too lived there. In fact my wife and children are still in Kaskaskia."

"Yes, I know," admitted Lauren looking down as if ashamed of her deception. "I know more about you than you realize, Lieutenant. We have met, but you do not remember me."

He stared at Lauren trying to remember her, and for the first time she noticed the heavy lines in his tanned face. He smiled and shook his head. "I am sorry, Madame but--"

"Many years back at *Fort De Chartres*. I came to you about the suspicious nature of my mistress's death, Madame Aberjon."

Brobriant smile dropped. He gasped, "You! You are the girl?" Stepping back he looked Lauren up and down. "Where did you go? I searched for you and you had disappeared."

"The Aberjons made sure I was far away, Lieutenant."

His scowled and he said, "They made sure I was sent far away as well. I would like nothing more that to expose those scoundrels."

"I agree, Lieutenant."

"Do you know the son is here, Madame?"

Lauren's heart lurched in her chest. Her mouth went dry, and she struggled to speak but no words would come.

Brobriant watched her and nodded.

Finally she gasped, "Claude! Claude Aberjon is here?"

"Not here at the fort but nearby in Montreal, I have learned that New France is a much smaller place than I had ever realized."

Lauren shook her head in disbelief. "Why is he here?"

Brobriant shrugged and said, "He lives with his cousin, Julien Gautier."

Chapter 50

The trapper watched the woman named Lauren walk from the shoreline alongside the commanding officer of the fort. He was told she would be easy to find. "Look for the woman with hair the color of a fox," they said.

This animal would be easy to track, thought the trapper. *Females like that standout and are easy to cut out from the herd.* He hated her already. In the world of man, females like that rebuffed him, scorned his thick features, bushy dark hair and low forehead. His size intimidated them and somehow they sensed he could crush them with one hand if he chose. He ran his eyes over the woman's figure and his loins tightened. He reminded himself he was not to touch her in that way. They had made that perfectly clear.

The trapper watched her close the door on the little shack. Soon she would open the shutters and sell her wares to the soldiers. He would mix among his French comrades talking of the price of hides or the next rendezvous, but all time he would be watching and waiting.

* * *

Lieutenant Brobriant and Lauren agreed to meet that night over supper. Lauren woke Isi that morning with the news of Claude being in Quebec with his cousin, Julien Gautier. The women spoke in low tones for almost an hour, trying to sort out the implications of their old enemy being in this part of New France. It was not until there was a knock on the shutters that they realized it was time to open for business.

It was another dry, sultry day in the North Country. The sun scorched the earth and leeched water from Lake Champlain as the men bent their backs to the burning rays, chopping and framing a fortification which would guard the passage to a continent.

Business was slow during the daylight hours but at nightfall, when the men were off duty, they beat a steady path to the sutler window. Lauren asked Brobriant to send a regular to stand guard by the shack to make sure Isi was safe during the final hours of business that night when she was gone.

Lauren had no clothing suitable to be dining with a ranking officer. She searched her trunk finally pulling out an old pink gown with a cream-colored stomacher. The material was worn and threadbare, but the gown had belonged to Madame Aberjon and she found the choice more than appropriate for that evening.

After sponging off the perspiration and grime of the day, Lauren slipped on the gown, placed combs in her hair, and then smudged some charcoal on her eyelids and berry stain on her lips. These ministrations would lead the men to believe she was paying an amorous visit to the commanding officer.

She was escorted to Lieutenant Brobriant's tent by one of the minor officers and played the coquette while the young man was in attendance. She flattered Brobriant's physique insisting he leave his topcoat off during supper, cooed over the rich food being served and flashed her pirate smile seductively at both males. The moment the young officer left the tent she dropped her ruse and was all business.

"Please tell me what you know about the Aberjons, Lieutenant."

Brobriant leaned back in his chair studying Lauren. He took his fist away from his mouth and said, "No, Madame. Suppose you tell me first about who you are. You are no sutler."

Lauren raised an eyebrow and murmured, "No sir. I am not."

He sipped some wine and stated, "I want more information about you before I go on."

Lauren chose her words carefully. "After I left Kaskaskia, I lived for a time in the English Colonies. Not by choice. I hated the Aberjons for banishing me from Kaskaskia and separating me from those I loved in the Illinois Country, but I buried my rage and carried on, much like you."

"You carried on in what profession, Madame?" he pressed.

"I spent some years as a courtesan," she shrugged. "Some years as a cook and innkeeper."

"But you never forgot," he added.

Lauren shook her head.

"I too never forgot," Brobriant said leaning forward. "I remembered when you came to me years ago, and it was because of you that I suspected Aberjon of murder several years later when his second wife died suddenly. Jean-Baptiste and his son Claude had exhausted this woman's funds and needed to make yet another prosperous marriage. I started asking questions about her death and they did not like it. With this second murder they had grown smug and complaisant *and* careless. They did not even bother to find a scapegoat to take the blame for the second treachery. They shrugged and said, "Such is life and death, Lieutenant."

Lauren closed her eyes trying to control the memories flooding her mind; Jean-Baptist drinking in the sitting room, the sound of Madame's music box, the red blood on the snow the day she broke Claude's nose. She opened her eyes and looked at Lieutenant Brobriant.

"I conducted an investigation," he continued. "And found poison in Claude Aberjon's possession. The poison that most likely killed the first Madame Aberjon, but it was too late. My orders came and I was immediately transferred to Montreal where I learned I would work under the Marquis de Lotbiniere in the building of Fort Carillion. They had sealed my fate."

"And your family could not accompany you?"

His expression grew dark. "No, my daughter was not strong enough to make the journey. She had consumption. That was the last time I saw her. She died several months later. She was only twelve."

Lauren jawed tightened. There seemed to be no end to the lives the Aberjon's had ruined. She murmured, "My most heartfelt condolences."

Collecting himself Brobriant took a deep breath and continued, "And that is why having Claude Aberjon nearby in Montreal is opening old wounds again."

"Indeed it is, Lieutenant. Please tell me. Claude's cousin is Julien Gautier?"

"Yes, Jean Baptiste is the brother of Gautier's mother."

"Why is Claude here?"

"It seems Claude and his father are destitute once more. Claude lost the lead mine in a card game early last autumn in New Orleans. He encountered the infamous Adair Heathstone, a renowned card shark from the English Colonies. In a last minute attempt to make good, he lost the family business."

Lauren's body went rigid. Her mind began to race and her heart pound. Before she could speak Brobriant continued. "This Heathstone character gambles for a smuggler by the name of--," he shook his head. "It always escapes me."

"James St. Clare," she whispered.

"Yes that's it. The Aberjons were not concerned about the loss of the family business to St. Clare because Englishmen cannot own French property, particularly in time of war, but the man surprised them. This St. Clare sent a vessel this spring up the Mississippi blockading all convoys coming up or down the river. When St. Clare's men encounter a bateaux they confiscate the lead, supplies or whatever booty they can find and keep it for their own."

Lauren swallowed and said with a shaky voice, "He sounds like a pirate."

Brobriant chuckled, "Well, call him what you will; I enjoy his creative debt collection."

*   *   *

Lauren felt as taut as the hemp on a bow. She thought she would snap as she followed the guard back to the shack. Not only had the information from Brobriant been unnerving, but she had the distinct feeling she was being watched. She wanted nothing more than to bolt and run from this web of treachery.

She decided not to tell Isi what she had learned. The girl had not been well since she heard of the close proximity of the Aberjons. Since then she had been sleeping little and eating even less, and Lauren knew that all the horrifying memories haunted her once more.

Lauren spent the night staring at the ceiling, trying to sort through all she had heard from Brobriant and struggling to make sense of the dangerous game James St. Clare was playing in the Illinois Country. She suspected that her husband taunted the Aberjons because of the pain they had caused Isi and herself, and she knew that she was the only one who could put an end to this perilous game of chess.

St. Clare had already made an enemy of Gautier, threatening to steal his merchant monopoly in New France, but now she realized he ruined Jean-Baptiste and Claude Aberjon as well, the most powerful French merchants in the west. There was no doubt in her mind that they were responsible for the extensive attacks on The Pride of the King.

The next day she told Isi that she had learned nothing of importance. Then that afternoon, Lauren pinned her indigo skirt to the clothesline along with the rest of the laundry in back of the shack. Isi did not notice the signal, and when Gunnar brought supplies the next day Lauren spoke privately with him.

"Isi is not well and she is in danger here," she whispered to the boy. "The only way she will leave my side is if she believes her husband is ill. I want you to take her back to Cavendish Ferry then return to the Claus homestead and check every few days for my signal. Do you understand?"

"I understand," the boy murmured.

"Now take her and leave immediately," Lauren ordered.

Gunnar replaced his floppy hat and unloaded the donkey cart. Lauren wiped her hands on her apron and went back to work feeling confident that Gunnar would deliver her friend to safety.

The boy had Isi on the donkey cart that afternoon. Isi's face was pinched with fear and anxiety. "I am so scared, Lauren. I don't want to leave you, but I must. Something feels wrong here."

Lauren assured her that she had a new and powerful friend in Lieutenant Brobriant, and that he would post a guard near the shack for her. She would be quite safe here at Fort Carillion. This didn't seem to comfort Isi. She continued to look back from the cart, watching Lauren until the thick pines swallowed them up. Lauren on the other hand felt relieved. She knew that a reunion with her husband would quell Isi's anxieties and that distance would ease the burden of her memories of Kaskaskia.

That night she requested a meeting with Brobriant. When she arrived at his tent she suggested they take a walk. He lit a lantern and they walked down to the lake. There was no moon that night, and the lieutenant held the lantern high to light their way.

"Why so clandestine, Madame?" he asked stopping by the shore. The candlelight flickered over him throwing his face into angular shadows.

"Because I believe your tent may have ears, Lieutenant. What I am about to propose will cause great repercussions."

He sat down on a boulder and set the lantern beside him.

Lauren remained standing. "I will be completely frank with you," she said. "I am the wife of James St. Clare, the leader of the organization The Pride of the King."

He straightened up and said, "What!"

"Please, Lieutenant. I beg you to let me finish."

Lauren could see his eyes narrow in the lantern light. He was suspicious of her now. "I have come to Lake Champlain to end the bloodshed in the settlements just south of here. I now realize that Gautier and the Aberjons are behind it. They have been trying to kill my husband and me over the past month and cripple our organization. In the process many innocents have died or been displaced. I am here, without my husband's knowledge, to try to identify the men behind these machinations and to undo them." Lauren paused and looked at Brobriant.

His jaw was clenched as her studied her face, "Go on," he ordered.

"I suggest we entrap these vermin with promises of power and monopoly. Their lust for money and supremacy supersedes any sense of moral obligation to King or country." Lauren swallowed hard and continued, "I propose entrapment."

She expected Brobriant to react as he had years ago in Kaskaskia when she suggested the Aberjons were guilty of murder. His reaction then was outrage and disbelief. This time he stood up, rubbed his chin and began to pace.

He turned and said, "How?"

A smile of relief flickered on Lauren's lips. "I will approach them as a representative of James St. Clare and The Pride of the King. I will propose that St. Clare and his operation will leave New England and New France permanently if they provide him with information about the troop movements of the French here in Lake Champlain. St. Clare will in turn sell this information to the British. This money will enable him to leave this part of the continent for good and start over in the West Indies. St. Clare will disband The Pride of the King terminate the blockade on the Mississippi and leave Gautier with the smuggling monopoly in Lake Champlain."

Lauren could not see the Lieutenant's expression in the darkness, but she could feel his eyes on her.

"And if they comply?" he asked.

"The authorities will be outside the door waiting to arrest them for treason."

He sighed and said, "How can you think they won't be suspicious?"

"Oh, they *will* be suspicious, but I believe their greed will cloud their judgment and more importantly, I believe *I* will cloud their judgment. These three men have a fundamental distain and hatred for women which is paramount and to admit that a lowly servant girl could be a threat to them would be unthinkable."

There was a pause and Brobriant said, "You are very sure of yourself."

"No, Lieutenant. I am very sure of them."

"And if they refuse?"

Lauren shrugged. "Then everything remains as it is, nothing more, nothing less."

"Why do you approach me?" he asked.

"You know where to find them. I need you to set up a meeting."

She heard him chuckle. "Impossible. They would have nothing to do with me."

"Well could you send me to--"

"Wait," he interrupted and he began to pace again. "There is a possibility. I know someone who loathes them as much as I do, but he conceals his true opinion. They would listen to him."

"Is it Dazemard de Lusignan from Fort Frederic?"

"No, but he hates them too. His name is Sebastian Dubois. He is the commander of Fort Saint-Jean on the Richelieu River."

"And you trust this Dubois?"

"I do. I will be meeting with him within the week, but he is unpredictable. This may not be to his liking."

"I will be waiting for your answer," said Lauren.

She turned and started back to her cabin leaving the Lieutenant on the shore watching her shadow move into the distance. The night breeze carried her scent to his nostrils and he remembered once more that she was a woman.

Chapter 51

The sun was relentless that summer and the rain nonexistent. Wildfires left a constant stench of smoke in the air and every living thing seemed on edge. Lauren longed for a fresh breath as she walked on the deer path heading to the north. She followed a group of soldiers, native women and trappers bound for a rendezvous on Lake Champlain, halfway between Carillon and Frederic. After several minutes the path turned downhill and they came out by the lake which flooded them with breezes and fresh air. Lauren heard several of the group sigh with relief.

The waterway was busy with canoes and bateaux bulging with furs and trade goods for the merchants and businessmen to inspect at the rendezvous, but this was only a small part of the grand meeting. At its core it was a celebration. A celebration of another year of survival in the rugged and dangerous interior, a celebration of the easy days of summer, a celebration of companionship and good will.

Strains of a bagpipe reached Lauren's ears, and she heard the hearty laughter of men. Because of the abundance of males, Lauren had stuffed her long, auburn hair under a floppy hat and clothed herself in her buckskin shift. For much of the way

Lauren thought she was the straggler on the trail, but hearing a twig snap, she looked behind her and saw a grizzly trapper following her. He kept his distance, but she felt his eyes on her the whole time.

Lieutenant Brobriants's instructions had been scant. He informed her that Julien Gautier, Jean Baptiste and Claude were purchasing furs at the rendezvous, and Lauren was to meet with them at a tavern at midday. Her contact was a *coureur des bois* or trader by the name of Guilliume Golon who had set up everything. Gautier and the Aberjons were ignorant of Dubois' involvement.

The festivities were in full force. Everywhere Lauren looked there was activity. Tents and campfires were scattered near the lake, circles of men gambling, fiddlers and dancers, men leaning on barrels drinking and telling stories of their adventures and there were women, many more women than Lauren had expected. Native and European women were cooking, dancing, mingling with the men. Many dressed in buckskin or loose blouses, skirts and aprons. Some appeared to be wives, mothers or cooks, some sold companionship.

She was told this Golon was an expert tomahawk thrower, and Lauren knew that she could find him near that competition. Brobriant said that everyone knew the large grey haired trader and finding him would not be a problem.

Lauren noticed people looking at the tall, black clouds beginning to build overhead. They all welcomed the rain and when large drops started to splash down there were cheers. Some ran to their tents, but most of the traders and voyageurs remained in the elements, thinking nothing of the wind and the rain.

Lauren spotted a large raw boned man pulling targets off the bark of a tree holding three tomahawks. He wore his long, grey hair tied back under a dirty three-cornered hat, and Lauren guessed this rough looking character was her contact.

Rain was running off her floppy hat in a steady stream, and the man bent down under the brim to see her face. "Well, well! There is somebody under there!" he boomed. Lauren smiled and he smiled back with a large toothless grin. "Couldn't tell there was such a pretty little thing under that hat."

"Are you Monsieur Golon?" she asked.

"That I am. What can I do for you?"

"I am here to meet Messieurs Julien Gautier, Jean Baptiste and Claude Aberjon." Guilliume Golon's smile dropped. Taking Lauren by the elbow he escorted her into a nearby tent. He took his hat off and slapped it against his knee to knock the water from it. Searching her face he asked, "Do you know what kind of men they are?"

Lauren took a breath and said, "I do."

After a moment's hesitation he shrugged and said, "Very well, little one." He walked her to the only structure on the site, a tall two story log tavern with a fieldstone foundation. Golon held the door, and she saw the trapper who had been following her on the trail walking in behind him. Golon and Lauren passed through a drinking establishment filled with smoke and boisterous unwashed voyageurs and up a staircase. When Lauren looked back, the stranger had taken a seat at a table in the corner of the room. Golon escorted her down a hall then disappeared into a one of the chambers. Lauren could hear murmuring then two squat men in stocking caps emerged and started down the stairs. Jerking his head Golon said, "You can go in now."

He went downstairs leaving her alone outside the door. The rain was drumming on the roof, and there was laughter downstairs, but Lauren heard none of it. She took off her hat letting her tresses fall about her shoulders, took a deep breath and entered the room.

Julien was the first one she saw, standing as usual with his hand on his hip by the fire. Her mouth went dry. When their eyes met he lifted his chin. Lauren noticed his face was still scarred from her fingernails.

Jean-Baptiste sat at a table, a quill in hand. He was a bit greyer and his right eyelid now completely obscured his eye. Claude she did not see anywhere. The room was dark because of the storm, and not until he spoke did she realize he was in the shadows on the bed, reclining on his side, his head on his hand.

He was the first to speak, and his voice felt like a barb in her belly. "So good to see you again, dear," he rubbed the bridge of his nose and said, "I just realized you have been responsible for rearranging two of our faces. No one could ever call you a shrinking violet. Father, today could be your turn."

"I am here to present an offer to you," Lauren said standing with her shoulders squared.

Putting down his quill, Jean-Baptiste said in a voice heavy with sarcasm, "Your husband shows great courage sending a woman to do his dirty work."

Lauren stepped forward and asked, "May I sit down?"

Julien, who was snacking on nuts, stopped chewing stunned by her aplomb. Without waiting for an answer she pulled a chair out and sat down at the table across from Jean-Baptiste. Out of the corner of her eye, she saw Claude sit up.

"Here is what we offer," she said. "St. Clare will agree to lift the blockade on the Mississippi permanently and pull his marketing operation out of New France and New England completely if you give us pertinent details about French troop movements."

There was silence in the room then Gautier laughed. "Blackmail."

Lauren raised her eyebrows and shrugged. "A simple cost free proposition which would solve all of our problems."

"He will sell the information to the British?" Gautier asked.

"Indeed," said Lauren. "It will fund his new operation in the West Indies."

Jean-Baptiste sat back in his chair, and it made a creaking sound as he reclined. He crossed his arms and said, "Your bravado enchants me. Claude was right. I should have taken you years ago."

She continued, "If you do not agree, St. Clare has no choice but to remain."

Claude rose off the bed and walked over to the hearth. He still wore thick white makeup and several patches around his mouth. Lauren wondered if these were to hide sores from the whore's disease.

He said, "What's to prevent us from ransoming you?"

Lauren sighed, dropped her eyes for a moment then explained, "Gentleman. I will be frank. If that had been something St. Clare feared he would not have sent me at all. I have found that ours is strictly a business arrangement."

"Then why did he come for you at Fort Frederic?" challenged Gautier, his eyes narrowing.

"He was interested in retaining his only French born contact. That matters little now. The *Melungion* girl who accompanied him was the one you should have ransomed. He loved her not me. Instead you killed her."

There was silence in the room as the thunder rumbled.

"How did you know where to find us?" Jean-Baptiste asked suspiciously.

"Wherever you can find someone who likes money, James St. Clare has spies."

Gautier lit some tobacco as Claude continued to watch Lauren closely. Jean-Baptiste said finally, "We will consider your proposition but," and he paused, "you will not have your answer tonight."

"Very well," said Lauren shrugging. "I will return before the sun sets tomorrow."

*   *   *

The moment Lauren left the room Gautier said, "That woman is not to be trusted."

"Oh really cousin? How perceptive you are," said Claude.

"I don't like it," said Jean-Baptiste frowning. "I don't like any of it. It's a trap."

"Yes, it could be a trap, Father," said Claude slumping down into a chair. "But who is behind it? Brobriant? He is terrified of us. Dazemard de Lusignan or Dubois? We line their pockets. It is absurd to think they would listen to an insignificant servant girl."

Gautier walked to the window, took a puff of his tobacco, blew out the smoke then said, "This St. Clare could be out of our hair forever."

"You cannot underestimate the man," argued Jean-Baptiste. "His powers are far reaching."

Claude threw his hands into the air and jumped up. "Just what do you suggest, Father! He has the Mississippi bottled up. There is no money coming from Kaskaskia. He threatens to cripple Julien's trade at Champlain, and our creditors grow impatient. Unless you have a wealthy wife hiding somewhere who will die in a week, we have little choice!"

The only sound in the room was the crackling of the fire as Jean Baptiste burned a look into his son. Finally he rubbed his forehead and said, "Very well. Julien get the information. We will meet here at sunset tomorrow."

* * *

After informing Golon of the meeting the next day at sunset, Lauren set out to find a place to sleep. The ground was dry again after the brief shower, and she found a family who allowed her to place her bedroll behind their tent. She took great care not to be seen, and when if finally grew dark she lay with her knife and flintlock by her side. She watched the bonfires, listened to music and laughter.

It had been unnerving seeing the Aberjons and Gautier again, and she slept fitfully having bizarre dreams of Fort St. Frederic and Kaskaskia throughout the night. When morning came she longed for the comfort and security *The Pride of the King,* and she wondered if they were on the Hudson or out to sea. She sat up feeling nauseated and thoroughly fatigued.

All day she stayed in back of the tent, out of sight, going to purchase porridge and cider for breakfast and stew with bread and cheese for supper. Being an unescorted female was dangerous, and Lauren counted the hours until sundown. After her meeting she would return to her sutler cottage, meet Gunnar and they would start their journey back to the Hudson River Valley immediately.

At last the hour came and every muscle in Lauren's body ached with tension. When she entered the tavern she saw several officers and regulars. She wondered if these were the men Dubois had posted for the arrest. She clenched her teeth, walked through the bar room, ignoring the lewd comments and lecherous gropes of the men and marched up the stairs knocking on the door at the end of the hall

This time when she entered the room Julien was seated at the table with Jean-Baptiste. They had some maps and documents in front of them, and when Lauren started across the room to examine the document Jean-Baptiste said, "Not so fast. We wait for Claude."

Lauren pursed her lips and sighed, stepping back. Julien jumped up and looked out the window while Jean-Baptiste watched Lauren. Her heart was thumping so hard she was afraid he could see it. Outwardly she remained calm touching her waist once to make sure her knife was still there, moving her shoulder to adjust the strap of the flintlock. Jean-Baptiste cleared his throat. There was cheering in the distance from some competition.

"Why the hell must we wait for him?" barked Julien.

Lauren looked at Jean-Baptiste, and he replied coolly, "A moment longer."

Reaching for a decanter of spirits on the table, he poured himself a drink. Tossing the contents down his throat in one gulp, he grumbled at last, "That damned fool. I suppose it matters not."

Julien returned to the table helping Jean-Baptiste roll up the maps and documents. Lauren looked at them with surprise and Jean-Baptiste said, "Why do you need to see them? You wouldn't understand them anyway."

"If these are false, St. Clare will be obliged to remain."

Julien handed her the documents and said, "Everything is in order. Now get out."

Lauren could feel the perspiration roll down her back as she started for the door. Her hand was on her knife in case either of them attempted to jump her. Her thoughts raced. *Where are Dubois' men? Has he betrayed me?*

Just as she lifted the latch on the door four guards burst in the room grabbing Lauren and yanking Jean-Baptiste and Julien to their feet, lashing their hands.

Julien screamed, "No!" and struggled violently.

Jean-Baptiste roared at Lauren, "You filthy slut. You-" but he was cut short by Claude strutting into the room with a portly man in uniform wearing a powdered wig. Lauren knew this must be Sebastian Dubois.

"Father, I am so disappointed in you," said Claude clucking his tongue. He pouted his lips mockingly. "How could you betray the Crown?" Then turning to Julian, he said, "Sadly, Cousin no one will be surprised by *your* involvement in this affair."

Jean-Baptiste and Julien were too stunned to speak. Lauren realized then that Claude had seen his opportunity to usurp ownership of the lead mine and seize his cousin's trade venture by informing on them all. Too spineless to admit his own involvement, Dubois chose to betray Lauren and save himself.

Sebastian Dubois stepped forward and stated, "Gentlemen, you are under arrest for treason." and jerking his head said to the guards, "Take them away."

The guards pushed them out of the room leaving Lauren with her hands tied behind her back, her firearm and knife confiscated.

Claude smiled, cocked his head at Lauren and said, "And you my dear are a spy. Don't be alarmed though. We won't kill you because I want you to take this message to St. Clare. I have sent a party down to the Hudson River to clean up that family of freaks that sail *The Pride of the King.* They will be dead by the time you reach St. Clare, but I want him to know that this is just a little sample of things to come. He deals with *me* now."

The blood drained from Lauren's face as she tried in vain to find the right words to injure Claude. She instead she took a deep breath and spit in his face. His smirk dropped and his eyes bulged with anger as he lunged at her with his long nails. He was caught instantly by Dubois.

"Outside," he ordered.

The guard dragged Lauren down the stairs and through the tap room where the men roared with laughter and hurled obscenities at her. The crowd followed her outside where she realized she was to become the next form of entertainment at the rendezvous. Two soldiers rushed up to her pushing her face down on the ground while a circle formed.

The roar was deafening with cheers and applause as one soldier straddled her, the other held her arms and third gathered her hair. In three strokes he had slashed her hair off, narrowly missing her scalp. Lauren sobbed from fear and humiliation, her heart drumming in her chest, but she did not move as the soldier took a straight razor and began to shave her head. He started at the base of her neck, moved around her ears where he slipped several times drawing blood. He ended at her forehead. The was crowd cheering and laughing uproariously. When he finished, he stood up with her auburn hair in his hand and they roared.

They pulled Lauren to her feet for everyone to see. She was completely bald with only a few turfs of hair remaining, blood running down her scalp and neck.

They grabbed her chin as tears ran down her cheeks and announced, "Behold! She wears the brand of a spy. Everywhere she ventures, they will know she is not to be trusted!"

The crowd cheered. The soldiers began to disperse men, informing them that the show was over demanding they find entertainment elsewhere. Lauren dropped to her knees sobbing, burying her head in her hands filled with shame and fear. Stunned and battered, she cried for James.

Suddenly, she was yanked to her feet, and she felt an arm go around her waist. It was large trapper with greasy red hair and beard. Lauren was pressed against his bare chest as he dragged her into the woods. She struggled wildly, but it was useless against his strength. He was followed closely by a group of men roaring, "I'm next!"

The man's breathing quickened as he pulled into the brush and pulled up her shift putting his hand between her legs. Suddenly her face was sprayed with blood and the man fell back, choking and sputtering. Putting the heels of her hands to her eyes to clear her vision, Lauren saw the man writhing on the ground with his throat slit.

A trapper jumped front of her holding a knife out. "I'll kill all of you!" he bellowed.

"Whoa, my friend. We are leaving!" cried one of them backing away, his hands in the air. The group dispersed instantly hurling insults at him. Lauren realized this was the trapper who had been following her at the rendezvous.

He reached out and she recoiled. Clamping down hard on her wrist he said, "St. Clare sent me to watch over you."

*   *   *

It was dark when they arrived at the sutler hut on Lake Champlain. Breathlessly she thanked the man and assured him Captain St. Clare would reward him handsomely. He nodded, lumbered off into the darkness and was gone.

Not far from the shack by the woods, Gunnar waited for Lauren staring wide eyed at her altered appearance. Asking him to wait she stumbled into the shack, poured some water into a bowl, washed her hands and face and cleansed her scalp wounds. She held a candle up and looked in the small mirror Isi had hung over the washstand. Her amber eyes filled with tears when she saw her reflection. "Oh, merciful God in Heaven!" she sobbed, dropping onto a chair. She felt hideous and ashamed. She didn't want to face James. She didn't want to see the pity and revulsion in his eyes.

Suddenly, she remembered what Claude had said about attacking the crew of *The Pride of the King*, and she jumped to her feet. After wrapping some bandages around the cuts and abrasions, she ran down to the lake to wash the stench of the soldiers and trappers off of her body. She was grateful for the lack of moonlight as she hastily soaped her skin, pulled on her shift and returned to Gunnar.

Putting her hat on, she said. "I am ready now," and climbed onto the cart. They traveled as quickly as the donkey and cart would allow down the path toward the Hudson River, bumping and jostling until Lauren's teeth hurt. They allowed themselves one night at the Claus residence then took turns sleeping in the back of the cart while the other drove. Lauren knew she was exhausted from worry and anxiety, but something else plagued her, a gnawing feeling in her belly, a restless, driving desire to find comfort and safety as soon as possible. It was not until they had reached Cavendish Tavern that she realized she was pregnant with James' child.

Chapter 52

The sign looked worn and the hats in the window faded as James stepped into Madame Vanoss' millinery shop on Broad Street. He stopped for a moment inside the front room and looked at the fabrics and ribbons spilling out of drawers, at the flowers and feathers heavy with dust on hats no woman would ever wear. He sighed and walked to a door at the back of the shop.

He did not like coming here. He did not like seeing Kaatje Vanoss. It brought back memories of his experiences here as a youth. He remembered her taking his hand, leading him to the back of the shop where she introduced him to a world of carnal pleasures and erotic experiences. For most of his life James had believed this was the true nature of love. He had never experienced the unconditional devotion of a parent or the bonds of a true friendship, and when he witnessed affection between couples he assumed it was merely a prelude to sexual gratification. Over time he began to see love as a trap people fell into, becoming slaves to their lusts and desires. He never understood the true spiritual awakening, until Lauren. Without question he would lay down his life for her, and now he too became a willing victim of his desire, but this time he realized that love transcended mere carnal pleasure.

When Kaatje Vanoss opened the door and smiled seductively at him, his stomach churned. She represented a tawdry past he would rather forget. Her eyes moved across his broad shoulders, lingering where his shirt was open. "It's charming to see you again, James," she murmured holding out her hand.

St. Clare bent over it briefly, making a pretense at kissing it. He had to admit, by most standards, she was still a handsome woman. Her figure was still firm and her eyes a stunning blue, but he was repulsed by her presence.

"Are Heloise and Cornelius in?" he asked."

"They certainly are," she said sweeping her arm. "Right this way."

It was midday and the house was just beginning to stir. James could hear several of the girls moving about in their rooms. Although the shop was neglected, Madame Vanoss kept the rest of the house clean and in good repair. Many of the walls were richly paneled or wainscoted. Some rooms were painted with landscapes or flowers and all the chambers had luxurious carpets. They climbed a flight of stairs to the rooms Heloise and Cornelius' occupied. They had insisted on the finest rooms in the home, and Madame Vanoss had indulged the two knowing that they would only stay a short time.

"Oh my God, I feel like a prisoner here!" gasped Cornelius after Madame Vanoss left the room. "When can we go?" he asked James.

St. Clare sighed. He was weary and not looking forward to a fight.

Heloise who was seated by the window fanned herself and said, "The heat is oppressive here, and the noises I hear coming from downstairs turn my stomach."

"I came to tell you that it will be just a few weeks longer then you may return to Duke Street," St. Clare said. "It will not be safe for you until the snows begin in the north."

"We were just beginning to catch up with everyone in New York when word came we must go into hiding. They probably have forgotten us by now," whined Corny.

"Don't worry, Cornelius. You're hard to forget," said James feeling edgy. This confused Corny long enough for James to continue. "*Everyone* is in hiding. Not just you. The fluyt has been on the Schuylkill in Pennsylvania most of the summer, our Providence connections went inland and those from the north have dispersed to the mountains of the western interior."

"Have the Chickasaw and Prussian mercenaries been successful with your blockade on the Mississippi?" asked Heloise.

"Yes. I received word a week ago. No convoys are coming or going from the lead mine."

"Have you ever thought the mine owners might be behind these slaughters?"

"Of course," said James, picking up a cupid figurine and looking at it with distaste. "Initially I thought it implausible, but now I think they may be responsible for the strikes everywhere."

"And what of Lauren?" said Heloise noting the dark circles under his eyes and his unshaven face. James said nothing.

"Where is the girl?" she demanded.

"In the north with Cavendish, gathering refugees from the Northern communities."

"What! How could you leave her there!" cried Heloise.

James felt his palms began to perspire. He tightened his jaw and turned toward the door. With his hand on the latch he stated, "You will receive word when it is safe to return to Duke Street," and he left the room.

Another month passed as James monitored the safety of the members of The Pride of the King on the Hudson and through the colonies to the south. He also continued business on a limited basis while his members were in hiding trying to generate some revenue while the organization was down. The strain began to show on his face, and his brief happiness with Lauren seemed now like a distant dream.

Late one September afternoon after a meeting with one of the local patroons, Ben Groot handed St. Clare a note. "This came for you while you were inside, Captain."

James read the message and said, "So the fluyt is here."

"Yes sir," was the giant's reply.

"Any word about--"

Ben's brown eyes sparkled, and he handed him another note, "And this came too."

James stared at Ben a moment stunned, then tore the note open, read it and breathed a sigh of relief. "All this news in one afternoon," James said.

"Is she safe, sir?"

"She is safe and waiting for us at Cavendish Landing."

James put his arms back and stretched. For the first time in months, he noticed the afternoon sun streaming through the colorful autumn leaves and the sparkling water of the Hudson. He put his tricorn on and announced, "*The Pride of the King* awaits, Mr. Groot!"

*   *   *

Lauren watched the canoe approach Cavendish Landing in the twilight. She was told James was hiding *The Pride of the King* on Popple Creek and that he would look for her on shore when the sun had set. She saw him climb out of out the canoe with Ben Groot and another man she assumed to be his new first mate.

Stepping back into the shadows, Lauren held her breath struggling to find the nerve to approach him. She watched James scan the shoreline as his companions started for the tavern. Drunken soldiers and whores loitered outside in the balmy night air laughing and shouting obscenities at one another. Patrons came and went and still he waited, arms crossed, then he began to pace. Suddenly, he shook his head and started for the inn. Lauren's heart jumped. She knew that she should not allow him to look for her inside. It was far too dangerous. Someone would recognize him. Even Cavendish Landing was no longer a safe haven for members of The Pride of the King.

She stepped out from the shelter of the trees and started toward him. She wore a simple blue skirt and bodice with a white kerchief on her head. When James saw her he grinned, took several strides then broke into a full run. She watched him a moment then something inside of her snapped. She picked up her skirts and ran from him bolting back into the woods and down the trail.

James stopped, looking confused. He called to her then dashed down the trail after her. When he finally reached her down by the river, he yanked her into his arms and exclaimed, "What's wrong with you!"

Lauren pushed away from him her eyes down. Suddenly, he saw her bare forehead and his jaw dropped. His eyes ran over her as tears rolled down her face. Slowly and carefully he reached up and lowered the kerchief. Lauren swallowed hard as he looked at her shaven head. She reached up and tied the kerchief back on.

"Who did this to you," he said through his teeth.

She whispered, "French soldiers. I was branded as a spy."

"How is it you were in French territory?"

His voice sounded threatening.

"I was gathering information. I found out that Julien Gautier, Jean-Baptiste and Claude Aberjon are responsible for the raids. Two of them are being tried for treason, but Claude remains free and vows to destroy us."

There was a long silence while James absorbed the news. His jaw tightened and he began to pace the shoreline, rocks and twigs crunching under his boots. Lauren stood with her eyes down, feeling ashamed and embarrassed. Her fists were clenched at her sides and she hung her head.

He walked up suddenly and stroked her cheek. "My beauty," he whispered then he took his face in his hands and kissed her. Lauren put her arms around him, tears streaming down her face. He ran his lips over her cheeks.

"Don't ever leave me again," he said. "At last I understand. At last I understand." He repeated the words to her again and again as he kissed her.

*　　　*　　　*

The crew of the *Pride of the King* guarded the mouth of Popple Creek as James and Lauren canoed back to his hideaway. Their passion for each other, frenzied at first with fire and desperation melted into contentment and serenity. They spent hours together drowsing by the stream, sunlight filtering through the trees, dancing across their entangled limbs. The talked long into the night at the kitchen table by candlelight.

It was late one afternoon by the creek when Lauren told him of their unborn child. James stared at her in disbelief than rolled onto his back on the moss and laughed with joy. "A child! Why did you not tell me sooner?"

"I wanted it to be a quiet moment such as this."

"A child who shall have a name."

"Yes," Lauren agreed. "And a child who will have a home."

Pulling Lauren down into his arms he murmured, "And they will know their birthday."

Several days passed and James began to grow restless. Lauren knew he was worried about the safety of the crew, and to ease his burden she suggested they return to the fluyt. She too could not fully appreciate their time together knowing that Claude may strike before winter approached.

The next day they returned to the vessel. The first thing James did was consult with the first mate. She overheard Mr. Duerr say in his thick Prussian accent, "Ya Captain, Robert, Mr. Bologne and a few others may go ashore."

"Fine, they can watch each other. The crew needs shore leave. I know the doldrums are upon them."

Lauren missed Isaac, and she knew James did too, but Duerr was a diligent and responsible first mate. She nodded a greeting to him then followed James down the companionway to his quarters. It feels wonderful to be home again, thought Lauren. She loved her husband's cabin. It still smelled of spicy soap and cedar and the barrel still sat by the bed with the name, *Chateaux St. Clare, Provence.*

James worked at his desk all afternoon while Lauren rested. She had been fatigued lately never seeming to get enough sleep. The baby demanded constant food and rest from her. Sliding under the covers she wiggled her toes and watched James work at his desk then peacefully drifted off to sleep.

She awoke many hours later to find the cabin dark and James gone. All was quiet above, and when she looked out the moon was high in the sky. Pulling a gown over her shift she went barefoot onto the deck. The only sound was the water sloshing against the hull and a light breeze rustling the dry leaves on shore. She wondered who was on night watch. She leaned on the rail and looked out at the silent woods then up at the moon.

She listened once more for movement and heard nothing. She walked toward the stern and tripped on a large bundle on the deck. Stepping to the side, her foot slipped on something slick. She realized it was not a bundle. The moonlight cast a pale light on the lifeless face of Josef Duerr. His throat had been cut. Lauren realized she was standing in his blood.

Her heart drumming in her chest, she scanned the deck for danger, realizing she must grab her rifle before she too became a victim. Dashing down the companionway she ran into the cabin and locked the door. She loaded her firearm with trembling hands. Taking a deep breath she took the stairs two at a time and rushed onto the deck, rifle in hand ready to fire, but nothing moved, and no one lunged at her from the shadows. The only movement came from the trees swaying in the night breeze.

Lauren's legs were so wobbly she wasn't sure she could walk. Nevertheless, she moved toward the bow where she saw another form leaning against the rail. As she drew closer, she realized it was Ben Groot his throat also cut. Across from him sprawled face down on the deck was old Mathias. She put her hand to her mouth to stifle a sob and bile began to rise in her throat. She felt her head start to spin. The grizzly scene was overwhelming.

She took a deep breath and steadier herself. If she was going to survive, she must not lose her head. Lauren realized Claude had fulfilled his promise. Jumping down onto the lower deck she searched madly for other victims especially for James. Finding no one else, she strained to see the shore. St. Clare usually posted a sentry on land, but she saw no one. Having searched every inch of the fluyt, Lauren stopped a moment clenching her fists. Her heart was pounding so wildly it was hard to collect her thoughts. *How could this have happened while she slept? They must have taken the crew by surprise.*

She assumed whoever committed this treachery did not know she was in the cabin otherwise she too would be dead. She knew she must find James and the others, so without delay she lowered herself into a canoe and set off for the Cavendish settlement. She looked over her shoulder at the macabre specter of the ship in the moonlight and shuddered.

The woods seemed alive as she paddled down stream, the brittle dry underbrush making snapping sounds as night creatures moved through it. Lauren stopped before Cavendish landing coming ashore at the clearing where she had met Isi by the bonfire months earlier. She pulled the canoe up onto the sand and the rocks making certain the cabin was dark and silent before she started up the path.

When she reached Cavendish settlement, she paused in the shadows. The tavern was ablaze with light and activity. Loud voices came from inside the establishment, and Lauren noted several patrons outside the door waving their arms and gesturing toward the river and woods. Several British soldiers ran down to the landing, loaded onto bateaux and pushed off down the Hudson. Lauren spotted Gunnar in back of the tavern returning from the necessary. She scanned the clearing then dashed toward him, startling him.

He cried, "Damn it, Miss!"

She grabbed him and dragged him into the woods. "*Mon Dieu, Gunnar, what is happening?*" she panted.

He looked furtively at the tavern then said, "It's a lynching. Cavendish's wife says she saw one of your crew using a child."

"What! Who did she accuse?"

"The one that's slow."

"Who? Robert!"

"Ya, that's the one. I saw that woman talking to him earlier, all fancy like. I saw her pull him upstairs, nuzzling up to him. A moment later she came down holding Lucy's little girl and shouted that she caught Robert with the child."

Lauren put her hands to her cheeks and repeated, "*Oh, mon Dieu! Oh mon Dieu!*"

"She is going after the whole crew saying they are cripples and misfits and can't be trusted."

"Where is Captain St. Clare?"

"No one knows. The soldiers were taking him to the fort, but those Indian friends of yours opened fire. He ran into the woods with them."

"Good," said Lauren breathing a sigh of relief. "And what of Robert?"

Gunnar looked down. Lauren knew that he was dead. "Gunnar, we must find Captain St. Clare."

"Ya, Miss, but the soldiers and townspeople are all over the woods."

Gunnar stared at Lauren waiting for her to make a decision. She unconsciously touched her belly as if to protect her baby then said, "I think I know where they are."

Chapter 53

The crowd at Cavendish Tavern did not disperse for many hours reveling in the excitement of a lynching. The troops from the fort made an attempt to put the mob down, but the soldiers seemed to enjoy the hanging as much as the crowd. The mob called for vengeance and hanged the terrified Robert from the nearest tree.

John Cavendish watched in horror, impotent to stop the maelstrom of hatred. St. Clare and the rest had been taken to the fort to be detained until morning when they would most certainly hang. It was late before John could convince the last patron of Cavendish Tavern to go home.

Anxious and distraught, trying to devise a plan to free St. Clare and the others, Cavendish paced the bar room. After several hours, Georgiana came through the front door. She had been drinking heavily with one of the soldiers down by the river.

Throwing herself into a chair, she declared, "Well, quite the night!"

Cavendish he did not respond. He squatted down and began banking the fire. She leaned forward and said, "Are you deaf?"

He turned his scarred face toward her and mumbled, "I heard you."

Georgiana stood up and staggered to the bar, pulled the cork out of a bottle and poured herself a drink. "Well, since you can hear me, listen to this. I am leaving tomorrow in the morning."

Still John did not turn around.

"I have been waiting for my opportunity to get out of this stinking hole for too long. Now I can go." She bent her head back and threw the drink down her throat.

John stood up slowly putting his hand on the mantle, still not looking at her. "Where are you going?"

"North, if that's any of your business."

She picked up a bottle and a mug and headed for the bed chamber. Pouring herself another drink she started to stuff clothes into a bag. John stood in the door, his berry colored face expressionless. Georgiana's blonde hair was disheveled and the charcoal on her lashes had smeared under her eyes.

"Don't try to get me to stay," she sneered.

"You lied about that boy, didn't you?" he said.

She cocked her head and replied; "Now what if I did?" She staggered a few steps backward, catching herself on the commode.

"Who paid you?"

"I would have done it for free. St. Clare and that group of freaks disgust me. I didn't think that French slut of his would make it back from Champlain." Then sweeping her arm she said thickly. "But she did." Pushing her dirty hair off her face she poured herself another drink.

"Who paid you?" he demanded.

Hearing the rage in his voice, Georgiana's eyebrows shot up with surprise. "Never met him. A messenger came down from Champlain." She continued to look at him and swayed. "He was sent by some Frenchman, a cousin of Gautiers'."

John stared at her for a moment then closed his eyes. He remembered the first time he met Georgiana in Albany; she was a barmaid then at his modest tavern on State Street. How captivating she was, so beautiful and so full of life and all the men wanted her. John had never been the kind of man to turn a woman's head, so when Georgiana consented to marry him a few months later, he felt like Heaven had blessed him. He opened his eyes again. He watched her drop her gown onto the floor and fall onto the bed, the alcohol dragging her into a dreamless sleep.

He paced again for a long time trying to figure out what to do. He rubbed his forehead and mumbled to himself. He knew that he should tell the authorities, but in the end he decided to keep her secret. He loathed himself for his weakness, but his wife meant everything to him.

John pulled the covers over Georgiana and lovingly brushed back her hair. There was a chill in the air, and he moved to the fireplace to light a fire. It sprang to life, flames of gold and blue warming the room. Cavendish stood up and sighed, looking at Georgiana. He picked up a broom and walked to the hearth. When the straw was ablaze he turned and lit his wife's bed on fire.

* * *

Lauren and Gunnar found St. Clare, Samuel Claypool and Henry Bologne at the hideaway on Popple Creek. Flooded with relief, Lauren ran to James then embraced Henry and Samuel. Tears rolled down Henry's face and he said, "Glad I am to see my girl."

"We went to the fluyt, but it was too late," said James. "They were dead and you were gone. What happened? Did you see anything?"

Lauren shook her head slowly. "The soldiers moved quickly and quietly. I came on deck and found the bodies then canoed down to Cavendish Landing and found Gunnar right away."

"I am grateful to you for keeping my wife safe," said St. Clare to the boy. Gunnar sat in the corner on the floor with his knees drawn up. He simply nodded.

James bent over the fire and lit his tobacco. Blowing out the smoke he said, "Isi and the other Chickasaws ambushed the British on the road and broke us free. If it wasn't for them we would be swinging from a noose this morning."

"Where are they?" asked Lauren.

"They have gone back to their posts. We need our couriers up and running again."

What?" cried Lauren. "Certainly you don't believe the threat is over? "

Samuel chimed in, his white eyeballs rolling, "Oh it most certainly is over! The Captain has sent his calling card to your French friend from the West."

Lauren looked at James, but he dismissed the subject by walking to the window. She wondered how he would have Claude killed. If he would send a henchman to strangle him in the night or have him assassinated at some gambling table. Either way she knew the deed would be done.

The conversation continued, but St. Clare did not listen. He cursed himself for not feeling grief like the others. After all the horror that day, he could feel only frigid numbness. He watched the sun rising through the trees.

He straightened up suddenly and leaned out the window. He realized with a jolt that he was not looking to the east at all. "That is not the sunrise!" he exclaimed. "That's fire!"

Springing to action, James and Samuel put Henry in a canoe and pushed off shore, followed closely by Lauren and Gunnar in their own craft. Henry drove the paddles deep as James guided them down Popple Creek. Samuel sat on the floor of the canoe, his chin held high using his keen sense of hearing to alert them to danger.

"I believe the fire is at Cavendish Landing," called James.

"And north of it," replied Samuel.

Gunnar and Lauren paddled furiously keeping pace with the three men. The light from the flames lit up the sky ahead of them, and smoke began to fill the air between the tree trunks, rolling quickly toward them. In spite of the sun rising, the light began to fade as the group came closer to the Hudson. A scorching wind carried the scent of burning resin to Lauren's nostrils, and she remembered the tinder dry debris strewn up and down the Hudson River and around Lake Champlain, debris from hastily built forts and cabins. Treetops, dry leaves and stumps which had never been cleared littered the floor of an already parched forest. All summer Lauren had smelled smoke from wildfires, but she never believed it would go beyond an isolated eruption.

Suddenly several explosions sounded in the distance as if cannons were being shot off from the fort.

"Why the hell are they shooting cannon!" shouted Henry.

Samuel shouted back, "That's not cannon, Bologne. Those are fire balls!"

There was another report behind them this time sounding like thunder as a globe of flame burst high into the sky. Sweat began to roll down Lauren's back as the heat intensified and the anxiety. Now with flames on both sides, the group had no choice but to flee downstream to *The Pride of the King*. The smoke thickened into a grayish mass and the two canoes became barely visible to each other. Lauren and Gunnar covered their faces with neckerchiefs and paddled on at top speed, their eyes running from the fumes.

James jerked back as Samuel cried, "Oh my God!" Something slammed into their canoe. Water splashed as something heavy hit Lauren's craft. Gunnar held a paddle up to protect himself as a terrified doe smashed into his face. Another panicked buck put his hoof into their canoe, tipping the craft onto its side. Lauren screamed and threw her body in the other direction. The buck reared up onto its hind legs and withdrew, leaping off into the brush behind them.

"Lauren!" called James.

"We are safe!" she cried picking up her paddle with trembling hands. Blood streamed out of Gunnar's nose, but he resumed paddling without words.

Samuel was the first to be aware of *The Pride of the King* and called, "I can hear the old girl. She is just ahead."

At last the hull of *The Pride of the King* loomed large in front of them, a ghostly giant waiting in the smoky shadows to carry them to safety. James scrambled onto the deck then lowered a platform for Henry Bologne and lines for the rest of the group. The skeleton crew burst into action, scampering about, taking comfort in being back on board once more.

Lauren noticed the corpses were gone. St. Clare had thrown them overboard earlier. With no time to lose, she turned her attention to easing the sheets as Gunnar carried out commands from Henry and Samuel.

"It is a hot unpredictable wind we must fight," cried James at the helm as the fluyt heaved forward. "Steady now!"

Careening out onto the river they got their first glimpse of Cavendish Landing. In a sky black as night, gargantuan flames illuminated the settlement. Fire raged along the river banks, deep into the woods and up to the fort. Except for the chimney, Cavendish tavern was gone and the cabins and outbuildings surrounding it crumbled in the blaze. The burning trees surrounding the settlement shot fire high into the black sky showering the fluyt with a rain of ash and sparks.

The firelight illuminated the soot-covered face of St. Clare as he called for buckets of water. He commanded everyone to drench themselves to keep their hair and clothing from igniting and to be ready to douse the sheets if necessary. He watched Lauren anxiously as she scrambled about the deck, her wet gown clinging to her belly. James caught her by the wrist as she raced past. Just as he was about to say something, Henry shouted, "Cap'n look!"

Wading into the water by Cavendish Landing were a score of people waving their arms wildly and calling to the fluyt. Many were naked, their clothing burned away from their bodies, some were holding children screaming in pain from injuries, and still others held their chests, rendered mute from scarred lungs. Several soldiers attempted to swim out to the vessel but stopped when a regular began to struggle in the current and was pulled under.

Setting his jaw, St. Clare turned back to the helm and commanded, "Sail on!"

The crew did not move, too stunned to obey.

"James!" screamed Lauren. "What are you doing? These people need us!"

As if possessed, James turned on her; his face contorted with rage and screamed, "What a short memory you have, Lauren! These are the people who killed my crew!"

Their eyes locked, sparks spiraling around them. Lauren knew he spoke the truth.

She heard a child crying and said, "There are innocents among them, James. Innocents like our child."

St. Clare hesitated a moment, grimaced then barked, "Mr. Bologne we head for Cavendish Landing."

The crew turned their soot-covered faces toward shore. St Clare looked up at the sky. He knew that at any moment a fireball could explode, jumping the river and igniting the vessel. He gripped the wheel so tightly his fingers began to bruise.

As they approached shore, the crew raced to the side of the vessel hauling the children first onto the fluyt, then the injured. Many fell onto the deck coughing and gasping for air, their eyes swollen shut, others babbled incoherently. Lauren held a toddler under her arm as she examined the wounds of the mother. St. Clare and Henry pulled up four regulars and an officer from the fort. The men fell onto the deck drenched and gasping for air.

"John Cavendish, the tavern owner," urged St. Clare. "Does he live?"

The officer shook his head, panting. "The fire started there, at his tavern. He and his wife were lost."

James turned to Henry, "Mr. Bologne. Is that everyone?"

"Aye. Captain!"

Sails surging in the hot wind *The Pride of the King* groaned into motion sweeping rapidly down the Hudson. In the few moments that they had paused to take on the injured, the blaze had rolled ahead of them downriver showering the Hudson as far as the eye could see with a rain of fire.

Gunnar scampered up the main mast to douse the sheets as Henry passed buckets of water up to him. Sustaining only minor burns, the soldiers put out fires on deck as Lauren ministered to the sick and injured. Claypool drenched in sweat, helped Captain St. Clare maneuver the fluyt through the tricky, unpredictable winds.

Several cows, dogs and some hogs took refuge in the river as well as a herd of deer. A black bear bawled loudly from the shoreline, terrified and overcome from the heat.

Just as Lauren finished bandaging a small boy, cool air filled her lungs. The *Pride of the King* had outrun the fire and pushed confidently on into fresh breezes. She looked up at the helm where St. Clare stood, his long hair loose and tangled, his jaw set, still intent on putting distance between them and the fire. Several of the settlers fell to their knees thanking the Lord for deliverance while others cried tears of joy. Lauren heaved a sigh and started for the helm but was stopped by one of the regulars.

"No, you don't," he ordered.

Lauren's jaw dropped. She was about to protest when three soldiers grabbed James and jerked his hands behind his back. "What!" she screamed, trying to wrench free.

"Your Captain is under arrest," said the regular holding her back.

Lauren called to James, but he would not look at her. His attention was riveted on the fire's approach from behind.

"You damn fools," he said through his teeth. "You don't know how to sail her in this wind!"

The officer took the wheel as the regulars pulled James roughly down the stairs. All at once sparks began to rain down on the fluyt again.

Rushing up Henry Bologne cried, "What the hell is going on!"

Lauren heard someone scream from the stern. She looked aft and saw a compact mass of black smoke rolling up the waterway. Before she could drop onto the deck a thunderous blast shook everything. Fire sprang to life again, this time on both sides of the river and flames shot up on *The Pride of the King*.

Gunnar jumped down from the mast and began to run madly, his clothing on fire. Quick as lightening Lauren doused him with a bucket of water.

The regulars were so stunned by the commotion; they didn't notice Claypool loosening the rope on St. Clare's hands. Grabbing a bucket, the Captain began to climb the main mast to put out the fire on the canvas while Henry filled buckets.

The settlers began to jump overboard howling in terror. In a flash a scorching hot wind encircled the fluyt like a cyclone and the flames jumped high into the sky. Lauren realized her gown was ablaze. Tongues of fire climbed up her legs, scorching her skin. The pain was intense. She slapped at them frantically trying to snuff them out. Gunnar dragged her to the railing and yanked them both backward, down into the waters of the Hudson.

The water gurgled around Lauren's ears, muffling the cries of anguish overhead. When she came to the surface she was near shore and pulled herself to her feet not far from Gunnar. The entire ship was a mass of flames and she cried out in horror. No one was left on the *Pride of the King* except James and a British officer whose uniform was ablaze. Overcome with panic, Lauren lunged toward the water, but Gunnar stopped her. "The Captain told me to protect you," he shouted.

Lauren watched as James struggled with the man to pull him overboard to douse the flames. Convinced St. Clare meant him harm, the man punched James in the face knocking him to the deck. James jumped to his feet once more and tried to pull the crazed man into the water, but the officer fought back with a vengeance.

Suddenly, there was a loud groaning sound as *The Pride of the King* began to shudder. Next there was a loud, crack as the main mast began to split. James looked up and tried to jump out of the way, but the officer, unaware of the danger, restrained him. The mast swayed ominously in the wind then began to fall. Lauren screamed as the flaming timber toppled down crushing the officer and her husband under its vast weight.

Chapter 54

Heartbroken and lost Lauren returned to New Orleans where the good sisters of the Ursaline Order helped her give birth to little Janie St. Clare. The child was beautiful and healthy, and for Lauren it was love at first sight. Simone was there too, older and more at peace with herself, fawning and fussing over her little niece.

In spite of the love and comfort, Lauren did not wish to stay. Even though she was of French birth her home was now in the English Colonies, and as soon as the child could travel she returned to the Hudson River Valley. She felt nearest to James there, and more than anything she wanted their daughter to know the beautiful river her father had sailed.

She hired Gunnar and another young man to build her a small cottage on her parcel of land and had him clear some trees, so she could see the river. Mrs. Quill, no longer able to run the Boar's Head, sold the tavern to Lauren for a modest sum, and Polly Quackenboss stayed on to help Lauren run the inn. Gunnar did odd jobs for a year then he found an apprenticeship with the local blacksmith.

The Pride of the King

The Pride of the King dissolved after James St. Clare's death. Henry Bologne and Samuel Claypool came to visit Lauren on one occasion, but after that she never heard from them again. She suspected that life had become difficult for them after The Pride of the King disbanded. She understood entirely. It had become difficult for her too. Isi visited as well, but eventually she was called back to her people on the Mississippi.

Lauren frequently thought of Heloise and Cornelius, Rene and his mother Anne, and those had given their lives for The Pride. They were all lost to her now, but in their place she had James' child. As the years passed so did her grief. She devoted her life entirely to Janie and her home on the Hudson where she had found happiness.

One spring afternoon when the river had been open for several weeks, and the trees had sprouted their pale green leaves, Lauren stood on a ladder trying to hook a newly painted sign to the bracket outside of the tavern. Her copper-colored tresses had returned tumbling down her back as always an unruly mess. Janie sat under a tree, now three years of age, playing with a cornhusk doll Gunnar had fashioned for her.

A donkey cart bumped down the road and Lauren looked up. It was driven by one of the boys from town, and someone shouted from the back seat, "Haven't you put that sign up yet!"

Lauren climbed down and waved to Mrs. Quill, who was sitting in the back of the wagon her legs dangling. The boy stopped the cart at the steps of the inn and helped Mrs. Quill down, removing her trunk and thumping it up the steps. Stiff and sore from the ride, the matron complained excessively to the young man but pressed a generous tip into his hand.

"How was Albany?" Lauren asked helping the woman to a bench under a maple tree. Mrs. Quill could see the Hudson glisten in the distance, the water open at last, fresh and cold from recently melted ice.

"It was tolerable," she replied removing her hat. Mrs. Quill ran her eyes over Lauren then the child. "You two look well."

"So do you," agreed Lauren.

"It was good to be gone from this brutal place during the winter," Mrs. Quill commented with a shiver.

"Gunnar looked after us and Polly too."

"I see you are putting up the new sign," the woman said nodding.

Lauren held it on her hip and scrutinized it. "Polly is talented at painting. The fluyt is perfect."

"*The Pride of the King*," read Mrs. Quill. "It's a good solid name for an inn."

"I am glad it lives on," said Lauren wistfully. She reached over and tousled Jane's curly auburn hair, set the sign down, then picked up a broom and started to sweep the steps. "Tell me about your stay. Does your cousin enjoy her new home in Albany?"

"She does," said Mrs. Quill, brushing some dust off her sleeve. "She had several other guests there as well. They were tiresome flibbertigibbets, but my cousin was impressed with them. They once owned property up here on the Hudson. The mother and son that is--"

Lauren stopped sweeping and looked up. "Mother and son, do you remember their names?"

Mrs. Quill sighed, "Oh, I don't know."

"Bench? Was it Bench?"

"Why yes, that's it," Mrs. Quill said, frowning. "My Heaven's do you know those pretentious snobs?"

Lauren dropped her broom and began to laugh. "Why yes I know them, Heloise and Cornelius Bench! Tell me everything," demanded Lauren, sitting down and grabbing Mrs. Quill's wrinkled hands. "Tell me where they have been, what they have been doing."

Mrs. Quill blinked several times looking at Lauren, surprised at her enthusiasm. "Well, my, my," the matron said leaning back. "They said they were in London for several years, then the West Indies."

"The West Indies!" gasped Lauren, shaking her head and smiling.

"They had an enjoyable time there, living supposedly with some well-to-do family. My cousin told me in confidence, that the old gentlemen that was with them had been convicted of some crimes here in New York and imprisoned in the Indies for several years."

The smile dropped from Lauren's face.

Mrs. Quill continued, "The man's health had been bad--"

"Old gentleman," Lauren interrupted. "There was an old man with them?"

"Yes, a most disagreeable sort, such a gravelly voice. I do believe he was enamored with me," she said grimacing. "He was constantly asking me questions."

Lauren jumped up, her heart pounding and grabbed Mrs. Quill by the arms. "What was his name?" she demanded.

"What? Well, I don't remember! Honestly! What is wrong with you?"

"Was it Fitch? Leopold Fitch?"

The matron blinked and replied, "Why, yes. It was."

Lauren threw her head back and laughed. "Ha! He survived. Somehow that man always survives!" She began to pace back and forth, shaking her head and laughing.

"Have you lost your mind!" Mrs. Quill barked, but Lauren didn't hear her.

She dashed up the stairs into the tavern, returning a moment later with a bag stuffed full of clothes. She threw a cloak over her arm and said breathlessly, "What time does the packet return to Albany?"

"At--ah--at half past four," she said looking at Lauren as if she was daft.

Lauren scooped Janie under her arm and ran down the road, her hair flying in the wind. Over her shoulder she cried, "Tell

Polly to take care of the tavern. It may be a while, but when I return, it will be on *The Pride of the King*!"

About the Author

All her life Amanda Hughes has been a Walter Mitty, spending more time in heroic daydreams than the real world. At last she found an outlet writing adventures about audacious women in the 18th Century.

Her debut novel, *Beyond the Cliffs of Kerry* was published in 2002, followed by *The Pride of the King* in 2011. Amanda is a graduate of the University of Minnesota, and when she isn't off tilting windmills, she lives and writes in Minneapolis, Minnesota.

Made in the USA
Charleston, SC
06 December 2011